HARMFUL
INTENT

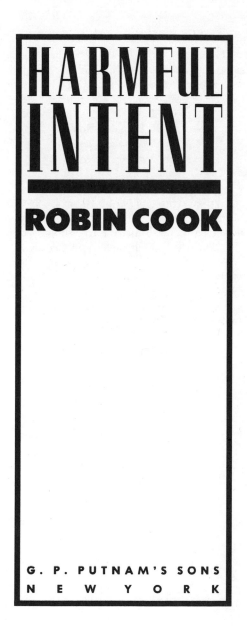

HARMFUL INTENT

ROBIN COOK

G. P. PUTNAM'S SONS
NEW YORK

This is a work of fiction. The characters
and events described in this book are imaginary,
and any resemblance to actual persons, living
or dead, is purely coincidental.

G. P. Putnam's Sons
Publishers Since 1838
200 Madison Avenue
New York, NY 10016

Library of Congress Cataloging-in-Publication Data

Cook, Robin, date.
Harmful intent/Robin Cook.—1st American ed.
p.   cm.
ISBN 0-399-13481-6
I. Title.
PS3553.O5545H37   1990   89-39756 CIP
813'.54—dc20

Printed in the United States of America
1   2   3   4   5   6   7   8   9   10

ACKNOWLEDGMENTS

As with all my projects, I have benefited significantly from the experience and expertise of friends, colleagues, and friends of friends for the writing of *Harmful Intent*. Since the story bridges two professions, it is understandable that professionals have been the primary source. Those whom I would particularly like to acknowledge are:

Physicians: Tom Cook
Chuck Karpas
Stan Kessler

Attorneys: Joe Cox
Victoria Ho
Leslie McClellan

Judge: Tom Trettis

School-based therapist: Jean Reeds

All of them generously donated many hours of their valuable time.

Once again for Audrey Cook, my wonderful mother

"The first thing we do, let's kill all the lawyers."

—*Henry VI, Part II*

PROLOGUE

From the first twinges of cramps that began around nine-thirty that morning, Patty Owen was sure that this was it. She had been worried that when the time came she wouldn't be able to distinguish between the contractions that signaled the onset of labor and the little kicks and general discomfort of the final trimester of her pregnancy. But her apprehension proved groundless; the twisting and grinding pain she was experiencing was entirely different from anything she had ever felt. It was familiar only in the sense that it was so classically textbook in its nature and regularity. Every twenty minutes, like clockwork, Patty felt a steady stab of pain in her lower back. In the intervals between, the pain vanished only to flare again. Despite the increasingly acute agony she was only beginning to endure, Patty couldn't repress a fleeting smile. She knew little Mark was on his way into the world.

Trying to remain calm, Patty searched through the scattered papers on the planning desk in the kitchen for the phone number of the hotel that Clark had given her the day before. He would have preferred to have skipped this business trip since Patty was so close to term, but the bank hadn't given him much choice. His boss had insisted that he follow through with the final round of negotiations that would close a deal he'd been working on for three months. As a compromise, the two men had agreed that no matter the state of the negotiations, Clark would be gone for only two days. He'd still hated to leave, but at least he'd be back a full week before Patty was due to deliver . . .

Patty found the hotel's number. She dialed and was put through to Clark's room by a friendly hotel operator. When he didn't pick up by the second ring, Patty knew Clark had already left for his meeting. Just to be sure, she let it ring five more times in hopes that Clark was in the shower and would suddenly answer, out of breath. She was desperate to hear his reassuring voice.

While the phone rang, Patty shook her head, fighting back tears. For as happy as she'd been to be pregnant this, her first time, she had been troubled by a vague premonition from the start that something bad would happen. When Clark had come home with the news that he had to go out of town at such a critical juncture, Patty had seen her sense of foreboding confirmed. After all the Lamaze classes and exercises they'd done together, she would have to tough it out alone. Clark had assured her she was overly concerned, which was natural, and that he'd be back in plenty of time for the delivery.

The hotel operator came back on the line and asked if Patty wanted to leave a message. Patty told her that she wanted her husband to call her as soon as possible. She left the number for Boston Memorial Hospital. She knew that such a terse message was bound to upset Clark, but it served him right for going away at a time like this.

Next, Patty called Dr. Ralph Simarian's office. The doctor's booming, high-spirited voice momentarily quelled her fears. He told her to have Clark take her over to the BM, as he humorously referred to the Boston Memorial, and get her admitted. He'd see them there in a couple of hours. He told her that twenty-minute intervals meant she had a lot of time.

"Dr. Simarian?" Patty said as the doctor was about to disconnect. "Clark is out of town on a business trip. I'll be coming in by myself."

"Great timing!" Dr. Simarian said with a laugh. "Just like a male. They like to have the fun, then disappear when there's a little work to be done."

"He thought there was another week," Patty explained, feeling like she had to defend Clark. She could be irritated at him but no one else could.

"Just joking," Dr. Simarian said. "I'm sure he will be crushed not to be involved. When he comes back, we'll have a little surprise for him. Now don't be a bit alarmed. Everything's going to be okay. Do you have a way of getting to the hospital?"

Patty said she had a neighbor who had agreed to drive her in case there were any surprises while Clark was away.

"Dr. Simarian," Patty added, hesitantly, "with my Lamaze partner gone, I think I really am too nervous to go through this. I don't want to do anything to hurt the baby, but if you think I could be anesthetized the way we discussed . . ."

"No problem," Dr. Simarian said, without letting her finish. "Don't you worry your pretty little head about these details. I'll handle everything. I'm going to call over there right this minute and tell them that you want the epidural, okay?"

Patty thanked Dr. Simarian and hung up the phone just in time to bite her lip as she felt the beginnings of another contraction.

There was no reason to worry, she told herself sternly. She still had plenty of time to make it to the hospital. Dr. Simarian had everything in hand. She knew her baby was healthy. She had insisted on ultrasound and amniocentesis, even though Dr. Simarian had advised it was unnecessary since Patty was only twenty-four years old. But between her ominous premonition and genuine concern, Patty's determination carried the day. The results of the tests were extremely encouraging: the child she was carrying was a healthy, normal boy. Within a week of receiving the results, Patty and Clark were painting the baby's room blue and deciding on names, ultimately settling on Mark.

All in all, there was no reason to expect anything but a normal delivery and a normal birth.

As Patty turned, intending to retrieve her packed overnight bag from the bedroom closet, she noticed the dramatic change in weather outside. The bright September sunlight which had been streaming through the bay window had been eclipsed by a dark cloud that had blown in suddenly from the west, plunging the family room into near darkness. A distant rumble of thunder sent a shiver down Patty's spine.

Not superstitious by nature, Patty refused to take this storm as an omen. She edged over to the family room couch and sat down. She thought she'd call her neighbor as soon as this contraction was over. That way they'd almost be at the hospital by the time the next one began.

As the pain reached a crescendo, the confidence that Dr. Simarian had engendered disappeared. Anxiety swept through Patty's mind just as a sudden gust of wind raked across the backyard, bending the birches, and bringing the first droplets of rain. Patty shuddered. She wished it were all over. She might not be superstitious, but she was frightened. All the timing—this storm, Clark's business trip, her going into labor a week early—seemed off. Tears rolled down Patty's cheeks as she waited to phone her neighbor. She only wished she weren't so afraid.

"Oh, wonderful," Dr. Jeffrey Rhodes said sarcastically as he glanced up at the main anesthesia scheduling board in the anesthesia office. A new case had appeared: Patty Owen, a delivery with a specific request for an epidural. Jeffrey shook his head, knowing full well that he was the only anesthesiologist currently available. Everyone else on the day shift was tied up on a case. Jeffrey called the delivery area to check on the patient's status and was told there wasn't any rush since the woman hadn't arrived from admitting yet.

"Any complications I should know about?" Jeffrey asked, almost afraid to hear. Things hadn't been going well for him on this particular day.

"Looks routine," the nurse said. "Primipara. Twenty-four. Healthy."

"Who's the attending?"

"Simarian," the nurse replied.

Jeffrey said he'd be over shortly and hung up the phone. Simarian, Jeffrey pondered, thinking it a wash. The guy was technically fine but Jeffrey found his patronizing manner toward patients a bit trying. Thank God it wasn't Braxton or Hicks. He wanted the case to go smoothly and hopefully quickly; if it had been either of the others, that wouldn't have been the case.

Leaving the anesthesia office, he headed down the main OR corridor, passing the scheduling desk and its attendant bustle of activity. The evening shift was due in a few minutes; the changing of the guard inevitably spelled momentary chaos.

Jeffrey pushed through the double swing doors of the surgical lounge and yanked off the mask which hung limply on his chest, dangling by its elastic. He tossed it into the waste receptacle with relief; he'd been breathing through the blasted thing for the last six hours.

The lounge was abuzz with staff members coming on shift. Jeffrey ignored them and passed through to the locker room, which was just as crowded. He paused in front of the mirror, curious to see if he looked as bad as he felt. He did. His eyes seemed to have receded, they appeared so sunken. Below each was a dark indelible crescent-shaped smudge. Even Jeffrey's mustache seemed the worse for wear and tear, though what could he expect after having kept it under the wraps of the surgical mask for six solid hours.

Like most doctors resisting the chronic hypochondriasis induced by medical school, Jeffrey often erred at the other extreme: he denied or ignored every symptom of illness or sign of fatigue, until it threatened to overwhelm him. Today was no exception. From the moment he'd awakened that morning at six, he'd felt terrible. Although he'd been feeling run-down for days, he first ascribed the light-headedness and chills to something he'd eaten the night before. When the waves of nausea came midmorning, Jeffrey was quick to attribute it to too much coffee. And when the headache and the diarrhea started in the early afternoon, he pinned it on the soup he'd had for lunch in the hospital cafeteria.

Only as he confronted his haggard reflection in the mirror of the surgical locker room did Jeffrey finally admit he was ill. He was probably coming down with the flu that had been going around the hospital for the last month. He put the flat of his wrist to his forehead for a rough check of his temperature. There was no doubt about it: it was hot.

Leaving the sink, Jeffrey went to his locker, grateful that the day was almost over. The idea of bed was the most appealing vision he could conjure.

Jeffrey sat on the bench, oblivious to the chatting crowd, and began to twirl his combination lock. He felt worse than ever. His stomach gurgled unpleasantly; his intestines were in agony. A passing cramp brought beads of perspiration to his brow. Unless someone could relieve him, he'd still be on duty for another few hours.

Stopping at the final number, Jeffrey opened his locker. Reaching within the neatly arranged interior, he retrieved a bottle of paregoric, an old remedy his mother used to force on him when he was a child. His mother had consistently diagnosed him as suffering from either constipation or diarrhea. It wasn't until he got to high school that Jeffrey realized these diagnoses were just excuses to get him to take his mother's cherished cure-all. Over the years, Jeffrey had developed a confidence in paregoric, if not in his mother's diagnostic skills. He always kept a bottle on hand.

Unscrewing the cap, he tilted his head back and took a healthy swig. Wiping his mouth, he noticed an orderly sitting next to him watching his every move.

"Want a swig?" Jeffrey asked, grinning, extending the bottle toward the man. "Great stuff."

The man gave him a disgusted look and got up and left.

Jeffrey shook his head at the man's lack of a sense of humor. From his reaction you'd have thought he'd offered him poison. With uncharacteristic slowness, Jeffrey took off his scrubs. Briefly massaging his temples, he then pushed himself to his feet and went in to shower. After sudsing and rinsing, he stood under the rushing water five minutes before stepping out and drying himself briskly. Brushing his wavy, sandy-brown hair, Jeffrey dressed in clean scrubs, donned a new mask and a new hat. He felt considerably better now. Except for an occasional gurgle, even his colon seemed to be cooperating—at least for the moment.

Jeffrey retraced his steps through the surgical lounge and

down the OR corridor and pushed through the connecting door that led to the delivery area. The decor there was a welcome antidote to the stark utilitarian tile of the OR. The individual delivery rooms may have been as sterile, but the delivery area and labor rooms were painted in pastels, with framed Impressionist prints on the walls. The windows even had curtains. The feeling was more like a hotel than a major urban hospital.

Jeffrey went to the main desk and inquired about his patient.

"Patty Owen is in fifteen," a tall, handsome black woman said. Her name was Monica Carver, and she was the nursing supervisor for the evening shift.

Jeffrey leaned over the desk, thankful for the momentary rest. "How's she doing?" he asked.

"Just fine," Monica said. "But it's going to be awhile. Her contractions aren't strong or frequent, and she's only dilated four centimeters."

Jeffrey nodded. He would have preferred to have things further along. It was standard practice to wait until the patient had dilated six centimeters to put in an epidural. Monica handed Jeffrey Patty's chart. He went through it quickly. There wasn't much there. The woman was obviously healthy. At least that was good.

"I'll have a chat with her," Jeffrey said, "then I'll be back in the OR. If something changes, give me a page."

"Sure thing," Monica said cheerfully.

Jeffrey started down toward room fifteen. About halfway down the hall he got another intestinal cramp. He had to stop and lean against the wall until it passed. What a nuisance, he thought. When he felt well enough, he continued to room fifteen and knocked. A pleasant voice told him to come in.

"I'm Dr. Jeffrey Rhodes," Jeffrey said, extending his hand. "I'll be your anesthesiologist."

Patty Owen grasped his outstretched hand. Her palm was damp, her fingers cold. She appeared considerably younger than twenty-four. Her hair was blond and her wide eyes looked like those of a vulnerable child. Jeffrey could tell the woman was frightened.

"Am I glad to see you!" Patty said, not willing to let go of

Jeffrey's hand immediately. "I want to tell you straight off that I'm a coward. I'm really not very good with pain."

"I'm sure we can help you," Jeffrey said reassuringly.

"I want an epidural," Patty said. "My doctor said I could have it."

"I understand," Jeffrey said, "and have it you will. Everything is going to be fine. We have a lot of deliveries here at the Boston Memorial. We'll take good care of you and after all is said and done, you'll wonder why you were so apprehensive in the first place."

"Really?" Patty asked.

"If we didn't have so many happy customers, do you think so many women would be coming back a second, a third, or even fourth time?"

Patty smiled wanly.

Jeffrey spent another quarter hour with her, questioning her about her health and allergies. He sympathized with her when she told him her husband was out of town on a business trip. Her familiarity with epidural anesthesia surprised him. She confided that not only had she read about it, her sister had had it for her two deliveries. Jeffrey explained why he wouldn't be giving her the epidural immediately. When he told her that she could get some Demerol in the meantime if she wanted it, Patty relaxed. Before leaving her, Jeffrey reminded her that any drugs she got, the baby got. Then he told her again there was no reason to worry; she was in good hands.

Coming out of Patty's labor room and suffering through another intestinal cramp, Jeffrey realized he would have to take more drastic steps against his own symptoms if he was to get through Patty's delivery. Despite the paregoric, he was feeling progressively worse.

Passing back through the connecting doors to the OR suite, Jeffrey returned to the anesthesia alcove next to the OR, where he'd spent most of the day. The room was empty and probably wouldn't be used again until the following morning.

Glancing up and down the OR corridor to make sure the coast was clear, Jeffrey pulled the drape closed. Although he'd finally acknowledged being sick, he wasn't about to admit it to anyone else.

From the drawer of his Narcomed III anesthesia machine, Jeffrey got out a small-gauge intravenous scalp needle and an infusion setup. He pulled a bottle of Ringer's Lactate IV fluid down from the shelf and snapped off the cover over the rubber port. With a decisive shove, he pushed the IV tubing into the bottle and hung the bottle up on the IV stand over the anesthesia machine. He ran fluid through the tubing until it was free of air bubbles, then he closed the plastic stopcock.

Jeffrey had only started IVs on himself a couple of times, but he was practiced enough in the procedure to be adept. Using his teeth to hold one end of the tourniquet, he secured it around his bicep and watched as his veins began to distend.

What Jeffrey had in mind was a trick that he'd learned as a resident. Back then, he and his colleagues, especially the surgical residents, refused to take any sick time for fear they'd lose the competitive edge. If they got the flu or symptoms like the ones Jeffrey was now experiencing, they would simply take time out to run in a liter of IV fluid. The results were almost guaranteed, suggesting most flu symptoms were due to dehydration. With a liter of Ringer's Lactate coursing through your veins, it was hard not to feel better. It had been ages since Jeffrey had last resorted to an IV. He only hoped the efficacy would be as strong as it had been when he'd been a resident. Now forty-two, he found it hard to believe that last time he had been almost twenty years younger.

Jeffrey was about to push the needle in when the curtain to the alcove was pulled aside. Jeffrey looked up into the surprised face of Regina Vinson, one of the evening nurses.

"Oh!" Regina exclaimed. "Excuse me."

"No problem," Jeffrey started to say, but Regina was gone as quickly as she had appeared. As long as she'd inadvertently caught him in the act, Jeffrey had half a mind to ask her to lend a hand by attaching the IV to the scalp needle once he got it into the vein. Reaching out, he pulled back the curtain in hopes of catching her, but Regina was already far down the crowded hall. He let the curtain fall back into place. He was just as well off without her.

Once the IV tubing was attached, he opened the stopcock. Almost at once he felt the cool sensation of the fluid as it flowed rapidly into the arm. By the time most of the bottle had run in, Jeffrey's upper arm was cool to the touch. After he pulled out the IV needle, he put an alcohol swab over the site and bent his elbow to hold it in place. He disposed of the IV paraphernalia in the wastebasket, then stood up. He waited for a moment to see how he felt. The light-headedness and headache were totally gone. So was the nausea. Pleased with the speedy results, Jeffrey pulled open the curtain and headed back to the locker room. Only his colon still troubled him.

The evening shift had now taken over and the day shift was in the process of leaving. The locker room was full of cheerful people. Most of the showers were occupied. First Jeffrey used the toilet. Then he got out his paregoric and took another hefty swig. He shuddered at the taste and wondered what made it so bitter. He tossed the now empty bottle into the wastebasket. Then he took a second shower and put on another set of clean scrub clothes.

When he walked out into the surgical lounge he almost felt human. He intended to sit down for a half hour or so and read the paper but before he had a chance his beeper went off. He recognized the number. It was delivery.

"Mrs. Owen is asking for you," Monica Carver told him when he phoned.

"How is she doing?" Jeffrey asked.

"Just fine," Monica said. "She's a little apprehensive, but she hasn't even asked for analgesia even though her contractions are now coming frequently. She's somewhere between five and six centimeters."

"Perfect," Jeffrey said. He was pleased. "I'll be right over."

En route to the delivery area, Jeffrey stopped at the anesthesia office to glance at the big board to see about the evening assignments. As he expected, everyone was busy with ongoing cases. He took a piece of chalk and wrote that whenever someone was free he or she should come over to delivery and relieve him.

When Jeffrey arrived in labor room fifteen, Patty was in the middle of a contraction. An experienced LPN was with her and the two women were functioning like a practiced team. Beads of sweat dotted Patty's brow. Her eyes were shut tightly, and she was gripping the nurse's hands with both of hers. Strapped to her abdomen was the rubber monitor keeping track of the progress of the labor as well as the fetal heartbeat.

"Ah, my white knight in blue," Patty said as the pain abated and she opened her eyes to see Jeffrey standing at the foot of the bed. She smiled.

"How about that epidural?" Jeffrey suggested.

"How about it!" Patty echoed.

All the equipment Jeffrey needed was on a cart he had wheeled in with him upon his return. After putting a blood pressure cuff in place, Jeffrey removed the rubber monitor from Patty's abdomen and helped position her on her side. With gloved hands he prepped her back with an antiseptic solution.

"First I'm going to give you the local anesthetic we talked about," Jeffrey said as he prepared the injection. He made a small weal with the tiny needle midline in Patty's lower back. She was so relieved to be getting it, she didn't even flinch.

Next, he took a Touhey needle from the epidural tray and made sure the stylet was in place. Then, using both hands, he pushed the needle into Patty's back, advancing it slowly but deliberately until he was certain he had reached the ligamentous covering of the spinal canal. Withdrawing the stylet, he attached an empty glass syringe. Jeffrey put slight pressure on the syringe's plunger. Feeling resistance, he expertly returned to advancing the needle. Suddenly the resistance on the plunger disappeared. Jeffrey was pleased: he knew he was in the epidural space.

"Are you okay?" Jeffrey asked as he used a glass syringe to draw up a test dose of 2 cc's of sterile water containing a tiny amount of epinephrine.

"Are you finished?" Patty asked.

"Not quite," Jeffrey said. "Just a few minutes more." He injected the test dose and immediately tested Patty's blood pressure and pulse. There was no change. If the needle had been in a blood vessel, Patty's heart rate would have increased immediately in response to the epinephrine.

Only then did Jeffrey seize the small epidural catheter. With practiced care, he threaded it up the Touhey needle.

"I feel something funny in my leg," Patty said nervously.

Jeffrey stopped pushing the catheter. It was only in about one centimeter beyond the tip of the needle. He asked Patty about the sensation, then explained that it was common for the epidural catheter to touch peripheral nerves as they transversed the epidural space. That could account for what she was feeling. When the paresthesia subsided, Jeffrey gingerly advanced the catheter another one and a half centimeters. Patty didn't complain.

Finally, Jeffrey pulled the Touhey needle out, leaving the small plastic catheter in place. Then he prepared a second test dose of 2 cc's of .25% spinal-grade Marcaine with epinephrine. After injecting this second dose, he monitored Patty's blood pressure and her sense of touch on her lower extremities. When there were no changes even after several minutes, Jeffrey was absolutely sure that his catheter was in the proper place. Finally, he injected the therapeutic dose of anesthetic: 5 cc's of .25% Marcaine. Then he capped off the catheter.

"That's all there is to that," Jeffrey said as he put a sterile bandage over the puncture site. "But I want you to stay on your side for a while."

"But I don't feel anything," Patty complained.

"That's the idea," Jeffrey said with a smile.

"You're sure it's working?"

"Just wait until your next contraction," Jeffrey said with confidence.

Jeffrey conferred with the LPN to let her know how frequently he wanted Patty's blood pressure taken. Then he helped her put the labor monitor back in place. He remained in the labor room through Patty's next contraction, using the time to complete his habitually meticulous anesthesia record. Patty felt reassured. The discomfort she had been experiencing was much improved, and she thanked Jeffrey effusively.

After telling Monica Carver and the LPN where he would be, Jeffrey went into one of the darkened empty labor rooms to lie down. He was feeling better, but certainly not normal. Closing his eyes for what he thought would be just a few minutes and soothed by the sound of rain against the window, he surprised himself by falling fast asleep. He was dimly aware of the door being opened and closed several times as different people checked on him, but no one disturbed him until Monica came in and gently shook his shoulder.

"We've got a problem," Monica said.

Jeffrey swung his legs over the side of the bed and rubbed his eyes. "What's wrong?"

"Simarian has decided to do a Caesarean on Patty Owen."

"So soon?" Jeffrey asked. He glanced at his watch. He blinked several times. The room seemed dimmer than before. Checking his watch, he was surprised to see that he'd been asleep for an hour and a half.

"The baby is an occiput posterior and hasn't been progressing," Monica explained. "But the main problem is that the baby's heart has been slow to return to a normal rate after each contraction."

"Time to do a Caesarean," Jeffrey agreed as he got unsteadily to his feet. He waited a beat until his mild dizziness cleared.

"Are you all right?" Monica questioned.

"Just fine," Jeffrey said. He sat down on a chair to slip on his OR shoes. "What's the time frame?"

"Simarian will be here in twenty minutes or so," Monica said, studying Jeffrey's face.

"Is something wrong?" Jeffrey asked. He ran his fingers through his hair in fear it was standing on end.

"You look pale," Monica said. "Maybe it's the lack of light in here." Outside it was raining even harder.

"How's Patty doing?" Jeffrey asked, heading for the bathroom.

"She's apprehensive," Monica said from the door. "Painwise, she's fine, but you might consider giving her some kind of tranquilizer just to keep her calm."

Jeffrey nodded as he turned on the light in the bathroom. He wasn't wild about the idea of giving Patty a tranquilizer, but given the circumstances, he'd consider it. "Make sure she's on oxygen," he told Monica. "I'll be out in a second."

"She's on oxygen," Monica called over her shoulder as she left the room.

Jeffrey examined himself in the mirror. He did look pale.

Then he noticed something else. His pupils were so contracted, they looked like twin pencil points. They were as small as he'd ever seen them. No wonder he'd had trouble seeing his watch in the other room.

Jeffrey splashed his face with cold water, then dried it roughly. At least that woke him up. He looked at his pupils again. They were still miotic. He took a deep breath and promised himself that as soon as he got through this delivery, he would make tracks for home and put himself to bed. After adjusting his hair with his fingernails, he headed for labor room fifteen.

Monica had been right. Patty was embarrassed, scared, and nervous about the upcoming Caesarean. She was taking the failure of the labor personally. Tears came to her eyes when she again voiced anger at her husband's absence. Jeffrey felt sorry for her and made a big effort at reassuring her that everything would be fine and that she certainly wasn't at fault. He also gave her 5 mg of diazepam IV, which he thought would have minimal effect if any on the unborn child. It had a rapid calming effect on Patty.

"I'll be asleep during the Caesarean?" Patty asked.

"You'll be very comfortable," Jeffrey replied, skirting the question. "One of the big benefits of continuous epidural anesthesia is that I can extend it now that we need a higher level, without disturbing Patty junior."

"It's a boy," Patty said. "His name is Mark." She smiled weakly. Her lids had become a little droopy. The tranquilizer was clearly taking effect.

The transfer from the delivery area to the OR suite was accomplished without incident. Jeffrey kept Patty on oxygen by mask during the short trip.

The OR had been advised as to the decision to do a Caesarean. By the time Patty was transferred, the room was almost set up for the procedure. The scrub nurse, already scrubbed, was busy laying out the instruments. The circulating nurse helped guide the gurney into the room and transfer Patty to the OR table. Patty still had the fetal monitor on, which was left in place for the time being.

Jeffrey wasn't as familiar with the evening personnel, and he hadn't met the circulating nurse before. Her name tag read: Sheila Dodenhoff.

"I'm going to need some .5% Marcaine," Jeffrey told Sheila as he changed Patty from portable bottle oxygen to oxygen delivered through his Narcomed III anesthesia machine. He then reapplied the blood pressure cuff to Patty's left arm.

"Coming up," Sheila said cheerfully.

Jeffrey worked quickly but deliberately. He checked off every procedure in his anesthesia record once it had been performed. In sharp contrast to most other doctors, Jeffrey prided himself on his exquisitely legible handwriting.

After hooking up the EKG leads, he attached the pulse oximeter to Patty's left index finger. He was replacing Patty's IV with a more secure intracath when Sheila returned.

"Here you go," she said, handing Jeffrey a 30 cc glass vial of .5% Marcaine. Jeffrey took the drug and, as he always did, checked the label. He set the vial on top of his anesthesia machine. From the drawer, he took out a 2 cc ampule of spinal grade .5% Marcaine with epinephrine and drew it up into a syringe. Maneuvering Patty onto her right side, Jeffrey injected the 2 cc's into the epidural catheter.

"How's everything going?" a booming voice called out from the door.

Jeffrey turned to see Dr. Simarian holding a mask to his face while he held open the door.

"We'll be ready in a minute," Jeffrey said.

"How's the little one's ticker?" he asked.

"At the moment, fine," Jeffrey answered.

"I'll scrub up and we'll get this show on the road."

The door swung shut. Jeffrey gave Patty's shoulder a squeeze while he studied the EKG and the blood pressure readout. "You okay?" he asked her, moving the oxygen mask to the side.

"I think so," she said.

"I want you to tell me whatever you feel. Understand?" Jeffrey said. "Do your feet feel normal?"

Patty nodded. Jeffrey went around and tested her sensation. Coming back to the head of the table and checking the monitors again, he was sure that the epidural catheter had not

moved and had not penetrated either the spinal canal or one
of the pregnancy-dilated veins of Bateson.

Satisfied that all was in order, Jeffrey picked up the vial of
Marcaine Sheila had brought him. Using his thumb, he
snapped off the top of the sealed glass container. Once again
he checked the label, then drew up 12 cc's. He wanted anesthesia to extend at least to T6, and preferably to T4. As he put
the Marcaine down, his eyes caught Sheila's. She was standing
off to the left, staring at Jeffrey.

"Is something wrong?" Jeffrey asked.

Sheila held his gaze for a beat, then spun on her heels and
left the OR without speaking. Jeffrey turned to catch the eye
of the scrub nurse, but she was still busy setting up. Jeffrey
shrugged. Something was going on that he didn't know about.

Returning to Patty's side, he injected the Marcaine. Then he
capped off the epidural catheter and returned to the head of the
table. After putting down the syringe, he noted the time and
the exact amount of the injection in the record. A slight quickening of the beep of the pulse brought his eyes up to the EKG
monitor. If there was to be any change in the heart rate, Jeffrey
expected a slight slowing from progressive sympathetic blockade. Instead, there was the opposite. Patty's pulse was speeding
up. It was the first sign of the impending disaster.

Jeffrey's initial reaction was more of curiosity than concern.
His analytical mind groped for a logical explanation for what
he was witnessing. He glanced at the blood pressure readout
and then the oximeter LED. They were all fine. He looked
back at the EKG. The pulse was still quickening, and even
more disturbing, there was an ectopic, irregular heartbeat.
Under the circumstances, that was not a good sign.

Jeffrey swallowed hard as fear clutched at his throat. It had
only been seconds since he'd injected the Marcaine. Could it
have gone intravenous despite the test dose result? Jeffrey had
had one other adverse reaction to local anesthetic in his professional career. The incident had been harrowing.

The ectopic beats were increasing in frequency. Why would
the heart rate increase and why the irregular rhythm? If the
anesthetic dose did go intravenously, why wasn't the blood
pressure falling? Jeffrey had no immediate answers to these

questions, but his medical sixth sense, born of years of experience, set off alarm bells in his mind. Something abnormal was occurring. Something Jeffrey was at a loss to explain, much less understand.

"I don't feel good," Patty said, turning her head to talk out of the side of the mask.

Jeffrey looked down into Patty's face. He could see it was again clouded with fear. "What's the matter?" he asked, puzzled by these rapid events. He touched her shoulder.

"I feel funny," Patty said.

"How do you mean, funny?" Jeffrey's eyes went back to the monitors. There was always the fear of allergy to the local anesthetic, although developing allergy in the two hours since the first dose seemed a rather farfetched notion. He noticed the blood pressure had risen slightly.

"Ahhhhh!" Patty cried.

Jeffrey's eyes shot to her face. Patty's features were twisted in a horrible grimace.

"What is it, Patty?" Jeffrey demanded.

"I feel a pain in my stomach," Patty managed hoarsely through clenched teeth. "It's high up, under my ribs. It's different from the labor pain. Please . . ." Her voice trailed off.

Patty began to writhe on the table, drawing up her legs. Sheila reappeared along with a muscular male nurse who lent a hand in attempting to restrain her.

The blood pressure that had risen slightly now began to fall. "I want a wedge under her right side," Jeffrey yelled as he got ephedrine from the drawer and prepared it for injection. Mentally he calculated how far he'd let the blood pressure drop before he'd inject the pressor agent. He still had no idea of what was happening, and he preferred not to act before he knew exactly what he was up against.

A gurgling sound brought his attention back to Patty's face. He pulled off her oxygen mask. To his surprise and horror she was salivating like a mad dog. At the same time she was lacrimating profusely; tears were streaming down her face. A wet cough suggested that she was also forming increasing amounts of tracheo-bronchial secretions.

Jeffrey remained the ultimate professional. He had been

trained to deal with this type of emergency situation. His mind raced ahead, taking in all the information, making hypotheses, then ruling them out. Meanwhile, he dealt with the life-threatening symptoms. First he suctioned Patty's nasopharynx, then he injected atropine intravenously, followed by ephedrine. He suctioned Patty again, then injected a second dose of the atropine. The secretions slowed, the blood pressure plateaued, the oxygenation stayed normal, but Jeffrey still did not know the cause. All he could think of was an allergic reaction to the Marcaine. He watched the EKG, hoping that the atropine might have a positive effect on the irregular heartbeats. But they remained irregular. In fact, they became even more irregular as Patty's pulse quickened. Jeffrey prepared a 4 mg dose of propranolol, but before he could inject it, he noticed the muscle fasciculations that distorted Patty's features in a series of seemingly uncontrolled twists and spasms. The fasciculations rapidly spread to other muscles until her body became wracked by clonic jerks.

"Hold her, Trent!" Sheila cried to the male nurse. "Get her legs!"

Jeffrey injected the propranolol as the EKG began to register further bizarre changes, intimating there was diffuse involvement of the heart's electrical conduction system.

Patty spewed up green bile which Jeffrey quickly suctioned away. He glanced at the oximeter readout. That was still holding. Then the fetal monitor alarm began to go off; the baby's heart was slowing. Before anyone could react, Patty suffered a grand mal seizure. Her limbs flailed madly in all directions, then her back arched in awkward hyperextension.

"What the hell is going on?" Simarian shouted as he came flying through the door.

"The Marcaine," Jeffrey shouted. "She's having some sort of overwhelming reaction." Jeffrey didn't have time to elaborate as he drew up 75 mg of succinylcholine.

"Jesus Christ!" Simarian yelled, coming around the table to help hold Patty down.

Jeffrey injected the succinylcholine as well as an additional dose of diazepam. He was thankful that his compulsiveness had made him change the IV to a more secure one. The audio portion of the oximeter readout began to fall in pitch as Patty's oxygenation decreased. Jeffrey again cleared her airway and tried to bag her with the 100% oxygen.

Patty's seizure movements slowed as succinylcholine-induced paralysis took effect. Jeffrey slipped in an endotracheal tube, checked its position, and ventilated her well with the oxygen. The sound of the oximeter immediately returned to its higher pitch. But the fetal monitor was still sending out its alarm. The baby's heart had slowed and was not speeding back up.

"We gotta get the baby!" Simarian yelled. He grabbed sterile gloves from one of the side tables and yanked them on.

Jeffrey was still watching the blood pressure, which had started to fall again. He gave Patty another dose of ephedrine. The blood pressure started back up. He glanced at the EKG; it had not improved with the propranolol. Then to Jeffrey's horror, just as he was watching, the EKG disintegrated into senseless fibrillation. Patty's heart had stopped beating.

"She's arresting!" Jeffrey shouted. The blood pressure fell to zero. Both the EKG and the oximeter alarms began shrieking stridently.

"My God!" Simarian yelled. He had been hastily draping the patient. He moved up to the table and started external cardiac massage by compressing Patty's chest. Sheila put out the word to the OR desk. Help was on its way.

The crash cart arrived along with additional OR nurses. With lightning speed, they prepared the defibrillator. A nurse anesthetist also arrived. She went directly to Jeffrey's side.

The oxygen content of Patty's blood went up slightly. "Countershock her!" Jeffrey ordered.

Simarian took the defibrillator paddles from one of the nurses. He applied them to Patty's bare chest. Everyone stepped back from the OR table. Simarian pressed the button. Since Patty was paralyzed with the succinylcholine, there was no apparent effect from the electric current except on the EKG screen. The fibrillation disappeared, but when the phosphorescent blip returned, it did not show a normal heartbeat. Instead, it traced a completely flat line with only a few minor squiggles.

"Restart massage!" Jeffrey ordered. He stared at the EKG.

He couldn't believe there was no electrical activity. The muscular male nurse took over from Simarian and started compressing Patty's chest with good result.

The fetal monitor was still sounding. The child's heart rate was too slow. "We gotta get the baby!" Simarian snapped again. He changed his gloves and hastily took additional drapes from the scrub nurse. He positioned them as best he could despite the cardiac massage. He grabbed a knife from the instrument table and went to work. Using a generous vertical incision, he sliced Patty's lower abdomen open. With the reduced blood pressure there was very little bleeding. A pediatrician arrived on the scene and prepared to take the baby.

Jeffrey's attention stayed with Patty. He suctioned her and was surprised at the amount of secretions even after the two doses of atropine. Checking Patty's pupils, he was pleased they were not dilated. In fact, he was surprised to find them pinpoint. With oxygenation remaining up, Jeffrey decided to hold off introducing any more drugs into Patty's system until after the baby was delivered. Briefly, he explained what had happened to the nurse anesthetist.

"You think it's a reaction to the Marcaine?" she asked.

"That's all I can think of," Jeffrey admitted.

In the next minute a silent, blue, flaccid baby was pulled from Patty's abdomen. After the cord was severed, the child was quickly handed to the waiting pediatrician. He rushed the newborn to the infant care unit, where the baby was surrounded by his own resuscitation team. The nurse anesthetist joined that group.

"I don't like this flat EKG," Jeffrey said to himself as he injected a bolus of epinephrine. He watched the EKG. No response. He then tried another dose of atropine. Nothing. Exasperated, he drew an arterial blood sample and sent it off to the lab for a stat reading.

Ted Overstreet, one of the cardiac surgeons who had recently finished a bypass case, came in and stood next to Jeffrey. After Jeffrey explained the situation, Overstreet suggested opening her up.

The nurse anesthetist came back to report that the baby was not in good shape. "The Apgar is only three," she said. "He's breathing and his heart is beating, but not well. And his muscle tone is not good. In fact, it's weird."

"How so?" Jeffrey asked, fighting a wave of depression.

"His left leg moves okay, but not his right. The right one is completely flaccid. With his arms it's just the opposite."

Jeffrey shook his head. Obviously the child had been oxygen deprived in utero and was now brain damaged. The realization was crushing, but there was no time to wallow in regret. Just then his chief concern was Patty and how to get her heart started.

The stat lab work came back. Patty's pH was 7.28. Under the circumstances, Jeffrey thought, that was pretty good. Next he injected a dose of calcium chloride. Minutes dragged like hours as everyone watched the EKG, waiting for some sign of life, some response to treatment. But the monitor traced a frustratingly flat line.

The male nurse continued the chest compressions and the ventilator kept Patty's lungs filled with pure oxygen. Her pupils remained miotic, suggesting her brain was getting enough oxygen, but her heart stayed electrically and mechanically still. Jeffrey repeated all the textbook procedures but to no avail. He even had Patty shocked again with the defibrillator set at 400 joules.

Once the pediatrician had the newborn stabilized, he had the entire infant care unit vacate the OR along with its attendant clutch of residents and nurses. Little Mark was on his way to the neonatal intensive care unit. Jeffrey watched them go. He felt heartsick. Shaking his head in sorrow, he turned back to Patty. What to do?

Jeffrey looked up at Ted, who was still standing next to him. He asked Ted what he thought they should do. Jeffrey was desperate.

"Like I said, I think we should open her up and work on the heart directly. There's not much to lose at this point."

Jeffrey watched the flat EKG for another moment. Then he sighed. "Okay. Let's try it," he said reluctantly. He had no other ideas, and he didn't want to give up. As Ted pointed out, they had nothing to lose. It was worth a try.

Ted gowned and gloved in less than ten minutes. Once he

was prepared, he had the nurse stop compressing the chest so that he could rapidly drape and slice into it. Within seconds he was holding Patty's naked heart.

Ted massaged the heart with his gloved hand and even injected epinephrine directly into the left ventricle. When that failed to have an effect, he tried to pace the heart by attaching internal leads to the cardiac wall. That resulted in a complex on the EKG, but the heart itself did not respond.

Ted recommenced the internal cardiac massage. "No pun intended," he said after a couple of minutes, "but my heart is no longer in this. I'm afraid the ballgame is over unless you guys have a heart transplant waiting around here. This one is long gone."

Jeffrey knew that Ted didn't mean to sound callous and that his apparently flip attitude was more of a defense mechanism than a true lack of compassion, yet it cut Jeffrey to the quick. He had to restrain himself from lashing out verbally.

For as much as he'd given up, Ted continued the internal cardiac massage. The only sound in the OR came from the monitor recording the pacemaker's discharge and the low hum of the pulse oximeter as it responded to Ted's internal massage.

Simarian was the one who broke the silence. "I agree," he said simply. He snapped off his gloves.

Ted looked across the rapidly erected ether screen at Jeffrey. Jeffrey nodded. Ted stopped massaging the heart and pulled his hand from within Patty's chest. "Sorry," he said.

Jeffrey nodded again. He took a deep breath, then turned the ventilator off. He looked back at the sorry sight of Patty Owen with her abdomen and chest rudely sliced open. It was a terrible sight, one that would stay with Jeffrey for the rest of his life. The floor was littered with drug containers and wrappers.

Jeffrey felt crushed and numb. This was the nadir of his professional career. He'd witnessed other tragedies, but this was the worst, and most unexpected. His eyes drifted to his anesthesia machine. It too was covered with debris. Beneath the debris was the incomplete anesthesia record. He'd have to bring it up to date. In the fevered attempt to save Patty he'd had no time to do so. He looked for the half-empty vial of Marcaine, feeling an irrational antipathy toward it. Although it seemed unreasonable in light of the test dose results, he couldn't help but feel an allergic reaction to the drug was the root of this tragedy. He wanted to dash the vial against the wall, just to vent his frustration. Of course he knew he wouldn't actually throw the vial; he was too controlled for that. But he couldn't find it among the mess.

"Sheila," Jeffrey called to the circulating nurse who was starting the clean-up process, "what happened to the Marcaine vial?"

Sheila stopped what she was doing to glare at Jeffrey. "If you don't know where you put it, I certainly don't," she said angrily.

Jeffrey nodded and then turned his attention to unhooking Patty from the monitors. He could understand Sheila's anger. He was angry too. Patty didn't deserve this kind of fate. What Jeffrey didn't realize was that Sheila wasn't angry at fate. She was angry at Jeffrey. In fact, she was furious.

MONDAY,

MAY 15, 1989

11:15 A.M.

A shaft of golden morning sunlight filtered through a window high on the wall to Jeffrey's left and knifed down through the courtroom, hitting the paneled wall behind the judge's bench like a spotlight. Millions of tiny motes of dust sparkled and swirled in the intense beam of light. Ever since the beginning of this trial, Jeffrey had been struck by the theatric quality of the justice system. But this was no TV daytime drama. Jeffrey's career—his whole life—was on the line.

Jeffrey closed his eyes and leaned forward at the defendant's table, cradling his head in his hands. With his elbows splayed on the table, he roughly rubbed his eyes. The tension was about to drive him crazy.

Taking a deep breath, he opened his eyes, half hoping the scene before him would have magically disappeared and he would wake up from the worst nightmare of his life. But of course it wasn't a bad dream he was suffering. Jeffrey was involved in his second trial for Patty Owen's untimely death eight months previously. Just then he was sitting in a courtroom in the center of Boston, waiting to hear the jury deliver his fate on criminal charges.

Jeffrey glanced over his lawyer's head to scan the crowd. There was an excited, low-pitched babble of voices, a murmur of expectancy. Jeffrey averted his gaze, knowing that all the talk centered on him. He wished he could hide. He felt utterly humiliated by the public spectacle so rapidly unfolding. His entire life had unraveled and disintegrated. His career was going down the drain. He felt overwhelmed, yet oddly numb.

Jeffrey sighed. Randolph Bingham, his lawyer, had urged him to appear calm and controlled. Easier said than done, especially now. After all the heartache, anxiety, and sleepless nights, it was now down to the wire. The jury had reached its decision. The verdict was on its way.

Jeffrey studied Randolph's aristocratic profile. The man had become a father to him through these last eight harrowing months, even though he was only five years Jeffrey's senior. Sometimes Jeffrey had felt almost love for the man, other times something more akin to rage and hatred. But he'd always had confidence in his lawyer's skills, at least until this point.

Glancing at the prosecuting team, Jeffrey studied the district attorney. He had particular antipathy for this man, who seemed to have seized on the case as a vehicle for advancing his political career. Jeffrey could appreciate the man's native intelligence though he'd grown to despise him during the course of the four-day trial. But now, watching as the D.A. conversed animatedly with an assistant, Jeffrey realized he felt oddly devoid of emotion toward the man. For him, the whole business had been a job, no more, no less.

Jeffrey's eyes strayed beyond the district attorney toward the empty jury box. During the trial the realization that these twelve strangers held his fate in their hands had paralyzed Jeffrey. Never before had he experienced such vulnerability. Up until this episode, Jeffrey had been living under the delusion that his fate was largely in his own hands. This trial showed him just how mistaken he was.

The jury had been deliberating for two anxious days and—for Jeffrey—two sleepless nights. Now they were waiting for the jury to return to the courtroom. Jeffrey again wondered if two days of deliberation was a good sign or a bad. Randolph, in his irritatingly conservative manner, would not speculate.

Jeffrey felt the man could have lied just to give him a few hours of relative peace.

Despite his good intentions to refrain from fidgeting, Jeffrey began to stroke his mustache. When he realized what he was doing, he folded his hands and set them on the table in front of him.

He glanced over his left shoulder and caught sight of Carol, his soon to be ex-wife. Her head was down. She was reading. Jeffrey turned his gaze back to the judge's empty bench. He could have been irritated that she was relaxed enough to be able to read at this moment, but he wasn't. Instead, Jeffrey felt thankful that she was there and that she'd shown as much support as she had. After all, even before this legal nightmare had started, the two of them had come to the mutual conclusion that they had grown apart.

When they had first married eight years ago, it hadn't seemed important that Carol was extremely social and outgoing while he tended toward the opposite. It also hadn't bothered Jeffrey that Carol wanted to put off having a family while she advanced her career in banking, at least until Jeffrey found out that her idea of postponement meant never. And now she wanted to head west, to Los Angeles. Jeffrey could have lived with the idea of moving to California, but he had trouble with the family issue. Over the years he'd come to want a child more and more. To see Carol's hopes and aspirations move in an entirely different direction saddened him, but he found he didn't hold it against her. Jeffrey had fought the idea of divorce at first, but had finally given in. Somehow, they just weren't meant to be. But then, when Jeffrey's legal problems materialized, Carol had graciously offered to hold off on the domestic issue until Jeffrey's legal difficulties were resolved.

Jeffrey sighed again, more loudly than before. Randolph shot him a disapproving glare, but Jeffrey couldn't see that appearances mattered at this point. Whenever Jeffrey thought about the sequence of events, it had a dizzying effect on him. It had all happened so quickly. After the disastrous death of Patty Owen, the malpractice summons had arrived in short order. Under the current litigious climate, Jeffrey had not been surprised by the lawsuit, except perhaps by the speed.

From the start, Randolph had warned Jeffrey that it would

be a tough case. Jeffrey had had no idea how tough. That was right before Boston Memorial suspended him. At the time, such a move had seemed capricious and unreasonably vicious. It certainly wasn't the kind of support or vote of confidence Jeffrey had hoped for. Neither Jeffrey nor Randolph had had any inkling of the rationale for the suspension. Jeffrey had wanted to take action against Boston Memorial for this unwarranted act, but Randolph had advised him to sit tight. He thought that issue would be better resolved after the conclusion of the malpractice litigation.

But the suspension was only the harbinger of worse trouble to come. The malpractice plaintiff attorney was a young, aggressive fellow named Matthew Davidson from a firm in St. Louis specializing in malpractice litigation. He was also associated with a small general law firm in Massachusetts. He'd filed suit against Jeffrey, Simarian, Overstreet, the hospital, and even Arolen Pharmaceuticals, who'd manufactured the Marcaine. Jeffrey had never been the subject of a malpractice action before. Randolph had to explain that this was the "shotgun" approach. Litigators sued everybody with "deep pockets" whether or not there was any evidence of direct involvement in the alleged incident of malpractice.

Being one among many had initially provided some solace to Jeffrey, but not for long. It quickly became clear that Jeffrey would stand alone. He could remember the turning point as if it were yesterday. It had happened through the course of his own testimony in the early stages of the initial civil malpractice trial. He had been the first defendant to take the stand. Davidson had been asking cursory background questions, when he suddenly became harder hitting.

"Doctor," Davidson said, turning his thin, handsome face toward Jeffrey and putting a pejorative cast to the title. He walked directly to the witness stand and placed his face within inches of Jeffrey's. He was dressed in an impeccably tailored, dark pinstriped suit with a light lavender shirt and a dark purple paisley tie. He smelled of expensive cologne. "Have you ever been addicted to any drug?"

"Objection!" Randolph called out, rising to his feet.

Jeffrey had felt as if he were watching a scene in some drama, not a chapter in his life. Randolph elaborated on his objection:

"This question is immaterial to the issues at hand. The plaintiff attorney is trying to impugn my client."

"Not so," Davidson countered. "This issue is extremely germane to the current circumstances as will be brought out with the testimony of subsequent witnesses."

For a few moments silence reigned in the crowded courtroom. Publicity had brought notoriety to the case. People were standing along the back wall.

The judge was a heavyset black man named Wilson. He pushed his thick black-rimmed glasses higher on the bridge of his nose. Finally he cleared his throat. "If you're fooling with me, Mr. Davidson, there's going to be hell to pay."

"I certainly wouldn't choose to fool with you, Your Honor."

"Objection overruled," Judge Wilson said. He nodded toward Davidson. "You may proceed, Counselor."

"Thank you," Davidson said as he turned his attention back to Jeffrey. "Would you like me to repeat the question, Doctor?" he asked.

"No," Jeffrey said. He remembered the question well enough. He glanced at Randolph, but Randolph was busy writing on a yellow legal tablet. Jeffrey returned Davidson's steady glare. He had a premonition that trouble was ahead. "Yes, I had a mild drug problem once," he said in a subdued voice. This was an old secret that he'd never imagined would surface, especially not in a court of law. He had been reminded of it recently when he had to fill out the required form to renew his Massachusetts medical license. Yet he thought that information was confidential.

"Would you tell the jury what drug you were addicted to," Davidson asked, stepping away from Jeffrey as if he was too revolted to remain too close to him for any longer than necessary.

"Morphine," Jeffrey said with almost a defiant tone. "It was five years ago. I had trouble with back pain after a bad bicycle accident."

Out of the corner of his eye, Jeffrey saw Randolph scratching his right eyebrow. That was a previously arranged gesture to signal that he wanted Jeffrey to confine himself to the question at hand and not offer any information. But Jeffrey ignored him. Jeffrey was angry that this irrelevant piece of his past was being dredged up. He felt the urge to explain and defend himself. He certainly wasn't a drug addict by any stretch of the imagination.

"How long were you addicted?" Davidson asked.

"Less than a month," Jeffrey snapped. "It was a situation where need and desire had imperceptibly merged."

"I see," Davidson said, lifting his eyebrows in a dramatic gesture of understanding. "That's how you explained it to yourself?"

"It was how my treatment counselor explained it to me," Jeffrey shot back. He could see Randolph frantically scratching again, but Jeffrey continued to ignore him. "The bicycle accident occurred at a time of deepening domestic strain. I was prescribed the morphine by an orthopedic surgeon. I convinced myself that I needed it longer than I actually did. But I realized what was happening in a few weeks' time and I took sick leave from the hospital and volunteered for treatment. And also marriage counseling, I might add."

"During those weeks, did you ever administer anesthesia while . . ." Davidson paused as if he were trying to think how to word his question. ". . . while you were under the influence?"

"Objection!" Randolph called. "This line of questioning is absurd! It's nothing short of calumny."

The judge bent his head down to look over the top of his glasses, which had slid down his nose. "Mr. Davidson," he said patronizingly, "we're back to the same issue. I trust that you have some cogent reason for this apparent excursion."

"Absolutely, Your Honor," Davidson said. "We intend to show that this testimony has a direct bearing on the case at hand."

"Objection overruled," the judge said. "Proceed."

Davidson turned back to Jeffrey and repeated the question. He seemed to relish the phrase "under the influence."

Jeffrey glared back at the plaintiff attorney. The one thing in his life that he was absolutely sure of was his sense of professional responsibility, competence, and performance.

The fact that this man was suggesting something else in-
furiated him. "I have never compromised a patient," Jeffrey
snapped.

"That is not my question," Davidson said.

Randolph got to his feet and said, "Your Honor, I would like
to approach the bench."

"As you wish," the judge said.

Both Randolph and Davidson went up to the judge. Randolph was obviously incensed. He began talking in a hoarse
whisper. Even though Jeffrey was only ten feet away, he could
not hear the conversation clearly although he did hear the
word "recess" mentioned several times. Eventually, the judge
leaned back and looked at him.

"Dr. Rhodes," he said, "your counsel seems to think you
need a rest. Is that true?"

"I don't need any rest," Jeffrey said angrily.

Randolph threw up his hands in frustration.

"Good," the judge said. "Then let's get on with this examination, Mr. Davidson, so we can all get out for some lunch."

"All right, Doctor," Davidson said. "Have you ever administered anesthesia under the influence of morphine?"

"There may have been one or two times . . ." Jeffrey began,
"but—"

"Yes or no, Doctor!" Davidson cut in. "A simple yes or no
is all I want."

"Objection!" Randolph called. "The counselor is not letting
the witness answer the question."

"Quite the contrary," Davidson said. "It's a simple question
and I'm looking for a simple answer. Either yes or no."

"Overruled," the judge said. "The witness will have a
chance to elaborate on cross-examination. Please answer the
question, Dr. Rhodes."

"Yes," Jeffrey said. He could feel his blood boil. He wanted
to reach out and strangle the plaintiff attorney.

"Since your treatment for your addiction to morphine . . ."
Davidson began, walking away from Jeffrey. He emphasized
the words "addiction" and "morphine," then paused. He
stopped near the jury box, turned, then added: ". . . have you
ever taken morphine again?"

"No," Jeffrey said with forcefulness.

"Did you take morphine on the day you administered anesthesia to the unfortunate Patty Owen?"

"Absolutely not," Jeffrey said.

"Are you sure, Dr. Rhodes?"

"Yes!" Jeffrey shouted.

"No more questions," Davidson said, and he returned to his seat.

Randolph had done what he could on cross-examination, emphasizing that the addiction problem had been minor and short-lived, and that Jeffrey had never taken more than a therapeutic dose. Besides, Jeffrey had volunteered for treatment, had been certified "cured," and had not been subjected to any disciplinary action. But despite these assurances, Jeffrey and Randolph had both felt his case had been dealt a death blow.

Just then, Jeffrey was brought back to the present by the sudden appearance of a uniformed court officer at the door to the jury room. His pulse shot up. He thought the jury was about to be announced. But the court officer made his way over to the door to the judge's chambers and disappeared. Jeffrey's thoughts drifted back to the malpractice trial.

True to his word concerning its relevancy, Davidson brought the addiction issue back with further testimony that had been totally unexpected despite the discovery depositions. The first surprise came in the form of Regina Vinson.

After the usual introductory questions, Davidson asked her if she had seen Dr. Jeffrey Rhodes on the fateful day of Patty Owen's death.

"I did," Regina said, staring at Jeffrey.

Jeffrey knew Regina vaguely as one of the evening OR nurses. He didn't remember seeing her on the day that Patty died.

"Where was Dr. Rhodes when you saw him?" Davidson asked.

"He was in the anesthesia alcove for operating room eleven," Regina said, keeping her eyes directly on Jeffrey.

Again, Jeffrey had a premonition that something detrimental to his case was coming, but he couldn't guess what it would be. He remembered working in room eleven for most of the day. Randolph leaned over and asked in a hushed voice, "What is she leading up to?"

"I haven't the foggiest," Jeffrey whispered, unable to break eye contact with the nurse. What disturbed him was that he could sense real hostility in the woman.

"Did Dr. Rhodes see you?" Davidson asked.

"Yes," Regina replied.

All at once, Jeffrey remembered. In his mind's eye he saw the image of her startled face as she pulled the drape aside. The fact that he was sick that fateful day was something besides his addiction problem that he had failed to tell Randolph. He'd considered it, but had been afraid to tell him. At the time he thought of his behavior as evidence of his dedication and self-sacrifice. After the fact, he'd not been so sure. So he'd never told anyone. He started to reach for Randolph's arm, but it was far too late.

Davidson was looking at the jurors, one after another, as he posed the next question: "Was there something strange about Dr. Rhodes being in the alcove of operating room eleven?"

"Yes," Regina answered. "The curtain was closed and operating room eleven was not in use."

Davidson kept his eyes on the jurors. Then he said, "Please tell the court what Dr. Rhodes was doing in the anesthesia alcove of the empty operating room with the drapes closed."

"He was shooting up," Regina said angrily. "He was injecting himself intravenously."

An excited murmur rippled through the courtroom. Randolph turned to Jeffrey with a shocked expression. Jeffrey shook his head guiltily. "I can explain," he said lamely.

Davidson went on. "What did you do after you saw Dr. Rhodes 'shooting up'?"

"I went to the supervisor, who called the chief of anesthesia," Regina said. "Unfortunately, the chief of anesthesia was not reached until after the tragedy."

Immediately after Regina's damaging testimony, Randolph had been able to get a recess. When he was alone with Jeffrey he demanded to know about this "shooting-up" episode. Jeffrey confessed to having been ill that fateful day, and said that no one but he had been available for the delivery. He explained everything he'd done in order to keep working, including giving himself the IV and taking paregoric.

"What else haven't you told me?" Randolph demanded angrily.

"That's all," Jeffrey said.

"Why didn't you tell me this before?" Randolph snapped.

Jeffrey shook his head. In truth, he wasn't completely sure himself. "I don't know," he said. "I have never liked admitting when I'm sick even to myself, much less anyone else. Most doctors are like that. Maybe it's part of our defense about being around illness. We like to think we're invulnerable."

"I'm not asking for an editorial," Randolph practically shouted. "Save it for the *New England Journal of Medicine*. I want to know why *you* couldn't tell *me*, your lawyer, that you were seen 'shooting up' on the morning in question."

"I guess I was afraid to tell you," Jeffrey admitted. "I did everything possible for Patty Owen. Anyone can read the record and attest to that. The last thing I wanted to admit was that there could be a question of my having been in top form. Maybe I was afraid you wouldn't defend me with the same intensity if you thought I was even remotely culpable."

"Jesus Christ!" Randolph exclaimed.

Later, back in the courtroom, during the cross-examination, Randolph did as much damage control as he could. He brought out the fact that Regina did not know if Jeffrey was injecting himself with a drug or merely starting an IV to rehydrate himself.

But Davidson was not done yet. He brought Sheila Dodenhoff to the stand. And just like Regina, she glared at Jeffrey while she testified.

"Miss Dodenhoff," Davidson intoned, "as the circulating nurse during Mrs. Owen's tragedy, did you ever notice anything strange about the defendant, Dr. Rhodes?"

"Yes, I did," Sheila said triumphantly.

"Would you please tell the court what you noticed," Davidson said, obviously relishing the moment.

"I noticed his pupils were pinpoint," Sheila said. "I noticed it because his eyes are so blue. In fact, I could barely see his pupils at all."

Davidson's next witness was a world-famous ophthalmologist from New York who'd written an exhaustive tome on the function of the pupil. After establishing his eminent credentials, Davidson asked the doctor to name the most common drug to cause pupils to contract to pinpoints—miosis, as the doctor preferred to call the condition.

"You mean a systemic drug or an eye drop?" the ophthalmologist asked.

"A systemic drug," Davidson said.

"Morphine," the ophthalmologist said confidently. He then commenced an incomprehensible lecture about the Edinger-Westphal nucleus, but Davidson cut him off and turned the witness over to Randolph.

As the trial dragged on, Randolph had tried to rectify the damage, proposing that Jeffrey had taken paregoric for diarrhea. Since paregoric is compounded with tincture of opium, and since opium contains morphine, he proposed that the paregoric had caused Jeffrey's constricted pupils. He also explained that Jeffrey had given himself an IV to treat flu symptoms, which are frequently caused by dehydration. But it was apparent that the jury did not buy these explanations, especially after Davidson brought a well-known and respected internist to the stand.

"Tell me, Doctor," Davidson said unctuously, "is it common for doctors to give themselves IVs as it has been suggested that Dr. Rhodes had done?"

"No," the internist said. "I've heard some scuttlebutt about gung-ho surgical residents doing such a thing, but even if such reports are true, it's certainly not a common practice."

The final blow in the trial came when Davidson called Marvin Hickleman to the stand. He was one of the OR orderlies.

"Mr. Hickleman," Davidson said. "Did you clean OR fifteen after the Patty Owen case?"

"Yes, I did," Marvin said.

"I understand you found something in the biohazard disposal container on the side of the anesthesia machine. Could you tell the court what you found?"

Marvin cleared his throat. "I found an empty vial of Marcaine."

"What concentration was the vial?" Davidson asked.

"It was .75%," Marvin said.

Jeffrey had leaned over and whispered to Randolph, "I used .5%. I'm sure of it."

As if he'd overheard, Davidson then asked Hickleman: "Did you find any .5% vials?"

"No," Marvin said, "I did not."

On cross-examination, Randolph tried to discredit Marvin's testimony, but only made things worse. "Mr. Hickleman, do you always go through the trash when you clean an operating room and check the concentration of the various drug containers?"

"Nope!"

"But you did on this particular case."

"Yup!"

"Can you tell us why?"

"The nursing supervisor asked me to."

The final coup de grace was delivered by Dr. Leonard Simon from New York, a renowned anesthesiologist whom even Jeffrey recognized. Davidson got right to the point.

"Dr. Simon. Is .75% Marcaine recommended for obstetric epidural anesthesia?"

"Absolutely not," Dr. Simon said. "In fact it is contraindicated. The warning is clearly labeled in the package insert and in the *PDR*. Every anesthesiologist knows that."

"Can you tell us why it is contraindicated in obstetrics?"

"It was found to cause occasional serious reactions."

"What kind of reactions, Doctor?"

"Central nervous system toxicity . . ."

"Does that mean seizures, Doctor?"

"Yes, it has been known to cause seizures."

"What else?"

"Cardiac toxicity."

"Meaning . . . ?"

"Arrhythmias, cardiac arrest."

"And these reactions were occasionally fatal?"

"That's correct," Dr. Simon said, pounding in the final nail of Jeffrey's coffin.

The result had been that Jeffrey and Jeffrey alone was found guilty of malpractice. Simarian, Overstreet, the hospital, and the pharmaceutical company had been exonerated. The jury awarded the Patty Owen estate eleven million dollars: nine million more than Jeffrey's malpractice coverage.

At the end of the trial, Davidson had been openly disappointed that he'd done such a good job destroying Jeffrey. Since the other defendants and their deep pockets had been exculpated, there was little chance of collecting much above and beyond Jeffrey's insurance coverage even if Jeffrey's income was attached for the rest of his life.

For Jeffrey, the result was devastating, personally no less than professionally. His whole image of himself and his self-worth had been predicated on his sense of dedication, commitment, and sacrifice. The trial and the finding by the jury destroyed that. He even came to doubt himself. Maybe he *had* used the .75% Marcaine by accident.

Jeffrey could have become depressed, but he didn't have time to submit to depression. Between the widespread news reports of Jeffrey's having "operated under the influence" and the fierce antidrug sentiment of the times, the district attorney had felt compelled to file criminal charges. To Jeffrey's total disbelief, he now found himself charged with murder in the second degree. It was on this charge that Jeffrey was now awaiting the jury's verdict.

Jeffrey's musings were again interrupted by the uniformed court officer as he reappeared from the judge's chamber and slipped back into the jury room. Why were they drawing it out like this? It was torture for Jeffrey. He was plagued by an all-too-real sense of déjà vu, since the four-day criminal trial had not gone much differently than the previous civil trial. Only this time the stakes were higher.

Losing money, even if he didn't have it, was one thing. The specter of a criminal conviction and mandatory prison term was something else entirely. Jeffrey truly did not think he could withstand life behind bars. Whether it was due to a rational fear or an irrational phobia, he didn't know. Regardless, he'd told Carol he'd spend the rest of his life in another country rather than face a prison term.

Jeffrey raised his eyes to the empty judge's bench. Two days previously, the judge had charged the jury before they'd retired for their deliberations. Some of the judge's words reverberated in Jeffrey's mind and fanned his fears.

"Members of the jury," Judge Janice Maloney had said, "before you can find the defendant, Dr. Jeffrey Rhodes, guilty of second-degree murder, the Commonwealth must have proved beyond a reasonable doubt that Patty Owen's death was caused by an act of the defendant which was imminently dangerous to another person and evinced a depraved mind, indifferent to human life. An act is 'imminently dangerous' and 'evinces a depraved mind' if it is an act that a person of ordinary judgment would know is reasonably certain to kill or do serious bodily injury to another. It is also such an act if it comes from ill will, hatred, or harmful intent."

It seemed to Jeffrey that the outcome of the case hinged on whether the jury believed he had taken morphine or not. If they believed he had, then they would find he had acted with harmful intent. At least that was how Jeffrey would find if he were one of the jurors. After all, giving anesthesia was always imminently dangerous. The only thing that distinguished it from criminal battery was the informed consent.

But the judge's words to the jury that had most threatened Jeffrey involved the part about punishment. The judge had informed the jury that even a conviction of the lesser charge of manslaughter would require her to sentence Jeffrey to a minimum of three years in prison.

Three years! Jeffrey began to perspire and feel cold at the same moment. He wiped his brow and his fingers came away damp.

"All rise!" the court officer called out, having just stepped out of the jury room. Then he stood aside. Everyone in the courtroom scrambled to his feet. Many craned their necks, hoping to get a glimmer of the verdict from the jurors' expressions when they appeared.

Preoccupied with his thoughts, Jeffrey was caught off guard by the court officer's terse announcement. He overreacted, leaping to his feet. He felt momentarily dizzy and had to lean on the defendant's table a moment for support.

As the jurors filed in, none of them made eye contact with

Jeffrey. Was that a good or bad sign? Jeffrey wanted to ask Randolph but he was afraid to.

"The Honorable Judge Janice Maloney," the court officer called out as the judge appeared from her chambers and took her seat at the bench. She arranged things on the desk in front of her, moving the water pitcher to the side. She was a thin woman with intense eyes.

"You may be seated," the court officer called. "Members of the jury, please remain standing."

Jeffrey took his seat, still watching the jury. Not one of them would look at him, a fact that progressively disturbed him. Jeffrey focused on the white-haired grandmotherly figure who stood on the far left in the front row. During the trial she had frequently looked in his direction. It had been Jeffrey's intuition she'd felt some special warmth toward him. But not now. Her hands were clasped in front of her, her eyes downcast.

The clerk of the court adjusted his glasses. He was sitting at a desk just below the bench and to the right. The court recorder was directly in front of him.

"Will the defendant please stand and face the jury," the clerk said.

Jeffrey stood up again. This time he did it slowly. Now all the jurors were staring at him. Still, their faces remained stony. Jeffrey felt his pulse hammering in his ears.

"Madam Foreperson," the clerk called out. The foreperson was a handsome woman in her late thirties who looked professional. "Has the jury agreed upon a verdict?"

"Yes," the foreperson said.

"Bailiff, please get the verdict from the foreperson," the clerk directed.

The court officer stepped over to her and took a seemingly plain sheet of paper from her hands. Then he handed the sheet to the judge.

The judge read the note, tilting her head back to read through her bifocals. She took her time, nodded, then handed the paper to the clerk who had stood to receive it.

The clerk seemed to take his time, too. Jeffrey felt intense irritation at all this unnecessary delay as he stood facing the expressionless jurors. The court was taunting him, mocking him with its archaic protocol. His heart was beating faster now, and his palms were sweating. There was a burning in his chest.

After clearing his throat, the clerk turned to face the jury. "What say you, Madam Foreperson, is the defendant guilty or not guilty of the alleged complaint of second-degree murder?"

Jeffrey felt his legs tremble. His left hand leaned on the edge of the defendant's table. He wasn't specifically religious, but he found himself praying: *Please, God . . .*

"Guilty!" the foreperson called out with a clear, resonant voice.

Jeffrey felt his legs sway as the image of the courtroom momentarily swam before him. He grappled for the table with his right hand to steady himself. He felt Randolph grip his right arm.

"This is only the first round," Randolph whispered in his ear. "We'll appeal, just like we did the malpractice judgment."

The clerk looked over toward Jeffrey and Randolph reprovingly, then turned back to the jury and said: "Madam Foreperson and members of the jury, harken to your verdict as recorded by the court. The jurors upon their oath do say that the defendant is guilty as charged in said complaint. So say you, Madam Foreperson?"

"Yes," the forelady said.

"So say you, members of the jury?" the clerk asked.

"Yes," the jurors replied in unison.

The clerk turned his attention back to his books while the judge began to discharge the jury. She thanked them for their time and consideration of the case, praising their role in upholding a two-hundred-year tradition of justice.

Jeffrey sat down heavily, feeling numb and cold. Randolph was talking to him, reminding him that the judge of the malpractice case should never have allowed the question of his drug problem to stand.

"Besides," Randolph said, bending down and looking Jeffrey directly in the eye, "all the evidence is circumstantial. There was not one piece of definitive evidence that you had taken morphine. Not one!"

But Jeffrey was not listening. The ramifications of this verdict were too overwhelming to consider. Deep down he realized that for all his fears, he'd really never believed he'd be convicted—simply because he was not guilty. He'd never been involved in the legal system before, and he'd always trusted that "truth would out" if he ever was wrongly accused. But that belief had been false. Now he'd be going to prison.

Prison! As if to underscore his fate, the court officer came over to handcuff him. Jeffrey could only look on, incredulous. He stared at the polished surface of the handcuffs. It was as if the manacles had transformed him into a criminal, a convict, even more than the jury's verdict.

Randolph was murmuring encouragement. The judge was still discharging the jury. Jeffrey heard none of it. He felt depression descend like a leaden blanket. Competing with the depression was a sense of panic from imminent claustrophobia. The idea of being locked in a small room evoked scary images of being caught beneath the blankets when he was a young child by his older brother, filling him with a fear of being smothered.

"Your Honor," the district attorney said as soon as the jury had filed out. He got to his feet. "The Commonwealth moves for sentencing."

"Denied," the judge said. "The court will schedule penalty proceedings after a presentencing investigation by the probation department. When is an appropriate time, Mr. Lewis?"

The clerk flipped through the scheduling book. "July 7 looks good."

"July 7 it is," the judge said.

"The Commonwealth respectfully requests denying bail or a significant increase in bail," the district attorney said. "It is the Commonwealth's position that at a minimum, the bail should be raised from $50,000 to $500,000."

"All right, Mr. District Attorney," the judge said, "let's hear your argument."

The district attorney stepped from behind the prosecution table to face the judge. "The serious nature of the complaint combined with the verdict demands a significant bail, more in keeping with the severity of the crime of which he has been convicted. There also have been rumors that Dr. Jeffrey

Rhodes would prefer to flee rather than face the punishment of the court."

The judge turned toward Randolph. Randolph stood up. "Your Honor," he began, "I would like to emphasize to the court that my client has significant ties to the community. He has always demonstrated responsible behavior. He has no previous criminal record. In fact, he has been an exemplary member of society, productive and law-abiding. He has every intention to appear for sentencing. I feel that $50,000 is more than enough bail; $500,000 would be excessive."

"Has your client ever expressed an intention of avoiding punishment?" the judge asked, looking over the top of her glasses.

Randolph shot a glance at Jeffrey. Jeffrey's gaze fell to his hands. Turning back to the judge, Randolph said: "I do not believe my client would think or say such a thing."

The judge looked slowly back and forth between Randolph and the district attorney. Finally she said, "Bail set at $500,000 cash surety." Then, looking directly at Jeffrey, she said, "Dr. Rhodes, as a convicted felon you are not to leave the Commonwealth of Massachusetts. Is that clear?"

Jeffrey meekly nodded.

"Your Honor . . . !" Randolph protested.

But the judge only pounded her gavel once and stood up, clearly dismissive.

"All rise!" the court officer barked.

With swirling robes like a dervish, Judge Janice Maloney swept from her court and disappeared into her chambers. The courtroom erupted in conversation.

"This way, Dr. Rhodes," the court officer standing next to Jeffrey said, motioning toward a side door. Jeffrey stood and stumbled forward. He cast a quick glance in Carol's direction. She was looking at him sadly.

Jeffrey's panic grew as he was taken to a holding room furnished with a plain table and spartan wooden chairs. He sat in the chair Randolph steered him to. Although he did his best to maintain his composure, he couldn't keep his hands from trembling. He felt short of breath.

Randolph did his best to calm him. He was indignant about

the verdict and optimistic about the appeal. Just then, Carol was escorted into the narrow room. Randolph patted her on the back and said, "You talk to him. I'll go call the bail bonds-man."

Carol nodded and looked down at Jeffrey. "I'm sorry," she said after Randolph had left the room.

Jeffrey nodded. She had been good to stand by him. His eyes welled with tears. He bit his lip to keep from crying.

"It's so unfair," Carol said, sitting down next to him.

"I can't go to prison," was all Jeffrey could say. He shook his head. "I still can't believe this is happening."

"Randolph will appeal," Carol said. "It's not over yet."

"Appeal," Jeffrey said with disgust. "It will be just more of the same. I've lost two cases . . ."

"It's not the same," Carol said. "Only experienced judges will be looking at the evidence, not an emotional jury."

Randolph came back from the phone to say that Michael Mosconi, the bail bondsman, was on his way over. Randolph and Carol began an animated conversation about the process of appeal. Jeffrey put his elbows on the table and despite the handcuffs, rested his head in his hands. He was thinking about his medical license, wondering what would happen to it as a consequence of the verdict. Unfortunately, he had a pretty good idea.

Michael Mosconi arrived in short order with his briefcase. His office was only a few steps from the courthouse, in the curved building facing Government Center. He was not a big man, but his head was large and almost bald. What hair he had grew in a dark crescent that stretched around the back of his head from ear to ear. Some of the strands of dark hair were combed directly over the bald dome in a vain effort to provide a minimum of cover. He had intensely dark eyes that appeared to be all pupil. He was oddly dressed in a dark blue polyester suit with a black shirt and a white tie.

Mosconi set his briefcase on the table, snapped open the latches, and removed a file folder labeled with Jeffrey's name.

"Okay," he said, taking a seat at the table and opening the file. "How much is the increase in bail?" He had already put up the initial $50,000 bail, having collected $5,000 for his services.

"It's $450,000," Randolph said.

Mosconi whistled through his teeth, pausing in setting out the papers. "Who do they think they got here, Public Enemy Number One?" Neither Randolph nor Jeffrey felt they owed him the courtesy of an answer.

Mosconi's attention returned to his paperwork, unconcerned by his client's lack of response. He'd already done an O&E, an ownership and encumbrance check, on Jeffrey and Carol's Marblehead house when bail had initially been set, securing the first bond with a lien of $50,000 on the home. The house had a documented value of $800,000 with an existing mortgage of just over $300,000. "Well, isn't that convenient," he said. "I'll be able to post bond with an additional $450,000 lien against your little castle in Marblehead. How's that?"

Jeffrey nodded. Carol shrugged.

As Mosconi began filling out the papers, he said: "Then, of course, there is the little matter of my fee, which in this case will be $45,000. I'll want that in cash."

"I don't have that kind of cash," Jeffrey said.

Mosconi held up from completing the form.

"But I'm sure you can raise it," Randolph put in.

"I suppose," Jeffrey said. Depression was setting in.

"Either yes or no," Mosconi said. "I don't do this stuff for recreation."

"I'll raise it," Jeffrey said.

"Normally I require the fee up front," Mosconi added. "But since you are a doctor . . ." He laughed. "Let's just say I'm accustomed to dealing with a slightly different clientele. But for you, I'll take a check. But only if you can raise the money and have it in your account by, let's say, this time tomorrow. Is that possible?"

"I don't know," Jeffrey said.

"If you don't know, then you'll have to stay in custody until you got the money," Mosconi said.

"I'll raise it," Jeffrey said. The thought of even a few nights in jail was intolerable.

"Do you have a check with you?" Mosconi asked.

Jeffrey nodded.

Mosconi went back to filling out the form. "I hope you understand, Doctor," he said, "that I'm doing you a big favor by taking a check. My company would take a dim view, so let's just keep it between us. Now you'll have that money in your account in twenty-four hours?"

"I'll take care of it this afternoon," Jeffrey said.

"Wonderful," Mosconi said. He pushed the papers toward Jeffrey. "Now if you two will sign this note, I'll run down to the clerk's office and settle the score."

Jeffrey signed without reading what he was signing. Carol read it carefully, then signed. Carol got Jeffrey's checkbook out of his jacket pocket and held it while Jeffrey made out a check for $45,000. Mosconi took the check and put it in his briefcase. Then he got up and sauntered to the door. "I'll be back," he said with a sly smile.

"Charming fellow," Jeffrey said. "Does he have to dress that way?"

"He is doing you a favor," Randolph said. "But it's true, you're hardly one of the low-lifes he's accustomed to dealing with. Before he gets back, I think we should talk about the presentencing investigation and what it entails."

"When do we file the appeal?" Jeffrey asked.

"Immediately," Randolph said.

"And I'm on bail until the appeal is heard?"

"Most likely," Randolph said evasively.

"Thank God for small favors," Jeffrey said.

Randolph then explained the presentencing investigation and what Jeffrey might expect from the penalty proceedings. He didn't want to see Jeffrey any more demoralized than he already was, so he was careful to emphasize the more promising aspects of the appeal. But Jeffrey's spirits remained low.

"I have to admit I don't have a lot of faith left in this legal system," Jeffrey said.

"You've got to think positively," Carol said.

Jeffrey looked at his wife and began to appreciate how angry he was. Carol telling him he should think positively under the circumstances was eminently annoying. Suddenly Jeffrey realized he was angry at the system, angry at fate, angry at Carol, even angry at his attorney. At least anger was probably healthier than being depressed.

"All is in order," Mosconi said as he slipped in the door. He was waving an official-looking document. "If you would?" he said, motioning for the court officer to unhandcuff Jeffrey.

Jeffrey rubbed his wrists with relief when they were free from the shackles. What he wanted most was to get out of the courthouse. He stood up.

"I'm sure I don't have to remind you about the $45,000," Mosconi said. "Just remember, I'm putting my ass on the line for you."

"I appreciate it," Jeffrey said, trying to sound thankful.

They left the holding room together although Michael Mosconi hurried off in the opposite direction when they got to the hall.

Jeffrey had never been so consciously appreciative of the fresh, ocean-scented air as when he stepped from the courthouse onto the brick-paved plaza. It was a bright, midspring afternoon with puffy little white clouds scudding across a faraway blue sky. The sun was warm but the air crisp. It was amazing how the threat of prison had sharpened Jeffrey's perceptions.

Randolph took his leave on the wide plaza in front of the garishly modern Boston City Hall. "I'm sorry it turned out like this. I tried my best."

"I know," Jeffrey said. "I also know I was a lousy client and made it extra hard for you."

"We'll get right on the appeal. I'll be talking with you in the morning. Good-bye, Carol."

Carol waved, then she and Jeffrey watched Randolph stride off toward State Street, where he and his partners occupied an entire floor of one of the newer Boston office towers. "I don't know whether to love him or hate him," Jeffrey said. "I don't even know if he did a good job or not, especially since I got convicted."

"I personally don't think he was forceful enough," Carol said. She started toward the parking garage.

"Aren't you going back to work?" Jeffrey called after her. Carol worked for an investment banking firm located in the financial area. That was in the opposite direction.

"I took the day off," she said over her shoulder. She stopped when she saw that Jeffrey wasn't walking after her. "I didn't know how long rendering the verdict would take. Come on, you can give me a ride to my car."

Jeffrey caught up to her and they walked together, skirting City Hall. "How are you going to raise $45,000 in twenty-four hours?" Carol asked, tossing her head in her characteristic way. She had fine, straight, dirty-blond hair that she wore in a fashion that caused it to constantly blow in her face.

Jeffrey felt his irritation surface again. Finances had been one of the trouble points in their marriage. Carol liked to spend money, Jeffrey liked to save it. When they'd married, Jeffrey's salary was larger by far, so it was Jeffrey's salary Carol made it her business to spend. When Carol's salary began to climb, it all went into her investment portfolio while Jeffrey's salary was still used to pay all the expenses. Carol's rationale had been that if she didn't work, then they would be using Jeffrey's salary for all the expenses anyway.

Jeffrey didn't answer Carol's question immediately. He realized that in this instance his anger was misdirected. He wasn't angry with her. All their old financial disputes were water under the bridge, and wondering where $45,000 in cash was to come from was a legitimate concern. What angered him was the legal system and the lawyers who ran it. How could lawyers like the district attorney or the plaintiff attorney live with themselves when they lied so much? From the depositions Jeffrey knew they did not believe their own prosecution ploys. Each of Jeffrey's trials had been an amoral process in which the opposing attorneys had allowed ends to justify dishonest means.

Jeffrey got in behind the wheel of his car. He took a deep breath to control his anger, then turned to Carol. "I plan to increase the mortgage on the Marblehead house. In fact, we should stop at the bank on the way home."

"With the lien we just signed, I don't think the bank will up the mortgage," Carol said. She was something of an authority on the subject; this was her area of expertise.

"That's why I want to go right now," Jeffrey said. He started the car and drove out of the garage. "No one will be the wiser. It will take a day or two before that lien finds its way into their computers."

"Do you think you ought to do that?"

"Do you have any other ideas of how I can raise $45,000 by tomorrow afternoon?" Jeffrey asked.

"I guess not."

Jeffrey knew she had that kind of money in her investment portfolio, but he'd be damned if he'd ask her for it.

"See you at the bank," Carol said as she got out in front of the garage where her car was parked.

As Jeffrey drove north over the Tobin Bridge, exhaustion settled over him. It seemed that he had to make a conscious effort to breathe. He began to wonder why he was bothering with all this rigmarole. He wasn't worth it. Especially now that he was sure to lose his medical license. Other than medicine, in fact other than anesthesia, he didn't know much about anything. Except for a menial job like bagging at a grocery store, he couldn't think of anything else he was qualified to do. He was a convicted, worthless forty-two-year-old, an unemployable middle-aged nothing.

When Jeffrey arrived at the bank, he parked but didn't get out of the car. He slumped forward and let his forehead rest on the steering wheel. Maybe he should just forget everything, go home, and sleep.

When the passenger-side door opened, Jeffrey didn't even bother to look up.

"Are you all right?" Carol asked.

"I'm a little depressed," Jeffrey said.

"Well, that's understandable," Carol said. "But before you get too immobile, let's get this bank stuff out of the way."

"You're so understanding," Jeffrey said irritably.

"One of us has to be practical," Carol said. "And I don't want to see you going to jail. If you don't get that money in your checking account, that's where you'll end up."

"I have a terrible premonition that that's where I'm going to end up no matter what I do." With supreme effort, he got out of the car. He faced Carol over the roof of the car. "The one thing I find interesting," he added, "is that I'm going to prison and you're going to L.A., but I don't know who's worse off."

"Very funny," Carol said, relieved that he was at least making a joke, even if she failed to find it amusing.

Dudley Farnsworth was the manager of the Marblehead

branch of Jeffrey's bank. Years before, he'd happened to be the junior bank officer in the Boston branch of the bank that had handled Jeffrey's first real estate purchase. Jeffrey had been a resident in anesthesia at the time. Fourteen years previously, Jeffrey had bought a Cambridge three-decker and Dudley had arranged the financing.

Dudley saw them as soon as he could, taking them back to his private office and seating them in leather chairs facing his desk.

"What can I do for you?" Dudley said pleasantly. He was Jeffrey's age but looked older with his silver-white hair.

"We'd like to increase the mortgage on our house," Jeffrey said.

"I'm sure that won't be a problem," Dudley said. He went to a file drawer and pulled out a folder. "What kind of money are you looking for?"

"Forty-five thousand dollars," Jeffrey said.

Dudley sat down and opened the folder. "No problem," he said, looking at the figures. "You could take even more if you wish."

"Forty-five thousand will be enough," Jeffrey said. "But I need it by tomorrow."

"Ouch!" Dudley said. "That's going to be tough."

"Perhaps you could arrange a home equity loan," Carol suggested. "Then when the mortgage comes through, you can use that to pay off the loan."

Dudley nodded with eyebrows arched. "That's an idea. But I tell you what, let's go ahead and fill out the forms for the mortgage. I'll see what I can do. If the mortgage doesn't come through, then I'll take Carol's suggestion. Can you come in tomorrow morning?"

"If I can get out of bed," Jeffrey said with a sigh.

Dudley shot a glance at Jeffrey. He intuited that something was wrong, but he was too much of a gentleman to inquire.

After the bank business was concluded, Jeffrey and Carol walked out to their cars.

"Why don't I stop at the store and get something good for dinner?" Carol suggested. "What would you like tonight? How about your favorite: grilled veal chops."

"I'm not hungry," Jeffrey said.

"Maybe you're not hungry now, but you will be later."

"I doubt it," Jeffrey said.

"I know you and you'll be hungry. I'm going to stop at the grocery for food for tonight. So what'll it be?"

"Get whatever you want," Jeffrey said. He climbed into his car. "With the way I feel, I can't imagine I'm going to want to eat."

When Jeffrey reached home, he pulled into the garage, then went directly to his room. He and Carol had been occupying separate rooms for the past year. It had been Carol's idea, but Jeffrey surprised himself by warming to the idea right away. That had been one of the first clear signs that their marriage was not all it should be.

Jeffrey closed the door behind him and locked it. His eyes wandered to his books and periodicals carefully shelved according to height. He wasn't going to need them for a while. He walked over to the bookcase and pulled out Bromage's *Epidural Analgesia* and threw it against the wall. It poked a small hole in the plaster, then crashed to the floor. The gesture didn't make him feel any better. In fact it made him feel guilty, and the effort exhausted him even more. He picked up the book, smoothed out a few of the bent pages, then slipped it back into its designated spot. By habit, he lined the spine up with the other volumes.

Sitting down heavily in the wing chair by the window, Jeffrey vacantly stared out at the dogwood, whose wilting spring blossoms were past their prime. He was gripped by overwhelming sadness. He knew he had to shake this self-pity if he was to accomplish anything. He heard Carol's car pull up, then the door slam. A few minutes later there was a quiet knock at his door. He ignored it, thinking she'd guess he was asleep. He wanted to be alone.

Jeffrey struggled with his deepening sense of guilt. Perhaps that was the worst part of having been convicted. By undermining his confidence, he again worried that maybe he had erred in administering the anesthesia that fateful day. Maybe he had used the wrong concentration. Maybe Patty Owen's death was his fault.

Hours slipped by as Jeffrey's preoccupied mind wrestled with a growing sense of his worthlessness. Everything that he'd ever done seemed stupid and pointless. He'd failed at everything from being an anesthesiologist to being a husband. He couldn't think of one thing that he'd succeeded at. He'd even failed at making the basketball team in junior high school.

When the sun sagged down in the western sky and touched the horizon, Jeffrey had the sense it was setting on his life. He thought that few people could realize the tremendous toll malpractice litigation took on a practicing physician's emotional and professional life, especially when there was no malpractice involved. Even if Jeffrey had won the case, he knew that his life would have been changed forever. The fact that he lost was that much more devastating. And it had nothing to do with money.

Jeffrey watched the sky change from warm reds to cold purple and silver, while the light ebbed and the day died. As he sat there in the gathering gloom, he suddenly had an idea. It wasn't entirely true that he was helpless. There was something he could do to affect his destiny. With the first sense of purpose in weeks, Jeffrey pushed himself out of the wing chair and went to the closet. From it he pulled his large black doctor's bag and put it on the bureau.

From the doctor's bag he retrieved two small bottles of Ringer's Lactate intravenous fluid as well as two infusion kits and one small scalp needle. Then he took out two vials, one of succinylcholine, the other of morphine. Using a syringe, he drew up 75 mg of the succinylcholine and squirted it into one of the Ringer's Lactate bottles. Then he drew up 75 mg of morphine, a walloping dose.

One of the benefits of being an anesthesiologist was that Jeffrey knew the most efficient way to commit suicide. Other doctors didn't, though they tended to be more successful in their attempts than the general public. Some shot themselves, a messy method which, surprisingly enough, was not always effective. Others took overdoses, another method that often didn't yield the desired result. Too often the would-be suicides were caught in time to have their stomachs pumped. Other times the drugs injected were enough to bring on a coma but not death. Jeffrey shuddered at the haphazard consequences.

Jeffrey felt his depression lift slightly as he worked. It was heartening to have a goal. He took the painting that hung over the head of the bed down to use the hook to hang both IV bottles. He then sat down on the side of the bed and started the IV on the back of his left hand with the bottle containing only the Ringer's Lactate solution. He piggy-backed the bottle containing the succinylcholine onto the other, with only the thin blue stopcock separating him from its lethal contents.

Careful not to dislodge the IV, Jeffrey lay back on the bed. His plan was to inject the huge dose of morphine and then open the stopcock on the solution containing the succinylcholine. The morphine would send him to never-never-land long before the succinylcholine concentration paralyzed his respiratory system. Without a ventilator, he would die. It was as simple as that.

Gently, Jeffrey inserted the needle of the syringe containing the morphine into the IV port of the infusion line going into the vein on the back of his hand. Just as he was beginning to inject the narcotic, there was a soft knock on his door.

Jeffrey rolled his eyes. What a time for Carol to interrupt. He held off the injection but didn't respond to her knock, hoping she'd go away if she thought he was still asleep. Instead, she knocked louder, then louder still. "Jeffrey!" she called. "Jeffrey! I've made dinner."

There was a short silence that made Jeffrey think she'd given up. But then Jeffrey heard the knob turn and the door rattle against the jamb. "*Jeffrey—are you all right?*"

Jeffrey took a deep breath. He knew he had to say something or she might be concerned enough to force the door. The last thing he wanted was for her to come barging in and see the IV.

"I'm fine," Jeffrey called out at last.

"Then why didn't you answer me?" Carol demanded.

"I was asleep."

"Why is this door locked?" Carol asked.

"I guess I didn't want to be disturbed," Jeffrey replied with pointed irony.

"I've made dinner," Carol said.

"That's nice of you, but I'm still not hungry."

"I made veal chops, your favorite. I think you should eat."

"Please, Carol," Jeffrey said with exasperation. "I'm not hungry."

"Well, come eat for my sake. As a favor to me."

Fuming, Jeffrey set the syringe with the morphine on the night table and pulled out the IV. He went to the door and yanked it open, but not so far that Carol could see in. "Listen!" he snapped. "I told you earlier that I wasn't hungry then and I'm telling you that I'm not hungry now. I don't want to eat and I don't like you trying to make me feel guilty about it, understand?"

"Jeffrey, come on. I don't think you should be alone. Now I've gone to the trouble to shop for you and cook. The least you can do is come try it."

Jeffrey could see there would be no getting around her. When she'd made up her mind, she was not the type of person who could be easily dissuaded.

"All right," he said heavily. "All right."

"What's wrong with your hand?" Carol asked, noticing a drop of blood on the back of it.

"Nothing," Jeffrey said. "Nothing at all." He glanced at the back of his hand. Blood was oozing from the IV site. Frantically, he searched for an explanation.

"But it's bleeding."

"A paper cut," Jeffrey said. He was never good at fibbing. Then, with an irony only he could appreciate, he added, "I'll live. Believe me, I'll live. Look," he said, "I'll be down in a minute."

"Promise?" Carol said.

"I promise."

With Carol gone and the door relocked, Jeffrey removed the quarter-liter IV bottles and stored them in the back of his closet in his leather doctor's bag. He threw the wrappers from the infusion kits and the scalp needle into the wastebasket in the bathroom.

Carol had some sense of timing, he thought ruefully. Only as he packed away the medical paraphernalia did he realize how close he had come. He told himself he shouldn't give in to despair, at least not until all legal avenues had been exhausted.

Until this recent turn of events, Jeffrey had never seriously entertained thoughts of suicide. He was honestly baffled by the suicides he knew of, though intellectually he could appreciate the depths of despair that might prompt it.

Oddly enough, or perhaps not so oddly, the only suicides he had known were other doctors who'd been pushed to the brink by motives not unlike Jeffrey's. He recalled one friend in particular: Chris Everson. He couldn't remember exactly when Chris had died, but it had been within the last two years.

Chris had been a fellow anesthesiologist. Years before, he and Jeffrey had been residents together. Chris would have remembered the days when gung-ho residents warded off flu symptoms with Ringer's Lactate. What made thinking about Chris suddenly so poignant was the realization that he'd been sued for malpractice because one of his patients had had a terrible reaction to a local anesthetic during epidural anesthesia.

Jeffrey closed his eyes and tried to remember the details of the case. As best as he could recall, Chris's patient's heart had arrested as soon as Chris put in the test dose of only 2 cc's. Although they had been able to get the heart beating again, the patient ended up quadriplegic and semicomatose. Within a week after the event, Chris had been sued along with Valley Hospital and everyone else even remotely associated with the episode. The "deep pockets" strategy yet again.

But Chris never went to court. He committed suicide even before the discovery period had been completed. And even though the anesthesia procedure had been characterized as having been impeccable, the decision ultimately rendered found for the plaintiff. At the time, the settlement had been the largest award for malpractice in Massachusetts' history. But in the ensuing months, Jeffrey could think of at least two awards that had topped it.

Jeffrey could distinctly remember his reaction when he'd heard of Chris's suicide. It had been one of complete disbelief. Back then, before Jeffrey's current involvement with the legal system, he'd had no idea what could have pushed Chris to do such an awful thing. Chris enjoyed a reputation as a superb anesthesiologist, a doctor's doctor, one of the best. He'd recently married a beautiful OR nurse who worked in Valley Hospital. He seemed to have everything going for him. And then the nightmare struck . . .

A soft knock brought Jeffrey back to the present. Carol was at the door again.

"Jeffrey!" she called. "Better come before it gets cold."

"I'm on my way."

Now that he knew too well what Chris had only begun to go through, Jeffrey wished he'd stayed in touch at the time. He could have been a better friend. And even after the man ended his life, all Jeffrey had done was attend the funeral. He had never even contacted Kelly, Chris's wife, even though at the funeral he'd promised himself he would do so.

Such behavior wasn't like Jeffrey, and he wondered why he'd acted so heartlessly. The only excuse he could think of was his need to repress the episode. The suicide of a colleague with whom Jeffrey could so easily identify was a fundamentally disturbing event. Perhaps facing it squarely would have been too great a challenge for him. It was the kind of personal examination that Jeffrey and doctors in general had been taught to avoid, labeling it "clinical detachment."

What a terrible waste, he thought as he remembered Chris the last time he'd seen him, before all the tragedy struck. And if Carol hadn't interrupted, mightn't there be others thinking the same thoughts with respect to him?

No, Jeffrey thought vehemently, suicide wasn't an option. Certainly not yet. Jeffrey hated to sound mawkish, but where there was life, there was hope. And what had happened in the aftermath of Chris's suicide? With Chris dead, there was no one to defend or clear his name. For all his despair and developing depression, Jeffrey still was enraged by a system and process that had managed to convict him when he had honestly done no wrong. Could he really rest until he'd done his best to clear his name?

Jeffrey got angry just thinking about his case. To the lawyers involved, even Randolph, all this might be business as usual, but not so to Jeffrey. This was his life on the line. His career. Everything. The great irony was that the day of the Patty Owen tragedy, Jeffrey had done his utmost to do well by her.

He'd only run the IV and taken the paregoric so he could perform the job for which he'd been trained. Dedication was what had motivated him, and this was how he'd been repaid.

If Jeffrey ever was able to return to medicine, he would be afraid of the long-lasting effects this case would have on any medical decisions he would ever make. What kind of care could people come to expect from doctors who were forced to work in the current malpractice milieu and who had to restrain their best instincts and second-guess their every step? How had such a system evolved? Jeffrey wondered. It certainly wasn't eliminating the few "bad" doctors, since they ironically rarely got sued. What was happening was that a lot of good doctors were being destroyed.

As Jeffrey washed before descending to the kitchen, his mind dredged up another memory that he had unconsciously repressed. One of the best and most dedicated internists he'd ever met had killed himself five years ago on the same night he'd received a summons for malpractice. Shot himself through the mouth with a hunting rifle. He hadn't even waited for the discovery process to begin, much less the trial. At the time Jeffrey had been disturbingly mystified, since everyone knew the suit had been baseless. In fact the doctor had, ironically, saved the man's life. Jeffrey now had some idea of the source of the man's despair.

Finished in the bathroom, Jeffrey returned to his bedroom and changed into clean slacks and shirt. Opening his door, he smelled the food Carol had prepared. He still wasn't hungry, but he'd make an effort. Pausing at the top of the stairs, he vowed to fight the depressive thoughts he was bound to experience until this current episode had run its course. With that commitment in mind he started for the kitchen.

TUESDAY,

MAY 16, 1989

9:12 A.M.

Jeffrey woke up with a start and was amazed at the time. He'd first awakened around five A.M., surprised to find himself sitting in the wing chair by the window. Stiffly, he had removed his clothes and gotten into bed, thinking he would never be able to fall back asleep. But obviously he had.

He took a quick shower. Emerging from his room, he looked for Carol. Having recovered to an extent from the depressive depths of the previous day, he wanted some human contact and a bit of sympathy. He hoped that Carol had not left for work without talking to him. He wanted to apologize for his lack of appreciation for her efforts the night before. It was a good thing, he now realized, that she'd interrupted him, and that she'd gotten him irritated. Unknowingly she'd saved him from committing suicide. For the first time in his life, getting angry had had a positive effect.

But Carol was long gone. A note was leaning against a shredded wheat box on the kitchen table. It said that she'd not wanted to disturb him since she was sure he needed rest. She had to get to work early. She hoped he'd understand.

Jeffrey filled a bowl with cereal and got the milk from the

refrigerator. He envied Carol her job. He wished he had a job to go to. It would keep his mind occupied if nothing else. He would have liked to have made himself useful. It might have helped his self-esteem. He'd never realized quite how much his work defined his persona.

Back in his room, Jeffrey disposed of the IV paraphernalia by wrapping it in old newspapers and carrying it out to the trash barrels in the garage. He didn't want Carol to find it. He felt strange handling the material. It gave him a tremendous uneasiness to have been knowingly and voluntarily so close to death.

The idea of suicide had occurred to Jeffrey in the past, but always in a metaphorical context, and usually more as a retribution fantasy to get back at someone who he believed had wronged him in some emotional way, like when his girlfriend in the eighth grade had capriciously switched her affections to Jeffrey's best friend. But last night it had been different, and to think that he'd come within a hair's breadth of doing it made his legs feel weak.

Returning to the house, Jeffrey considered what effects his suicide would have had on his friends and family. It probably would have come as a relief to Carol. She wouldn't have had to go through with the divorce. He wondered if anyone would have missed him. Probably not . . .

"For Pete's sake," Jeffrey exclaimed, realizing the ridiculousness of this line of thought and remembering his vow to resist depressive thoughts. Would his thinking thrive on his low self-esteem for the rest of his days?

But the subject of suicide was hard to shake from his mind. He wondered again about Chris Everson. Had his suicide been the product of an acute depression that had struck like a sudden storm, like Jeffrey had felt the night before? Or had he planned it for some time? Either way, his death was a terrible loss for everyone—his family, the public, even the profession of medicine.

Jeffrey stopped en route to his room and stared out the living-room window with unseeing eyes. His situation was no less a waste. From the point of view of his productivity, the loss of his medical license and his going to prison was no less a waste than if he'd succeeded in committing suicide. "Damn!" he shouted as he grabbed one of the pillows from the couch and punched it repeatedly with his fist. "Damn, damn, damn!"

Jeffrey quickly wore himself out and replaced the pillow. Then he sat himself down dejectedly with his knees jutting up in front of him. He interwound his fingers and rested his elbows on his knees and tried to think of himself in prison. It was a horrid thought. What a travesty of justice! The malpractice stuff had been more than enough to seriously disrupt and alter his life, but this criminal nonsense was a quantum leap worse, like throwing salt into a mortal wound.

Jeffrey thought about his colleagues at the hospital and other physician friends. They had all been supportive at first, at least until the criminal indictment had been handed down. Then they had avoided Jeffrey as if he'd had some kind of infectious disease. Jeffrey felt isolated and alone. And more than anything, he felt angry.

"It's just not fair!" he said through clenched teeth.

Completely out of character, Jeffrey snatched up a piece of Carol's crystal bric-a-brac from a side table and in a moment of sheer frustration threw it with deadly accuracy at the glass-fronted sideboard that he could see through the arch leading to the dining room. There was a resounding shatter of glass that made him wince.

"Uh-oh!" Jeffrey said as he realized what he'd done. He got up and went for the dustpan and broom. By the time he'd picked up the mess, he'd come to a momentous conclusion: he wasn't going to prison! No way. Screw the appeal process. He had as much confidence in the legal system as he did in fairy tales.

The decision was made with a suddenness and resolve that left Jeffrey feeling exhilarated. He checked his watch. The bank would be open soon. Excitedly he went to his room and found his passport. He was lucky the court hadn't made him surrender it at the same time they'd increased his bail. Then he called Pan Am. He learned that he could shuttle to New York, bus to Kennedy, and then fly on to Rio. Considering all the carriers serving the market, he had a wide range of flights from which to choose, including one that left at 11:45 P.M. and made a few stops in exotic locations.

With his pulse racing in anticipation, Jeffrey called the bank and got Dudley on the line. He did his best to sound controlled. He asked about the progress on the loan.

"No problem," Dudley said proudly. "Pulling a few strings, I got it approved like that." Jeffrey could hear the man snap his fingers for his benefit. "When will you be coming in?" Dudley continued. "I'd like to be sure I'm here."

"I'll be in shortly," Jeffrey said, planning his schedule. Timing would be key. "I have one other request. I'd like to have the money in cash."

"You're joking," Dudley said.

"I'm serious," Jeffrey insisted.

"It's a bit irregular," Dudley said hesitantly.

Jeffrey hadn't given this issue much thought, and he could sense Dudley's hesitance. He realized he'd have to explain if he hoped to get the money, and he definitely needed the money. He couldn't leave for South America with only pocket change.

"Dudley," Jeffrey began, "I'm in some unfortunate trouble."

"I don't like the sound of this," Dudley said.

"It's not what you're thinking. It's not gambling or anything like that. The fact is, I have to pay it to a bail bondsman. Haven't you read about my troubles in the papers?"

"No, I haven't," Dudley said, warming up again.

"I got sued for malpractice and then indicted over a tragic anesthesia case. I won't burden you with the details at the moment. The problem is, I need the $45,000 to pay a bail bondsman who posted my bail. He said he wanted it in cash."

"I'm sure a cashier's check would be acceptable."

"Listen, Dudley," Jeffrey said. "The man told me cash. I promised him cash. What can I say? Do me this one favor. Don't make it any harder on me than it already is."

There was a pause. Jeffrey thought he heard Dudley sigh. "Are hundred-dollar bills okay?"

"Fine," Jeffrey said. "Hundreds would be perfect." He was wondering how much space four hundred and fifty hundred-dollar bills would take.

"I'll have it ready," Dudley said. "I just hope you're not planning on carrying this around for any length of time."

"Just into Boston," Jeffrey said.

Jeffrey hung up the phone. He hoped that Dudley wouldn't

call the police or try to check his story. Not that anything wouldn't have jibed. Jeffrey felt the fewer people thinking about him and asking questions, the better, at least until he was on the plane out of New York.

Sitting down with a writing tablet, Jeffrey started a note to Carol, telling her he was taking the $45,000 but that she could have everything else. But the letter sounded awkward. Besides, as he wrote he realized he didn't want to leave any evidence of his intentions in case he was delayed for some reason. He crumpled the paper, set a match to it, and tossed it in the fireplace. Instead of writing, he decided to call Carol from some foreign location and talk to her directly. It would be more personal than a letter. It would be safer, too.

The next issue was what he should take with him. He didn't want to be burdened with a lot of luggage. He settled on a small suitcase, which he loaded with basic casual clothes. He didn't imagine South America would be very formal. By the time he had packed everything he wanted, he had to sit on the suitcase to get it closed. Then he put some things in his brief-case, including his toiletries and clean underwear.

He was about to leave his closet when he eyed his doctor's bag. He hesitated for a moment, wondering what he would do if something went horribly wrong. To be on the safe side, he opened the doctor's bag and took out an IV setup, a few syringes, a quarter liter of IV fluid, and a vial each of succinyl-choline and morphine and packed them in his briefcase be-neath the underwear. He didn't like to think he was still entertaining thoughts of suicide, so he told himself that the drugs were like an insurance policy. He hoped he wouldn't need them, but they were there just in case . . .

Jeffrey felt strange and a little sad glancing around the house for what was probably the last time, knowing he might never lay eyes on it again. But walking from room to room, he was surprised not to be more upset. There was so much to remind him of past events, both good and bad. But more than anything else, Jeffrey realized that he associated the place with his failed marriage. And just like his malpractice case, he'd be better off leaving it behind. He felt energized for the first time in months. It felt like the first day of a new life.

With the suitcase in the trunk and his briefcase on the passenger seat beside him, Jeffrey drove out of the garage, beeped the door shut, and was on his way. He didn't look back. The first stop was the bank, and as he got closer, he began to get anxious. His new life was starting out in a unique fashion: he was deliberately planning to break the law by defying the court. He wondered if he would get away with it.

By the time he pulled into the bank's parking lot, he was very nervous. His mouth had gone dry. What if Dudley had called the police about his requesting the bail money in cash? It wouldn't take the intelligence of a rocket scientist to figure that Jeffrey might be planning on doing something else with the money rather than turn it over to the bail bondsman.

After sitting in his parked car for a moment to summon his courage, Jeffrey grabbed his briefcase and forced himself into the bank. In some respects he felt like a bank robber, even though the money he was seeking technically belonged to him. Taking a deep breath to steady himself, he went to the service desk and asked for Dudley.

Dudley came to meet him with smiles and small talk. He led Jeffrey back to his office and motioned to a chair. To judge by his demeanor, he didn't hold Jeffrey suspect. But Jeffrey's anxiety stayed razor sharp. He was trembling.

"Some coffee or a soft drink?" Dudley offered. Jeffrey decided he'd be better off without caffeine. He told Dudley some juice would be fine. He thought it best to give his hands something to do. Dudley smiled and said, "Sure thing." The man was being so cordial, Jeffrey was afraid it was a trap.

"I'll be right back with the cash," Dudley said after handing Jeffrey a glass of orange juice. He returned in a few minutes carrying a soiled canvas money bag. He dumped the contents onto his desk. There were nine packets of hundred-dollar bills, each containing fifty bills. Jeffrey had never seen so much money in one place. He felt increasingly uneasy.

"It took us a little doing to get this together so quickly," Dudley told him.

"I appreciate your effort," Jeffrey said.

"I suppose you'll want to count it," Dudley said, but Jeffrey declined.

Dudley had Jeffrey sign a receipt for the cash. "Are you sure you don't want a cashier's check?" Dudley asked as he took the signed paper from Jeffrey. "It's not safe carrying this kind of cash around. You could call your bail bondsman and have him pick it up here. And you know, a cashier's check is as good as cash. He could then go into one of our Boston offices and get cash if that's what he's after. It would make it safer for you."

"He said cash, so I'm giving him cash," Jeffrey said. He was actually touched by Dudley's concern. "His office isn't far," he explained.

"And you're sure you don't want to count it?"

Jeffrey's tension was beginning to evoke irritation, but he forced a smile. "No time. I was supposed to have this money in town before noon. I'm already late. Besides, I've been doing business long enough with you." He packed the money into his briefcase and stood up.

"If I'd known you weren't going to count it, I would have taken a few bills from each packet." Dudley laughed.

Jeffrey hurried out to the car, tossed in the briefcase, and drove out of the parking lot with extra care. All he needed was a speeding ticket! He checked the rearview mirror to make sure he wasn't being followed. So far so good.

Jeffrey drove directly to the airport and parked on the roof of the central parking building. He left the parking stub in the car's ashtray. When he called Carol from wherever, he'd tell her to pick the car up.

With the briefcase in one hand and the suitcase in the other, Jeffrey walked to the Pan Am ticket counter. He tried to behave like any businessman going off on a trip, but his nerves were shot; his stomach was in agony. If anyone recognized him, they'd know he was jumping bail. He'd been specifically told not to leave the state of Massachusetts.

Jeffrey's anxiety went up a notch every minute he waited in the ticket line. When his turn finally came, he bought a ticket for the New York to Rio flight as well as one for the 1:30 P.M. shuttle. The agent tried to convince him it would be far easier to take one of their late afternoon flights directly to Kennedy. That way Jeffrey wouldn't have to take the bus from La-Guardia to Kennedy. But Jeffrey wanted to go on the shuttle.

He felt the sooner he got out of Boston, the better he would feel.

Leaving the ticket area, Jeffrey approached security's X-ray machine. There was a uniformed state police officer casually lounging just beyond it. It was all Jeffrey could do not to turn around and run.

Right after he hoisted his briefcase and then the suitcase onto the conveyer belt and watched them disappear into the machine, Jeffrey had a sudden fright. What about the syringes and the ampule of morphine? What if they showed up on the X-ray, and he had to open the briefcase? Then they'd discover the stacks of money! What would they think of all that cash?

Jeffrey thought about trying to reach into the X-ray machine to yank his briefcase back, but it was too late. He glanced at the woman studying the screen. Her face was illuminated eerily by the light, but her eyes were glazed with boredom. Jeffrey felt himself being subtly urged on by the people waiting behind. He stepped through the metal detector, eyes on the policeman the whole time. The policeman caught his eye and smiled; Jeffrey managed a crooked smile in return. Jeffrey looked back at the woman studying the screen. Her blank face looked suddenly puzzled by something. She had stopped the conveyor belt and was motioning for another woman to look at the screen.

Jeffrey's heart sank. The two were examining the contents of his briefcase as it appeared on the screen. The policeman hadn't noticed yet. Jeffrey caught him yawning.

Then the conveyor belt started again. The briefcase came out, but the second of the two women stepped over and put her hand on it.

"Is this yours?" she asked Jeffrey.

Jeffrey hesitated, but there was no denying it was his. His passport was in it.

"Yes," he said weakly.

"Do you have a Dopp Kit in there with a small pair of scissors?"

Jeffrey nodded.

"Okay," she said, giving the briefcase a push toward him.

Stunned but relieved, Jeffrey quickly took his belongings to a far corner of the waiting area and sat down. He picked up a discarded newspaper and hid behind it. If he hadn't felt like a criminal when the jury handed down its verdict, he felt like one now.

As soon as his flight was called, Jeffrey pressed to get on. He couldn't wait to get on the plane. Once he was on, he couldn't wait to take his seat.

Jeffrey was in an aisle seat fairly close to the front of the plane. With his suitcase secured in the overhead compartment and his briefcase tucked under his feet, Jeffrey leaned back and closed his eyes. His heart was still racing but at least he could now try to relax. He had just about made it.

But it was difficult to calm down. Sitting there in that plane, the seriousness and irreversibility of what he was about to do finally began to sink in. So far, he hadn't broken any law. But as soon as the plane crossed from Massachusetts into another state, he would have. And there would be no turning back.

Jeffrey checked his watch. He began to perspire. It was one twenty-seven. Only three minutes to go before the door would be sealed. Then takeoff. Was he doing the right thing? For the first time since he'd come to this decision that morning, Jeffrey felt real doubt. The experience of a lifetime argued against it. He'd always followed the law and respected authority.

Jeffrey began to shake all over. He'd never experienced such agonizing indecision and confusion. He looked at his watch again. It was twenty-nine after the hour. The cabin attendants were busy slamming all the overhead compartments, and the crashing noise threatened to drive him mad. The door to the cockpit was closed with a resounding click. A gate agent came onto the plane and gave a final manifest. All the passengers were in their seats. In a way he was ending the life he had always known, as surely as if he'd released the stopcock the night before.

He wondered how running away would affect his appeal. Wouldn't it make him appear the guiltier? And if he was ever brought to justice, would he have to serve extra time for fleeing? Just what did he plan to do in South America? He didn't even speak Spanish or Portuguese. In a flash, the full horror of his action hit home. He just couldn't go through with it.

"Wait!" Jeffrey shouted as he heard the sounds of the plane's door closing. All eyes turned on him. "Wait! I have to get off!" He undid the seat belt, then tried to pull his briefcase from under the seat. It opened and some of the contents, including a stack of hundred-dollar bills, fell out. Hastily, he jammed the things back inside, then got his suitcase from the overhead compartment. No one spoke. Everyone was watching Jeffrey's panic with stunned curiosity.

Jeffrey rushed forward and confronted the cabin attendant. "I have to get off!" he repeated. Perspiration was running down his forehead, blurring his vision. He looked crazed. "I'm a doctor," he added, as if to explain. "It's an emergency."

"Okay, okay," the cabin attendant said calmly. She pounded on the door, then made a gesture through the window at the gate agent who was still standing on the jetway on the other side. The door was opened, too slowly for Jeffrey's taste.

As soon as the passage was clear, Jeffrey rushed from the plane. Luckily, no one confronted him to ask for his reasons for deplaning. He ran up the jetway. The door to the terminal was closed, but it was unlocked. He started across the boarding area, but he didn't get far. The gate agent called him over to the boarding podium.

"Your name, please?" he asked with no expression.

Jeffrey hesitated. He hated to say. He didn't want to have to explain himself to the authorities.

"I can't give you your ticket back unless you give me your name," the agent said, slightly irritated.

Jeffrey relented, and the gate agent returned his ticket. Pushing it hastily into his pocket, he then walked past the security check and went into the men's room. He had to calm down. He was a nervous wreck. He put down his hand luggage and leaned on the edge of the sink. He hated himself for vacillating, first with suicide, now with fleeing. In both cases Jeffrey still felt he made the right choice, but now what were his options? He felt depression threaten to return but he fought against it.

At least Chris Everson had had the fortitude to follow through with his decision, albeit a misguided one. Jeffrey cursed himself again for not having been a better friend. If only he knew then what he knew now, he might have been able to save the man. Only now did Jeffrey have an appreciation of what Chris had been going through. Jeffrey hated himself for not having called the man, and for compounding the oversight by failing to call his young widow, Kelly.

Jeffrey splashed his face with cold water. When he'd regained some semblance of composure, he picked up his belongings and emerged from the rest room. Despite the bustle of the airport, he felt horribly alone and isolated. The thought of going home to an empty house was oppressive. But he didn't know where else to go. Directionless, he headed for the parking garage.

Reaching his car, Jeffrey put the suitcase in the trunk and the briefcase on the passenger-side seat. He got in behind the wheel and sat, blankly staring ahead, waiting for inspiration.

For several hours he sat there running through all his failings. Never had he been so low. Obsessed about Chris Everson, he eventually began to wonder what had happened to Kelly Everson. He'd met her on three or four social occasions prior to Chris's death. He could even remember having made some complimentary remarks about her to Carol. Carol hadn't been pleased to hear them at the time.

Jeffrey wondered if Kelly still worked at Valley Hospital, or, for that matter, if she still lived in the Boston vicinity. He remembered her as being about five-four or five, with a slim, athletic build. Her hair had been brown with highlights of red and gold, which she'd wear long, clasped with a single barrette. He recalled her face as being broad with dark brown eyes and small, full features that frequently broke into a bright smile. But what he remembered most was her aura. She'd had a playfulness that had melded wonderfully with a feminine warmth and sincerity that made people like her instantly.

As Jeffrey's thoughts switched from Chris to Kelly, he found himself thinking that she, more than anyone else, would have some insight into what Jeffrey was now going through. Having lost a husband through the emotional devastation caused by a malpractice case, she'd probably be acutely sensitive to Jeffrey's emotional plight. She might even have some suggestions for dealing with it. At the very least she might provide some much needed sympathy. And if nothing else, at least his conscience would be assuaged by finally making a call he'd been vaguely meaning to make.

Jeffrey returned to the terminal. At the first bank of phones
he came to, he used a directory to look up Kelly Everson. He
held his breath as his index finger trailed down the names. He
stopped on K. C. Everson in Brookline. That was promising.
He put in his coin and dialed. The phone rang once, twice,
then a third time. He was about to hang up when someone at
the other end picked up. A cheerful voice came through the
receiver.

Jeffrey realized he hadn't given a thought as to how to begin.
Abruptly, he said hello and gave his name. He was so unsure
of himself, he was afraid she wouldn't remember him, but
before he could offer something to jog her memory, he heard
her ebullient "Hello, Jeffrey!" She sounded genuinely glad to
hear from him and didn't sound at all surprised.

"I'm so pleased you called," she said. "I'd thought about
calling you when I read about your legal problems, but I just
couldn't get myself to do it. I was afraid you might not even
remember me."

Afraid that *he* wouldn't remember *her!* Jeffrey assured her
that wouldn't have been the case. Taking her lead, he apologized profusely for not having called her sooner as he'd promised.

"You don't have to apologize," she said. "I know tragedies
intimidate people, the way cancer does, or used to. And I know
that doctors have a hard time dealing with a suicide of a colleague. I didn't expect you to call, but I was moved you'd taken
the time to come to the funeral. Chris would have been pleased
to know you cared. He really respected you. He once told me
that he thought you were the best anesthesiologist he knew. So
I was honored you were there. A few of his other friends didn't
come. But I understood."

Jeffrey didn't know what to say. Here Kelly was forgiving
him completely, even complimenting him. Yet the more she
said, the more he felt like a heel. Not knowing how to respond,
he changed the subject. He said he was glad to find her home.

"This is a good time to catch me. I just got home from work.
I guess you know I don't work at the Valley anymore."

"No, I didn't know that."

"After Chris's death I thought it would be healthy for me
to go elsewhere," Kelly said. "So I moved into town. I'm

working at St. Joe's now. In the intensive care unit. I like it better than recovery. I guess you're still at Boston Memorial?"

"Sort of," Jeffrey said evasively. He felt awkward and indecisive. He was afraid she'd refuse to see him. After all, what did she owe him? She had a life of her own. But he'd gotten this far; he had to try. "Kelly," he said at last, "I was wondering if I could drop by and talk with you for a moment."

"When did you have in mind?" Kelly asked without missing a beat.

"Whenever's good for you. I . . . I could come by now if you're not too busy."

"Well, sure," Kelly said.

"If it's inconvenient, I could . . ."

"No, no! It's fine. Come on over," Kelly said before Jeffrey had a chance to finish. Then she gave him directions to her house.

Michael Mosconi had Jeffrey's check on his blotter in front of him when he placed the call to Owen Shatterly at the Boston National Bank. He didn't think he'd be nervous, but his stomach filled with butterflies the instant he dialed. He had taken a personal check only once before in his bail bondsman career. That transaction had turned out fine. He hadn't been burned. But Michael had heard horror stories from colleagues. Of course if anything did go wrong, Mosconi's biggest problem was that his underwriting company forbade him to take checks in the first place. As Michael had explained it to Jeffrey, he was putting his ass on the line. He didn't know why he was getting to be such a soft touch. Then again, it was a unique case. The guy was a doctor, for chrissake. Also, a $45,000 fee came along only once in a blue moon. Michael had not wanted to lose the case to his competition. So, in his way, he'd offered better terms. It had been an executive decision.

Someone at the bank answered, then put Michael on hold. Muzak floated out of the receiver. Michael drummed his fingers on the desk top. It was close to four in the afternoon. All he wanted to do was make sure the doc's check would clear before he deposited it. Shatterly had been a friend for a long time; Michael knew there would be no problem finding out from him.

When Shatterly came on the line, Michael explained the information he needed. He didn't have to say more. Shatterly only said, "Just a sec." Michael could hear him tapping his computer keys.

"How much is the check?" Shatterly asked.

"Forty-five grand," Michael said.

Shatterly laughed. "The account only has twenty-three dollars and change."

There was a pause. Michael stopped his drumming. He got a sinking feeling in the pit of his stomach. "You sure there's been no deposits today?" he asked.

"Nothing like $45,000," Shatterly said.

Michael hung up the phone.

"Trouble?" Devlin O'Shea asked, peering over the top of an old *Penthouse* magazine. Devlin was a big man who looked more like a sixties-style biker than a former Boston policeman. Dangling from his left earlobe was a small, gold Maltese cross earring. He even wore his hair in a neat little ponytail. Besides helping with his work, his appearance was his small way of thumbing his nose at authority now that he didn't have to trouble himself with rules like dress codes anymore. O'Shea had been dropped from the force after a bribery conviction.

Devlin was making himself comfortable on a vinyl couch facing Michael's desk. He was dressed in the clothes that had pretty much become his uniform since his leaving the force: a denim jacket, acid-washed jeans, and black cowboy boots.

Michael didn't say anything, which was enough of an answer for Devlin. "Anything I can help with?" Devlin asked.

Michael studied Devlin, taking in the man's massive forearms and their lattice of tattoos. One of Devlin's front teeth was gone, giving him the look of the barroom brawler he occasionally was.

"Maybe," Michael said. He was beginning to form a plan.

Devlin had dropped by Mosconi's office that afternoon because he was between jobs. He'd just brought back a killer who'd jumped bail and fled to Canada. Devlin was one of the bounty hunters that Michael used when the need arose.

Michael felt that Devlin was just the man to send to remind Jeffrey about his obligation. Michael thought that Devlin would be far more persuasive than he could be.

Leaning back in his desk chair, Michael explained the situation. Devlin tossed the *Penthouse* aside and stood up. He was six-foot-five and weighed two hundred and sixty-eight pounds. His rotund belly spilled over the large silver buckle of his belt. But underneath the layer of fat was a lot of muscle.

"Sure, I can talk to him," Devlin said.

"Be nice," Michael said. "Just be persuasive. Remember, he's a doctor. I just don't want him to forget about me."

"I'm always nice," Devlin said. "Considerate, well-groomed, well-mannered. That's my charm."

Devlin left the office, glad to have something to do. He hated just sitting around. The only problem was that he wished the task was a bit more lucrative. But he looked forward to the ride out to Marblehead. Maybe he'd hit that Italian restaurant up there and then go and have a few beers at his favorite harbor bar.

Kelly's house was a charming two-story colonial with mullioned windows. It was painted white with black shutters. The two chimneys on either end were surfaced with old brick. A two-car garage was to the right of the house, a screened porch off the left.

Jeffrey stopped in the street across from the house and pulled up to the curb. He studied the house through the car window, hoping to nerve up enough to cross the street and ring the bell. He was surprised to see so many trees so close to downtown Boston. The house was nestled in a cozy stand of maples, oaks, and birches.

As he sat there, Jeffrey tried to think of what he would say. Never before had he gone to someone's house looking for "sympathy and understanding." And there was always the concern of rejection despite her warmth on the phone. If he didn't know she was waiting for him, he wouldn't have been able to go through with it.

Marshaling his courage, he put the car in gear and turned into Kelly's driveway. He went up to the front door, briefcase in hand. He felt ridiculous holding it—as a doctor, he wasn't even used to carrying one—but he was afraid to leave so much cash in the car.

Kelly opened the door before he had a chance to ring the bell. She was dressed in black tights with a pink leotard and pink headband and warm-up leggings. "I go to an aerobics class most afternoons," she explained, blushing slightly. Then she gave Jeffrey a big hug. Tears almost came to his eyes when he realized he couldn't remember the last time someone had hugged him. It took him a moment to catch his balance and hug her back.

Still holding his arms, she leaned back so she could look up into his eyes. Jeffrey was a good six inches taller than she was. "I'm so glad you came over," she said. She held his gaze for a beat, then added: "Come in, come in!" She took him by the hand and led him inside, giving the door a kick closed with her stockinged foot.

Jeffrey found himself in a wide foyer with archways into a dining room on the right and a living room on the left. There was a small table supporting a silver tea service. At the end of the foyer, toward the back of the house, an elegant staircase curved up to the second floor.

"How about some tea?" Kelly offered.

"I don't want to be a bother," Jeffrey said.

Kelly clucked her tongue. "What do you mean, bother?" She led him, still holding his hand, through the dining room and into the kitchen. Extending off the back of the house and open to the kitchen was a comfortable family room. It seemed to be part of an addition. There was a garden outside the broad bow window. The garden appeared as if it could use a little attention. Inside, the house was spotless.

Kelly sat Jeffrey on a gingham couch. Jeffrey put down his briefcase.

"What's with the briefcase?" Kelly asked as she went over to put some water on to boil. "I thought doctors carried little black bags when they made house calls. It makes you look more like an insurance salesman." She laughed a crystalline laugh as she went to the refrigerator and pulled a cheesecake from the freezer.

"If I showed you what was in this briefcase you wouldn't believe it," Jeffrey said.

"What makes you say that?"

Jeffrey didn't answer, but she graciously let it pass. She pulled a knife from a rack above the sink and cut two pieces of cheesecake.

"I'm glad you decided to come over," she said, licking the knife. "I only bring out the cheesecake when I have company." She put a large tea bag in the teapot and got out cups.

The kettle began to whistle fiercely. Kelly pulled it off the range and poured the boiling water into the teapot. She put everything on a tray and carried it to a coffee table in front of the family room couch.

"There!" she said, setting it down. "Did I forget anything?" Kelly surveyed the tray. "Napkins!" she cried, and returned to the kitchen area. When she returned, she sat down. She smiled at Jeffrey. "Really," she said, pouring the tea. "I'm glad you came over, and not just because of the cheesecake."

Jeffrey realized he'd not eaten since the shredded wheat that morning. The cheesecake was a delight.

"Was there something in particular that you wanted to talk about?" Kelly asked, setting her teacup down.

Jeffrey admired her frankness. It made it easier for him.

"For starters, I guess I want to apologize for not having been much of a friend to Chris," Jeffrey said. "After what I've been through in the past few months, I have an appreciation of what Chris went through. At the time, I had no idea."

"I guess no one did," Kelly said sadly. "Even I didn't."

"I don't mean to dredge up painful memories for you," Jeffrey said when he saw the change in Kelly's expression.

"Don't worry. I've finally come to terms with it," she said. "But that's all the more reason I should have called you. How are you holding up?"

Jeffrey hadn't expected the conversation to shift to his troubles so quickly. How *was* he holding up? In the last twenty-four hours he'd attempted suicide and, failing that, had tried to leave the country. "It's been difficult," was all he managed.

Kelly reached over and squeezed his hand. "I don't think people have any idea of the toll malpractice takes and I'm not talking about money."

"You know better than most," Jeffrey said. "You and Chris paid the highest price."

"Is it true you are going to prison?" Kelly asked.

Jeffrey sighed. "It looks that way."

"That's absurd!" Kelly said with a vehemence that surprised Jeffrey.

"We're filing an appeal," he said, "but I don't have much faith in the process. Not anymore."

"How did you become the scapegoat?" Kelly asked. "What happened to the other doctors and the hospital? Weren't they sued?"

"They were all dropped from the case," Jeffrey explained. "I had a brief problem with morphine a few years back. Standard story: it was prescribed for a back injury I suffered in a bike accident. During the trial, they suggested that I'd mainlined some morphine shortly before I came on the case. Then someone found an empty vial of .75% Marcaine in the disposal of the anesthesia machine I was using—.75% Marcaine is contraindicated for obstetric anesthesia. No one found the .5% vial."

"But you didn't use .75%, did you?" Kelly asked.

"I always check the label of any medication," Jeffrey said. "But it's that type of reflex behavior that's hard to specifically remember. I can't believe I used .75%. But what can I say? They found what they found."

"Hey," Kelly said. "Don't start to doubt yourself. That's what Chris started to do."

"Easier said than done."

"What is .75% Marcaine used for?" Kelly asked.

"Quite a few things," Jeffrey said. "Whenever you want a particularly long-acting block with little volume. It's used a lot in eye surgery."

"Had there been any eye cases in the OR where your accident occurred or any operations that might have required .75% Marcaine?"

Jeffrey thought for a moment. He shook his head. "I don't think so, but I don't know for sure."

"It might be worth looking into," Kelly said. "It wouldn't have much legal import, but if you could explain the .75% Marcaine, at least to yourself, it would go a long way in helping rebuild your confidence. I really think that where malpractice is concerned, doctors need to be as diligent in guarding their self-esteem as they are in preparing their court cases."

"You're right about that," Jeffrey said, but he was still thinking about Kelly's questions regarding the .75% Marcaine. He
couldn't believe that no one had thought to ask about cases
prior to Patty Owen's in the same OR. He sure hadn't thought
of it. He wondered how he'd go about inquiring now that he
didn't enjoy the access to the hospital he once had.

"Speaking of self-esteem, how's yours?" Kelly smiled, but
Jeffrey could tell that despite her apparent lightheartedness,
she was dead serious.

"I have the feeling I'm talking to an expert," Jeffrey said.
"Have you been reading a bit of psychiatry on the side?"

"Hardly," Kelly said. "Unfortunately, I learned about the
importance of self-esteem the hard way, by experience." She
took a sip of tea. For a moment she was lost in her own
sorrowful reverie, staring out the bay window at the overgrown garden. Then, just as abruptly, she snapped out of her
momentary trance. She looked at Jeffrey, without her smile.
"I'm convinced it was through low self-esteem that Chris committed suicide. He couldn't have done what he did if he felt
better about himself. I just know it. It wasn't the fact of the
tragedy that pushed him over the edge. It certainly wasn't
guilt. Chris was like you, in that he had nothing to feel guilty
about. It was the sudden erosion of confidence, the damage
done to how he thought about himself, that made Chris take
his life. People have no idea how sensitive even the most accomplished doctors are to the impact of being sued. In fact, the
better the doctor the more it hurts. The fact that the suit is
baseless has nothing to do with it."

"You're so right," Jeffrey said. "Back when I heard that
Chris had killed himself, I was astounded. I knew what kind
of man he was, what kind of doctor he was. Now his suicide
doesn't astound me at all. In fact, from where I sit now, I'm
surprised more doctors sued for malpractice aren't drawn to it.
In fact, I tried it last night."

"Tried what?" Kelly asked sharply. She knew what Jeffrey
meant but she didn't want to believe it.

Jeffrey sighed. He couldn't look at her. "Last night I tried
to commit suicide," he said simply. "I came within an inch of
doing the same thing that Chris did. You know, the succinyl-

choline and morphine trick. I had the IV running and everything."

Kelly dropped her cup of tea. She lunged forward and,
grabbing Jeffrey by his shoulders, she shook him. The move
startled him. She caught him completely unaware.

"Don't you dare do such a thing. Don't even think about it!"

Kelly was glaring at him, still clutching his shoulders. Finally Jeffrey mumbled that she needn't worry, since he'd
lacked the courage to go through with it.

Kelly shook him again, reacting to his comments.

Jeffrey didn't know what to do, much less say.

Kelly kept shaking him, her passions inflamed. "Suicide is
not courageous," she said angrily. "It is the opposite. It's the
cowardly thing to do. And it's selfish. It hurts everyone you
leave behind, everyone who loves you. I want you to promise
me that if you ever have thoughts of suicide again, you'll call
me immediately, no matter what time of day or night. Think
of your wife. Chris's suicide filled me with such guilt, you have
no idea. I was crushed. I felt that somehow I had failed him.
I know that's not true now, but his death is something I'll
probably never get over completely."

"Carol and I are getting a divorce," Jeffrey blurted.

Kelly's expression softened. "Because of the malpractice
suit?"

Jeffrey shook his head. "We'd planned it before all this
started. Carol was just nice enough to put it off for the time
being."

"You poor man," Kelly said. "I can't imagine trying to deal
with being sued for malpractice and a breakup of a marriage
at the same time."

"My marital problems are the least of my worries," Jeffrey
said.

"I'm serious about your promising me you'll call before you
do anything foolish," Kelly said.

"I'm not thinking . . ."

"Promise!" Kelly insisted.

"All right, I promise," Jeffrey said.

Satisfied, Kelly got up and cleaned up the mess that she'd
made when she'd dropped her teacup. As she picked up the

pieces of broken china, she said: "I wish more than anything that I'd had the slightest indication of what Chris had been planning. One minute it seemed that he'd been full of fight, talking about the anesthetic complication being secondary to a contaminant in the local, the next minute he was dead."

Jeffrey watched Kelly as she threw the shards of china away. It took a few moments for her last words to sink in. When she returned and took her seat again, Jeffrey asked, "What made Chris think of a contaminant in the local anesthetic?"

Kelly shrugged. "I haven't the faintest idea. But he seemed to be genuinely excited about the possibility. I encouraged him. Just before that he'd been depressed. Very depressed. The idea of a contaminant gave him a real boost. He spent several days poring over pharmacology and physiology textbooks. He made lots of notes. He was working on it the night he . . . I'd gone to bed. I found him the next morning with an IV in place, the bottle empty."

"How awful," Jeffrey said.

"It was the worst experience of my life," Kelly admitted.

For an instant, Jeffrey envied Chris, not because he'd succeeded where Jeffrey had failed, but because he'd left behind someone who obviously loved him so deeply. If Jeffrey had followed through, would anyone be that sorry about it? Jeffrey tried to shake the thought. Instead, he considered the notion of a contaminant in the local anesthetic. It was a curious thought.

"What kind of contaminant was Chris thinking about?" Jeffrey asked.

"I really don't know," Kelly answered. "It was two years ago, and Chris never did go into much detail about it. At least not with me."

"Did you mention his theory to anybody at the time?"

"I told the lawyers. Why?"

"It's an intriguing idea," Jeffrey said.

"I still have Chris's notes," Kelly said. "You're welcome to see them if you'd like."

"I would," Jeffrey said.

Kelly stood up and led Jeffrey back through the kitchen and dining room, across the foyer and through the living room. She stopped at a closed door.

"I think I'd better explain," she said. "This was Chris's study. I know it probably wasn't all that healthy, but after Chris's death I just closed the door to this room and left everything the way it was. Don't ask me why. At the time it made me feel better, as if some part of him was still here. So be prepared. It might be a little on the dusty side." She opened the door and stepped aside.

Jeffrey walked into the study. In contrast to the rest of the house, it was disheveled and musty. A thick layer of dust coated everything. There were even a few cobwebs hanging from the cciling. The blinds were closed tight. On one wall was a floor-to-ceiling bookcase filled with volumes that Jeffrey recognized immediately. Most of them were standard texts for anesthesia. The others dealt with more general medical topics.

In the center of the room stood an old partners' desk, heaped with papers and books. In the corner of the room was an Eames chair upholstered in black leather that had dried and cracked. Next to the chair was a tall stack of books.

Kelly was leaning against the doorjamb with her arms folded as if she was reluctant to enter. "Quite a mess," she said.

"You don't mind if I look around?" Jeffrey asked. He felt a certain kinship with his dead colleague but did not want to trespass on Kelly's feelings.

"Be my guest," she said. "As I told you, I've finally come to terms with Chris's passing. I've been meaning to clean this room for some time. I just haven't gotten around to it."

Jeffrey circled the desk. There was a lamp on it, which he turned on. He wasn't superstitious; he did not believe in the supernatural. Yet somehow he felt Chris was trying to tell him something.

Open on the desk's blotter was a familiar textbook: Goodman and Gillman's *Pharmacological Basis of Therapeutics.* Next to it was *Clinical Toxicology.* Beside both books was a pile of handwritten notes. Bending over the desk, Jeffrey noted that the Goodman and Gillman was open to the section on Marcaine. The potential adverse side effects were heavily underlined.

"Did Chris's case involve Marcaine as well?" Jeffrey asked.

"Yes," Kelly said. "I thought you knew that."

"Not really," Jeffrey said. He'd not heard which of the local anesthetics Chris had used. Occasional complications were seen with all of them.

Jeffrey picked up the stack of notes. Almost immediately he felt a tickle in his nose. He sneezed.

Kelly put the back of her hand to her lips to hide her smile. "I warned you it might be dusty."

Jeffrey sneezed again.

"Why don't you get what you want and we can retreat to the family room," Kelly suggested.

Through watery eyes, Jeffrey picked up the pharmacology and toxicology books, along with the notes, and carried them out with him. He sneezed a third time before Kelly shut the study door.

When they got back to the kitchen, Kelly offered a suggestion. "Why don't you stay for an early dinner? I can whip us up something. It won't be gourmet, but it'll be healthy."

"I thought you were off to an aerobics class," Jeffrey said. He was delighted by her offer, but didn't want to inconvenience her any more than he already had.

"I can work out any day," Kelly said. "Besides, I think you need a little TLC."

"Well, if it wouldn't be a bother," Jeffrey said. He was amazed by her kindness.

"I'll enjoy it," Kelly said. "Now you make yourself comfortable on the couch. Take your shoes off if you like."

Jeffrey took her at her word. He sat down and laid the books on the coffee table. He watched her for a moment as she bustled about the kitchen, looking in the refrigerator and various cabinets. Then he kicked off his shoes and settled back to shuffle through Chris's notes. The first thing he came across was a handwritten summary of the anesthetic complication in Chris's tragic case.

"I'm going to run to the store," Kelly said. "You just stay put."

"I don't want you going to any trouble," Jeffrey said, making a motion as if to get up. But it wasn't true. He loved the fact that Kelly was willing to make such an effort for him.

"Nonsense," Kelly said. "I'll be back in a flash."

Jeffrey wasn't sure if Kelly had said nonsense because she saw through his fib or because to her it was no trouble. She was gone in the blink of an eye. Jeffrey heard her start her car in the garage, pull out, and accelerate down the street.

He glanced around at the comfortable family room and kitchen, pleased that he'd made the decision to call Kelly. Aside from deciding not to kill himself and not to fly away, in the last twenty-four hours it was the best decision he'd made.

Settling back again, Jeffrey turned his attention to the summary of Chris's anesthetic complication:

Henry Noble, a fifty-seven-year-old white male, entered the Valley Hospital to undergo a total prostatectomy for cancer. The request from Dr. Wallenstern was for continuous epidural anesthesia. I visited the man the evening before his surgery. He was mildly apprehensive. His health was good. Cardiac status was normal with a normal EKG. Blood pressure was normal. Neurological exam was normal. He had no allergies. Specifically, he had no drug allergies. He'd had general anesthesia for a hernia operation in 1977 with no problems. He'd had local anesthesia for multiple dental procedures with no problems. Because of his apprehension I wrote an order for 10 mg of diazepam to be given by mouth one hour prior to coming to surgery. The following morning he arrived in good spirits. The diazepam had had good effect. The patient was mildly sleepy but could be roused. He was taken to the anesthesia room and placed in a right lateral position. An epidural puncture was made with an 18-gauge Touhey needle without problems. There was no reaction to 2 cc's of Lidocaine utilized to facilitate the epidural stick. Confirmation of the epidural location was made with 2 cc's of sterile water with epinephrine. A small-bore epidural catheter was threaded through the Touhey needle. The patient was returned to a supine position. A test dose of .5% Marcaine with a small amount of epinephrine was then prepared from a 30 ml vial. This test dose was injected. As soon as the test dose was injected the patient complained of what he described as dizziness, followed by severe intestinal cramping. The heart rate began to increase but not to the extent expected if the test dose had inadvertently been injected intravenously. Generalized muscular fasciculations then appeared, suggesting a hyperesthesia state. Massive salivation intervened, suggesting a parasympathetic reaction. Atropine was given intravenously. Miotic pupils were noted. The patient then had a grand mal seizure which was treated with succinylcholine and Valium intravenously. The patient was intubated and maintained on oxygen. The patient then had a cardiac arrest. The heart proved to be extremely resistant to drugs, but finally a sinus rhythm was achieved. The patient was stabilized but did not return to consciousness. The patient was moved to the surgical intensive care unit, where he remained comatose for one week, suffering multiple cardiac arrests. It was also documented that the patient had a total paralysis following his anesthetic complication that involved not only the spinal cord but cranial nerves as well. At the end of the week, the patient had a final cardiac arrest from which the heart could not be started.

Jeffrey looked up from the notes. Reading Chris's terse history of his complication recreated the terror that Jeffrey had felt when he'd desperately fought to save Patty Owen. The memory was so poignant that it brought perspiration to Jeffrey's hands. What made it so poignant were the striking similarities in the two cases, and it wasn't just the dramatic seizures and cardiac arrests. Jeffrey could remember with startling clarity the moment he'd seen salivation and lacrimation that Patty had had. And besides that there was the abdominal pain and the small pupils. None of these responses were usual side effects of local anesthetics, although local anesthetics were capable of causing an extraordinarily wide range of adverse neurological and cardiac effects in a few unfortunate individuals.

Jeffrey studied the next page of the notes. There were a number of words printed in bold letters. Two of them were "muscarinic" and "nicotinic." Jeffrey recognized them, mostly from his medical school days. They had to do with autonomic nervous system function. Then there was the phrase "irreversible high spinal blockade with cranial nerve involvement," followed by a series of exclamation points.

Jeffrey heard Kelly's car pull up the drive and enter the garage. He glanced at his watch. She was a fast shopper.

The next item in Chris's pile was an NMR—nuclear magnetic resonance—report on Henry Noble during the time he was paralyzed and comatose. The results recorded were normal.

"Hi," Kelly called brightly as she came through the door. "Miss me?" She laughed as she dumped a parcel on the kitchen counter top. Then she stepped up to the back of the couch and looked over Jeffrey's shoulder. "What does all this stuff mean?" She pointed to the words and phrases Jeffrey had been reading.

"I don't know," Jeffrey admitted. "But these notes are fascinating. There are so many similarities between Chris's case and mine. I don't know what to make of it."

"Well, I'm glad someone's getting some use out of that stuff," Kelly said as she went back into the kitchen. "It makes me feel less weird for having saved it all."

"I don't think your saving it was weird at all," Jeffrey said, turning to the next page. It was a typed summary of Henry Noble's autopsy, which had been performed by the medical examiner. Chris had underlined the phrase "axonal degeneration seen on microscopic sections" and had followed it up with a series of question marks. Then he'd underlined the phrase "toxicology negative" and capped it off by an emphatic exclamation point. Jeffrey was mystified.

The rest of the notes were outlines of articles taken mostly from the Goodman and Gillman book on pharmacology. A quick glance suggested to Jeffrey that they chiefly dealt with the function of the autonomic nervous system. He decided to look at the material later. He stacked the papers and set them on the table with the two medical volumes serving to anchor them.

Jeffrey joined Kelly by the kitchen sink. "What can I do?" he asked her.

"You're supposed to be relaxing," Kelly said as she rinsed the lettuce.

"I'd prefer to help," Jeffrey said.

"Suit yourself. How about firing up the barbie on the back porch? The matches are in that drawer." Kelly pointed with a lettuce leaf.

Jeffrey grabbed a book of matches and went outside. The barbecue was one of those domed types powered by a cylinder of propane. He quickly figured out how the valve worked and lit it, then closed the dome.

Before going back inside, Jeffrey looked around the untended yard. The tall grass was a fresh spring green. There had been a lot of rain that spring, so all the vegetation was particularly healthy and lush. Lacy fern fronds could be seen within the thicket of trees.

Jeffrey shook his head in disbelief. It seemed almost inconceivable that only last night he had come so close to committing suicide. And only that afternoon he'd tried to flee to South America for good. And now here he was standing on a porch in Brookline getting ready to have a barbecue with an attractive, sensitive, disarmingly demonstrative woman. It almost seemed too good to be true. Then Jeffrey realized with a shock that it was; before too long he'd probably be confined to prison.

Jeffrey took in a deep breath of the cool, late-afternoon air, enjoying its purity. He watched a robin yank a worm from the moist soil. Then he went back inside to see what else he could do to help.

The dinner was delicious and a great success. In spite of the rather dire circumstances, Jeffrey managed to enjoy himself immensely. Conversation with Kelly was natural and easy. They dined on marinated tuna steaks, rice pilaf, and a mixed green salad. Kelly had a bottle of chardonnay hidden in the back of her refrigerator. It was cold and crisp. Jeffrey found himself laughing for the first time in months. That in itself was a major accomplishment.

With coffee and more of the frozen cheesecake, they retired to the gingham couch. Chris's notes and the textbooks brought Jeffrey's mind back to more serious thoughts.

"I hate to revert to unpleasant subjects," Jeffrey said after a pause in the conversation, "but what was the outcome of Chris's malpractice case?"

"The jury found for the plaintiff's estate," Kelly said. "Payment of the settlement was divided between the hospital, Chris, and the surgeon according to some complicated plan. I think that Chris's insurance paid most of it, but I don't know for sure. Fortunately this house was in my name only, so they couldn't count that among his available assets."

"I read a summary that Chris had written," Jeffrey said. "There certainly wasn't any malpractice involved."

"With that kind of emotionally charged case," Kelly said, "whether there was actual malpractice or not isn't all that important. A good plaintiff attorney can always get the jury to identify with the patient."

Jeffrey nodded. Unfortunately, it was true. "I have a favor to ask," Jeffrey said after a pause. "Would you mind terribly if I borrowed these notes?" He patted the pile.

"Heavens no," Kelly said. "Be my guest. May I ask why you're so interested in them?"

"They remind me of questions I'd had about my own case," Jeffrey said. "There were some mild inconsistencies that I could never explain. I'm surprised to see that the same inconsistencies appeared in Chris's case. The thought of a contaminant hadn't occurred to me. I'd like to go over his notes a few more times. It's not immediately apparent what he was thinking. "Besides," Jeffrey added with a smile, "borrowing them will give me a good excuse for coming back."

"You hardly need an excuse," Kelly said. "You're welcome here anytime."

Jeffrey left soon after they finished their dessert. Kelly walked him out to his car. They had eaten so early that it was still daylight outside. Jeffrey thanked her effusively for her spontaneous hospitality. "You have no idea how much I've enjoyed this visit," he said with sincerity.

After Jeffrey had climbed into his car, along with his briefcase, which now contained Chris's notes, Kelly stuck her head in through the open window. "Remember your promise!" she warned. "If you start thinking foolish thoughts, you have to get in touch with me."

"I'll remember," Jeffrey assured her. He drove home in quiet contentment. Spending a few hours with Kelly had done much to elevate his mood. Under the circumstances it amazed him that he'd been able to respond in such a normal fashion. But he knew it had more to do with Kelly's psyche than his. Making the final turn onto his street, Jeffrey reached out to steady his briefcase, which threatened to fall from the seat. With his hand on it, he thought of its strange contents. Toiletries, underwear, $45,000 in cash, and a pile of notes written by a suicide victim.

Although he didn't expect to find anything absolving in the notes, just having them in his possession gave him a feeling of hope. Maybe he could learn something from Chris's experience that he hadn't been able to see himself.

And although he'd been sorry to say good-bye to Kelly, Jeffrey was glad to be getting home so early. He planned to go through Chris's notes more thoroughly and pull out a few books of his own for some serious reading.

Jeffrey stopped just short of the garage door, got out of the car, and stretched. He could smell the ocean. As a peninsula that jutted into the Atlantic Ocean, all of Marblehead was near to the water. Bending back into the car, Jeffrey dragged his briefcase toward him and hefted it into the air. He slammed the car door and started up the front steps.

As he walked he noted the beauty that was all around him. Songbirds were going crazy in the evergreen tree in the front lawn and a sea gull shrieked in the distance. A bank of rhododendrons was in full bloom in a riot of color along the front of the house. Having been preoccupied by his problems during the last months, Jeffrey had completely missed the enchanting transition from bleak New England winter to glorious springtime. He was appreciating it now for the first time that year. The effect of having visited Kelly was still very much on his mind.

Reaching the front door, Jeffrey remembered his suitcase. He hesitated a moment, then decided he could get it later. He put his key in the front door and went inside.

Carol was standing in the entranceway, her hands on her hips. He could tell by her expression that she was angry. Wel-

come home, thought Jeffrey. And how was *your* day? He put
his briefcase down.

"It's almost eight o'clock," Carol said with undisguised im-
patience.

"I'm quite aware of the time."

"Where have you been?"

Jeffrey hung up his jacket. Carol's inquisitional attitude
irked him. Maybe he should have called. In the old days, he
would have, but these weren't normal times by any stretch of
the imagination.

"I don't ask you where you've been," Jeffrey said.

"If I'm going to be delayed until almost eight at night I
always call," Carol said. "It's just common courtesy."

"I suppose I'm not a courteous person," Jeffrey said. He was
too tired to argue the point. He picked up his briefcase, intending to go directly to his room. He wasn't interested in fighting
with Carol. But then he stopped. A large man had appeared,
leaning casually against the doorjamb leading into the kitchen.
Jeffrey's eyes immediately took in the ponytail, the denim
clothes, the cowboy boots, and the tattoos. He had a gold
earring in one ear and was holding a bottle of Kronenbourg
in his hand.

Jeffrey gave Carol a questioning look.

"While you are out doing God knows what," Carol
snapped, "I've been here putting up with this pig of a man.
And all because of you. Where have you been?"

Jeffrey's eyes went from Carol to the stranger and back
again. He had no idea what was going on. The stranger winked
and smiled at Carol's unflattering reference as if it had been a
compliment.

"I'd also like to know where you've been, sport," the thug
said. "I already know where you haven't been." He took a pull
on the beer and smiled. He acted as if he were enjoying himself.

"Who is this man?" Jeffrey asked Carol.

"Devlin O'Shea," the stranger offered. He pushed off the
doorjamb and stepped beside Carol. "Me and the cute little
missus here have been waiting for you for hours." He reached
out to pinch Carol's cheek, but she batted his hand away.
"Feisty little thing." He laughed.

"I want to know what's going on here," Jeffrey demanded.

"Mr. O'Shea is the charming emissary of Mr. Michael Mosconi," Carol said angrily.

"Emissary?" Devlin questioned. "Ooh, I like that. Sounds sexy."

"Did you go to the bank to see Dudley?" Carol demanded, ignoring Devlin.

"Of course," Jeffrey said. Suddenly he realized why Devlin was there.

"And what happened?" Carol demanded.

"Yeah, what happened?" Devlin chimed in. "Our sources report that there was no deposit like was promised. That's unfortunate."

"There was a problem . . ." Jeffrey stammered. He'd not been prepared for this interrogation.

"What kind of a problem?" Devlin asked, stepping forward and poking Jeffrey repeatedly in the chest with his index finger, keeping the pressure on. He felt Jeffrey wasn't coming clean.

"Paperwork," Jeffrey said, trying to fend off Devlin's jabs. "The kind of red tape you always get at a bank."

"What if I don't believe you?" Devlin said. He smacked Jeffrey on the side of the head with an open palm.

Jeffrey's hand went to his ear. The blow stung him and startled him. His ear was ringing.

"You can't come in here and push me around," Jeffrey said, trying to be authoritative.

"Oh, no?" Devlin said in an artificially high voice. He switched the beer to his right hand and then with his left he smacked Jeffrey on the other side of the head. His movement was so swift, Jeffrey had no time to react. He stumbled back against the wall, cowering in front of this behemoth.

"Let me remind you of something," Devlin said, staring down at Jeffrey. "You are a convicted felon, my friend, and the only reason you're not rotting in prison at this moment is because of the generosity of Mr. Mosconi."

"Carol!" Jeffrey yelled. He felt a mixture of terror and anger. "Call the police!"

"Ha!" Devlin laughed, throwing his head back. " 'Call the

police!' You're too much, Doc. You really are. I'm the one with
the law behind me—not you. I'm just here as an . . ." Devlin
paused, then looked back at Carol. "Hey, dearie, what was that
you called me?"

"An emissary," Carol said, hoping to appease the man. She
was appalled at this scene but had no idea what to do.

"Like she said, I'm an emissary," Devlin repeated, turning
back to Jeffrey. "I'm an emissary to remind you about your
deal with Mr. Mosconi. He was a little disappointed this afternoon when he called the bank. What happened to the money
that was supposed to be in your checking account?"

"It was the bank's fault," Jeffrey repeated. He hoped to God
this giant didn't look in his briefcase, which he was still holding. If he saw the cash, he'd guess that Jeffrey had been planning to flee. "It was some minor bureaucratic holdup, but the
money will be in the account in the morning. All the paperwork is done."

"You wouldn't be jerking me around, would you?" Devlin
asked. He flicked the end of Jeffrey's nose with the nail of his
index finger. Jeffrey winced. His nose felt like it had been
stung by a bee.

"They assured me there would be no further problems,"
Jeffrey said. He touched the tip of his nose and looked at his
finger. He expected to see blood but there wasn't any.

"So the money will be there tomorrow morning?"

"Absolutely."

"Well, in that case I guess I'll be going," Devlin said. "Needless to say, if the money doesn't appear, I'll be back." Devlin
turned from Jeffrey and stepped over to Carol. He extended
the beer. "Thanks for the brew, honey."

She took the bottle. Devlin again made a motion to pinch her
cheek. Carol tried to slap him, but he caught her arm. "You
certainly are feisty," he said with a laugh. She yanked her arm
free.

"I'm sure you're both sorry to see me go," Devlin said at the
door. "I'd love to stay for dinner but I'm supposed to meet a
group of nuns over at Rosalie's." He laughed a hoarse laugh
as he pulled the door closed behind himself.

For a few moments neither Jeffrey nor Carol moved. They

could hear a car start out in the street, then pull away. Carol was the one to break the silence: "What happened at the bank?" she demanded. She was furious. "Why didn't they have the money for you?"

Jeffrey didn't answer. He just looked at his wife dumbly. He was shaking from his reaction to Devlin. The balance between anger and terror had tilted to terror. Devlin was the embodiment of Jeffrey's worst fears, especially since he understood he had no defense against him and no protection from the law. Devlin was just the kind of person Jeffrey imagined populated the prisons. Jeffrey was surprised the man hadn't threatened to break his kneecaps. Despite his Irish name, he seemed like a character straight from the Mafia.

"Answer me!" Carol demanded. "Where have you been?"

With his briefcase still in hand, Jeffrey started for his room. He wanted to be alone. The nightmare vision of a prison filled with inmates all like Devlin came to him in a dizzying rush.

Carol grabbed his arm. "I'm talking to you!" she snapped.

Jeffrey stopped and looked down at Carol's hand gripping his arm. "Let go of me," he said in a controlled voice.

"Not until you talk to me and tell me where you've been."

"Let go of me," Jeffrey said menacingly.

Thinking better of it, Carol let go of his arm. Again he started for his room. She quickly fell in behind him. "You are not the only one around here who has been under strain," she yelled after him. "I think I deserve some kind of explanation. I had to entertain that animal for hours."

Jeffrey stopped at his door. "I'm sorry," he said. He owed her that. Carol was right behind him.

"I think I've been pretty understanding through all this," Carol said. "Now I want to know what happened at the bank. Dudley said yesterday there would be no problems."

"I'll talk to you about it later." He needed a few minutes to calm down.

"I want to talk about it now," Carol persisted.

Jeffrey opened his door and stepped into the room. Carol tried to push through after him, but Jeffrey blocked her way. "Later!" he said, louder than he'd meant to. He closed the door on her. Carol heard the lock click into place.

She pounded on the door in frustration and began to cry. "You're impossible! I don't know why I was willing to wait on the divorce. This is the thanks I get." Sobbing, she gave the door a kick, then ran down the hall to her own room.

Jeffrey slammed the briefcase down on his bed, then sat down next to it. He didn't mean to aggravate Carol like that, but he couldn't help it. How could he explain what he was going through when there hadn't been any real communication between them for years? He knew he owed her an explanation, but he didn't want to confide in her until he'd decided what to do. If he told her he had the cash in hand, she'd make him take it to the bank first thing. But Jeffrey needed time to think first. For what felt like the fortieth time that day alone, he wasn't sure what he would do.

For the moment, he got up and went into the bathroom. He filled a glass with water and held it with both hands as he drank. He was still shaking from a whirlpool of emotions. He looked at himself in the mirror. There was a scratch on the end of his nose where Devlin had flicked him. Both his ears were bright red. He shuddered when he recalled how defenseless he'd felt in front of the man.

Jeffrey returned to the bedroom and eyed the briefcase. Flipping open the latches, he lifted the lid and pushed aside Chris Everson's notes. He looked at the neat packets of hundred-dollar bills and found himself wishing that he'd stayed on the plane that afternoon. If he had, he'd now be well on his way to Rio and some sort of new life. Anything had to be better than what he was going through now. The warm moments with Kelly, that great dinner, seemed to have happened to him in another life.

Glancing at his watch, Jeffrey noticed it was a little after eight. The last Pan Am shuttle was at nine-thirty. He could make it if he left soon.

He remembered how awful he'd felt on the plane that afternoon. Could he really go through with it? Jeffrey went back into the bathroom and again examined his inflamed ears and scratched nose. What else was a man like Devlin capable of if they were locked in the same room day in, day out?

Jeffrey turned and went back to the briefcase. He closed the lid and locked it up. He was going to Brazil.

When Devlin left the Rhodes's house, he fully intended to follow his original plan of Italian food, followed by beers at the harbor. But when he got about three blocks away, intuition made him pull over to the side of the road. In his mind's eye, he replayed the conversation he'd had with the good doctor. From the moment Jeffrey had blamed the bank for not coming through with the money, Devlin knew he'd been lying. Now he started wondering why. "Doctors!" Devlin said. "They always think they're smarter than everybody else."

Doing a U-turn, Devlin drove back the way he'd come and cruised by the Rhodes's house, trying to decide how to proceed. About a block beyond it, he made a second U-turn and passed the house again. This time he slowed down. He found a parking place and pulled in.

The way he saw it, he had two choices. Either he could go back inside the Rhodes's house and ask the doc why he was lying, or he could sit tight and wait awhile. He knew he'd put the fear of God into the man. That had been his intention. Often people who felt guilty about something reacted to confrontation by hastily committing some telltale act. Devlin decided to wait Rhodes out. If nothing happened in an hour or so, then he'd go get some food and come back for a visit afterward.

Turning off the motor, Devlin scrunched down as best he could behind the steering wheel. He thought about Jeffrey Rhodes, wondering what the guy had been convicted of. Mosconi hadn't told him that. To Devlin, Rhodes didn't seem like the criminal type, even the white-collar variety.

A few mosquitoes disturbed Devlin's reverie. After rolling up the windows, the temperature inside the car climbed. Devlin began to rethink his plans. Just as he was about to start the car, he saw movement at the far edge of the garage. "Now what have we here?" he said, hunching low in his seat.

At first Devlin couldn't tell who it was, the Mr. or the Mrs. Then Jeffrey stepped around the edge of the garage, making a beeline for his car. He was carrying his briefcase, and he ran kind'a hunched over, as if he didn't want to be seen by anyone inside the house.

"This is getting interesting," Devlin whispered. If Devlin could prove Jeffrey was trying to jump bail and caught him, and dragged him to jail, some big money would be coming his way.

Without closing the car door for fear that Carol might hear it, Jeffrey released the emergency brake and let the auto slip silently down the driveway and out into the street. Only then did he start the motor and drive off. He craned his neck for a view of the house for as long as he could, but Carol never appeared. A block away he slammed the door properly and put on his seat belt. It had been easier to get away than he'd thought.

By the time Jeffrey got to the congested Lynn Way with its used-car lots and gaudy neon signs, he began to calm down. He was still somewhat shaky from Devlin's visit, but it was a relief to know that he would soon be putting the man and the threat of prison far behind him.

As he got closer to Logan International Airport, he began to feel the same misgivings he had had that morning. But all he had to do was touch his tender ears to rekindle his resolve. This time he was committed to following through, no matter his qualms, no matter how high his anxiety.

Jeffrey had a few minutes' leeway, so he went to the ticket counter to have the agent change his Rio de Janeiro ticket. He knew the shuttle ticket was still fine. As it turned out, the night flight to Rio was cheaper than the afternoon flight, and Jeffrey got a considerable refund.

Holding his ticket in his mouth, the suitcase in one hand, and the briefcase in the other, he hurried toward security. It had taken longer than he'd expected to exchange the ticket. That was one flight he didn't want to miss.

Jeffrey went directly to the X-ray machine and hoisted the suitcase onto the conveyor belt. He was about to do the same with his briefcase when someone grabbed his collar from behind.

"Going on vacation, Doctor?" Devlin asked with a wry smile. He snatched the airline ticket from Jeffrey's mouth.

Holding on to Jeffrey's collar with his left hand, Devlin flipped open the ticket folder and read the destination. When he saw Rio de Janeiro, he said "Bingo!" with a broad smile. He could already see himself at one of the gaming tables in Vegas. He was in the money now.

Stuffing Jeffrey's ticket into his denim jacket pocket, Devlin reached around to his back pocket and pulled out his handcuffs. A few people who had backed up behind Jeffrey to get at the X-ray machine stood gawking in open-mouthed disbelief.

The familiar sight of handcuffs jolted Jeffrey from his paralysis. With a sudden, unexpected move, he swung his briefcase in a violent arc aimed at Devlin. Devlin, concentrating on opening the handcuffs with his free hand, didn't see the blow coming.

The briefcase hit Devlin on the left temple, just above the ear, sending him crashing into the side of the X-ray machine. The handcuffs clattered to the floor.

The female attendant behind the X-ray machine screamed. A uniformed state police officer looked up from the sports page of the *Herald*. Jeffrey took off like a rabbit, sprinting back toward the terminal and ticket counters. Devlin put a hand to his head, and it came away with blood on it.

For Jeffrey it was like broken-field running as he tried to skirt passengers, missing some, colliding into others. As he came to the junction of the concourse with the terminal proper, he glanced back at the security area. He could see Devlin pointing in his direction with the uniformed policeman at his side. Other people were looking in Jeffrey's direction as well, mainly those he'd run into.

In front of Jeffrey was an escalator bringing people up from the floor below. Jeffrey ran for it and charged down, pushing irate passengers out of his way along with their luggage. On the arrival floor below there was a crowd milling about, since several flights had recently landed. Worming his way through the newly arrived, Jeffrey skirted the baggage area as fast as he could and ran out through the electronic doors to the street.

Gasping for breath, he paused at the curb, trying to decide where to go next. He knew he had to get out of the airport immediately. The question was how. There were a few taxis lined up, but there was also a long line of people waiting for them. Jeffrey didn't have much time. He could run over to the parking garage and get his car, but something told him that would be a dead end. For starters, Devlin probably knew where it was. He'd probably trailed Jeffrey to the airport. How else would he have known where to find him?

As Jeffrey weighed his alternatives, the intraterminal bus came lumbering along the roadway. Without a second's hesitation, Jeffrey rushed into the street and stood directly in its path, flailing his arms wildly.

The bus screeched to a halt. The driver opened the door. As Jeffrey jumped on, the driver said, "Man, you are either stupid or crazy and I hope it's stupid 'cause I'd hate to have a nut on board." He shook his head in disbelief, put the bus in gear, and hit the gas pedal.

Steadying himself by clutching the overhead rack, Jeffrey stooped to get a look out the window. He caught sight of Devlin and the policeman threading their way through the crowds at the baggage carousel. Jeffrey couldn't believe his luck. They hadn't seen him.

Jeffrey took a seat and set his briefcase on his lap. He still had to catch his breath. The next stop was the central terminal, serving Delta, United, and TWA. That's where Jeffrey got off. Dodging traffic, he ran over to the taxi line. As before, there was a considerable number of people waiting.

Jeffrey hesitated for a moment, running through his alternatives. Marshaling his courage, he walked directly to the taxi dispatcher.

"I'm a doctor and I need a cab immediately," he said with as much authority as he could muster. Even in emergency situations, Jeffrey was loath to take advantage of his professional status.

Holding a clipboard and a stub of a pencil, the man looked Jeffrey up and down. Without saying a word, he pointed to the next cab in line. As Jeffrey hustled in, some of the people queued up grumbled.

Jeffrey slammed the taxi's door. The driver looked at him through his rearview mirror. He was a young fellow with long, stringy hair. "Where to?" he asked.

Hunching low, Jeffrey told him just to drive out of the airport. The cabbie turned around to look Jeffrey in the eye.

"I need a destination, man!" he said.

"All right—downtown."

"Where downtown?" the cabbie asked irritably.

"I'll decide when we get there," Jeffrey said, turning around to peek out the rear window. "Just go!"

"Jesus!" the driver murmured, shaking his head in disbelief. He was doubly irritated to get such a short fare. He'd been waiting in the pool for half an hour and had hopes for a run to someplace like Weston. And on top of the short fare, his passenger was a weirdo or maybe worse. When they drove past a police car at the far end of the terminal, the guy lay flat across the backseat. Just what he needed: a weirdo on the lam.

Jeffrey lifted his head slowly, even though the cab had to be well beyond the squad car. He turned and peered out the rear window. No one seemed to be following. There were certainly no sirens or flashing lights. He turned around and faced forward. Night had finally fallen. Ahead lay a sea of bobbing taillights. Jeffrey tried to clear his head enough to think.

Had he done the right thing? His reflex had been to flee. He was understandably terrified of Devlin, but should he have run, especially with the policeman there?

With a shock, Jeffrey remembered that Devlin had seized his ticket, proof he had intended to jump bail. That was reason enough to toss him in jail. What effect would his attempt to flee have on the appeal process? Jeffrey didn't want to be around when Randolph found out.

Jeffrey didn't know much about the finer points of the law, but this much he did know: with his bumbling, indecisive behavior he had managed to turn himself into a true fugitive. Now he would have to face an entirely separate charge, maybe a separate set of charges.

The cab plunged into the Sumner Tunnel. Traffic was relatively light, so they moved ahead swiftly. Jeffrey wondered if he should go directly to the police. Would it be better to own up and turn himself in? Maybe he should go to the bus station and get out of town. He thought about renting a car, since he'd have more independence that way. But the trouble with that idea was that the only car rental places open at that time of the night were at the airport.

Jeffrey was at a loss. He had no idea what he should do. Every plan of action he could think of had disadvantages. And every time he thought he'd reached rock bottom, he managed to find an even deeper quagmire.

"I got good news and I got bad news," Devlin said to Michael Mosconi. "Which do you want to hear first?" Devlin was calling from one of the airport phones in the baggage section beneath the Pan Am departure gates. He had combed the terminal searching for Jeffrey, with no luck. The policeman had gone off to alert the other officers at the airport. Devlin was calling Michael Mosconi for additional backup. Devlin was surprised that the doc was lucky enough to have slipped away.

"I'm not in any mood to be playing games," Mosconi said irritably. "Just tell me what you have to tell me and be done with it."

"Come on, lighten up. Good news or bad?" Devlin enjoyed teasing Mosconi because Mosconi was such an easy target.

"I'll take the good news," Mosconi fumed, swearing under his breath. "And it better be good."

"Depends on your point of view," Devlin said cheerfully. "The good news is that you owe me a few bucks. Minutes ago I stopped the good doctor from boarding a plane for Rio de Janeiro."

"No shit?" Mosconi said.

"No shit—and I have the ticket to prove it!"

"That's *great,* Dev!" Mosconi said excitedly. "My God, the man's bail is five hundred thousand dollars! That would have ruined me. How the hell did you do it? I mean, how did you know he was going to try to jump? I got to hand it to you. You're amazing, Dev!"

"It's so nice to be loved," Devlin said. "But you're forgetting the bad news." Devlin smiled into the receiver mischievously, knowing what Mosconi's reaction was soon to be.

There was a brief pause before Mosconi said with a groan, "All right, give me the bad news!"

"At the moment, I don't know where the good doc is. He's on the loose in Boston someplace. I got ahold of him, but the skinny bastard hit me with his briefcase before I could 'cuff him. I never expected it, him being a doctor and all that."

"*You got to find him!*" Mosconi shouted. "Why the hell did I trust him? I should have my head examined."

"I've explained the situation to the airport police," Devlin said. "So they'll be on the lookout for him. My hunch is, he won't try to fly away again. At least not from Logan. Oh, and I had his car impounded."

"I want that guy found!" Mosconi said menacingly. "I want him delivered to the jail. Pronto. You hear me, Devlin?"

"I hear you, man, but I don't hear any numbers. What are you offering me to bring in this dangerous criminal?"

"Quit joking around, Dev!"

"Hey, I'm not joking. The doctor might not be all that dangerous, but I want to know how serious you are about this guy. The best way you can tell me is what kind of reward I'll be getting."

"Get him, then we'll talk numbers."

"Michael, what do you take me for, a fool?"

There was a strained silence. Devlin broke it. "Well, maybe I'll go have some dinner, then take in a show. See you around, sport."

"Wait!" Michael said. "All right—I'll split the fee. Twenty-five thousand."

"Split the fee?" Devlin said. "That's not the usual rate, my friend."

"Yeah, but this guy is hardly the cold-blooded, armed killers that you usually have to deal with."

"I don't see where that makes any difference," Devlin said. "If you call in anybody else, they'll demand the whole ten percent. That's fifty grand. But I tell you what. Since we go back a long way, I'll do it for forty grand and you can keep ten for filling out those papers."

Mosconi hated to give in, but he was in no position to bargain. "All right, you bastard," he said. "But I want the doctor in the slammer ASAP, before they forfeit the bond. Understand?"

"I'll give the matter my undivided attention," Devlin said. "Especially now that you have insisted on being so generous. In the meantime, we got to block the usual exits from the city. The airport is already covered, but that leaves the bus station, the railroads, and the car rental agencies."

"I'll call the duty police sergeant," Mosconi said. "Tonight it should be Albert Norstadt, so there won't be any problem there. What are you going to do?"

"I'll stake out the doc's house," Devlin said. "My guess is that he will either show up there or call his wife. If he calls his wife, then she'll probably go to wherever he is."

"When you get to him, treat him like he's murdered twelve people," Mosconi said. "Don't go soft on him. And Dev, I mean business on this. At this point I really don't much care whether you bring him in alive or dead."

"So long as you make sure he stays in town, I'll get him. If you have any problems with the police, you can reach me on the car phone."

Jeffrey's cabbie's mood improved as the fare mounted on the meter. Unable to decide where to go, Jeffrey had the man drive aimlessly around Boston. As they cruised the periphery of the Boston Garden for the third time, the meter hit thirty dollars.

Jeffrey was afraid to go home. His house was sure to be the first place Devlin would go to look for him. In fact, Jeffrey was afraid to go anyplace. He was afraid of going to the bus or train station for fear the authorities had already been put on some alert. For all he knew, every policeman in Boston could be looking for him.

Jeffrey thought he'd try to call Randolph to see what the lawyer could do—if anything—to turn things back to the pre-airport status quo. Jeffrey wasn't optimistic but the possibility was worth pursuing. At the same time, he decided he'd do well to check into a hotel, though not one of the better ones. The good hotels would probably be the second place Devlin would look for him.

Scooting forward against the Plexiglas divider, Jeffrey asked the cabbie if he knew of any cheap hotels. The cabbie thought for a moment. "Well," he said, "there's the Plymouth Hotel."

The Plymouth was a large motor inn. "Something less well-known. I don't care if it's a little on the seedy side. I'm looking for something out-of-the-way, nondescript."

"There's the Essex," the cabbie said.

"Where's that?" Jeffrey asked.

"Other side of the combat zone," the driver said. He eyed Jeffrey in the rearview mirror to see if he registered a flicker of recognition. The Essex was a dump, more of a flophouse than a hotel. It was frequented by many of the zone's call girls.

"So it's kind of low-key?" Jeffrey asked.

"About as low as I'd care to sink."

"Sounds perfect," Jeffrey said. "Let's go there." He slid back in the seat. The fact that he'd never heard of the Essex sounded promising, since he'd been in the Boston area for almost twenty years, right from the beginning of medical school.

The driver took a left off Arlington Street onto Boylston, then made his way downtown. There, the neighborhood took a nosedive. In contrast to the genteel areas around the Boston Garden, there were abandoned buildings, porn shops, and garbage-strewn streets. The homeless were scattered in alleyways and huddled on tenement steps. When the cab was stopped waiting for a light to change, a pimply-faced girl in an obscenely short skirt raised her eyebrows at Jeffrey suggestively. She looked like she couldn't have been more than fifteen.

The red neon sign in front of the Essex Hotel had aptly been amended to SEX EL; the other letters were out. Seeing how decrepit the place seemed, Jeffrey felt a moment's hesitation.

Peering out the window from the safety of his cab, he warily surveyed the hotel's dirty brick façade. Seedy was too kind an adjective. A drunk, still clutching his brown-paper-bag-wrapped bottle, was passed out to the right of the front steps.

"You wanted cheap," the cabbie said. "Cheap it is."

Jeffrey handed him a hundred-dollar bill from the briefcase. "You don't have anything smaller?" the cabbie complained.

Jeffrey shook his head. "I don't have forty-two dollars."

The cabbie sighed and made an elaborate passive-aggressive ritual of giving Jeffrey his change. Deciding he'd be better off not leaving an angry cabbie in his wake, Jeffrey gave him an extra ten. The driver even said thanks and have a nice night before driving off.

Jeffrey studied the hotel again. On the right was an empty building whose windows except for the ground floor were covered with plywood. On the ground floor there was a pawnshop and an X-rated video store. On the left was an office building in equal disrepair to the Essex Hotel. Beyond the office building was a liquor store, whose windows were barred like a fortress. Beyond the liquor store was an empty lot that was strewn with litter and broken bricks.

With his briefcase in hand and looking distinctly out of place, Jeffrey climbed the steps and entered the Essex Hotel.

The hotel's interior was about as classy as the exterior. The lobby furnishings consisted of a single threadbare couch and a half-dozen folding metal chairs. A bare pay phone was the wall's sole decoration. There was an elevator but the sign across its doors said OUT OF ORDER. Next to the elevator was a heavy door with a wire-embedded window leading to a stairwell. With a sinking feeling in his stomach, Jeffrey stepped up to the reception desk.

Behind the desk, a shabbily dressed man in his early sixties eyed Jeffrey suspiciously. Only drug dealers came to the Essex with briefcases. The clerk had been watching a small-screen black-and-white TV complete with old-fashioned rabbit-ear antennae. He had unkempt hair and sported a three-day-old beard. He had on a tie, but it was loosened at the collar and had a line of gravy stains across the lower third.

"Can I help you?" he asked, giving Jeffrey the once-over. Helping seemed the last thing he was inclined to do.

Jeffrey nodded. "I'd like a room."

"You got a reservation?" the man asked.

Jeffrey couldn't believe the man was serious. Reservations in a flophouse like this? But he didn't want to offend him. Jeffrey decided to play along.

"No reservation," he told him.

"Rates are ten dollars an hour or twenty-five a night," the man said.

"How about two nights?" Jeffrey said.

The man shrugged. "Fifty dollars plus tax, in advance," he said.

Jeffrey signed "Richard Bard." He gave the clerk the change he'd gotten from the taxi driver and added a five and a few singles from his wallet. The man gave him a key with an attached chain and a metal plaque that had *5F* etched into its surface.

The staircase provided the first and only hint that the building had once been almost elegant. The treads and risers were white marble, now long since stained and marred. The ornate balustrade was wrought iron festooned with decorative swirls and curlicues.

The room Jeffrey had been given faced the street. When he opened the door, the room's only illumination came from the blood-red glow of the dilapidated neon sign over the entrance four stories below. Switching on the light, Jeffrey surveyed his new home. The walls hadn't been painted for ages. What paint remained was scarred and peeling. It was difficult to determine what the original color had been; it seemed to be somewhere between gray and green. The sparse furnishings consisted of a single bed, a nightstand with a lamp minus the shade, a card table, and a single wooden chair. The bedspread was chenille with several greenish stains. A thin-paneled door led to a bathroom.

For a moment, Jeffrey hesitated to enter, but what was his choice? He decided to try to make the best of his predicament, or at least make do. Stepping over the threshold, he closed and locked his door. He felt terribly alone and isolated. He truly could not sink any deeper than this.

Jeffrey sat on the bed, then lay down across it, keeping both feet firmly planted on the floor. He didn't realize how exhausted he was until his back hit the mattress. He would have loved to curl up for a few hours, as much to escape as to rest, but he knew this was no time for napping. He had to come up with a strategy, some plan. But first he had to make a few phone calls.

Since there was no phone in the shabby hotel room, Jeffrey had to go to the lobby to place the calls. He took his briefcase with him, afraid to leave it unattended even for a minute or two.

Downstairs, the clerk reluctantly left his Red Sox game to make change so Jeffrey could use the phone.

His first call was to Randolph Bingham. Jeffrey didn't have to be a lawyer to know he desperately needed sound legal advice. While Jeffrey waited for the call to go through, the same pimply-faced girl he'd seen through the cab window entered the front door. She had a nervous-appearing, bald-headed man with her who had a sticker attached to his lapel that said: *Hi! I'm Harry.* He was obviously a conventioneer who was seeking the thrill of putting his life in jeopardy. Jeffrey turned his back on the transaction at the front desk. Randolph answered the phone with his familiar aristocratic accent.

"I've got a problem," Jeffrey said without even saying who he was. But Randolph recognized his voice immediately. In a few simple sentences, Jeffrey brought Randolph up to date. He left nothing out, including his striking Devlin with the briefcase in full view of a policeman and the subsequent chase through the airport terminal.

"My good God," was all Randolph could say by the time Jeffrey had finished. Then, almost angrily, he added, "You know, this is not going to help your appeal. And when it comes to sentencing, it is certainly going to have an influence."

"I know," Jeffrey said. "I could have guessed as much. But I didn't call you to tell me I'm in trouble. I had that figured without benefit of counsel. I need to know what you can do to help."

"Well, before I do anything, you have to turn yourself in."

"But . . ."

"No buts. You've already put yourself in an extremely precarious position with regard to the court."

"And if I do turn myself in, won't the court be likely to deny bail entirely?"

"Jeffrey, you have no choice. In light of your attempt to flee the country, you haven't exactly done much to encourage its trust."

Randolph started to say more, but Jeffrey cut him off. "I'm sorry, but I'm not prepared to go to jail. Under any circumstances. Please do whatever you can from your end. I'll get back to you." Jeffrey slammed the receiver down. He couldn't blame Randolph for the advice he had given. In some respects it was just like medicine: sometimes the patient just didn't want to hear the doctor's proposed therapy.

With his hand still resting on the receiver, Jeffrey turned back into the reception area to see if anyone had overheard his conversation. The young miniskirted girl and her john had disappeared upstairs, and the clerk was again glued to his tiny TV set. Another man, who looked to be in his seventies, had appeared and was sitting on the tattered couch, thumbing through a magazine.

Dropping another coin into the phone, Jeffrey called home.

"Where are you?" Carol demanded as soon as Jeffrey muttered a dull hello.

"I'm in Boston," he told her. He wasn't about to tell her anything more specific, but he felt he owed her that much. He knew she would be furious that he had left without a word, but he wanted to warn her in case Devlin headed back. And he wanted her to pick up the car. Beyond that, he didn't expect anything along the lines of sympathy. An earful of fury was what he got.

"Why didn't you tell me you were leaving the house?" Carol snarled. "Here I've been patient, standing by you all these months, and this is the thanks I get. I looked all over the house before I realized your car was gone."

"It's the car I need to talk to you about," Jeffrey said.

"I'm not interested in your car," Carol snapped.

"Carol, listen to me!" Jeffrey yelled. When he heard that she was going to give him a chance to speak, he lowered his voice, cupping a hand around the receiver. "My car is at the airport at central parking. The ticket stub is in the ashtray."

"Are you planning on forfeiting bail?" Carol asked incredulously. "We'll lose the house! I signed that lien in good faith . . ."

"There are some things more important than the house!" Jeffrey snapped in spite of himself. He lowered his voice again. "Besides, the house on the Cape has no mortgage. You can have that if money's your worry."

"You still haven't answered me," Carol said. "Are you planning to forfeit the bail?"

"I don't know," Jeffrey sighed. He really didn't. It was the truth. He still hadn't had time to think things through. "Look, the car's there on the second level. If you want it, fine. If not, that's fine too."

"I want to talk to you about our divorce," Carol said. "It's been on hold long enough. As much as I sympathize with your problems, and I do, I have to get on with my life."

"I'll have to get back to you," Jeffrey said irritably. Then he hung up on her as well.

He shook his head sadly. He couldn't even remember a time when there had been warmth between Carol and him. Dying relationships were so ugly. Here he was on the run and all she could worry about was property and the divorce. Well, she had her life to get on with, he supposed. One way or the other, it wouldn't be much longer. She'd be rid of him for good.

He looked at the phone. What he wanted to do was call Kelly. But what would he say? Would he admit to having tried to flee and failed? Jeffrey was filled with indecision and confusion.

Picking up his briefcase, he strode across the lobby, consciously avoiding looking at the two men.

Feeling even more alone than he had before, he climbed the four flights of twisting, filthy stairs, and returned to his depressing room. He stood at the window, bathed in the red neon glow, wondering what he should do. Oh, how he wanted to call Kelly, but he couldn't. He was too embarrassed. Stepping over to the bed, he wondered if he could sleep. He had to do something. He eyed his briefcase.

The only light in the room came from the television set. A forty-five-caliber pistol and a half-dozen vials of Marcaine on a bureau by the TV glimmered in the soft light. On the screen, three Jamaican men stood in a cramped hotel room and all three were visibly edgy. Each one was carrying an AK-47 assault rifle. The burliest of the three kept glancing at his watch. Perspiration stood on their foreheads. The obvious tension of the Jamaicans stood in sharp contrast to the sonorous reggae rhythm that pealed from a radio on the nightstand. Then the door burst open.

Crockett entered first, clutching a nine-millimeter automatic with the barrel pointed to the ceiling. With one swift, catlike move, he put the barrel against the first Jamaican's chest and pumped one silent, deadly bullet into him. Crockett had his second bullet into the second man by the time Tubbs cleared the doorway in time to take care of the third. It was all over in the blink of an eye.

Crockett shook his head. He was dressed in his usual: an expensive linen jacket by Armani over a casual cotton T-shirt. "Good timing, Tubbs," he said. "I would have had trouble nailing the third dude."

As the closing credits came onto the TV screen, Trent Harding high-fived an imaginary companion. "All *right!*" he exclaimed in triumph. TV violence had a stimulating effect on Trent. It charged him with aggressive energy that demanded expression. He lived to picture himself pumping bullets into chests the way Don Johnson did so regularly. Sometimes Trent thought he should have gone into law enforcement. If only he'd elected to join the military police when he enlisted in the Navy. Instead, Trent had decided to become a Navy corpsman. He'd liked it okay. It had been a challenge and he'd learned some far-out stuff. He'd never thought about being a corpsman before going into the Navy. The first time he thought of it had been when he'd heard a talk during basic training. He found the idea of performing physicals oddly appealing, and he liked the idea of guys coming to him for help so that he could tell them what to do.

Trent got up from the living room couch and walked into his kitchen. It was a comfortable apartment with one bedroom and two baths. Trent could afford better, but he liked it fine where he was. He lived on the top floor of a five-story building on the back side of Beacon Hill. The bedroom and the living room windows looked out onto Garden Street. The kitchen and the larger of the two bathrooms faced an inner courtyard.

Pulling an Amstel Light from the refrigerator, Trent popped the top and took a long, satisfying gulp. He thought the beer might calm him down some. He was anxious and edgy from the hour of *Miami Vice.* Even reruns got him riled up enough to want to hit one of the local bars to see if he could scare up some trouble. He could usually find a homo or two along Cambridge Street to rough up.

Trent looked like a man who was looking for trouble. He also looked like he'd found it more than a couple of times. A stocky, muscular man of twenty-eight, Trent wore his bleach-blond hair in the severe, flat-topped hairstyle popularly known as a fade. His eyes were a piercing crystal blue. He had a scar below his left eye that ran back to his ear. He'd gotten it from being on the wrong end of a broken beer bottle in a barroom scuffle in San Diego. It had taken a few stitches but the other guy had had to have his entire face rearranged. The guy had made the mistake of telling Trent that he thought he had a cute ass. Trent still got hot every time he thought of the episode. What a creep, that goddamned fag.

Trent went back to his bedroom and set his beer down on top of the TV. He picked up the military-issue .45 pistol that he'd "cumshawed" from a Marine for amphetamines. It felt comfortable in his large hand. Gripping the pistol with both hands, Trent leveled the barrel straight at the TV screen with arms stiff and elbows locked. He spun around to point the gun out the open window.

Across the street a woman was opening her bedroom window. "Tough luck, baby," Trent whispered. He aimed the pistol carefully, lowering the barrel until the front and rear sights lined up perfectly, targeting the woman's torso. Slowly, deliberately, Trent pulled the cold steel of the trigger.

As the firing mechanism clicked, Trent called out "Pow!" as he pretended the gun kicked in the air from its recoil. He smiled. He could have drilled the woman if he'd put in the clip. In his mind's eye he saw her hurled back into her apartment, a neat hole through her chest and blood squirting out.

Laying the pistol on the TV next to his beer bottle, Trent grabbed one of the vials of Marcaine from the bureau. Tossing it in the air, he caught it with his other hand behind his back. He calmly sauntered back to the kitchen to retrieve the necessary paraphernalia from its hiding place.

First he had to remove the glasses from the shelf of one of his kitchen cabinets next to the refrigerator. Then he gently lifted the plywood square that led to his secret cache: a small vault of space between the cabinet's back and the exterior wall. Trent brought out a single vial filled with yellow fluid and an array of 18-gauge syringes. He'd picked up the vial from a Colombian in Miami. The syringes easily came into his possession through his hospital job. He carried both vials and the syringes back to his bedroom along with a propane torch he kept under the kitchen sink.

Trent reached for his bottle and took another swig of beer. He set the propane torch on a small tripod he kept folded under his bed. Taking a cigarette from the pack by the television set, he lit it with a match.

Trent took a long drag, then lit the propane torch with the

cigarette. Next, he took one of the 18-gauge needles. After drawing up a tiny amount of the yellow fluid, he heated the tip of the needle until it glowed red hot. Keeping the needle in the flame, he picked up the vial of Marcaine and heated its top until it too started to become red. With deft, practiced moves, he pushed the hot needle through the molten glass and deposited a drop of the yellow fluid. Next was the trickiest part. After disposing of the needle, Trent began to twirl the vial, slipping it back into the hottest part of the flame. He kept it there for a few seconds, long enough for the puncture site to fuse closed.

He continued to twirl the vial even after he pulled it from the flame. He didn't stop until the glass had cooled considerably.

"Shit!" Trent said as he watched the very end of the vial suddenly dimple into an unwanted depression. Though virtually unnoticeable, Trent couldn't risk the blemish. If someone was careful enough to notice, they'd discard the vial as a defect. Or worse, someone on the ball might get suspicious. Disgusted, Trent tossed the vial into the trash.

"Dammit," he thought as he grabbed another vial of Marcaine. He'd have to try again. As he repeated the process, he became more and more intense, angrily cursing when even the third attempt ended in failure. Finally, on the fourth try, the puncture site sealed properly; the curved tip maintained its smooth hemispherical contour.

Holding the ampule up to the light, he inspected it carefully. It was close to perfect. He could still tell that the tube had been punctured, but he had to look carefully. He thought it might have been the best one he'd ever done. It gave him great satisfaction to have mastered such a difficult process. When he'd first thought of it a number of years ago, he'd had no idea if it would work. It used to take him hours to do what he could now do in minutes.

Once he had accomplished what he'd set out to do, Trent returned the vial of yellow fluid, the .45 pistol, and the remaining vials of Marcaine to the hiding place. He replaced the false back of the cabinet and put the glasses back.

Picking up the doctored Marcaine vial, he gave it a good

shake. The drop of yellow fluid had long since dissolved. He turned the ampule upside down, checking to see if there was a leak. But the puncture site was as he expected it to be: airtight.

Trent gleefully considered the effect his vial would soon have in St. Joseph's OR. He thought particularly about the high-and-mighty doctors, the havoc he would wreak in that lofty quarter. In his wildest dreams, Trent couldn't have settled on a better career.

Trent hated doctors. They always acted as if they knew everything, when in reality many didn't know their ass from a hole in the wall, especially in the Navy. Most of the time Trent knew twice as much as the doctor did, yet he had to do their bidding. In particular, Trent loathed that true pig of a Navy doctor who'd turned him in for pocketing a few am- phetamines. What a hypocrite. Everybody knew the doctors had been making off with drugs and instruments and all sorts of other loot for years. Then there was that real pervert doctor who complained to Trent's commanding officer about Trent's alleged homosexual behavior. That had been the straw that broke the camel's back. Instead of going through some stupid court-martial or whatever the hell they were planning to do, Trent had resigned.

At least by the time he got out, he was properly trained. He had no trouble getting nursing jobs. With nursing shortages widespread, he found he could work anywhere he pleased. Every hospital wanted him, especially since he liked working in the OR and had experience in that area from his stint in the Navy.

The only trouble with working in a civilian hospital, aside from the doctors, was the rest of the nursing staff. Some of them were as bad as the doctors, particularly the supervisors. They were always trying to tell him something he already knew. But Trent didn't find them as irritating as the doctors. After all, it was the doctors who conspired to limit the auton- omy Trent had had to practice routine medicine in the Navy.

Trent put the doctored ampule of Marcaine in the pocket of his white hospital coat, which hung in the front closet. Think- ing about doctors reminded him of Dr. Doherty. He clenched his teeth at the thought of the man. But it wasn't enough. Trent couldn't contain himself. He slammed the closet door with such force it seemed to jar the whole building. Just that day, Doherty, one of the anesthesiologists, had had the nerve to criticize Trent in front of several nurses. Doherty had chastised him for what he referred to as sloppy sterile technique. And this was coming from the moron who didn't put on his scrub hat or surgical mask properly! Half the time Doherty didn't even have his nose covered. Trent was enraged.

"I hope Doherty gets the vial," Trent snarled. Unfortunately, there wasn't any way he could ensure Doherty's getting it. The chances were about one in twenty unless he waited until Doherty was scheduled for an epidural. "Ah, who cares," Trent said with a wave of dismissal. It would be entertaining no matter who got the vial.

Although Jeffrey's new fugitive status heightened his indecision and confusion, he no longer had the slightest inclination toward suicide. He didn't know if he was acting courageously or cowardly, but he wasn't about to agonize further. Yet with all that had happened, he was understandably concerned about the possibility of a new round of depression. Thinking it better to throw temptation away, he took the step of getting the morphine vial from the briefcase, popping its lid, and flushing the contents down the toilet.

Having at least made a decision about one issue, Jeffrey felt slightly more in control. To make himself feel even more organized, he occupied himself by rearranging the contents of his briefcase. He stacked the money carefully, in the base, covering it with the underwear. He then rearranged the contents of the accordion-style file area under the lid to make room for Chris Everson's notes. Turning his attention to the notes, he organized them according to size. Some of them were on Chris's notepaper, which had *From the Desk of Christopher Everson* printed on top. Others were written on sheets of yellow legal paper.

Jeffrey began to scan the notes, almost without meaning to. He was glad for anything that took his mind away from his current predicament. Henry Noble's case history was espe-

cially fascinating the second time around. Once again, Jeffrey
was struck by the similarities between Chris's unhappy experience with the man and his own with Patty Owen, particularly
with respect to each patient's initial symptoms. The major
difference between the two cases was that Patty's had been
more fulminating and overwhelming. Since Marcaine had
been involved in both cases, the fact that the symptoms were
similar was not surprising. What seemed extraordinary was
that in both situations the initial symptoms were not what was
expected in an adverse reaction to a local anesthetic.

Having been a practicing anesthesiologist for some years,
Jeffrey was familiar with the kinds of symptoms that could
occur when a patient had an adverse reaction to a local anesthetic. Trouble invariably arose due to an overdose reaching
the bloodstream, where it could affect either the heart or the
nervous system. Considering the nervous system, it was usually the central or the autonomic system that caused problems,
either through stimulation or depression, or a combination of
the two.

All this covered a lot of territory, but of all the reactions
Jeffrey had studied, heard about, or witnessed, none had been
anything like Patty Owen's, not with the excessive salivation,
the tearing, the sudden perspiration, the abdominal pain, and
the constricted, or miotic, pupils. Some of these responses
might occur in an allergic reaction, but not from an overdose,
and Jeffrey had reason to believe that Patty Owen had not been
allergic to Marcaine.

Obviously, to judge by his notes, Chris Everson had been
comparably troubled. Chris noted that Henry Noble's symptoms were more muscarinic than anything else, meaning the
kind that were expected when parts of the parasympathetic
nervous system were stimulated. They were called muscarinic
because they mirrored the effect of a drug called muscarine,
which came from a type of mushroom. But parasympathetic
stimulation was not expected with a local anesthetic like Marcaine. If not, then why the muscarine symptoms? It was puz-
zling.

Jeffrey closed his eyes. It was all very complicated, and,
unfortunately, although he knew the basics, much of the physi-

ological details were not fresh in his mind. But he remembered enough to know that the sympathetic division of the autonomic nervous system was the part affected by local anesthetics, not the parasympathetic part apparently affected in the Noble and Owen cases. There was no immediate explanation for it.

Jeffrey's deep concentration was interrupted by a thump against the wall, then some exaggerated moaning of feigned ecstasy coming from the neighboring room. He had an unwelcome image of the pimply-faced girl and the bald man. The moaning reached a crescendo of sorts and then diminished.

Jeffrey stepped over to the window to stretch. He was again bathed in the red neon light. A group of homeless people was milling around to the right of the Essex's stoop, presumably in front of the liquor store. Several young hookers were working the street. Off to the side were young toughs who seemed to take a proprietary interest in the goings-on of the area. Whether they were pimps or drug dealers, Jeffrey couldn't say. What a neighborhood, he thought.

He turned away from the window. Jeffrey had seen enough. Chris's notes were sprawled across the bed. The moans from next door had stopped. Jeffrey tried to review the list of possibilities for the Noble and Owen mishaps. Once more he focused on the notion that had so consumed Chris through the course of his last days: the possibility of a contaminant in the Marcaine. Assuming that neither he nor Chris had made a gross medical error—in the Owen case, for example, that he had not used the .75% Marcaine that had been found in his disposal—and in view of the fact that both patients had had unexpected parasympathetic symptoms without allergic or anaphylactic reactions, then Chris's theory of a contaminant had considerable validity.

Returning to the window, Jeffrey thought about the implications of a contaminant being in the Marcaine. If he could prove such a theory, it would go a long way toward absolving him from blame in the Owen case. Culpability would fall to the pharmaceutical company that had manufactured it. Jeffrey wasn't sure about how the legal machinery would work once such a theory was proven. Given his recent brushes with the judicial system, he knew the gears would turn slowly, but turn they would. Maybe old Randolph would be able to figure a way to get the wheels to turn faster. Jeffrey smiled at a wonderful thought: maybe his life and career could be salvaged. But how would he go about proving there had been a contaminant in a vial that had been used nine months earlier?

Suddenly, Jeffrey had a thought. He rushed back to Chris's notes to read Henry Noble's case summary. Jeffrey was particularly interested in the initial sequence of events, when Chris was first administering the epidural anesthesia.

Chris had taken 2 cc's of Marcaine from a 30 cc ampule for his test dose, adding his own 1:200,000 epinephrine. It had been immediately after that test dose that Henry Noble's reaction began. With Patty Owen, Jeffrey had used a fresh 30 cc ampule of Marcaine in the OR. It was after this Marcaine was introduced into her system that her adverse reaction began. For the test dose, Jeffrey had used a separate 2 cc vial of spinal grade Marcaine, as was his custom. If a contaminant had been in the Marcaine, it had to have been in the 30 cc ampule in both situations. That would mean that Patty had gotten a substantially larger dose than Henry Noble—a full therapeutic dose as opposed to a test dose of 2 cc's. That would explain why Patty's reaction was so much more severe than Henry Noble's and why Noble had managed to live for a week.

For the first time in months, Jeffrey felt a glimmer of hope that his old life was still within reach. He could have it back again. During his defense, he'd never considered the possibility of a contaminant. Now, suddenly it seemed like a real possibility. But it would take time and some serious effort to investigate, much less prove. What was his first step?

First of all, he needed more information. That meant he'd have to bone up on the pharmakinetics of local anesthetics as well as the physiology of the autonomous nervous system. But that would be relatively easy. All he needed was books. The hard part would be looking into the idea of a contaminant. He'd need access to the full pathology report on Patty Owen. He'd seen only parts of it during the discovery process. Plus, there was the question Kelly had raised: what about an explanation for the .75% Marcaine vial found in the disposal container on the anesthesia machine? How could it have gotten there?

Investigating these issues would have been difficult under the best of circumstances. Now that he was a convict and a fugitive, it would be all but impossible. He would have to get into Boston Memorial. Could he do that?

Jeffrey went into the bathroom. Standing in front of the mirror, he evaluated his features in the raw fluorescent light. Could he change his appearance enough not to be recognized? He'd been associated with Boston Memorial since his clinical clerkships in medical school. Hundreds of people knew him by sight.

Jeffrey put a hand to his forehead and slicked back his light brown hair. He combed his hair to the side, parting it on the right. Holding it back made his forehead appear broader. He'd never worn glasses. Maybe he could get a pair now. And for most all of the years he'd been working at Boston Memorial, he'd had a mustache. He could shave it off.

Caught up with this intriguing thought, Jeffrey went to the other room to retrieve his Dopp Kit. He went back to the bathroom mirror. Soaping up, he quickly shaved off his mustache. It felt strange to run his tongue across a bare upper lip. Wetting his hair, he combed it straight back from his forehead. He was encouraged; already he was beginning to look like a new man.

Next, Jeffrey shaved off his moderate sideburns. The difference wasn't much but he figured everything helped. Could he pass for another M.D.? He had the know-how; what he needed was an ID. Security at Boston Memorial had been beefed up considerably, a sign of the times. If he was challenged and couldn't produce an ID, he would be caught. Yet he needed the access, and it was the doctors who had access to all areas of the hospital.

Jeffrey kept thinking. He wouldn't despair. There was another group in the hospital that had wide access: housekeeping. No one questioned housekeeping. Having spent many nights on call in the hospital, Jeffrey could recall seeing housekeeping staff everywhere. No one ever wondered about them. He also knew there was a housekeeping graveyard shift from eleven

P.M. to seven A.M., which they always had a hard time filling. The graveyard shift would be perfect, Jeffrey figured. He'd be less likely to bump into people who knew him. For the past few years, he'd worked mainly during the day.

Energized by this new crusade, Jeffrey yearned to start immediately. That meant a trip to the library. If he left right away, he would have about an hour before closing. Before he had time for second thoughts, he slipped Chris's notes into the spot he'd prepared for them in his briefcase and closed and latched the lid.

For what it was worth, Jeffrey locked the door behind him. As he made his way down the stairs, he hesitated. The musty, sour smell reminded him of Devlin. Jeffrey had gotten a whiff of his breath when Devlin nabbed him at the airport.

In considering his plan of action, Jeffrey neglected to factor in Devlin. Jeffrey knew something about bounty hunters, and that's what Devlin undoubtedly was. Jeffrey harbored no illusions of what would happen if Devlin caught him again, especially after the episode at the airport. After a moment's indecision, Jeffrey resignedly continued down the stairs. If he wanted to do any investigating, he'd have to take some chances, but it still behooved him to remain constantly alert. In addition, he'd have to think ahead so that if he was unlucky enough to confront Devlin, he'd have some sort of plan. Downstairs, the man with the magazine was gone, but the clerk was still watching the Red Sox game. Jeffrey slipped out without being noticed. A good sign, he joked to himself. His first try at not being seen was a success. At least he still had a sense of humor.

Any lightheartedness that Jeffrey had been able to call up faded as he surveyed the street scene in front of him. He felt a wave of acute paranoia as he reminded himself of the double reality of being a fugitive and carrying around $45,000 in cash. Directly across from Jeffrey, in the shadows of a doorway of a deserted building, the two men he'd seen from the window were smoking crack.

Clutching his briefcase, Jeffrey descended the Essex's front steps. He avoided stepping on the poor man who was still lolling on the pavement with his brown-bagged bottle. Jeffrey turned to the right. He planned to walk the five or six blocks to the Lafayette Center, which included a good hotel. There he'd find a cab.

Jeffrey was abreast of the liquor store when he spotted a police car heading in his direction. Without a moment's hesitation, he ducked into the store. The jangle of bells attached to the door wore on Jeffrey's nerves. As crazy as it seemed, he didn't know whom he was more afraid of, the street people or the police.

"Can I help you?" a bearded man asked from behind a counter. The police car slowed, then went past. Jeffrey took a breath. This wasn't going to be easy.

"Can I help you?" the clerk repeated.

Jeffrey bought a pint-sized bottle of vodka. If the police cruised back, he wanted his visit to the store to appear legitimate. But it wasn't necessary. When he emerged from the store, the police car was nowhere in sight. Relieved, Jeffrey turned to the right, intending to hurry. But he pulled up short, practically colliding with one of the homeless men he'd seen earlier. Startled, Jeffrey raised his free hand to protect himself.

"Got any spare change, buddy?" the man asked unsteadily. He was obviously drunk. He had a fresh cut just by his temple. One of the lenses of his black-rimmed glasses was cracked.

Jeffrey recoiled from the man. He was about Jeffrey's height but with dark, almost black hair. His face was covered with a heavy stubble, suggesting he'd not shaved for a month. But what caught Jeffrey's attention was the man's clothes. He was dressed in a tattered suit complete with a button-down blue oxford shirt that was soiled and missing a few buttons. He had on a regimental striped tie that was loosened at the collar and spotted with green stains. Jeffrey's impression was that the man had dressed for work one day, then never gone home.

"What's the matter?" the man asked in a wavering, drunken voice. "Don't you speak English?"

Jeffrey dug into his trouser pocket for the change he'd received from his purchase of vodka. As he dropped the money in the man's palm, Jeffrey studied his face. His eyes, though glassy, looked kind. Jeffrey wondered what had driven the man to such desperate circumstances. He felt an odd kinship with

this homeless person and his unknown plight. He shuddered
to think of how fine a line separated him from a similar fate.
The identification was made easier since the man appeared to
be close to Jeffrey's age.

As he'd expected, Jeffrey hailed a taxi easily at the nearby
luxury hotel. From there it took only fifteen minutes to get out
to Harvard's medical area. It was just a little after eleven when
Jeffrey walked into the Countway Medical Library.

Among the books and narrow study cubicles, Jeffrey felt at
home. He used one of the computer terminals to get the call
numbers for several books on the physiology of the autonomic
nervous system and the pharmacology of local anesthetics.
With these books in hand he went into one of the carrels facing
the inner court and closed the door. Within minutes he was
lost in the intricacies of nerve impulse conduction.

It wasn't long before Jeffrey understood why Chris had
highlighted the word "nicotinic." Although most people
thought of nicotine as an active ingredient in cigarettes, it was
actually a drug, more specifically a poison, which caused a
stimulation and then blockade of autonomic ganglia. Many of
the symptoms associated with nicotine were the same as those
caused by muscarine: salivation, sweating, abdominal pain, and
lacrimation—the very same symptoms that had appeared in
Patty Owen and Henry Noble. It even caused death in surprisingly low concentrations.

All this meant to Jeffrey that if he was thinking of a contaminant, it would have to have been a compound that mirrored
local anesthetics to an extent, something like nicotine. But it
couldn't have been nicotine, thought Jeffrey. The toxicology
report on Henry Noble had been negative; something like
nicotine would have shown up.

If there had been a contaminant it would also have to have
been in an extremely small, nanomolar amount. Therefore it
would have to have been something extraordinarily potent. As
to what that could have been, Jeffrey hadn't a clue. But in his
reading Jeffrey stumbled across something he'd remembered
from medical school, but had not thought of since. Botulinum
toxin, one of the most toxic substances known to man, mirrored local anesthetics in its ability to "freeze" neural cell

membranes at the synapse. Yet Jeffrey knew he was not seeing botulinum poisoning. Its symptoms were totally different; muscarinic effects were blocked, not stimulated.

Never had time passed so quickly. Before Jeffrey knew it, the library was about to close for the night. Reluctantly, he gathered up Chris Everson's notes as well as his own that he'd just made. Carrying the books in one hand and his briefcase in the other, he descended to the first floor. He left the books on the counter to be reshelved and started for the door. He stopped abruptly.

Ahead people were being stopped by an attendant to open their parcels, knapsacks, and, of course, briefcases. It was standard practice to keep the loss of books to a minimum, but it was a practice Jeffrey had forgotten about. He hated to think what the reaction might be if the library guard got a look at his stacks of hundred-dollar bills. So much for staying low profile.

Jeffrey doubled back to the periodical section and ducked behind a shoulder-high display case. He opened his briefcase and began to jam the packets of paper money in his pockets. To make room, he pulled the pint of vodka from his jacket side pocket and packed it in the briefcase. Better to let the guard think he was a tippler than a drug dealer or thief.

Jeffrey was able to leave the library without incident. He felt a little conspicuous with all his pockets bulging, but there was nothing to be done about it just then.

There were practically no cabs on Huntington Avenue at that time of night. After he tried for ten minutes to no avail, the Green Line trolley came along. Jeffrey got on, feeling it was more prudent to keep moving.

Jeffrey took one of the seats oriented parallel to the car and balanced the briefcase on his knees. He could feel all of the packets of money that were in his pants, particularly the ones he was sitting on. As the trolley lurched forward, Jeffrey allowed his eyes to roam around the car. Consistent with his experience on Boston subways, no one said a word. Everyone stared ahead expressionlessly as if in a trance. Jeffrey's eyes met those of the other travelers who were sitting across from him. The people who sullenly returned his stare made him feel transparent. He was amazed at how many of them in his mind looked as if they were criminals.

Closing his eyes, Jeffrey went over some of the material he'd just read, considering it in light of the experience he'd had with Patty Owen and Chris's with Henry Noble. He'd been sur- prised by one piece of information about local anesthetics. Under a section marked "adverse reactions," he'd read that occasionally miotic or constricted pupils were seen. That was new to Jeffrey. Except for Patty Owen and Henry Noble, he'd never seen it clinically or read it before. There was no explana- tion of the physiological mechanism, and Jeffrey couldn't ex- plain it. Then in the same article it was written that usually mydriasis, or enlargement, of the pupils was seen. At that point Jeffrey gave up the issue of pupillary size. It all didn't make much sense to him and only added to his confusion.

When the trolley suddenly plunged underground, the sound startled Jeffrey. He opened his eyes in terror and let out a little gasp. He hadn't realized how jumpy he was. He began to take deep, steady breaths in order to calm himself.

After a minute or two, Jeffrey's thoughts returned to the cases. He realized there was another similarity between the Noble and Owen cases that he'd not considered. Henry Noble had been paralyzed for the week he'd lived. It was as if he'd had total irreversible spinal anesthesia. Since Patty had died, Jeffrey had no idea if she would have suffered paralysis had she lived. But her baby had survived and did display marked resid- ual paralysis. It had been assumed that the baby's paralysis stemmed from a lack of oxygen to his brain, but now Jeffrey wasn't so sure. The strange, asymmetric distribution had al- ways troubled him. Maybe this paralysis was an additional clue, one that might be of use in identifying a contaminant.

Jeffrey got off the subway at Park Street and climbed the stairs. Giving wide berth to several policemen, he hurried down Winter Street, leaving the crowded Park Street area behind. As he walked, he thought more seriously about getting back into Boston Memorial Hospital now that he'd done his reading.

The idea of becoming part of the housekeeping staff had a lot of merit except for one problem: to apply for a job he'd need to provide some sort of identification as well as a valid social security number. In this day of computers, Jeffrey knew he couldn't expect to get by by making one up.

He was wrestling with the problem of identification when he turned onto the street where the Essex Hotel stood. Half a block away from the liquor store, which was still open, he paused. A vision of the man in the tattered suit came back to him. The two of them had been about the same height and age.

Crossing the street, Jeffrey approached the empty lot next to the liquor store. A strategically placed streetlamp threw a good deal of light into the area. About a quarter of the way into the lot there was a concrete overhang sticking out of one of the bordering buildings that looked like it could have been an old loading dock. Beneath it Jeffrey could make out a number of figures, some sitting, some passed out on the ground.

Stopping and listening, Jeffrey could hear conversation. Overpowering any misgivings, he started toward the group. Stepping gingerly on a bed of broken bricks, Jeffrey approached the overhang. A fetid odor of unwashed humans assaulted his senses. The conversation stopped. A number of rheumy eyes regarded him suspiciously in the semidarkness.

Jeffrey felt he was an intruder in another world. With rising anxiety, he searched for the man in the tattered suit, moving his eyes quickly from one dark figure to the next. What would he do if these men suddenly sprang at him?

Jeffrey saw the man he was looking for. He was one of the men sitting in the semicircle. Forcing himself forward, Jeffrey approached closer. No one spoke. There was an electric charge of expectation in the air as if a spark could cause an explosion. Every eye was now following Jeffrey. Even some of the people who'd been lying down were now sitting up, staring at him.

"Hello," Jeffrey said limply when he was in front of the man. The man didn't move. Nor did anyone else. "Remember me?" Jeffrey asked. He felt foolish, but he couldn't think of what else to say. "I gave you some change an hour or so ago. Back there, in front of the liquor store." Jeffrey pointed over his shoulder.

The man didn't respond.

"I thought maybe you could use a little more," Jeffrey said.

He reached into his pocket, and pushing away the packet of hundred-dollar bills, pulled out some change and several smaller bills. He extended the change. The man reached forward and took the coins.

"Thanks, buddy," he managed, trying to see the coins in the darkness.

"I've got more," Jeffrey said. "In fact, I've got a five-dollar bill here, and I'm willing to bet that you're so drunk, you can't remember your social security number."

"Whaddya mean?" the man mumbled as he struggled to his feet. Two of the other men followed suit. The man Jeffrey was interested in swayed as if he were about to fall, but caught himself. He appeared drunker than he'd been earlier. "It's 139-32-1560. That's my social security number."

"Oh, sure!" Jeffrey said with a wave of dismissal. "You just made that up."

"The hell I did!" the man said indignantly. With a sweeping gesture that almost knocked him off his feet, he reached for his wallet. He staggered again, struggling to lift the wallet from his trouser pocket. After he got it out, he fumbled to remove not a Social Security card, but his driver's license. He dropped the wallet in the process. Jeffrey bent down to pick it up. He noticed there was no money in it.

"Lookit right here!" the man said. "Just like I said."

Jeffrey handed him the wallet and took the license. He couldn't see the number but that wasn't the point. "My word, I guess you were right," he said after he pretended to study it. He handed over the five-dollar bill, which the man grabbed eagerly. But one of the other men grabbed it out of his hand.

"Gimme that back!" the man yelled.

Another of the men had advanced behind Jeffrey. Jeffrey reached into his pocket and pulled out more coins. "There's some for everybody," he said as he tossed them on the ground. They clinked against the broken brick. There was a rush as everyone but Jeffrey dropped to his hands and knees in the darkness. Jeffrey took advantage of the diversion to turn and run as quickly as he dared across the rubble-strewn lot toward the street.

Back in his hotel room, he propped the license up on the

edge of the sink and compared his image to that of the photo on the license. The nose was completely different. Nothing could be done about that. Yet if he darkened his hair and combed it straight back with some gel the way he'd thought he would, and if he added some black-framed glasses, maybe it would work. But at the very least, he had a valid social security number associated with a real name and address: Frank Amendola, of 1617 Sparrow Lane, Framingham, Massachusetts.

6

WEDNESDAY,

MAY 17, 1989

6:15 A.M.

Trent Harding wasn't due to start work until seven, but at six-fifteen he was already pulling off his street clothes in the locker room off the surgical lounge of St. Joseph's Hospital. From where he was standing, he had a straight shot to the sinks and he could see himself in the over-the-basin mirrors. He flexed his arm and neck muscles so that they bulged. He hunched over slightly to check their definition. Trent liked what he saw.

Trent went to his health club at least four times a week to use the Nautilus equipment to the point of exhaustion. His body was like a piece of sculpture. People noticed and admired it, Trent was sure. Yet he wasn't satisfied. He thought he could stand to beef up his biceps a bit more. On his legs, his quads could use tightening. He planned to concentrate on both in the coming weeks.

Trent was in the habit of arriving early, but on this particular morning, he was earlier than usual. In his excitement he'd awakened before his alarm and could not go back to sleep, so he'd decided to get to work early. Besides, he liked to take his time. There was something unbelievably exhilarating about placing one of his doctored Marcaine ampules in the Marcaine supply. It gave him shivers of pleasure—like planting a time bomb. He was the only one who knew about the imminent danger. He was the one who controlled it.

After he'd gotten into his scrub outfit, Trent glanced around him. A few people who were going off shift had come into the locker room. One was in the shower singing a Stevie Wonder tune; another was in one of the toilet stalls; and a third was at his locker well out of sight.

Trent reached into the pocket of his white hospital jacket and pulled out the doctored ampule of Marcaine. Palming it in case someone unexpectedly appeared, Trent slipped it into his briefs. It felt cold and uncomfortable at first; he grimaced as he adjusted it. Then he closed his locker and started walking toward the lounge area.

In the surgical lounge, fresh coffee was softly perking, filling the room with its pleasant aroma. Nurses, nurse anesthetists, a few doctors, and orderlies were gathered there. Soon they'd be going off shift. There were no emergency cases in progress, and all the preparations for the day's schedule for which the night shift was responsible were complete. The room rang with happy conversation.

No one acknowledged Trent, nor did he try to say hello to anyone. Most of the staff didn't recognize him since he was not a member of the night shift. Trent passed through the lounge and entered the OR area itself. No one was at the main scheduling desk. The huge blackboard was already chalked with the upcoming day's schedule. Trent paused briefly, scanning the big board for two things: to see which room he was assigned to for the day and to see if there were any spinal or epidural cases scheduled. To his delight there was a handful. Another shiver of excitement went down his spine. Having a number of such cases meant there was a good chance his Marcaine would be used that very day.

Trent continued down the main OR corridor and turned into Central Supply, which was conveniently located in the middle of the OR area. The operating room complex at St. Joe's was shaped like the letter U with the ORs lining the outside of the U and Central Supply occupying the interior.

Moving with a sense of purpose, as if he were heading into Central Supply to get a setup pack for one of the ORs, Trent took a loop around the whole area. As usual, no one was there. There was always a hiatus between six-fifteen and six forty-five when Central Supply was unoccupied. Satisfied, Trent went directly into the section that housed the IV fluids and the non-narcotic and uncontrolled drugs. He did not have to search for the local anesthetics. He'd scouted them out long ago.

With one more quick glance around, Trent reached for an open pack of 30 cc .5% Marcaine. Deftly he raised the lid. There were three ampules remaining in the box where there originally had been five. Trent exchanged one of the good ampules for the one in his briefs. He winced again. It was surprising how cold room temperature glass could feel. He closed the lid of the Marcaine box and carefully slid it back into its original position.

Again Trent glanced around Central Supply. No one had appeared. He looked back at the box of Marcaine. Once more an almost sensual excitement rippled through his body. He'd done it again, and no one would ever have a clue. It was so damned easy, and depending on the OR schedule and a little luck, the vial would be used soon, maybe even that morning.

For a brief moment, Trent thought about removing the other two good vials from the box just to speed things up. Now that the vial was placed, he was impatient to enjoy the chaos it would cause. But he decided against removing the other vials. He'd never taken any chances in the past, and it wasn't a good time to start. What if someone was keeping track of how many vials of Marcaine were on hand?

Trent emerged from Central Supply and headed back to his locker to tuck away the ampule that was now in his briefs. Then he'd get himself a nice cup of coffee. Later that afternoon, if nothing had happened, he'd return to Central Supply to see if the doctored vial had been taken. If it was used that day, he'd know about it soon enough. News of a major complication spread like wildfire in the OR suite.

In his mind's eye, Trent could see the vial resting so innocently in the box. It was a kind of Russian roulette. He felt a stirring of sexual excitement. He hurried into the locker room, trying to contain himself. If only it could be Doherty who'd get it, thought Trent. That would make it perfect.

Trent's jaw tightened as he thought of the anesthesiologist.

The man's name re-ignited his anger from the previous day's humiliation. Arriving at his locker, Trent gave it a resounding thump with his open palm. A few people looked in his direction. Trent ignored them. The irony was that before the humiliating episode, Trent had liked Doherty. He'd even been nice to the jerk.

Angrily, Trent twirled his combination lock and got his locker door open. Pressing in against it, he slipped the ampule of Marcaine from his shorts and eased it into the pocket of his white jacket hanging within the locker. Maybe he'd have to make some special arrangements for Doherty.

Breathing a sigh of relief, Jeffrey closed the door to his room at the Essex Hotel. It was just after eleven in the morning. He'd been on the go since nine-thirty when he left the hotel to do some shopping. Every moment he'd been terrified of being discovered by an acquaintance, Devlin, or the police. He'd seen several police officers, but he'd avoided any direct confrontation. Even so, it had been a nerve-racking venture.

Jeffrey put his packages and his briefcase on the bed and opened the smallest bag. Among its contents was a hair rinse. The color was called Midnight Black. Taking off his clothes, Jeffrey went directly into the bathroom and followed the directions on the box. By the time he put the styling gel in his hair and brushed it straight back from his forehead, he looked like a different person. He thought he looked like a used car salesman or like someone out of a 1930s movie. Comparing his image with the small photo on the license, he thought he could pass for Frank Amendola if no one looked too closely. And he still wasn't finished.

Back in the bedroom, Jeffrey opened the larger of the packages and took out a new dark blue polyester suit he'd bought in Filene's Basement and had altered at Pacifici of Boston. Mike, the head tailor, had been happy to do the alterations while Jeffrey waited. Jeffrey didn't have much done to the suit because he didn't want it to fit too well. In fact, he had to resist some of Mike's suggestions.

Going back to his parcels, Jeffrey pulled out several white shirts and a couple of unattractive ties. He put on one of the shirts and a tie, then slipped on the suit. Finally he searched

through the bags until he found a pair of dark-rimmed protective glasses. After he put them on, he returned to the bathroom
mirror. Again he compared his image with the photo on the
license. In spite of himself, he had to smile. From a general
point of view, he looked terrible. In terms of looking like Frank
Amendola, he looked reasonably good. It surprised him how
little facial features mattered in generating an overall impression.

One of the other parcels contained a new duffel bag with a
shoulder strap and a half-dozen compartments. Jeffrey transferred the packets of money to these. He'd felt conspicuous
carrying the briefcase with him and was afraid it might be a
way for the police to recognize him. He even guessed it might
be mentioned as part of his description.

Going back to the briefcase, Jeffrey took out a syringe and
the vial of succinylcholine. Having worried all morning about
Devlin suddenly appearing as he had at the airport, Jeffrey had
come up with an idea. He carefully drew up 40 mg of succinylcholine in the syringe, then capped it. He put the syringe in
the side pocket of his jacket. He wasn't sure how he would use
the succinylcholine, but it was there just in case. It was more
of a psychological support than anything else.

With his plano glasses on and his duffel bag over his shoulder, Jeffrey took one last glance around his room, wondering
if he was forgetting anything. He was hesitant to leave because
he knew the moment he stepped out of the room, the anxiety
of being recognized would return. But he wanted to get into
Boston Memorial Hospital, and the only way that was going
to happen was if he went over there and applied for a housekeeping job.

Devlin rudely shoved his way out of the elevator on his way
to Michael Mosconi's office without giving the other passengers time to get out of his way. He got perverse pleasure out
of provoking the people, especially men in business suits, and
he half hoped one of them would try to be a gallant hero.

Devlin was in a foul mood. He'd been awake for most of the
night, uncomfortably propped up in the front seat of his car
watching the Rhodes's house. He'd fully expected Jeffrey to

come sneaking home in the middle of the night. Or at the very least, he expected Carol to leave suddenly. But nothing happened until just after eight in the morning, when Carol came out of the garage like the Green Hornet in her Mazda RX7 and left a patch of rubber in the middle of the street.

With great difficulty and not very high hopes, Devlin had followed Carol through the morning traffic. She drove like an Indy 500 driver, the way she weaved in and out of the traffic. She led him all the way downtown, but she'd merely gone to her office on the twenty-second floor of one of the newer office buildings. Devlin decided to give up on her for the time being. He needed more information on Jeffrey to decide what to do next.

"Well?" Michael asked expectantly as Devlin came through the door.

Devlin didn't answer immediately, which he knew would drive Michael crazy. The guy was always so wound up. Devlin dropped onto the vinyl couch that faced Michael's desk and put his cowboy boots on top of the small coffee table. "Well what?" he said irritably.

"Where's the doctor?" He thought Devlin was about to tell him he'd already delivered Rhodes to the jailhouse.

"Beats me," Devlin said.

"What does that mean?" There was still a chance Devlin was teasing him.

"I think it's pretty clear," Devlin said.

"It might be clear for you, but it's not clear to me," Michael said.

"I don't know where the little bastard is," Devlin finally admitted.

"For chrissake!" Michael said, throwing up his hands in disgust. "You told me you'd get the guy, no problem. You gotta find him! This is no longer a joke."

"He never showed up at home," Devlin said.

"Damn, damn, damn!" Michael said with progressive panic. His swivel chair squeaked as he tipped forward and stood up. "I'm going to be out of business."

Devlin frowned. Michael was more wound up than usual. This missing doctor was really getting to him. "Don't worry," he told Michael. "I'll find him. What else do you know about him?"

"Nothing!" Michael yelled. "I told you everything I know."

"You haven't told me squat," Devlin said. "What about other family, things like that? What about friends?"

"I'm telling you, I don't know anything about the guy," Michael admitted. "All I did was an O and E on his house. And you know something else? The bastard screwed me there too. This morning I got a call from Owen Shatterly at the bank, telling me he just learned Jeffrey Rhodes had upped his mortgage before my lien was filed. Now even the collateral doesn't cover the bond."

Devlin laughed.

"What the hell's so funny?" Michael demanded.

Devlin shook his head. "It tickles me that this little piss-ant doctor is causing so much trouble."

"I fail to find anything about this funny," Michael said. "Owen also told me that the doctor took the forty-five thousand he'd upped his mortgage in cash."

"Geez, no wonder the guy's briefcase hurt," Devlin said with a smile. "I've never been hit with that kind of dough."

"Very funny," Michael snapped. "The trouble is that the situation is going from bad to worse. Thank God for my friend Albert Norstadt down at police headquarters. The police weren't going to do a goddamn thing until he got involved."

"They think Rhodes is still in town?" Devlin questioned.

"As far as I know," Michael said. "They haven't been doing much, but at least they've been covering the airport, bus and train stations, rent-a-car agencies, and even taxi companies."

"That's plenty," Devlin said. He certainly didn't want the police to catch Jeffrey. "If he's in town, I'll find him in the next day or so. If he's skipped, it will take a little longer, but I'll get him. Relax."

"I want him found today!" Michael said, working himself up into a renewed frenzy. He started to pace behind his desk. "If you can't find the bastard, I'll bring in some other talent."

"Now hold on," Devlin said, bringing his legs off the coffee table and sitting up. He didn't want anybody else horning in on this job. "I'm doing the best anybody could do. I'll find the guy, no sweat."

"I want him now, not next year," Michael said.

"Relax, It's only been twelve hours," Devlin said.

"What the hell are you sitting around here for?" Michael snapped. "With forty-five grand in his pocket, he's not going to hang around forever. I want you to go back to the airport and see if you can pick up his trail from there. He had to get into town somehow. He sure as hell didn't walk. Get your ass out there and talk to the MBTA people. Maybe somebody will remember a skinny guy with a mustache and a briefcase."

"I think it's better to cover the wife," Devlin said.

"They didn't strike me as being so lovey-dovey," Michael said. "I want you to try the airport. If you don't, I'll send someone else."

"All right, all right!" Devlin said, getting to his feet. "If you want me to try the airport, I'll try the airport."

"Good," Michael said. "And keep me informed."

Devlin let himself out of Michael's office. His mood had not improved. Normally he'd never let someone like Michael tell him how to do his job, but in this instance, he thought he'd better humor the man. The last thing he wanted was competition. Especially on this job. The only trouble was that now that he had to go to the airport, he'd have to hire someone to follow the wife and watch the house. As Devlin waited for the elevator, he thought about whom he could call.

Jeffrey paused on the broad steps of Boston Memorial's entrance to marshal his courage. Despite his efforts at disguise, he was apprehensive now that he had reached the hospital's threshold. He was worried he'd be recognized by the first person who knew him.

He could even imagine their words: "Jeffrey Rhodes, is that you? What are you doing, going to a masquerade ball? We heard the police are looking for you, is that true? Sorry about your being convicted of second-degree murder. Sure does prove it's getting harder and harder to practice medicine in Massachusetts."

Taking a step back and switching his duffel bag to the other shoulder, Jeffrey tipped his head to look up at the Gothic details over the lintel of the front entrance. There was a plaque that read: THE BOSTON MEMORIAL HOSPITAL ERECTED AS A HOUSE

OF REFUGE FOR THE SICK, INFIRM, AND TROUBLED. He wasn't sick or infirm, but he was certainly troubled. The longer he hesitated, the harder it was to go inside. He was locked in indecision when he spotted Mark Wilson.

Mark was a fellow anesthesiologist whom Jeffrey knew well. They'd trained together at the Memorial. Jeffrey had been a year ahead. Mark was a large black man whose own mustache had always made Jeffrey's appear sparse by comparison; it had always been a point of humor between them. Mark seemed to be enjoying the brisk spring day. He was approaching from Beacon Street, heading for the front entrance—and straight for Jeffrey.

It was the kick Jeffrey needed. In a panic, he went through the revolving door and into the main lobby. He was immediately swept up in a sea of people. The lobby served not only as an entrance but as the confluence of three main corridors that led to the hospital's three towers.

Fearing that Mark was on his heels, Jeffrey hurried around the circular information booth in the center of the domed lobby and walked down the central corridor. He figured Mark would be heading left to the bank of elevators that led to the OR complex.

Tense with fear of discovery, Jeffrey walked down the hall trying to appear casual. When he finally turned to glance behind him, Mark was nowhere in sight.

Although he'd been affiliated with the hospital for almost twenty years, Jeffrey was not acquainted with anyone in personnel. Even so, he was wary when he entered the employment office and took the application a friendly clerk handed him. Just because he wasn't familiar with personnel staff didn't mean they weren't familiar with him.

He filled out the application, using Frank Amendola's name, social security number, and his Framingham address. In the section asking for work preference, Jeffrey indicated housekeeping. In the section asking for shift preference if applicable, he wrote "night." For references, Jeffrey listed several hospitals where he'd visited for anesthesia meetings. It was his hope that it would take time for personnel to follow up on the references, if follow-ups were done at all. Between the high demand for hospital workers and the low wages offered, Jeffrey figured it was an applicant's market. He didn't think that his employment in a position in housekeeping would be predicated on a reference check.

After he handed in his completed application, Jeffrey was offered the choice of being interviewed immediately or having an interview scheduled for a future date. He said he'd be pleased to be interviewed at personnel's earliest convenience.

After a brief wait, he was ushered into Carl Bodanski's windowless office. Bodanski was one of the Memorial's personnel officers. One wall of his small room was dominated by a huge board with hundreds of name tags hanging from small hooks. A calendar was on another wall. Double doors filled the third. It was all very neat and utilitarian.

Carl Bodanski was in his mid to late thirties. He had dark hair, a handsome face, and was neatly if not too stylishly dressed in a dull business suit. Jeffrey realized he'd seen the man many times in the hospital cafeteria, but the two had never spoken. When Jeffrey entered, Bodanski was hunched over his desk.

"Please sit down," Bodanski said warmly, not yet looking up. Jeffrey could see that he was going over his application. When Bodanski finally turned his attention to Jeffrey, Jeffrey held his breath. He was afraid he'd see some sudden evidence of recognition. But he didn't. Instead, Bodanski asked Jeffrey if he would care for anything to drink, coffee, maybe a Coke.

Jeffrey nervously declined. He studied Bodanski's face. Bodanski smiled in return.

"So you've worked in hospitals?"

"Oh, yes," Jeffrey answered. "Quite a bit." Jeffrey smiled weakly. He was starting to relax.

"And you want to work the night shift in housekeeping?" Bodanski wanted to make sure there hadn't been a mistake. As far as he was concerned, this was too good to be true: an applicant for housekeeping's night shift who didn't look like a criminal or an illegal alien, and who spoke English.

"That's what I'd prefer," Jeffrey said. He realized it was a bit unexpected. On the spur of the moment he presented an explanation: "I'm planning on taking a few courses at Suffolk

University during the day or perhaps evening. Have to support myself."

"What kind of courses?" Bodanski asked.

"Law," Jeffrey responded. It was the first subject that came to mind.

"Very ambitious. So you'll be going to law school for a number of years?"

"I hope to," Jeffrey said enthusiastically. He could see Bodanski's eyes had brightened. Besides recruitment, housekeeping had a problem of a high turnover rate, especially on the night shift. If Bodanski thought Jeffrey would stay for several years on nights, he'd think it was his lucky day.

"When would you be interested in starting?" Bodanski asked.

"As soon as possible," Jeffrey said. "As early as tonight."

"Tonight?" Bodanski repeated with disbelief. This was really too good to be true.

Jeffrey shrugged his shoulders. "I've just come to town and I need work. Gotta eat."

"From Framingham?" Bodanski asked, glancing at the application.

"That's correct," Jeffrey said. He didn't want to get into any discussion about where he'd never been, so he said: "If Boston Memorial can't use me, I can head over to St. Joseph's or Boston City."

"Oh, no. No need for that," Bodanski said quickly. "It's just that things take a little time. I'm sure you understand. You'll have to have a uniform and an ID card. Also there's some paperwork that has to be done before you can start."

"Well, here I am," Jeffrey said. "Why can't we just get it all over with right away?"

Bodanski paused for a beat, then said, "Just one moment." He got up from behind his desk and left the office.

Jeffrey stayed in his seat. He hoped he hadn't been too eager about starting so soon. He looked around Bodanski's office to pass the time. There was a silver-framed photo on the desk: a woman standing behind two rosy-cheeked children. It was the only personal touch in the whole room, but a nice one, Jeffrey thought.

Bodanski returned with a short man with shiny black hair and a friendly smile. He was dressed in a dark green housekeeping uniform. Bodanski introduced him as Jose Martinez. Jeffrey stood up and shook the man's hand. He'd seen Martinez many times. He watched the man's face as he had with Bodanski, but could detect no sign of recognition.

"Jose is our head of housekeeping," Bodanski said, with a hand on Martinez's shoulder. "I've explained to Jose your wish to get to work right away. Jose is willing to expedite the process, so I'll turn you over to him."

"Does that mean I'm hired?" Jeffrey asked.

"Absolutely," Bodanski said. "Glad to have you part of the Memorial team. After Jose has finished with you, come back here. You'll need a Polaroid for your ID. Also, we have to sign you up for either Blue Cross/Blue Shield, or one of the HMOs. Any idea of your preference?"

"Doesn't matter," Jeffrey said.

Martinez took Jeffrey to the housekeeping headquarters, located on the first basement level. He had a pleasant Spanish accent and an infectious sense of humor. In fact, he found most everything funny enough to giggle at, especially the first pair of trousers he held up to Jeffrey. The legs only reached as far as Jeffrey's knees.

"I think we'll have to amputate," he said with a laugh.

After several tries, they found a uniform that fit. Then Jeffrey was assigned a locker. For the moment, Martinez told him to change into the shirt. "You can leave your own pants on," he added.

Martinez explained that he would be giving Jeffrey a tour of the hospital. The housekeeping shirt would do in lieu of an ID for the moment.

"I hate to take any more of your time," Jeffrey said quickly. The last thing he wanted to do was walk around the hospital during the day when he was most likely to be recognized.

"I got the time," Martinez said. "No problem. Besides, it's part of our usual orientation."

Afraid to make an issue of this, Jeffrey reluctantly put on the dark green housekeeping shirt and stored his street clothes in the locker. Keeping the duffel bag on his shoulder, he prepared himself to follow wherever Martinez led. What he wished he could do was put a bag over his head.

Martinez kept up a steady chatter as he showed Jeffrey around. First he introduced him to what housekeeping staff was present. Then they went into the laundry where everyone was too busy to pay much attention. Next was the cafeteria, where everyone was decidedly unfriendly. Luckily there was no one sitting in the cafeteria whom Jeffrey knew well.

Climbing the stairs to the first floor, Martinez took Jeffrey through the outpatient clinics and the emergency room. In the emergency room, Jeffrey wanted to turn and duck down the hall at the sight of several surgical residents he'd come to know quite well after their rotations through anesthesia. Luckily for him, they didn't look in his direction. They were preoccupied with trauma cases from an auto accident.

After the emergency room, Martinez took Jeffrey to the main elevators in the north tower. "Now I want to show you the labs," Martinez said. "And then the OR area."

Jeffrey gulped. "Shouldn't we be getting back to Mr. Bodanski?" he asked.

"We can take all the time we need," Martinez answered. He motioned for Jeffrey to get on the elevator whose doors had just opened. "Besides, it's important for you to see pathology, chemistry, and the OR. You'll be up there tonight. The night shift always cleans them. Night's the only time we can get in."

Jeffrey moved to the back of the elevator. Martinez joined him. "You'll be working with four other people," Martinez explained. "The shift supervisor's name is David Arnold. He's a good man."

Jeffrey nodded. As they approached the OR and lab floor, Jeffrey began to feel a burning sensation in his stomach. He jumped when Martinez grabbed his arm and urged him forward, saying, "This is our floor."

Jeffrey took a deep breath as he prepared to step off the elevator into the part of the hospital where he'd practically lived for almost two decades.

Jeffrey's jaw dropped. For a second he couldn't move. Directly in front of him was Mark Wilson, waiting to board the elevator. His dark eyes bore into Jeffrey. Mark's eyes narrowed, then he started to speak. Jeffrey expected to hear "Jeffrey, is that you?"

"Are you getting off or what?" Mark asked Jeffrey.

"We're getting off," Martinez said, giving Jeffrey a slight shove.

It took Jeffrey a few seconds to comprehend that Mark hadn't recognized him. He turned around just as the elevator doors closed, and caught Mark's eyes a second time. There wasn't the slightest trace of recognition.

Jeffrey pushed his glasses higher on his nose. They'd slipped down when he'd stumbled off the elevator.

"Are you okay?" Martinez questioned.

"Fine," Jeffrey said. He actually was much better. The fact that Mark hadn't recognized him was a heartening sign.

The tour through the chemistry and pathology labs was less stressful than the elevator ride. Jeffrey certainly saw plenty of people he knew, but no one recognized him any more than Mark Wilson had.

The real stress returned when Martinez took Jeffrey to the surgical lounge. At that time of the early afternoon, there were at least twenty people whom Jeffrey knew well, sitting in the lounge having coffee, enjoying conversation, or reading the newspaper. All it would take was for one of them to realize who he was, then it would be all over. While Martinez ticked off the nightly procedures, Jeffrey studied his shoes. He kept his eye contact with others at a minimum but after almost fifteen minutes of tense anticipation, Jeffrey realized that no one was paying him any attention. He and Martinez could have been invisible for all the notice they attracted.

In the men's locker room Jeffrey passed another test as rigorous as his brush with Mark Wilson. He came face to face with another anesthesiologist whom he knew extremely well. They did a kind of shadow dance in an attempt to pass each other by the sinks. When this doctor failed to recognize him even after such close scrutiny, Jeffrey was amazed and pleased. His disguise was even better than he'd hoped.

"Have you had any experience with scrub clothes?" Martinez asked as they stopped in front of the cabinets that contained the scrub clothing.

"Yes," Jeffrey said.

"Good," Martinez said. "I don't think we should go in there now. David Arnold will have to show you around the OR tonight. It's much too busy at this time."

"I understand," Jeffrey said.

Jeffrey, relieved to get the tour over with, put on his street clothes. Then Martinez led him back to Carl Bodanski's office. After shaking hands, Martinez wished Jeffrey well before returning to his duties. Bodanski had a withholding statement and a health care form for Jeffrey to sign. As nervous as he still was, Jeffrey started to sign his real name before he caught himself and scribbled Frank Amendola's name in the requisite blanks.

Only after he went through the revolving door at the front entrance of the hospital and reached the street did Jeffrey feel his anxiety lift. He even felt encouraged. So far, everything was moving along according to plan.

Devlin climbed the stairs from the inbound side of the MBTA airport station. The metal heel savers on the heels of his cowboy boots clicked loudly against the dirty concrete. He felt like strangling somebody and he wasn't terribly choosy. Anybody would do.

His mood had deteriorated further since leaving Michael Mosconi's office. As he expected, the airport had so far been a total waste of time. He'd talked to the parking attendants to see if any of them had noticed the guy who pulled in around 9:00 P.M. with a cream-colored Mercedes 240D. Of course, no one had.

Next, Devlin had gone to the MBTA stop and gotten the name and phone number of the fellow who had manned the token booth the previous evening. Just getting the number was like pulling teeth. When he finally was able to reach the man, it proved as futile as he'd suspected it would. The guy wouldn't have remembered if his mother had come by to buy a token.

Reaching the bus platform, Devlin waited for the intraterminal bus to come by. When a bus finally arrived, he boarded by the front door. At first he tried to be nice.

"Excuse me," he said. The driver was a thin black fellow

with round, metal-rimmed glasses. "Maybe you can give me some information," Devlin said.

The driver blinked, then glanced down at Devlin's tattooed arm before looking back up into his face. "I can't close the door until you sit down," he said. "And I can't drive the bus until the door is closed."

Devlin rolled his eyes. He looked into the bus. A few other passengers had boarded from the rear door and were busy storing their luggage in the luggage rack.

"This will only take a second," Devlin said, restraining himself. "You see, I'm looking for a man who might have boarded one of these buses last night around nine-thirty. He's a skinny white dude with a mustache, carrying a briefcase. No other luggage. What I was wondering is—"

"I'd appreciate it if you'd sit down," the driver said, interrupting Devlin.

"Listen, friend," Devlin said, his voice dropping an octave. "I'm trying to be nice."

"You're wasting your time," the driver said. "I get off at three-thirty."

"I understand," Devlin said, doing his utmost to remain composed. "But could you tell me the names of the drivers who were driving last night?"

"Why don't you go to the transportation office?" the driver said. "Now if you'll take a seat."

Devlin closed his eyes. This little squirt was pushing his luck.

"Either sit down or get off the bus," the driver said.

That was the last straw. Devlin moved quickly, grabbing the driver by the front of his shirt and lifting him off the seat. He pulled the man's face within inches of his own.

"You know something, buddy?" Devlin asked. "I don't think I like your attitude. All I want is a simple answer to a simple question."

"Hey!" one of the passengers yelled.

Still holding the terrified driver off his seat, Devlin turned toward the back of the bus. A man in a business suit came up to him. His face was flushed with indignation. "What's going on here?" he demanded.

Devlin reached out with his left hand and grabbed the passenger's head as if he were palming a basketball. First he pulled the man a step forward, then he gave him a powerful shove back. The man stumbled and fell over backward in the aisle. The other passengers just gawked. No one else tried to come to the driver's rescue.

Meanwhile, the driver was making an attempt to speak. Devlin lowered him into his seat. The driver coughed. Then, in a hoarse voice, he gave Devlin two names. "I don't know their numbers, but they both live in Chelsea."

Devlin wrote the names down in a small notebook he carried in the left front pocket of his denim shirt. Then his beeper went off. He snapped the beeper from his belt, pushed the button and watched the LED screen. Michael Mosconi's number flashed into view.

"Thanks, buddy," Devlin said to the driver. He turned and got off the bus. The bus pulled away in a cloud of diesel smoke, its door still open.

Devlin watched it go, wondering if a squad car would be descending on him in the next few minutes. If so, chances were he'd know the cops. He'd been off the police force for over five years, but he still had a lot of friends. Except for the rookies, he knew most everybody.

Returning inside the station, Devlin used a pay phone to call Michael. He wondered if Michael was checking up on him to see if he'd gone to the airport.

"Got some good news, pal," Michael said when the connection went through. "I shouldn't even be telling you this. Makes your job too easy. I know where Jeffrey Rhodes is holed up."

"Where?" Devlin asked.

"Not so fast," Michael said. "If I tell you and you waltz over there and pick him up, it ain't worth forty grand. I can call someone else. You get my point?"

"How'd you come by this information?" Devlin asked.

"Norstadt from police headquarters," Michael said triumphantly. "While they were covering the cab companies, one of the drivers came forward to say that he'd picked up a guy who matched Jeffrey Rhodes's description. The driver said that Rhodes had acted strange. At first he didn't even have a destination. He said they just drove around aimlessly."

"How come the police haven't nabbed him?" Devlin asked.

"They will. Eventually," Michael said. "But they're a little preoccupied right now. Some rock group is coming to town. Besides, they don't view Rhodes as much of a threat to anybody."

"So what's the deal?"

"Ten grand," Michael said. "Take it or leave it."

Devlin only had to think for a moment. "I'll take it," he said.

"The Essex Hotel," Michael said. "And, Dev—kick him around a little. The guy's caused me a lot of aggravation."

"It'll be my pleasure," Devlin said, and he meant it. Not only had Jeffrey hit him with his briefcase, now he'd managed to screw Devlin out of thirty thousand dollars. But then again, maybe he hadn't.

Back on the bus platform, Devlin managed to flag down a cab. He had the cabbie drive him to his car in central parking for five dollars.

By the time Devlin drove out of the airport, his attitude had considerably improved. It was a shame to lose thirty grand, if that's what ended up happening, but ten grand was nothing to sneeze at either. Besides, he could have a little fun with Jeffrey. And now that he knew Jeffrey's location, the job was a snap. Piece of cake.

Devlin drove directly to the Essex Hotel. He parked by a fire hydrant just across the street. He knew the Essex. When he'd been on the police force, he'd participated in a couple of drug busts in the hotel.

Devlin mounted the steps. Before pulling open the door, he reached beneath his denim jacket under his left arm and unsnapped the strap that buckled over the hammer of his snub-nosed .38. Although he was certain Jeffrey would not be armed, one could never be too careful. The doc had surprised him before. But that wouldn't happen again.

One quick glance around the interior told Devlin that the Essex had not changed one iota since his last visit. He even remembered the odor. It was the same musty smell as always, as if they had mushrooms growing in the basement. Devlin walked over to the front desk. When the clerk got up from his TV, Devlin remembered him too. The guys on the force re-

ferred to him as Drool because his lower lip hung down like
a bulldog's.

"Can I help you?" the clerk asked, eyeing Devlin with obvious distaste. He stayed several feet back from the desk as if he
were afraid Devlin was about to reach out and grab him.

"I'm looking for one of your guests," Devlin said. "His
name is Jeffrey Rhodes, but that might not be the name he's
registered under."

"We don't give out information about our guests," the clerk
said primly.

Devlin leaned intimidatingly toward the clerk. He paused
long enough to make the clerk uncomfortable. "So you don't
give out any information on your guests?" he repeated, nod-
ding his head as if he understood.

"That's right," the clerk said uncertainly.

"What the hell do you think this is, the Ritz-Carlton?" Devlin asked sarcastically. "All you usually got here is a bunch of
pimps, prostitutes, and druggies."

The clerk took a step back, watching Devlin with alarm.

With lightning speed, Devlin slammed his palm down on
the desk top with thunderous effect. The clerk winced. He was
visibly cowed.

"People have been giving me a hard time all day," Devlin
roared. Then he lowered his voice. "I'm only asking a simple
question."

"We don't have a Jeffrey Rhodes registered," the clerk stammered.

Devlin nodded. "Not surprising," he said. "But let me de-
scribe him. He's about your height, about forty or so, with a
mustache, kinda thin, brown hair. Nice looking. And he would
have been carrying a briefcase."

"Could be Richard Bard," the clerk said obligingly.

"And when did Mr. Bard check into this palatial establish-
ment?" Devlin asked.

"Last night around ten," the clerk said. Hoping to ward off
Devlin's anger, the clerk turned over a page in the register and
pointed to a name with a trembling hand. "See, that's where
he signed in, right there."

"Is Mr. Bard currently in residence?" Devlin asked.

The clerk shook his head no. "He went out about noon," he said. "But he looked very different. His hair was black and he'd shaved off his mustache."

"Well now," Devlin said. "I think that just about clinches it. What room would Mr. Bard be in?"

"Five-F."

"I don't suppose it would be asking too much for you to take me up there, now would it?"

The clerk shook his head. He locked the cash drawer, grabbed a spare key, and came out from behind the desk. Devlin followed him to the stairwell.

Devlin pointed at the elevator. "Things move at a slow pace around here. When I was in here on a drug bust five years ago, that elevator had the same sign on it."

"Are you a cop?" the clerk asked.

"Sort of," Devlin said.

They climbed in silence. By the time they got to the fifth floor, Devlin thought the clerk was about to have a heart attack. He was breathing heavily and perspiring profusely. Devlin let him catch his breath before they went down the hall to 5F.

Just to be on the safe side, Devlin knocked on the door. When there was no answer, he stepped aside and let the clerk open it. Devlin made a quick tour. The room was empty.

"I think I'll wait for Mr. Bard here," Devlin said as he walked over to the window and glanced out. He turned back to the clerk. "But I don't want you to say anything to him when he comes in. Let's just think of me as a little surprise. Understand?"

The clerk nodded vigorously.

"Mr. Rhodes, alias Mr. Bard, is a fugitive from justice," Devlin said. "There's a warrant for his arrest. He's a dangerous man, convicted of murder. If you say anything to arouse his suspicion, there's no telling how he may react. You know what I'm saying?"

"Absolutely," the clerk said. "Mr. Bard acted strange when he first came in. I was thinking of calling the police."

"Sure you were," Devlin said sarcastically.

"I won't say a word to anyone," the clerk said as he retreated out the door.

"I'm counting on you," Devlin said. He locked the door behind the clerk.

As soon as he was alone, Devlin dashed over to the briefcase and slung it onto the bed. With trembling hands he undid the latches and lifted the lid. He riffled through the papers but came up with nothing. Next he unsnapped the accordion file and went through each compartment rapidly.

"Damn!" he yelled. He'd hoped Jeffrey would have been foolish enough to have left the money in the briefcase. But all it contained was a bunch of papers and underwear. Devlin picked up one of the sheets that had "From the Desk of Christopher Everson" printed on the top. It was filled with scientific jargon. Devlin wondered who Christopher Everson was.

Dropping the paper, Devlin made a complete search of the room in case Jeffrey had hidden the money. But it wasn't there. Devlin guessed that Jeffrey would have the money on him. It was the main reason he'd agreed to Michael's deal so quickly. Devlin planned to pocket the forty-five grand Jeffrey was supposed to have, in addition to the ten Michael would be giving him.

Stretching out on the bed, Devlin pulled his handgun from his holster. The good doctor was a constant source of surprises. Devlin decided he'd better be ready for anything.

Jeffrey felt considerably more at ease with his disguise and new identity after his trip to Boston Memorial had gone without a hitch. If people he knew intimately didn't recognize him, he had nothing to fear out in public, at least in terms of having his identity revealed. Bolstered by his new confidence, Jeffrey caught a cab and headed over to St. Joseph's Hospital.

He was still conscious of carrying so much cash, but he was a lot more comfortable toting it around in the duffel bag than he had been carrying the briefcase.

St. Joseph's Hospital was considerably older than the Memorial. It was a turn-of-the-century brick structure that had been refurbished several times. Set in a wooded grove adjacent to the Arnold Arboretum in Jamaica Plain, its grounds and location were considerably more attractive than the Memorial's.

The hospital had originally been built as a Catholic charity hospital, but over the years it had been transformed to a busy community hospital. Since St. Joseph's was in Boston's suburbs, it lacked the gritty, urban feeling of an inner-city hospital that bore the brunt of the country's social problems.

Jeffrey stopped and asked for directions to the intensive care unit from one of the pink-smocked, snowy-haired women volunteers who manned the hospital's information booth. With a smile, the elderly woman directed him to the second floor.

Jeffrey found the intensive care unit without difficulty and walked in.

As an anesthesiologist, Jeffrey felt right at home in the seemingly chaotic, high-tech unit. Every bed was occupied. Machines hissed and beeped. Clusters of IV bottles hung on the tops of poles like glass fruit. Tubes and wires were everywhere.

In the middle of all this electronic hustle-bustle were the nurses. As usual, they were so preoccupied with their responsibilities they didn't even acknowledge Jeffrey's presence.

Jeffrey spotted Kelly by the nursing station. She had just picked up a phone when Jeffrey stepped up to the desk. Their eyes met briefly and Kelly indicated for Jeffrey to wait for a moment. He noticed she was taking down some stat laboratory values.

Once Kelly had hung up, she called out to one of the other nurses and yelled out the results. From across the room the nurse made a motion that she understood and adjusted the flow of the IV to compensate.

"Can I help you?" Kelly asked once she directed her attention to Jeffrey. She was dressed in a white blouse and white slacks. Her hair was pulled back in a French knot.

"You already have," Jeffrey said with a smile.

"Excuse me?" Kelly asked, clearly puzzled.

Jeffrey laughed. "It's me! Jeffrey!"

"Jeffrey?" Kelly squinted.

"Jeffrey Rhodes," he said. "I can't believe that no one recognizes me! It's not as if I had plastic surgery."

Kelly brought a hand up to hide her smile. "What are you doing here? What happened to your mustache? And your hair?"

"It's kind of a long story. Do you have a minute?"

"Sure." Kelly told another nurse that she was taking her break. "Come on," she said to Jeffrey, pointing to a door behind the nurses' station. She took him into a back room that the nurses used for storage as well as a makeshift lounge.

"How about some coffee?" Kelly asked. Jeffrey said he'd love a cup. Kelly poured one for him and one for herself. "So what's with this disguise?"

Jeffrey put down his duffel bag and removed his glasses. They had started to irritate the bridge of his nose. He took the coffee and sat down. Kelly leaned against the counter, holding her coffee mug in both hands.

Starting from the time he left her house the evening before, Jeffrey told Kelly everything that had happened: the fiasco at the airport, the fact that he had become a fugitive, assaulting Devlin with his briefcase, the scuffle with the handcuffs.

"So you were going to leave the country?" Kelly asked.

"That had been my intention," Jeffrey admitted.

"And you weren't going to call and tell me?"

"I would have called you as soon as I could," Jeffrey said. "I wasn't thinking too clearly."

"Where are you staying?"

"At a flophouse in downtown Boston," Jeffrey said.

Kelly shook her head in dismay. "Oh, Jeffrey. This all sounds pretty bad. Maybe you should just turn yourself in. This can't help your appeal."

"If I turn myself in, they'll put me in jail and probably deny bail. Even if they gave me bond, I don't think I could raise it now. But my appeal really should remain a separate issue. Anyway, I can't go to jail because I have too much to do."

"What does that mean?" Kelly asked.

"I've been going over Chris's notes," Jeffrey said, barely able to contain his excitement. "I've even spent some time doing research at the library. I think Chris might have been onto something when he suspected a contaminant being in the Marcaine he'd administered to Henry Noble. And now I'm beginning to suspect the same about the Marcaine I gave to Patty Owen. What I want to do is investigate both incidents more thoroughly."

"This gives me a bad sense of déjà vu," Kelly said.

"What do you mean?" Jeffrey asked.

"You're sounding exactly the way Chris did when he first began to suspect a contaminant. The next thing I knew, he'd committed suicide."

"I'm sorry," Jeffrey said. "I don't mean to bring back painful thoughts for you by dredging up the past."

"It's not the past that worries me," Kelly said. "It's you. I'm worried about you. Yesterday you were depressed, today you're a little manic. What will it be tomorrow?"

"I'll be fine," Jeffrey said. "Honest! I really think I'm onto something."

Kelly cocked her head to the side and raised one eyebrow as she looked at Jeffrey questioningly. "I want to be sure you remember your promise to me," Kelly said.

"I remember."

"You'd better," Kelly said sternly. Then she smiled. "Now that we have that understood, you can tell me what's made you so excited over the contaminant idea."

"A number of things. Henry Noble's persistent paralysis, for one. Apparently he'd even lost function of cranial nerves. That doesn't happen with spinal anesthesia, so it couldn't have been 'irreversible spinal anesthesia' like they said. And in my case, the child had persistent paralysis with an asymmetric distribution."

"Wasn't Noble's paralysis thought to be secondary to lack of oxygen because of the seizures and cardiac arrests?"

"That's right," Jeffrey said. "But at autopsy, Chris wrote that axonal or nerve cell degeneration had been seen on microscopic sections."

"You're getting beyond me," Kelly admitted.

"You wouldn't see axonal degeneration with the degree of oxygen deprivation that Henry Noble had experienced— if he had any oxygen deprivation at all. If he had been deprived of oxygen enough to cause axonal degeneration, they wouldn't have been able to resuscitate him. And you certainly don't see axonal degeneration with local anesthetics. Local anesthetics block function. They definitely aren't cellular poisons."

"Suppose you're right," Kelly said. "How are you going to prove it?"

"It's not going to be easy," Jeffrey admitted, "especially with my being a fugitive. But I'm going to give it a shot just the same. I wanted to ask you if you would consider lending a hand. If my theory is right and I can prove it, it would clear Chris's name as well as mine."

"Of course I'll help," Kelly said. "Did you really think you had to ask?"

"I want you to think seriously about this before you agree," Jeffrey told her. "There could be a problem because of my fugitive status. Any aid you give me could be interpreted as abetting a fugitive. If so, it could be a felony itself. I just don't know."

"I'll take my chances," Kelly said. "I'd do anything to clear Chris's name. And besides"—she added, blushing slightly—"I'd like to do what I can to help you."

"The first step will be to document that the two ampules of Marcaine came from the same pharmaceutical manufacturer. That should be easy enough. It will be more difficult to find out if they came from the same batch, which is what I suspect. Even though Chris's case and mine were a number of months apart, it's still possible they could have come from the same production run. What worries me is that there might be more contaminated vials out there."

"God! What a creepy thought! A tragedy waiting to happen."

"Are you still friendly with someone out at Valley Hospital who could tell you the company that supplies their Marcaine? I happen to know that the Memorial gets theirs from Arolen Pharmaceuticals in New Jersey."

"Heavens, yes," Kelly said. "Most of the staff I worked with when I was at Valley is still there. Charlotte Henning is the OR supervisor. I talk to her at least once a week. I'll call her as soon as I get off work."

"That would be terrific," Jeffrey said. "As for me, I'm the newest member of the Boston Memorial housekeeping team."

"What!"

Jeffrey explained how he'd gone to Boston Memorial in his new disguise to apply for a position in housekeeping's night shift.

"I'm not surprised no one recognized you," Kelly said. "I sure didn't."

"But these are people I've worked with for years and years," Jeffrey said.

The door to the intensive care unit cracked open and one of the nurses stuck her head in. "Kelly, we're going to need you in a few minutes. We're getting an admission."

Kelly told her that she'd be there shortly. The nurse nodded, then discreetly retreated.

"So they hired you right off the bat?" Kelly asked.

"They sure did," Jeffrey said. "I'm starting tonight."

"What are you going to do once you're inside the hospital?" Kelly asked.

"One thing is to take you up on your suggestion," Jeffrey said. "I'm going to try to explain the vial of .75% Marcaine that was found in my anesthesia machine. I plan to look up what other surgeries were performed in that OR that day. The other thing I want to try to do is see the whole pathology report on Patty Owen. I'm curious whether they did any peripheral nerve sections on her at autopsy. I'm also curious to know if they did any toxicology."

"All I can say is you better be careful," Kelly said. Then she polished off the dregs of her coffee and rinsed her mug at the sink. "Sorry, I have to get back to work."

Jeffrey went to the sink and rinsed his cup. "Thanks for taking the time to talk with me," he said as she opened the door. The sounds of the respirators drifted into the room. Jeffrey picked up his duffel bag, put on his glasses, and followed her out the door.

"You'll call me tonight?" she asked before they parted. "I'll speak to Charlotte as soon as I can."

"What time do you go to bed?" Jeffrey asked.

"Not before eleven," Kelly said.

"I'll call before I go to work," Jeffrey said.

Kelly watched him go. She wished she'd had the courage to ask him if he wanted to stay with her.

*

As far as Carl Bodanski was concerned, it had been an extraordinarily productive day. Many unpleasant loose ends that had been bothering him had been solved. The biggest had been finding an additional worker for housekeeping's night shift. At that very moment Bodanski was busy at the big board, hanging its newest name tag. It read: FRANK AMENDOLA.

Stepping back from the board, Bodanski eyed it critically. It wasn't quite right. Frank Amendola's name was slightly cockeyed. He gingerly bent the tiny metal hooks that held the name tag, then stepped back. Much better.

There was a quiet knock on his door. "Come in," he called. The door opened. It was his secretary, Martha Reton. She stepped into the room and closed the door behind her. Something was up. Martha was behaving strangely.

"Sorry to bother you, Mr. Bodanski," she said.

"Quite all right," Bodanski said. "What's wrong?" Bodanski was an individual who saw any change in routine as threatening.

"There's a man here to see you," Martha said.

"Who is it?" Bodanski asked. Plenty of people came to see him. It was the personnel department. Why was she making an issue of it?

"His name is Horace Mannly," Martha said. "He's from the FBI."

An imperceptible tremor went down Bodanski's spine. The FBI, he thought with alarm. He ran through the various minor offenses he'd committed in the past few months. There was the parking ticket he'd ignored. There was the deduction of the fax machine for his home that he'd included on last year's income tax, even though he hadn't purchased the machine for business purposes.

Bodanski arranged himself in the seat behind his desk as if by looking professional he might ward off suspicion. "Send Mr. Mannly in," he said nervously.

Martha disappeared. An instant later, a rather obese man entered Bodanski's office.

"Mr. Bodanski," the FBI man said as he sauntered to Bodanski's desk. "Agent Mannly." He extended his hand.

Bodanski shook it. It was clammy; Bodanski stifled a grimace. The agent had a large dewlap that practically covered the
knot of his tie. His eyes, nose, and mouth seemed remarkably
small, centered in the large, pale sphere of his face.

"Sit down," Bondanski offered. After they were both seated,
he asked, "Now what can I do for you?"

"Computers are supposed to help us but sometimes they just
create work," Mannly said with a sigh. "You know what I
mean?"

"Certainly do," Bodanski said, but he didn't know if he
agreed or not. Yet he wasn't about to contradict an FBI agent.

"Some big computer someplace just spit out the name Frank
Amendola," Mannly said. "Is it true this guy is working for
you? Hey—you mind if I smoke?"

"Yes. No. I mean, I did just hire a Frank Amendola. And
no, I don't mind if you smoke." Although he was relieved not
to be the object of an inquiry, he was disappointed to learn that
Frank Amendola was. He should have known hiring him for
the night shift was too good to be true.

Horace Mannly lit up. "Our office got a tip from the Bureau
about you hiring this Frank Amendola," Mannly explained.

"We hired him today," Bodanski said. "Is he wanted?"

"Oh, he's wanted all right, but it's nothing criminal. It's his
wife that wants him, not the FBI. A domestic issue. Sometimes
we get involved. It depends. His wife's apparently made a big
fuss, writing to her congressman and to the Bureau and all that
jazz. So his social security number was flagged as a missing
person. You guys run your cross-check, his social security
number rings our bell. Bingo. So how'd this guy act, normal
or what?"

"He seemed a bit nervous," Bodanski said with relief. At
least the guy wasn't dangerous. "Otherwise, he acted normal.
He seemed intelligent. He talked of taking classes at law
school. We thought he was a good candidate for employment.
Is there something we should do?"

"I don't know," Mannly said. "I don't think so. I was just
supposed to come down here and check it out. See if he really
had reappeared. Tell you what. Don't do anything until you
hear from us. How's that?"

"We'll be happy to cooperate in any way we can."

"Wonderful," Mannly said. His face reddened as he struggled to his feet. "Thanks for your time. I'll give you a call as soon as I know anything."

Horace Mannly left but the stench from his cigarette hung around. Bodanski tapped his fingers on his desk, hoping that some problems on Frank's home front wouldn't rob him of a good potential employee.

Not even the run-down area around the Essex nor the hotel itself could dampen Jeffrey's spirits as he climbed the six steps to the front door. Maybe he was a bit manic, but at least he had the feeling that things had finally begun to tip in his direction. For the first time since he could remember, he felt like he was somewhat in control of events rather than vice versa.

As he'd taxied back from seeing Kelly at St. Joe's, he'd reviewed the case for his contaminant theory. More than anything else, it was the paralysis issue that made him sure something had to be wrong with the sealed ampules of Marcaine.

Jeffrey started across the lobby, then abruptly slowed down. The clerk wasn't watching his TV. Instead, he'd retreated to a storeroom just behind the reception desk. Previously the door had always been closed. The clerk nodded, nervously, Jeffrey thought, the moment their eyes met. It was as though the man was afraid of him.

Jeffrey went to the stairs and started up to his room. He couldn't account for the clerk's odd behavior. The man had struck Jeffrey as being a bit eccentric, but not this weird. Jeffrey wondered what it could mean. He hoped nothing.

When he got to the fifth floor, Jeffrey bent over the balustrade and looked down. The clerk was on the ground floor, looking up at him. He ducked out of view as soon as he saw Jeffrey look down.

So it wasn't his imagination, thought Jeffrey as he went through the stairwell door to the hallway. The man was obviously keeping an eye on him from a very deliberate distance. But why?

Jeffrey started down the hall, preoccupied with explaining the clerk's disturbing behavior. Then he remembered his disguise. Of course! That had to be it. Maybe the clerk didn't recognize him and thought he was a stranger. What if he decided to call the police?

Arriving at his door, Jeffrey searched his pockets for his key. Then he remembered he'd put it in his duffel bag. As he swung the bag around in front of him to unzip the central compartment, he thought about moving to another hotel. With all the other things he had to think about, he didn't want to have to worry about a hotel clerk.

Jeffrey slipped the key in the door and unlocked it. He put the key back in the duffel bag so he'd know where it was when he wanted to leave the room. He was already back to thinking of the contaminant theory when he walked through the door. Then he froze.

"Welcome home, doc," Devlin said. He was lounging on the bed with his revolver dangling carelessly at his side. "You have no idea how much I've been looking forward to seeing you again since you were so rude at our last encounter."

Devlin pushed himself up on one elbow. He squinted at Jeffrey. "You do look different! I'm not sure I would have recognized you." He laughed a hearty, deep laugh that evolved into a hacking cigarette cough.

Devlin spit over the side of the bed and thumped his chest with his fist. He cleared his throat and said hoarsely, "Don't just stand there. Come in and have a seat. Make yourself comfortable."

With the same sort of unthinking reflex that had led him to slug Devlin with his briefcase at the airport, Jeffrey leaped out of the room. Yanking the door shut, he lost his balance and fell to his knees. As they hit the shabby carpet, an explosion sounded inside the room. The next thing Jeffrey knew, splinters of wood were raining down on him. Devlin's .38 slug had ripped through the thin-paneled door only to lodge in the opposite wall.

Jeffrey scrambled to his feet and ran headlong down the hall toward the stairwell. He couldn't believe that he'd been shot at. He knew that he was a wanted man, but surely he didn't fit the dead-or-alive category. Jeffrey thought Devlin had to be crazy.

As Jeffrey skidded to a stop at the stairwell, catching the

doorjamb with his hand to help change directions, he heard the
door to his room bang open behind him. Using his shoulder,
he burst through the stairwell door at the same moment he
heard a second report from Devlin's gun. This bullet whined
off the door casement just behind Jeffrey, to shatter a window
at the end of the hall. Jeffrey heard Devlin laugh. The man was
enjoying himself!

Jeffrey threw himself down the twisting stairs, using the
banister to maintain his balance. His feet hit only every fourth
or fifth stair. His shoulder bag trailed behind him like a heavy
pennant. Where to go? What to do? Devlin wasn't far behind
him.

As Jeffrey rounded the last turn before reaching the first
floor, he heard the door above slam open and heavy footfalls
echo in the stairwell. With his panic ever increasing, he leaped
onto the first-floor landing. He threw himself at the door and
grasped the vertical handle. He yanked on the door but it
didn't open. Frantically he yanked again. The door didn't
budge. It was locked!

Peering through the small, wire-embedded window, Jeffrey
saw the clerk cowering on the opposite side of the door. Behind him, Jeffrey could hear Devlin's footfalls getting closer.
He would be on him in seconds.

Frantically, Jeffrey pantomimed to the clerk that the stairwell door was locked. The clerk blankly shrugged his shoulders, pretending he didn't understand what Jeffrey was trying
to tell him. Jeffrey rattled the door, still pointing in the direction of the lock.

Abruptly the sound of Devlin's footfalls stopped. Jeffrey
slowly turned. Devlin had reached the top of the final flight of
stairs and was gazing down at his trapped prey. His gun was
pointing at Jeffrey. Jeffrey wondered if this was it. If this was
where his life was destined to end. But Devlin didn't pull the
trigger.

"Don't tell me the door is locked," Devlin said with false
sympathy. "I'm so sorry, Doc."

Devlin walked down the last few steps slowly, keeping the
gun pointed at Jeffrey's face. "Funny," he said. "I would have
preferred the door to be open. It would have been more sporting."

Devlin stepped directly up to Jeffrey. He was smiling with obvious satisfaction. "Turn around!" he ordered.

Jeffrey turned, raising his hands in the air even though Devlin had not asked him to. Devlin pushed him roughly against the locked door and leaned his weight against him. He pulled the duffel bag from Jeffrey's shoulder and let it fall to the floor. Not taking any chances this time, he yanked Jeffrey's arms behind him and cuffed him before he did another thing. Once the cuffs were secure, he frisked Jeffrey for weapons. Then he turned Jeffrey back around and picked up the duffel bag.

"If this is what I think it is," Devlin said, "you're about to make me a happy man."

Devlin unzipped the bag and stuck his hand in it to grope around for the money. His mouth, which had assumed a pinched look of determination, suddenly curled into a broad smile. Triumphantly he pulled out a bound packet of hundred-dollar bills. "Now lookie here," he said. Then he stuffed the stack back into the duffel bag. He didn't want the clerk to see the cash and get any ideas.

Devlin slung the duffel bag over his shoulder and began to pound on the stairwell door. The clerk rushed forward to unlock it. Devlin grabbed Jeffrey by the scruff of the neck and pushed him into the lobby.

"Don't you know it's a code violation to have a lock on a stairwell door?" Devlin said to the clerk.

The clerk stammered that he didn't.

"Ignorance of the law is no defense," Devlin said. "Get it fixed or I'll have the building inspectors over here."

The clerk nodded. He'd expected some sort of thanks for having been so cooperative and helpful. But Devlin ignored him as he walked Jeffrey through the lobby and out the door.

Devlin marched Jeffrey across the street to his car, parked at the hydrant. Passers-by stopped to gawk. Devlin opened the passenger's door and shoved Jeffrey inside. He slammed the door, locked it, and started around the car.

With a presence of mind that he might not have expected under the circumstances, Jeffrey leaned forward in the seat and managed to get his right hand into the side pocket of his jacket. His fingers wrapped around the syringe he had put there. With his nail, he eased the cap off the needle. Jeffrey gingerly pulled the syringe from the pocket, then leaned back in the seat.

Devlin yanked the car door open, tossed the shoulder bag in the backseat, sat down, and put the key into the ignition. The instant he turned the key to start the car, Jeffrey lunged at the man, bracing his feet against the passenger-side door for leverage. Devlin was caught unaware. Before he could ward Jeffrey off, Jeffrey plunged the needle into his right hip and pressed the plunger.

"Shit!" Devlin screamed. He backhanded Jeffrey across the side of his head. The force of the blow sent Jeffrey reeling.

Devlin raised his arm to investigate the source of the stinging pain in his right buttock. Buried to the hilt was a 5 cc syringe. "Jesus," he said, gritting his teeth. "You freaking doctors are more trouble than serial killers." Daintily he pulled the needle out with a wince, then threw it into the backseat.

Jeffrey had recovered enough from Devlin's blow to try to unlock his door, but he couldn't get his handcuffed hands up high enough to reach. He was attempting to pull the lock with his teeth when Devlin grabbed him by the scruff of the neck once again and yanked him around like a rag doll.

"What the hell did you inject into me?" Devlin snarled. Jeffrey began to choke. "Answer me!" Devlin yelled as he gave Jeffrey another shake. Jeffrey could only gurgle. His eyes had begun to bulge. Then Devlin let go of Jeffrey and drew his arm back to strike him again. "Answer me!"

"Won't hurt," was all Jeffrey managed to gasp, "won't hurt you." He tried to raise his shoulder to block the blow he saw coming, but then the blow stalled.

With his arm poised to strike, Devlin's eyes went unfocused and he began to sway. His expression changed from anger to confusion. He clutched the steering wheel to support himself, but he couldn't manage to hold on. He slumped to the side, toward Jeffrey.

Devlin tried to talk but his speech was garbled.

"It won't hurt you," Jeffrey told him. "It's only a small dose of succinylcholine. You'll be all right in a few minutes. Don't panic."

Jeffrey shoved Devlin into a sitting position and managed to get a hand into the man's right pocket. But there was no handcuff key. Jeffrey scooted forward and let Devlin slump sideways on the seat. Jeffrey awkwardly searched the rest of Devlin's pockets. Still no key.

He was about to give up when he spotted a small key on the ring dangling from the ignition. It took some doing, but Jeffrey was able to yank the keys from the ignition by standing up, hunched over, facing out the passenger side. After a few futile tries, he succeeded in inserting the small key in the lock and getting the handcuffs off.

Reaching in the backseat, Jeffrey grabbed his duffel bag. Before getting out of the car, he checked Devlin. Devlin was just about completely paralyzed. His breathing was slow but steady. If Jeffrey had given him a much stronger dose, even Devlin's diaphragm would have been affected. He would have suffocated in minutes.

Ever the anesthesiologist, Jeffrey struggled to position Devlin so that he wouldn't compromise his circulation while he lay there. Then he got out of the car.

Jeffrey made a move toward the hotel. The clerk was nowhere in sight. Jeffrey paused. For a moment he debated about his belongings. He decided it was too risky to try to get his things. The clerk might have been dialing 911 that very moment. Besides, what did he have to lose? He was sorry to have to part with Chris Everson's notes, especially if Kelly wanted to keep them. But Kelly had said that she'd planned to get rid of all of Chris's material.

Jeffrey turned on his heels and fled. He headed in the direction of downtown. He wanted to lose himself in a crowd. Once he felt safer, he'd have a chance to think. And the further he got from Devlin, the better. Jeffrey still couldn't quite believe he'd managed to inject him with the succinylcholine. If Devlin had been angry with him over the episode at the airport, he'd be doubly furious now. Jeffrey only hoped he wouldn't run into the man again before he'd had a chance to prove his case.

The first chance Trent had to get back to Central Supply wasn't until well into the evening shift. Trent had been scrubbed on a particularly long aneurysm case. At the time of

the change of shifts, there'd been no one to relieve him.
Whether he liked it or not, he was forced into a little overtime.
It happened once in a while. It usually didn't bother him,
although on this particular occasion he found the timing inconvenient.

He'd been tense with anticipation since he'd arrived at the
hospital that morning. Each time the circulating nurse returned to the OR, he expected her to spread the news that there
had been a terrible anesthetic complication. But nothing had
happened. The day had remained stultifyingly routine.

At lunchtime in the cafeteria, his hopes were falsely raised
when one of the nurses who handled OB cases said, "Hey, did
you hear what happened in room eight?"

Once she had everyone's attention, she regaled them with a
story of how one of the surgical residents' pants had mysteriously become untied during a case and had slipped to his knees.
Everybody had a big laugh over that one. Everyone but Trent.

Trent paused outside of Central Supply. He'd already been
to his locker and had the good ampule of Marcaine hidden in
his briefs again. There were plenty of people moving in and
out of various ORs, but the confusion of the shift change had
dissipated.

He was not pleased with this situation. It was risky for him
to go into Central Supply at that time because he was not on
duty. If someone saw him and questioned his presence there,
he'd have little to say in defense. But he had no choice. He
couldn't leave the doctored vial unattended. He had made it a
practice to be around when one of his vials was used so that
in the ensuing confusion he could either remove the empty vial
from the scene, or at least dispose of any remaining contents.
He couldn't risk anyone's checking the Marcaine to see if
anything had been wrong with it.

Trent took a quick stroll around Central Supply before
going to the cabinet that contained the local anesthetics. So far
so good. With one last furtive look around to make sure no one
was watching, he lifted the lid of the open box of Marcaine and
peered in. There were two ampules left. One had been used
sometime that day.

Trent easily identified his doctored vial and quickly

switched it for the good one in his briefs. Then he closed the lid and pushed the box back into its original position. When he turned to head back to the locker room, he stopped in his tracks. He was dismayed to find his path blocked by a tall, blond nurse. She seemed as surprised to see him at the cabinet as he was to see her. She had her hands on her hips and her feet spread apart.

Trent felt his face redden as he tried to think of a plausible reason for being there. He hoped the tampered ampule in his briefs was not apparent.

"Can I help you?" the nurse asked. From her tone, Trent guessed the last thing in the world she wanted to do was help.

"No, thanks," he said. "I was just leaving." At last he thought of something: "I was returning some IV fluid we didn't get around to using on the aneurysm case in room five."

The nurse nodded but she seemed unconvinced. She extended her head to look over Trent's shoulder.

Trent looked at her name tag. It read Gail Shaffer. "The aneurysm went on for seven hours," Trent told her just to make conversation.

"I heard," Gail said. "Aren't you supposed to be off duty?"

"Finally," Trent said, regaining his composure. He rolled his eyes. "It's been a long day. Boy, am I looking forward to a few beers. Hope things are quiet for you this evening. Take care."

Trent edged by the nurse and started down the corridor toward the surgical lounge. After twenty or so steps, he glanced around. Gail Shaffer was still standing in the doorway to Central Supply, watching him. Damn, he thought. She was suspicious. He waved at her. She waved back.

Trent pushed through the swinging doors into the lounge. Where the hell had Gail Shaffer come from so quickly? He was irritated at himself for not having been more careful. He'd never been caught in the supply cabinet before.

Prior to going into the locker room, Trent stopped at the bulletin board in the lounge. Among the notices and schedules he found Gail Shaffer's name listed with the hospital softball team. Each player's telephone number was listed on the bulletin board in one form or another. On a piece of scrap paper,

Jeffrey wrote Gail's number down. From the first three digits, he guessed it was a Back Bay exchange.

What a pain, thought Trent, as he went into the dressing area to put on his street clothes. He slipped the vial back into his white hospital coat.

As Trent headed for the elevators and then home, he realized he'd have to do something about Gail Shaffer. In his position he couldn't afford to ignore loose ends.

WEDNESDAY,

MAY 17, 1989

4:37 P.M.

Devlin had always hated hospitals. Ever since he was a little boy growing up in Dorchester, Massachusetts, he'd been afraid of them. His mother had played on his fear to threaten him: If you don't do this or you don't do that, I'll take you to the hospital and the doctor will give you a shot. Devlin hated shots. That was one of the reasons he now wanted to get Jeffrey Rhodes whether Michael Mosconi paid him or not. Well, that wasn't completely true.

Devlin shuddered. Thinking about Jeffrey reminded him of the terror he'd just experienced. Throughout the whole ordeal, he'd remained conscious and aware of everything that had happened. It had felt like gravity had suddenly increased a thousandfold. He'd been completely paralyzed, even unable to speak. He'd been able to breathe, but only with great effort and concentration. Every second he'd had the terror that he was about to suffocate.

The idiot of a clerk from the Essex Hotel had come out only after Jeffrey was long gone. He'd tapped repeatedly on the glass, calling to Devlin to see if he was okay. It had taken the fool ten minutes to open the damn door. Then he asked Devlin

ten more times if he was okay before he had enough sense to
go back into the hotel and call an ambulance.

By the time Devlin arrived at the hospital, forty minutes had
passed. To his great relief, the paralysis had passed. The leaden
feeling had vanished during the ambulance ride. But, terrified
it might come back, Devlin had allowed himself to be wheeled
into the emergency room to be examined despite his fear of
hospitals.

In the emergency room, Devlin had been ignored except for
a quick visit by a uniformed policeman. Officer Hank Stanley,
whom Devlin knew vaguely, had come in to have a chat.
Apparently one of the ambulance drivers had seen Devlin's
gun. Of course once Stanley recognized him, there had been
no problem. Devlin's gun was properly registered and li-
censed.

Finally, Devlin had been seen by a doctor who looked like
he was barely old enough to drive. His name was Dr. Tardoff
and he had skin like a baby's behind. Devlin wondered if he'd
started shaving yet. He had told the doctor what had happened.
The doctor had examined him, then had disappeared without
saying a word, leaving Devlin alone in one of the emergency
room cubicles.

Devlin swung his legs over the side of the examining table
and stood up. His clothes were in a heap on a chair. "Screw
this!" he said to himself. It seemed like he'd been waiting for
hours. Removing the hospital johnny, Devlin quickly dressed
and pulled on his boots. Walking out to the main desk, he asked
for his gun. They'd insisted he leave it there.

"Dr. Tardoff hasn't finished with you yet," the nurse said.
She was a huge woman, about Devlin's size, and looked about
as tough as he did.

"I'm afraid I'll die of old age before he gets back," Devlin
said.

At that very moment, Dr. Tardoff appeared from one of the
examining rooms, snapping off rubber gloves. He saw Devlin
and came over. "Sorry to have kept you waiting," he said. "I
had to sew up a laceration. I talked with an anesthesiologist
about your case and he said that you'd been injected with a
paralyzing drug."

Devlin lifted both hands to his face and rubbed his eyes as he took a deep breath. His patience had come to an end. "I didn't have to come all the way over here to this hospital to be told something I already knew," he said. "Is this what you've had me wait for?"

"Our guess is that it was succinylcholine," Dr. Tardoff said, ignoring Devlin's remark.

"I already told you that," Devlin said. He'd remembered what Jeffrey had told him. He hadn't quite gotten the name of the drug completely right when he'd repeated it to Dr. Tardoff, but he'd been close enough.

"It's a drug that's used routinely in anesthesia," the doctor continued, unruffled. "It's something like what the Amazon Indians use on their poison darts, although physiologically it involves a slightly different mechanism."

"Now that's a helpful little tidbit of information," Devlin said sarcastically. "Now maybe you could tell me something a little more practical, like whether I have to worry about paralysis recurring at some inconvenient moment, say when I'm behind the wheel of my car going ninety miles an hour."

"Absolutely not," Dr. Tardoff said. "Your body has completely metabolized the drug. To get the same effect, you'd have to have another dose injected."

"I think I'll pass." Devlin turned to the nurse. "How about my gun now?"

Devlin had to sign some papers, then they gave him the gun. They had placed it in a manila envelope and the cartridges in another. Devlin made a great show of loading the gun right at the emergency room desk, then putting it into its holster. He touched his index finger to his forehead in a kind of salute on his way out. Boy, was he glad to be out of there.

Devlin took a cab back to the Essex Hotel. His car was still parked in front of the fire hydrant. But before he picked it up, he stormed into the hotel.

The clerk was nervously solicitous about how Devlin was feeling.

"Fine, no thanks to you," Devlin told him. "Why'd it take you so long to call the ambulance? I could have died, for chrissake."

"I thought maybe you were sleeping," the clerk said feebly.

Devlin let that comment go. He knew if he thought about it, he'd probably want to strangle the idiot. As if he'd decide to take a catnap right after he'd apprehended a fugitive and handcuffed him at gunpoint. It was absurd!

"Did Mr. Bard come back inside after it looked like I fell asleep?" Devlin asked.

The clerk shook his head.

"Give me a key for 5F," Devlin demanded. "You haven't been up there, have you?"

"No, sir," the clerk said, handing the key to Devlin.

Devlin climbed the steps to Jeffrey's room slowly. There was no hurry now. He looked at the bullet hole and wondered how the slug had missed the doctor. It was centered on the door about four and a half feet from the floor. It should have hit something, and it should have stopped Jeffrey, even if by fright alone.

Opening the door, experience told Devlin that the clerk had been lying. He'd been in there searching for any valuables. Glancing in the bathroom, Devlin guessed that the clerk had taken most of the doc's toiletries. Devlin picked up some of the notepaper on the nightstand that had Christopher Everson's name on it. He wondered again who Christopher Everson was.

After his quick getaway, Jeffrey had wandered around the downtown section of Boston, avoiding any policeman he saw. He felt like everyone was watching him. He walked into Filene's and hung out in the basement. Crowds made him feel safer. He pretended to browse long enough to try to calm down and figure out what to do next.

He stayed in the store for almost an hour, until he realized that the security people were eyeing him as if they had reason to believe he was a shoplifter.

Once he left Filene's, Jeffrey headed up Winter Street to the area around the Park Street MBTA station. Rush hour was in full swing. Jeffrey felt envious of the commuters hurrying home. He wished he had a home he could go to. He hung out by a bank of telephones and watched the parade of people go by. But when a couple of mounted police appeared, coming against the traffic on Tremont Street, he decided to move into the Boston Common. For a moment, Jeffrey was tempted to go down into the MBTA station with the commuters and catch a Green Line trolley to Brookline. But at the last minute he couldn't let himself do it.

What Jeffrey longed to do was go directly to Kelly's. The memory of her cozy house beckoned. The thought of a cup of tea with her was so tempting. If only things weren't the way they were just then. But Jeffrey was a convicted criminal, a fugitive. He was one of the homeless now, aimlessly wandering the city. The only difference was that he was carrying a ton of money in his duffel bag.

As much as he wanted to go to Kelly's, he was reluctant to draw her into his whirlpool of troubles now, especially with a crazed, gun-toting bounty hunter on his trail. Jeffrey did not want to jeopardize Kelly's safety. He couldn't lead a fiend like Devlin to her door. He shuddered as he recalled the sound of Devlin's gun.

But where could he go? Wouldn't Devlin search all the hotels in the city? And Jeffrey realized that his disguise would be of no help now that Devlin had seen him. For all Jeffrey knew, there might be a revised APB out on him already.

Jeffrey crossed the edge of the Common and ended up at the corner of Beacon and Charles streets. He turned up Charles. A few doors in from Beacon was a busy grocery store called Deluca's. Jeffrey went in and bought some fruit. He'd not eaten much that day.

Eating his fruit, Jeffrey continued his wandering up Charles Street. Several taxis went by, and he stopped walking. He followed the cabs with his eyes while his mind came up with an explanation of Devlin's appearance. It had to have been the cabdriver who'd taken Jeffrey from the airport to the Essex. He'd probably reported Jeffrey to the police. Thinking back, Jeffrey had to admit that he'd acted rather strangely.

But if it had been the cabdriver who'd gone to the police, why hadn't the police come and not Devlin? Jeffrey started walking again. But he wouldn't let the issue drop. Finally he reasoned that it had been Devlin who'd gone to the cab companies on his own. The implications were that Devlin was more

than a fearful presence. He was also resourceful, and that being
the case, Jeffrey had better be significantly more careful. He
was learning that becoming a successful fugitive took some
effort and experience.

Reaching Charles Circle, where the MBTA emerged from
beneath Beacon Hill and ran across the Longfellow Bridge,
Jeffrey paused, not sure where he should go. He could turn
right on Cambridge Street and head back downtown. But that
didn't sound so good since he now associated downtown with
Devlin's presence. Squinting into the sun, Jeffrey saw the footbridge that spanned Storrow Drive to the Charles Street Embankment along the Charles River. That seemed like as good
a destination as any.

Reaching the river's edge, Jeffrey strolled along what used
to be elegant walkways, as evidenced by granite balustrades
and steps. It was now overgrown and unattended. The river
was pretty, but it was dirty and emanated a swampy smell.
There was a profusion of small sailboats dotted across its spar-
kling surface.

Reaching the esplanade in front of the Hatch Shell stage
where the Boston Pops gave free concerts in the summertime,
Jeffrey sat on one of the park benches under a row of oak trees.
He wasn't alone. There were numerous joggers, Frisbee toss-
ers, power walkers, and even roller skaters doing their thing
on the maze of walkways and stretches of grassy turf.

Even though there were still several hours of daylight remaining, the sun seemed to abruptly lose its strength. A haze
of high clouds had materialized that suggested the weather was
about to change. A wind picked up and blew chilly air from
over the water. Jeffrey shivered and put his arms around himself.

He had to be at the Memorial at eleven for work. He had no
place to go until then. Again, Jeffrey thought of Kelly. He
could remember how comfortable he'd felt in her home. It had
been so long since he'd confided in anyone; so long since
there'd been anyone to listen.

Jeffrey thought about going to Brookline again. Hadn't
Kelly encouraged him to stay in touch with her? Didn't she
want to clear Chris's name? She had a stake in this too, after

all. That was all the convincing Jeffrey needed. He really needed help and Kelly seemed willing. She'd said she was willing. Of course, that was before these latest developments. He would be completely frank with her and tell her what had happened, including the gunshots. He would give her the choice again. He could understand if she didn't want to stay involved now that Devlin was back in the picture. But at least he could try her. He rationalized that she was an adult and could make her own decision about risk.

Jeffrey decided that the best way to get to Kelly's would be by taking the MBTA from the Charles Street station. He broke into a jog at the thought of himself sitting by Kelly on her gingham couch with his legs on the coffee table, and she laughing her crystalline laugh.

Carol Rhodes had just gotten home from the office. It had been an exhausting but productive day. She'd finished turning most of her clients over to other officers in the bank in anticipation of her upcoming transfer to the Los Angeles branch. After seeing the transfer put off for so many months, she'd begun to doubt that it would ever happen. But now she was confident that before too long she would be in sunny southern California.

Opening the refrigerator door, she looked to see what she could make herself for dinner. There was the cold veal left over from the dinner she'd made for Jeffrey. A lot of thanks she'd gotten for that effort. And there were plenty of salad fixings.

Before tackling dinner, she glanced at the telephone answering machine. There were no messages. She hadn't heard from Jeffrey all day. She wondered where the hell he was and what he was up to. She found out only that day that Jeffrey had kept the money he'd been able to raise from the increase in the mortgage. Forty-five thousand in cash. Just what was he planning? If she'd known he was going to behave this irresponsibly, she would never have signed the new mortgage. Let him wait out the appeal in jail. She only wished their divorce was final. At this point she wondered what had ever attracted her to the man in the first place.

Carol had met Jeffrey when she'd come to Boston to attend

Harvard Business School. She'd come from the west coast where she'd studied as an undergrad at Stanford. Maybe she'd been attracted to Jeffrey because she had been so lonely. She had been living in a dorm in Allston and hadn't known a soul when they'd met. Never in a million years had she planned on staying in Boston. It was so provincial compared to L.A. She felt the people were as cold as the climate.

Well, it would all be behind her in another week. She'd deal with Jeffrey through her lawyer and throw herself into her new job.

Just then, the doorbell rang. Carol looked at her watch. It was almost seven. She wondered who it could be. Through force of habit, she checked through the peephole before opening up. She flinched when she saw who it was.

"My husband is not at home, Mr. O'Shea," Carol called through the door. "I have no idea where he is and I don't expect him."

"I'd like to talk to you for two minutes, Mrs. Rhodes."

"What about?" Carol said. She wasn't inclined to discuss anything with that vile man.

"It's a little hard conversing through the door," Devlin answered. "I'll only take a few moments of your time."

Carol thought about calling the police. But if she did call the police, what would she say? And how would she explain Jeffrey's absence? For all she knew, this O'Shea character might be perfectly within his rights. After all, Jeffrey hadn't come through with the money he owed Mosconi. She hoped Jeffrey wasn't getting into worse trouble still.

"I just want to ask you a few questions about your husband's whereabouts," Devlin said when it appeared Carol would not answer. "Let me tell you something. If I don't find him, Mosconi will be calling in some bad dudes. Your husband could get hurt. If I find him first, maybe we can resolve this whole thing before the bail is forfeited."

Carol hadn't quite realized that Jeffrey stood to forfeit the bail money. Maybe she should think again about talking to this O'Shea person.

In addition to the regular lock and a dead bolt, the front door had a security chain that Carol and Jeffrey never used. Carol

slipped the end of the chain into its track, then released the
dead bolt and opened the door. With the security chain in
place, the door opened only about three inches.

Carol started to tell Devlin again that she had no idea where
Jeffrey was, but she never got the words out. Before she knew
what had happened, the door flew completely open with a loud
splintering sound, leaving a fractured section of the doorjamb
dangling from the chain.

Carol's first reaction was to run, but Devlin grabbed her arm
and pulled her up short. He smiled at her and even laughed.

"You cannot come into my home!" Carol shouted. She
hoped to sound authoritative, even though she was scared.
Vainly she tried to wrench her arm free from Devlin's grip.

"Really?" Devlin said, feigning surprise. "But it seems I'm
already in. Besides, this is the doctor's house, too, and I'm
curious if the little devil snuck back here after he shot me in
the ass with some kind of arrow poison. I have to say I'm
getting a little tired of your husband."

"You're not the only one," Carol was tempted to say, but she
stopped herself.

"He's not here," she said instead.

"Oh yeah?" Devlin questioned. "Well, let's you and me take
a little look around."

"I want you out!" Carol yelled as she tried to resist. But it
was no use. Devlin had a good hold on her wrist as he dragged
her from room to room while he looked for any sign of Jeffrey's having been there.

Carol kept trying to pull herself free. Just before Devlin led
her upstairs, he gave her a sudden shake. "Will you calm
down," he shouted. "You know, hiding or abetting a convicted
felon who's jumped bail is itself a felony. If the doc's here, it
would be better for you that I find him and not the police."

"He's not here," Carol told him. "I don't know where he is
and frankly I don't care!"

"Uh-oh," Devlin said, surprised at this last comment. His
grip loosened. "Are we talking a little marital discord here?"

Carol took advantage of Devlin's genuine surprise to pull
her arm free. Without missing a beat, she slapped Devlin across
the face.

Devlin was stunned for a moment. Then he laughed aloud
as he re-seized her wrist. "You *are* a feisty little thing!" he said.
"Just like your husband. If only I could believe you. Now if
you'd be so kind, I'd like to have you show me around upstairs."

Carol shrieked in fear as Devlin pulled her rapidly up the
stairs. He moved so quickly that she had trouble keeping up
with him and tripped on several of the steps, bruising her
shins.

They made a rapid tour of the upstairs. Peering into the
bedroom, which was a mess, with dirty clothes piled everywhere, and into the closet, whose floor was a chaotic jumble
of shoes, Devlin said, "Not much of a homemaker, are you?"

Being in the bedroom terrified Carol, unsure of Devlin's
true intentions. She tried to get herself under control. She
had to think of something before this pig of a man fell on top
of her.

But Devlin was clearly not interested in Carol. He dragged
her up the folding stairs into the attic, then down two flights
into the basement. It was apparent that Jeffrey was not there
and had not been there. Satisfied, he walked Carol into the
kitchen and eyed the refrigerator.

"So you were telling the truth. Now I'm going to let go of
you, but I expect you to behave. Understand?"

Carol glared at him.

"Mrs. Rhodes, I said, Understand?"

Carol nodded.

Devlin let go of her wrist. "Well now," he said. "I think I'll
just stick around in case the doctor calls or comes in for clean
undies."

"I want you to leave," Carol said angrily. "Leave or I will
call the police."

"You can't call the police," Devlin said matter-of-factly, as
if he knew something Carol didn't.

"And why not?" Carol asked indignantly.

"Because I'm not going to let you," Devlin said. He laughed
his hoarse laugh and began to cough. When he got control of
himself, he added: "I hate to tell you this, but the police don't
have a lot of concern for Jeffrey Rhodes these days. Besides,

I'm the one who's working for law and order. Jeffrey lost his rights when the conviction was handed down."

"Jeffrey was convicted," Carol said. "I wasn't."

"A mere technicality," Devlin said with a wave of his hand. "But let's talk about something more important. What's for dinner?"

Jeffrey took the trolley to Cleveland Circle and then walked up Chestnut Hill Avenue before weaving his way through the quaint suburban streets toward Kelly's. Lights were coming on in kitchens, dogs were barking, and kids were playing outside. It was a picture-perfect neighborhood with Ford Taurus station wagons pulled up in front of freshly painted garage doors. The sun was low on the horizon. It was almost dark.

Once Jeffrey had decided to go to Kelly's, all he'd wanted to do was be there. But now that he was approaching her street, he felt indecision returning. Decision-making had never been a problem before. Jeffrey had decided on a career in medicine in junior high school. When it came to buying a home, he'd simply walked through the front door of the house in Marblehead and said, "This is it." He wasn't accustomed to being so genuinely torn. When he'd finally managed to make it up the walk to her front door and ring the bell, he almost wished she wouldn't be home to answer.

"Jeffrey!" Kelly exclaimed as she opened the door. "This is the day for surprises. Come in!"

Jeffrey stepped inside and instantly realized how relieved he was that Kelly was home.

"Let me have your jacket," she said. She helped him out of it and asked what had happened to his glasses.

Jeffrey put a hand to his face. For the first time he realized he'd lost them. He guessed they'd bounced off when he'd thrown himself out of the hotel room.

"Not that I'm not glad to see you—I am. But what are you doing here?" She led the way to the family room.

"I'm afraid I had company waiting for me when I got back to my hotel room," he said, following behind her.

"Oh, God. Tell me all about it."

Once again, Jeffrey filled Kelly in. He recounted the entire episode with Devlin at the Essex Hotel, including the gunshots and the injection of succinylcholine.

Despite her dismay, Kelly had to giggle. "Only an anesthesiologist would think of injecting a bounty hunter with succinylcholine," she said.

"There's nothing funny about all this," Jeffrey said ruefully. "The real problem is that the stakes are higher. And so are the risks. Especially if Devlin finds me again. I had a hard time deciding to come over here. I think you should reconsider your offer to help."

"Nonsense," Kelly said. "In fact, after you left the hospital today I could have kicked myself for not inviting you to stay here."

Jeffrey studied Kelly's face. Her sincerity was disarming. She was so obviously concerned. "This Devlin character shot at me," Jeffrey repeated. "Twice. Real bullets, and he was laughing like he was having a good time at a turkey shoot. I just want to make sure you understand the degree of danger that's involved here."

Kelly looked Jeffrey straight in the eye. "I understand perfectly," she said. "I also understand that I have a guest room and you are in need of a place to stay. In fact, I'll be offended if you don't take me up on my offer. Now is it a deal?"

"It's a deal," Jeffrey said, barely suppressing a smile.

"Good. Now that that's settled, let's get you something to eat. I'll bet you haven't had anything to eat all day."

"Not true," Jeffrey said. "I had an apple and a banana."

"How about some spaghetti?" Kelly said. "I can have that ready in half an hour."

"Spaghetti would be great."

Kelly went into the kitchen. In a few minutes she had some diced onions and garlic sautéing in an old iron skillet.

"I never went back to my hotel room once I got away from Devlin," Jeffrey told her. He was leaning over the back of the couch so he could watch Kelly's activities in the kitchen.

"Well, I should hope not." She got some ground beef from the refrigerator.

"I only mentioned it because I'm afraid I've lost Chris's notes—the ones I borrowed."

"No problem," Kelly said. "I told you I was going to get rid of them anyway. You saved me the trouble."

"I'm still sorry."

Kelly began to open a can of peeled Italian tomatoes with an electric opener. Over the whir of the motor she said, "By the way, I forgot to tell you. I talked to Charlotte Henning over at Valley Hospital. She told me that they get their Marcaine from Ridgeway Pharmaceuticals."

Jeffrey's jaw dropped. "Ridgeway?"

"That's right," Kelly said as she added the ground beef to the onions and the garlic. "She said Ridgeway's been their supplier since Marcaine went generic."

Jeffrey faced around on the couch and stared out the window at the darkened garden outside. He was stunned. The idea that the Marcaine from Memorial and Valley had come from the same pharmaceutical manufacturer was crucial to his theory of a contaminant. If the Marcaine used in the Noble and Owen operations were from different suppliers, there was no way to argue that they'd come from the same contaminated batch.

Unaware of the effect of her information on Jeffrey, Kelly added the tomatoes and some tomato paste to the beef and the onions and garlic. She sprinkled in some oregano, stirred, and lowered the gas for the mixture to simmer. She got out a large pot, filled it with water, and set it on the stove to boil.

Jeffrey joined her by the kitchen counter.

Kelly could sense something was wrong. "What's the matter?" she asked.

Jeffrey sighed. "If Valley uses Ridgeway, then the idea of a contaminant is out the window. Marcaine comes in sealed glass containers, and any contaminant would have to be introduced during manufacture."

Kelly wiped her hands on a towel. "Couldn't a contaminant be added later?"

"I doubt it."

"What about after the vial is opened?" Kelly suggested.

"No," Jeffrey said with finality. "I open my own vials and extract the drug immediately. I'm sure Chris would have done the same."

"Well, there has to be a way," Kelly said. "Don't give up so easily. That's probably what Chris did."

"To get a contaminant into one of those ampules would mean penetrating the glass," Jeffrey said almost angrily. "It can't be done. Capsules yes, glass ampules no." But even as he said this, Jeffrey began to wonder. He remembered chemistry lab in college, where he'd been required to fashion pipettes using a Bunsen burner and glass rods. He could remember the taffylike feel of the molten glass as he'd wait until it was red hot before he pulling it out into a wispy cylinder.

"Do you have any syringes here?" he asked.

"I still have Chris's medical bag," she said. "There might be some in there. Shall I get it?"

Jeffrey nodded, then went over to the stove and turned on one of the front burners next to the simmering spaghetti sauce. The flame would certainly be hot enough. When Kelly returned with Chris's bag, he took a few syringes and a couple of ampules of bicarbonate from it.

He heated the tip of the syringe until the metal glowed red hot. Taking it from the fire, he quickly tried to push it into the glass. It didn't penetrate well. Then he tried heating the glass and using a cold needle, but that didn't work either. Then he tried heating both the needle and the glass, and the needle went through easily.

Jeffrey pulled the needle out of the ampule and studied the glass. Its once smooth surface was misshapen and a tiny hole remained where the needle had been inserted. Placing the ampule back over the burner, the glass became soft again, but as he tried to rotate it, the molten glass distorted more, and he only succeeded in burning himself and making a mess of the whole end of the ampule.

"What do you think?" Kelly asked, squinting over his shoulder to see.

"I think you're right," Jeffrey said, newly hopeful. "It might be possible. It's not that easy. I certainly made a mess of this one. But it suggests it could be done. A hotter flame might help, or one that can be better directed."

Kelly got Jeffrey a piece of ice and wrapped it in a dishtowel for his burned finger. "What kind of contaminant are you thinking about?" she asked.

"I don't know specifically," Jeffrey admitted, "but I'm thinking about some kind of toxin. Whatever it is, it would have to exert its effects in very low concentration. Plus from what Chris had written, it would have to cause nerve cell damage without causing kidney or liver damage. That eliminates a lot of the usual poisons. Maybe I'll know more when I get my hands on Patty Owen's autopsy report. I'll be very interested to see the toxicology section. I'd seen it briefly during discovery for both trials and I remember it was negative except for a trace of Marcaine. But I'd never examined it closely. It hadn't seemed important at the time."

With the water boiling furiously in the pot, Kelly tossed in the pasta. She turned to face Jeffrey. "If this is how the toxin got in the Marcaine"—she pointed to the ampule and syringe Jeffrey had set on the counter—"it means that someone is tampering with Marcaine on purpose, deliberately poisoning."

"Murdering," Jeffrey said.

"My God," Kelly said. The full horror was beginning to dawn on her. "Why?" she asked with a shudder. "Why would someone do that?"

Jeffrey shrugged. "That's a question I'm not prepared to answer. It wouldn't be the first time someone's tampered with medication or purposely used it to no good. Who can say what the motivation is? The Tylenol killer. That New Jersey Doctor X, the one who killed patients with overdoses of succinylcholine."

"And now this." Kelly was visibly shaken. The idea of some crazy person stalking the halls of Boston hospitals was too much to take in. "If you believe this might be true," she said, "don't you think we should talk to the police?"

"I wish we could," Jeffrey said. "But we can't for two reasons. First of all, I'm a convicted criminal and a fugitive. But even if I weren't, we have to recognize that there is not the slightest bit of proof of any of this. If anyone went to the police with this story, I doubt very much they would do anything at all. We need some sort of evidence before we go to the authorities."

"But we have to stop this person!"

"I agree," Jeffrey said. "Before there are any more deaths and any more convicted physicians."

Kelly said her next words so softly that Jeffrey could barely hear. "Before there are any more suicides." Her eyes filled with tears.

To hold her emotions in check, Kelly turned to the boiling pasta. She fished out a strand of the spaghetti and threw it at the front of the dish cabinet. It stuck. Wiping her eyes, she said, "Let's eat."

"I'll call you as soon as the procedure is over," Karen Hodges told her mother. She'd been on the phone for almost an hour and was beginning to feel a little irritated. She felt like her mother should be trying to comfort her, not vice versa.

"Are you sure this doctor is okay?" Mrs. Hodges asked.

Karen rolled her eyes for the benefit of her roommate, Marcia Ginsburg, who smiled in sympathy. Marcia knew exactly what Karen was going through. Marcia's mother's calls were just as nagging. She was constantly warning her daughter about men, AIDS, drugs, and her weight.

"He's fine, Mother," Karen said without bothering to disguise her exasperation.

"Tell me again how you found him," Mrs. Hodges said.

"Mother—I told you a million times."

"All right, all right," Mrs. Hodges said. "You just be sure to call me as soon as you can, you hear?" She knew her daughter was annoyed, but she couldn't help being concerned. She'd suggested to her husband that they fly to Boston to be with Karen when she went in for the laparoscopy, but Mr. Hodges said he couldn't leave the office. Besides, as he'd pointed out, a laparoscopy was only a diagnostic procedure, not a "real operation."

"It's real if it concerns my baby," Mrs. Hodges had replied. But in the end she and Mr. Hodges remained in Chicago.

"I'll call you as soon as I can," Karen said.

"Tell me what kind of anesthesia you're going to have," Mrs. Hodges said, hoping to stall her daughter. She didn't want to hang up.

"Epidural," Karen told her.

"Spell it."

Karen spelled it.

"Don't they use that for deliveries?"

"Yes," Karen said. "And also for procedures like laparosco-
pies when they aren't sure how long it will take. The doctor
doesn't know what he's going to see. It might take awhile, and
he didn't want me unconscious."

"Come on, Ma, you went through this with Cheryl." Cheryl
was Karen's older sister, and she too had trouble with endometriosis.

"You're not having an abortion, are you?" Mrs. Hodges
asked.

"Mother, I have to go," Karen said. The last question had
pushed her over the edge. Now she was angry. After all this
talk, her mother thought she was lying to her. It was ridiculous.

"Call me," Mrs. Hodges managed to get in before Karen
hung up.

Karen turned to Marcia and the two women looked at each
other for a moment, then burst out laughing.

"Mothers!" Karen said.

"A unique species," Marcia said.

"She doesn't seem to want to believe that I'm twenty-three
and out of college," Karen said. "Three years from now when
I graduate from law school, I wonder if she'll still be treating
me the same way."

"No doubt in my mind," Marcia said.

Karen had graduated from Simmons College the year before
and was currently working as a legal secretary for an aggressive and successful divorce lawyer named Gerald McLellan.
McLellan had become more a mentor than a boss to her.
Recognizing her intelligence, he had urged her to go to law
school. She was scheduled to begin at Boston College in the
fall.

Although Karen was the picture of general health, she'd
suffered from endometriosis since puberty. Over the last year,
the problem had worsened. Her doctor had finally scheduled
her for a laparoscopy to decide on treatment.

"You have no idea how happy I am that you're going with
me tomorrow, not my mother," Karen said. "She'd drive me
bananas."

"It'll be my pleasure," Marcia said. She'd arranged to take the day off from work at the Bank of Boston to accompany Karen to day surgery and then escort her home unless it turned out Karen was to stay overnight. But Karen's doctor thought it very unlikely that would happen.

"I am a little worried about going tomorrow," Karen admitted. Except for a visit to an emergency room after falling from a bicycle when she was ten, she'd never been in a hospital.

"It will be a breeze," Marcia assured her. "I was worried before my appendectomy, but it was nothing. Really."

"I've never had any anesthesia," Karen said. "What if it doesn't work and I feel everything?"

"Haven't you ever had a shot at the dentist?"

Karen shook her head. "Nope. I've never had a cavity."

Trent Harding moved the glassware from the cabinet next to the refrigerator and took out the false back. Reaching in, he pulled out the .45 pistol and let it rest in his hand. He loved the gun. There was a slight smear of oil on the barrel from the last time he'd handled it. He took a paper towel and lovingly polished it.

Reaching back into the hiding place, he pulled out the clip loaded with shells. Holding the gun in his left hand, he inserted the clip in the bottom of the handle. Then he pushed it home so that it clicked in place. The maneuver gave him a feeling akin to sensual pleasure.

Hefting the gun again, it felt different now that it was loaded. Holding it the way Crockett had on *Miami Vice*, he aimed it through the kitchen door at the Harley-Davidson poster that hung on the living room wall. For a second he debated with himself if he could get away with firing the pistol in his own apartment. But he decided it wasn't worth the risk. A .45 made one hell of a bang. He didn't want the neighbors calling the cops.

He laid the gun on the table and went back to his secret cache. He reached in and pulled out the small vial with the yellow fluid. He shook it and looked at it in the light. For the life of him, he had no idea how they got the liquid from the skin of frogs. He'd bought it from a Colombian drug dealer in

Miami. The stuff was great. It had turned out to be everything the guy had promised it would be.

With a small 5 cc syringe, Trent drew up a tiny bit of the fluid, then diluted it with sterile water. Under the circumstances, he didn't have any idea how much to use. He had no experience to rely on for what he was planning now.

Trent carefully returned the vial to its hiding place, then replaced the plywood and the glassware. He capped the syringe full of the diluted toxin and pocketed it. Then he tucked the pistol into his belt so that its barrel was cold against the small of his back.

Going to the front closet, Trent got out his Levi's denim jacket and put it on. Then he checked in his bathroom mirror to make sure the gun couldn't be seen. From the way the jacket was cut, there wasn't even a bulge.

He hated losing his parking spot on Beacon Hill, knowing he'd have a devil of a time finding another when he returned, but what were his options? He covered the distance to St. Joe's in a quarter of the time it took him to go there on public transportation. That was another thing that bothered him about doctors. They got to park at the hospital during the day. Nurses were not allowed unless they were supervisors, or they worked either the evening or the night shift.

Trent parked in the public lot, but chose a slot close to the employee parking area. He locked his car and strolled into the hospital. One of the lady volunteers asked if she could help him, but he said no, he was fine. He got a *Globe* from the hospitality shop and parked himself in the corner. He was early, but he didn't want to take any chances. He wanted to be there when Gail Shaffer got off work.

Devlin burped. Beer sometimes did that to him. He glanced over at Carol, who gave him a disgusted look. She was seated opposite him in the family room, leafing through magazines by angrily flipping the pages. She was obviously irritated.

Devlin switched his attention back to the Red Sox game, which he found relaxing. If they'd been winning, he'd have been nervous they would blow it. But they'd accommodated

him by being behind by six runs. It was pretty obvious they
were going to lose another one.

At least he'd eaten well. The cold veal chops and salad had
hit the spot. So did the four beers. He'd never heard of Kronenbourg before visiting the Rhodes's household. It wasn't bad,
even though he would still have preferred a Bud.

The doctor had failed to materialize or call. Although Devlin
had gotten a decent meal out of the vigil, he'd had to put up
with Carol. After an evening with her, he could see why the
good doctor didn't choose to come home.

Devlin let himself sink a little farther into the comfy couch
in front of the TV. He'd removed his cowboy boots and had
his stocking feet propped up on one of the straight-backed
kitchen chairs. He sighed. It was a hell of a lot better than
keeping watch in his car, even if the Sox were losing. Devlin
blinked. For a second he'd felt himself drifting off to sleep.

Carol couldn't believe this was how she was having to spend
one of her last nights in Boston: entertaining a thug who was
interested in Jeffrey's whereabouts. If she never saw her soon
to be ex-husband again, it would be too soon. Maybe she would
like to see him once, just so she could let him know what she
thought of him.

Carol had been watching Devlin out of the corner of her eye.
For a moment he seemed to be falling asleep. But then he got
up to get yet another beer. But soon he was back in the same
almost horizontal position with his eyes nearly closed.

Finally, during a commercial, Devlin's head dropped onto
his chest. The beer bottle he'd been holding tilted, to pour
some of its contents onto the carpeted floor. His breathing
became stertorous. He'd fallen sound asleep.

Carol stayed where she was, holding her magazine, afraid to
turn a page for fear of rousing Devlin. There was a sudden roar
from the TV set as one of the players hit a home run. Carol
winced, thinking the noise would surely wake Devlin, but he
only began to snore more loudly.

Carol slowly eased herself up out of the chair to a standing
position. She placed her magazine on top of the TV.

Taking a slow, deep breath, she tiptoed past Devlin, through
the kitchen, and up the stairs. The minute she got inside her

bedroom, she closed and locked her door and picked up the phone. Without hesitation, she dialed 911 and told the operator that she had an intruder in her house and needed the police immediately. She calmly gave her address. If Jeffrey could handle his problems his way, she could handle hers. The operator assured her that help was on its way.

Meanwhile, Carol went into her bathroom. For good measure, she closed and locked the door. She put down the seat on the toilet and sat down to wait. In less than ten minutes the front door chimes rang. Only then did Carol emerge from the bathroom, cross through the bedroom and listen at the door. She heard the front door open, then the murmur of voices.

Opening the bedroom door, Carol went to the top of the stairs. Below, she could hear conversation, and then, to her surprise, laughter!

She started down the stairs. In the foyer by the front door, two uniformed policemen were chuckling over something and thumping Devlin on the back as if they were all the best of friends.

"Excuse me!" Carol said in a loud voice from the bottom step.

The three looked up.

"Carol, dear," Devlin said, "there appears to be some kind of mixup. Somebody called the police about an intruder."

"I called the police," Carol said. She pointed at Devlin. "He's the intruder."

"Me?" Devlin said with exaggerated surprise. He turned his attention to the two policemen. "Now that's one for the books. I was in the family room, asleep in front of the TV. How's that for an intruder? In fact, Carol here had just fixed me a great dinner. She'd invited me . . ."

"I never invited him!" Carol yelled.

"If you boys would like to go into the kitchen you'll see the soiled dishes from our romantic dinner. I guess I was somewhat of a disappointment, falling asleep as I did."

The two policemen smiled in spite of themselves.

"He forced me to make dinner," Carol snapped.

Devlin seemed genuinely hurt.

With marked indignation, Carol strode across the foyer and

grasped the chain with its attached piece of doorjamb. She waved it at the policemen. "Does this look like I invited that pig in here?"

"I have no idea how that got broken," Devlin said. "I certainly had nothing to do with it." He rolled his eyes for the policemen's benefit. "But, Harold, Willy, if the little lady wants me to leave, I'll leave. I mean, she could have just asked me to go. I'd hate to stay where I'm not wanted."

"Willy, why don't you take Mr. O'Shea outside for a moment?" said the older of the two policemen. "I'll have a chat with Mrs. Rhodes."

Devlin had to go back into the family room for his boots. After he'd pulled them on, he and Willy went outside and stood next to the police cruiser. "Women," Devlin said, cocking his head toward the Rhodes's house. "They're such trouble. It's always something!"

"Wow, she's a fireball," Harold said, coming out of the house and joining the others. "Devlin, what the hell did you do to get her so riled up?"

Devlin shrugged. "Maybe I hurt her feelings. How was I to know she'd take my falling asleep so personal? All I want to do is find her husband, hopefully before his bail is forfeited."

"Well, I managed to calm her down," Harold said. "But please use discretion and don't break anything else."

"Discretion? Hell, that's my middle name," Devlin said with a laugh. "Sorry to cause you boys any inconvenience."

Harold went on to ask Devlin about one of the other Boston policemen who'd been bounced from the force along with Devlin during the bribery scandal. Devlin told him that the last he'd heard of the man was that he'd moved to Florida and was working as a private detective in the Miami area.

With final handshakes all around, they got in their cars and pulled away. When they got to West Shore Drive, the cops turned left, Devlin right. But Devlin didn't go far. He looped around and eventually cruised past the Rhodes's house again. He parked where he could keep the place under observation. Since Jeffrey hadn't shown up or called, he lamented the fact that he would have to rehire the guy he'd had following Carol.

But after this evening, he wasn't as confident as he had been that Carol would lead him to Jeffrey. Mosconi's comment about them not being so lovey-dovey, combined with Carol's behavior and a few stray comments here and there, made Devlin think he might have to come up with another idea for locating Jeffrey. But one thing that was going to make things easier was that he'd managed to put a bug on Carol's telephone while she'd been preparing their dinner. If Jeffrey did call, he'd know about it.

Looking around Kelly's guest room, Jeffrey decided to leave his duffel bag under the bed. He thought it would be as safe there as anyplace. He elected not to tell Kelly about the money lest it add to her worries.

Emerging from the guest room, Jeffrey found Kelly in her bedroom, propped up in bed with a novel. Her door was ajar as if she was expecting him to say good-bye when he left. She had on pink cotton pajamas with dark green piping. Curled up on her bed with her were two cats, one Siamese, the other a tawny tabby.

"Well, isn't this the picture of domesticity," Jeffrey said. He glanced around the room. It was wonderfully feminine, with French country-style wallpaper and matching drapes. It was easy to see that care had been taken with all the details. There were no clothes visible and Jeffrey couldn't help but contrast the scene with Carol's chaotic lair.

"I was just about to come in and make sure you were awake," Kelly said. "I guess we'll miss each other in the morning. I have to leave here by six forty-five. I'll put the front door key inside the carriage lamp."

"You haven't reconsidered my staying here?"

Kelly frowned in mock chagrin. "I thought we'd settled that. I definitely want you to stay. It was my impression we were in this together. Especially now, with that fiend out there."

Jeffrey stepped into the room and walked over to the side of the bed. The Siamese lifted its head and spat.

"Come on now, Samson, let's not be jealous," Kelly scolded. To Jeffrey she said, "He's not used to a man in the house."

"Who are these critters?" Jeffrey asked. "How come I haven't seen them before?"

"This is Samson," Kelly said, pointing to the Siamese. "He's out a good deal of the time, terrorizing the neighborhood. And this is Delilah. She's pregnant, as you can see. She sleeps all day in the pantry."

"They married?" Jeffrey asked.

Kelly laughed in her characteristic way. Jeffrey smiled. He didn't think his little joke was that funny, but Kelly's mirth was infectious.

Jeffrey cleared his throat. "Kelly," he began, "I don't know how to say this, but you don't have any idea how much I appreciate your understanding and hospitality. I can't thank you enough."

Kelly looked down at Delilah and gave her a loving stroke. Jeffrey thought she was blushing, but it was tough to judge in the light.

"I just wanted you to know that," Jeffrey added. Then, changing the subject, he said, "So I guess I'll talk to you sometime tomorrow."

"You be careful!" Kelly commanded. "And good luck. If you run into any problem, call me. I don't care about the time."

"There won't be any trouble," Jeffrey said confidently. But half an hour later, when he was climbing the steps to Boston Memorial, he wasn't so sure. Despite the confidence he'd gained through the course of his tour of the hospital with Martinez, Jeffrey was again concerned about running into someone he knew well. He wished he hadn't lost his glasses and only hoped they weren't crucial to his disguise.

Jeffrey felt somewhat more confident once he'd changed into his housekeeping uniform. There was even an envelope hanging on the outside of his locker, containing his name tag and a photo ID.

A tap on his shoulder made him jump and Jeffrey's sudden movement startled the person who'd tapped him.

"Cool it, man, you nervous or what?"

"I'm sorry," Jeffrey said. He was standing before a small fellow, about five-six, with a narrow face and dark features. "I guess I am a bit nervous. It's my first night on the job."

"No need to be nervous," the man said. "My name is David Arnold. I'm the shift supervisor. For the first couple of nights, we'll be working together. So don't worry. I'll show you the ropes."

"Glad to meet you," Jeffrey said. "But I do have a lot of hospital experience, so if you want me to go off on my own, I'm sure I'll be fine."

"I always spend the first couple of days with anybody new," David said. "Don't take it personally. It gives me a chance to show you exactly what is expected according to our routine here at the Memorial."

Jeffrey felt it best not to argue. David took him into a narrow, windowless lounge modestly furnished with a Formica table, a soft-drink vending machine, and an electric coffee maker. He introduced Jeffrey to the others who worked the graveyard shift. Two spoke only Spanish. Another spoke street slang, and he bounced and swayed to the rap music coming from a pair of headphones.

At one minute before eleven, David rallied his workers: "Okay, let's move out," reminding Jeffrey of patrols going out in war movies. They left the lounge and each picked out housekeeping carts. Each worker was responsible for stocking his own cart. Jeffrey followed the lead of the others, making sure his cart had the necessary complement of cleaning implements and solutions.

The carts were about twice the size of a normal shopping cart. One end had housing for long-handled equipment like mops, a long-handled duster, and brooms. The other end had a large plastic bag for refuse. The center portion had three shelves. They carried all sorts of things, like glass cleaner, tile cleaner, Formica cleaner, paper towels, even spare toilet paper rolls. There were soaps, waxes, polishes, and even WD-40 lubricant.

Jeffrey followed David to the elevators of the west tower. The choice was both encouraging and nerve-racking. The west tower included the ORs and labs. For as much as Jeffrey wanted to probe there, he remained apprehensive about whom he might run into.

"You and I will start up in the OR area," David explained, fanning Jeffrey's fears. "Have you ever put on a scrub suit?"

"Couple of times," Jeffrey said distractedly.

He began to worry that once he put on a scrub suit, he would be losing most of the rest of his disguise. He wished he had the black-rimmed glasses. The only thing he thought he could do would be to wear a surgical mask constantly. David would probably question that, since a mask was usually only worn in an OR when a case was under way. Jeffrey decided that he'd say he had a cold.

But they didn't go into the OR area immediately. David told Jeffrey that the surgical lounge and locker rooms had to be tackled first.

"Why don't you do the lounge, and I'll start in the locker rooms?" David said once they were in the area. Jeffrey nodded. He peeked into the room, then quickly pulled his head back out again. Two nurse-anesthetists were sitting on the couch having coffee. Jeffrey knew them both.

"Something wrong?" David asked.

"Not at all," Jeffrey said quickly.

"You're going to do fine," David told him. "Don't worry. First dust. Be sure to get the corners up by the ceiling. Then use a cleaner on the tables. Then mop. Okay?"

Jeffrey nodded.

David pushed his cart into the locker room and closed the door behind him.

Jeffrey swallowed. He had to start. Taking the long-handled duster from the cart, he went into the lounge. At first he tried to keep his face averted from the women. But they didn't pay him the slightest attention. His housekeeping uniform was as good as a cloak of invisibility.

With her knapsack over her shoulder, Gail Shaffer got off the elevator with Regina Puksar. They walked down the central corridor together toward the main entrance. The two had known each other for almost five years. They often discussed their personal problems even though they didn't socialize that much outside of the hospital. Gail had been telling Regina about the fight she'd had with her boyfriend of two years.

"I agree with you," Regina said. "If Robert suddenly said to me he wanted to date other people, I'd say fine, but that would be it in terms of us. A relationship can't go backward. Either it grows or it dies. At least that's been my experience."

"Mine too," Gail sighed.

Neither noticed as Trent folded his newspaper and got to his feet. As they went through the revolving door, Trent was right behind them. He could hear their conversation.

Certain that the women were headed to the employee parking lot, Trent gave them a little lead, but kept them in view. The two stood next to a sporty red Pontiac Fiero and talked for another few minutes. Finally, they said their good-byes. Then Gail got into the car. Regina went a few spaces over to her own car.

Trent went to his Corvette and climbed in. It wasn't the best car to tail someone in since it was so flashy, but he didn't think it would matter in this case. There was no reason for Gail to be suspicious.

Gail's car was equally as flashy, which made it easy to follow. She headed straight for Back Bay, just as Trent had guessed from her phone number. She double-parked on Boylston Street and disappeared into a Store-24.

Trent pulled across the street, since Boylston was one way, and stopped in a taxi area. From there he could easily keep an eye on the store and Gail's car. When Gail emerged with a single parcel and got back into her car, he waited for her to pull out. Then he slipped right in behind her.

She turned left on Berkeley, then slowed down. Trent could tell she'd begun to hunt for a parking place, no easy matter this time of night. He let the distance between them lengthen. She finally found a spot on Marlborough Street, but then took forever to back into it.

"Incompetent bitch," Trent murmured as he watched her third attempt to back in and parallel park. Trent had pulled into a no parking zone. He didn't care. If he got a ticket, so what? This was business; any expense he incurred would be a legitimate business expense. The only thing he didn't want was to have his car towed, but from experience he knew there was little chance of that happening.

Gail finally pulled in to her satisfaction, if not Trent's. The car was still a good foot from the curb. She got out, bundle in hand, locked her doors and started off on foot. Trent kept an eye on her but remained out of sight on the opposite side of the street. He watched Gail turn left on Berkeley and right on Beacon. A few doors down Beacon, she entered one of the brownstones.

After waiting a few minutes, Trent went into the building and scanned the list of names posted by each resident's buzzer. He found "G. Shaffer" listed along with an "A. Winthrop."

"Damn it to hell," Trent said under his breath. He'd hoped Gail lived alone. Nothing was ever easy, he thought. Still fuming, he went back out to the street. He couldn't go barging into Gail's apartment if she had a roommate. He couldn't have any witnesses. That would never do.

Trent glanced up Beacon Street, toward Boston Garden. He saw he was close to the popular bar made famous by the TV series *Cheers*. That's when a plan began to take shape in his mind. Maybe he could get Gail or her roommate out of the apartment.

Leaving the building, Trent walked the short distance to the Hampshire House. There he used a pay phone to dial the number for Gail that he'd taken from the bulletin board in the OR lounge. As the phone rang, he thought up various ploys. It all depended who answered. "Hello," said the voice at the other end of the line. It was Gail.

"Ms. Winthrop, please," Trent said.

"Sorry, she's not at home."

Trent's mood brightened. Maybe this was going to be easy after all. "Could you please tell me when she'll be in?"

"Who is this?"

"A friend of the family's," Trent said. "I'm in town on business and was given her number to say hello."

"She's currently working the night shift at St. Joseph's Hospital," Gail said. "Would you like that number? You could try her there. Otherwise, she'll be back here around seven-thirty tomorrow morning if you prefer to call back."

Trent pretended to take the St. Joseph's number, thanked Gail and hung up. He couldn't repress a smile.

Leaving Hampshire House, he hurried back to Gail's building. Now all he had to do was get in there. He stepped into the foyer and put on a pair of black driving gloves. Then he rang her buzzer.

In a minute, Gail's voice crackled through the mesh-covered speaker.

"Gail, is that you?" Trent asked, even though he was quite sure it was.

"Yes. Who's this?"

"Duncan Wagner," Trent said. It was the first name that came to his mind. The Wagners had lived next to the Hardings at the army base in San Antonio. Duncan was a few years older than Trent and they had played together until Duncan's father had deemed Trent a bad influence.

"Do I know you?" Gail questioned.

"By sight, if not by name," Trent said. "I work evenings in pedes." Trent thought pediatrics sounded the most benign.

"On the third floor?"

"That's right," Trent said. "I hope I'm not disturbing you, but a group of us from the hospital ended up at the Bull Finch Pub. Your name came up. Someone said you lived just up the street. We played Wales Tails to see who would come and get you to join us. Looks like I won."

"That's nice of you," Gail said, "but I just got home and just got off work."

"So did we. Come on over. You'll know everybody."

"Who else is there?"

"Regina Puksar, for one," Trent said.

"I just left her. She said she was going over to her boyfriend's."

"What can I say? Maybe she changed her mind. Maybe her boyfriend wasn't around. Anyway, she came in and joined us. She was big on having someone come get you. She thought you could use the break."

There was a pause. Trent smiled. He knew he had her.

"I'm still in my uniform," Gail said.

"So are a few of the others." Trent had an answer for everything.

"Well, I'd have to take a shower."

"No problem," Trent said. "I'll wait."

"I can meet you there."

"No, I'll wait. Just buzz me in."

"It will take me ten minutes or so," Gail said.

"Take all the time you need."

"Okay," Gail said. "If you don't mind waiting. I live in 3C."

Suddenly the lock on the inner door to the foyer began to buzz. Trent leaped for it and pushed. Stepping through, he smiled again. This wasn't just going to be easy, it was going to be fun. He checked his gun. It was still secure. Next he checked the syringe. It was safe in his pocket.

Trent climbed quickly to the third floor. The trick was to get into Gail's apartment before anyone saw him. If he ran into one of the other tenants in the hallway, he would pretend he was going somewhere else. But there was no one in sight in the third floor corridor. What's more, Gail had left her door open for him. He stepped inside and closed and locked the door. The last thing he wanted now was to be interrupted. Trent heard water running in the bathroom. Gail was already in the shower.

"Make yourself at home," Gail called once she heard the front door close. "I'll be out in a flash."

Trent took a look around. First he went to the kitchen. No one was there. Then he checked the second bedroom. Turning on the light, he saw that it was empty. Gail was by herself. The setup was perfect.

Taking out his beloved gun, Trent wrapped his hand around the grip, gently resting a finger on the trigger. It was such a perfect fit. Stepping over to Gail's bedroom door, Trent gave it a careful push. The door swung open a few inches. Trent looked in. The bed was unmade. Gail's nurse's uniform was casually draped across it. On the floor was a pair of panties, a pair of white stockings, and a garter belt. The door to the bathroom was closed, but Trent could still hear water running.

Trent stepped over to the garter belt and nudged it with his foot. His mother had always worn one. She'd told him a dozen times that pantyhose were uncomfortable. Since his mother insisted he sleep with her while his father was off on his numerous army missions, Trent grew up seeing a lot more of the garter belts than he would have liked.

Trent quietly edged over to the bathroom door and tried it. The knob turned easily. He cracked the door open about an inch. A waft of warm, moist air escaped. Trent pointed the gun barrel at the ceiling, like Don Johnson in *Miami Vice*. He was holding it with both hands. Using his foot, he pushed the door completely open. The bathroom fixtures were old-fashioned. The tub was an old porcelain model on legs with claw-shaped feet. The white shower curtain with large irises printed across it was drawn. Behind the curtain, Trent could make out Gail's silhouette as she shampooed her hair. Trent took two steps toward the tub and yanked the curtain back with one fluid move. The curtain rod gave way and clattered to the floor, along with the curtain.

Gail put her arms across her chest. "What . . . Who the . . ." she sputtered. Then, angrily, she shouted, "Get out!"

Water streamed down Gail's well-lathered body. It took a

moment for Trent to regain his composure. Gail certainly had
a better figure than Trent's mother had had.

"Get out of the shower," he said, coolly leveling the gun at
Gail so she would be sure to see.

"Out!" he said again when she didn't move. But Gail was
frozen in terror. Trent put the gun to her head to urge her out.

Gail started to scream. Within the confines of the bathroom,
it was a horrid screech. To stop her quickly, Trent lifted the
gun high and brought the butt down on her head hard. He hit
her just at the hairline.

The instant he struck her he knew he'd hit her too hard. Gail
crumpled into the tub in a limp heap. A long gash ran across
her forehead and down as far as her ear. The wound looked
deep, and Trent could see bone at its base. In only a minute
there was so much blood that it turned the whole tub pink.

Trent leaned in and turned off the shower. Then he darted
into the living room to listen for sounds of help on the way.
Somewhere a TV set was on. Other than that, there wasn't a
sound. He put his ear to the door; the hallway was quiet. No
one had heard Gail's scream; if they had, it didn't seem as if
anyone was coming to her aid. Trent went back to the bathroom.

Gail had ended up in a semi-sitting position, with her legs
tucked underneath her and her head resting in the corner
against the wall. Her eyes were closed. The gash was oozing
blood but the flow had slowed without the shower water hitting it.

Shoving his pistol back into his belt, Trent grabbed Gail by
her legs and began to pull her out lengthwise. But he stopped.
He felt his anger flare. Seeing Gail's naked body lying before
him he expected to feel some kind of sexual arousal, but he
didn't feel anything except perhaps disgust. Maybe a little
panic.

With sudden rage, he pulled his gun back out. Holding it
by the barrel, he raised the butt high over his head. He wanted
to smash Gail's calm face. He was just about to bring his arm
down hard when he caught himself. Slowly he lowered the
gun. For as much as he wanted to mutilate her, he knew it
would be a mistake. The beauty of his plan was that Gail's

death would seem to have been due to natural causes, not murder.

Putting his gun back in his belt, Trent pulled out the syringe. Removing the cap from the needle, he bent over. Taking advantage of the gash, and thereby avoiding a puncture site, he injected the contents of the syringe directly into the wound.

Trent stood up. He put the cap back on the needle and slipped the empty syringe back into his pocket. Then he waited and watched. Within a minute, muscle fasciculations contorted Gail's face, distorting her still, placid lips into a grotesque grimace. The fasciculations quickly spread to the rest of her body. After a few minutes more, the muscle twitches coalesced into violent jerks followed by a full-blown seizure. Gail's head smashed helplessly against the hard tile wall, then even against the hardware, with a sickening sound. Trent winced as he watched.

Trent backed away, awed by the drug's power. The effect was truly horrifying, especially when Gail was suddenly incontinent. Trent turned and fled into the living room.

Opening the door to the hallway, he glanced up and down the stairs. Thankfully, no one was there. Stepping out, he pulled the door shut. He then tiptoed to the stairs and made his way down to the ground floor. He left the building, making it a point to walk casually, as if he was simply out for a stroll. He wanted to be sure not to call attention to himself in any way.

Feeling nervous and upset, he turned right on Beacon Street and headed back to the Bull Finch Pub. He didn't understand why he felt so unsettled. He'd expected to be excited by the violence, like when he watched the *Miami Vice* reruns.

As he walked he told himself that Gail wasn't all that attractive. In fact she must have been pretty ugly. That had to be the explanation that her nakedness hadn't turned him on. She was just too damn skinny, with hardly any chest at all. The one thing Trent was sure of was that he wasn't a homosexual. The Navy had just used that as an excuse because he didn't get along with the doctors.

Just to prove to himself how normal he was, Trent made it a point to introduce himself to a perky brunette secretary at the

bar. She wasn't very attractive either. But it didn't matter. As
they chatted, he could tell she was impressed by his body. She
even asked him if he worked out. What a stupid question, he
thought. Any man who cared about himself worked out. The
only men that didn't work out were those limp-wristed fags
that Trent occasionally ran into on Cambridge Street when he
went out looking for a fight.

It didn't take long for Jeffrey to get the surgical lounge looking
cleaner than it had in years. Housekeeping had a closet in the
hall just outside the lounge. There, Jeffrey found a vacuum
cleaner. He used it to vacuum not only the lounge, but also the
dictation area and the hallway all the way to the elevators.
Next, he attacked the small kitchen off the surgical lounge.
He'd always felt the place was filthy. He actually enjoyed the
chance to clean it up. He even cleaned the refrigerator, stove,
and sink.

David still hadn't come back. Going into the locker room,
Jeffrey found out why. David's modus operandi was to work
for five or ten minutes, then take a five or ten minute break to
smoke a cigarette. Sometimes he broke for a cigarette and
coffee.

David didn't seem pleased that Jeffrey had accomplished so
much in so little time. He told Jeffrey to slow down or he'd
suffer a "cleaning burnout." But Jeffrey felt it harder to stand
around doing nothing than it was to work.

Once David gave up on any notion of the supervision game,
he gave Jeffrey his own set of passkeys. He told Jeffrey he
could head into the OR suite itself. "I'll stay here and finish the
locker room," he said. "Then I'll be in to help you. Start in the
OR corridor. Be sure to hit the big blackboard. In fact, do that
first. The director of nursing has a fit whenever we forget to
wash it down. Then hit any of the ORs that have been used
tonight. The others should have been cleaned during the evening shift."

Jeffrey would have preferred to go straight to pathology to
look up Patty Owen's pathology report, but he was happy to
get into the OR. He put on a scrub suit as he'd been instructed.
When he checked himself in the mirror, he was alarmed to see

that except for his new shade of hair and his bare upper lip, he looked much like his old self. He quickly put on a surgical mask as he'd planned.

"You don't need a mask," David said when he caught sight of him.

"I'm coming down with a cold," Jeffrey explained. "I think they'd want me to wear it."

David nodded. "Good thinking."

Pushing his cleaning cart ahead of him, Jeffrey went through the double doors to the OR. He hadn't been in there since the hospital had put him on leave, but the place looked exactly the same. As far as Jeffrey could tell, nothing had changed.

Following David's instructions, Jeffrey tackled the big blackboard first. A few staff members came and went as Jeffrey worked. Some of them Jeffrey knew by name, but none of them gave him a second look. Jeffrey had to believe his cleaning activities protected his true identity as much as his altered appearance did. He made it a point not to stray far from his mop and cleaning cart as he worked.

Even so, when an emergency appendectomy that had been in progress when he first entered the OR was at last completed and the operating team emerged, Jeffrey made it a point to keep his back to the group. The anesthesiologist and the surgeon were both good friends of his.

After the doors swung closed behind the departing team, a silence descended on the OR. Jeffrey could make out the faint sound of a radio coming from the direction of Central Supply. He mopped his way over to the main operating room desk.

The operating room desk was more of a long counter with several areas for people to sit. It served as the command post for moving people into and out of the ORs, calling to have patients brought up from their rooms, bringing in the patients from the holding area, and coordinating the flow of personnel. Under the center portion were a number of large file drawers. One was marked "scheduling."

Jeffrey glanced up and down the corridor to make sure it was truly deserted. Then he pulled open the drawer. Since the operating schedules were filed according to date, Jeffrey was soon able to find the schedule for the fateful day: September 9. He scanned the day's cases, looking for epidurals that might have required .75% Marcaine, but there were none to be found. There were a number of spinal cases, but they would have used spinal grade Marcaine if Marcaine had been used at all, not the 30 cc variety used for epidurals or regional blocks.

Going back in the drawer, Jeffrey pulled out the schedule for September 8. Although the biohazard disposal container on the side of the anesthesia machine was emptied every day, there was always a chance it had been missed for some reason. But the schedule for the 8th provided no more possible explanations than the one for the 9th had. Jeffrey was forced to wonder if he'd misread the Marcaine label for Patty Owen's epidural after all. How else could he account for the empty .75% Marcaine vial that had been found?

Just as Jeffrey was almost through, the swinging doors burst open. Jeffrey grabbed his mop and frantically started mopping. For a moment, he dared not look up. But after it became clear no one was approaching, he raised his head in time to see a surgical team rushing a patient on a gurney toward the OR set up for emergencies. Several units of blood were hanging above the stretcher. Jeffrey guessed the patient was a victim of an automobile accident.

Only after calm had returned did Jeffrey go back to the schedules. He replaced each one in its respective slot and closed the file drawer. The emergency case that had just gone by started him thinking. Emergencies wouldn't appear on an OR schedule. For that matter, neither would a case like Patty Owen's. Her Caesarean had not been anticipated. How could it have been scheduled? Jeffrey moved on to the previous year's scheduling book. This was the book that contained listings of all the OR cases, including emergencies and operations that may have been scheduled, only to be canceled or postponed.

Other than Caesareans, epidural anesthesia was not commonly used in emergencies. Jeffrey knew that, but he decided to check the scheduling book anyway, just to be sure. There were exceptions. He looked at entries on the 8th first, running his finger down the list. It was not easy to read since it was in longhand by many different hands. He found nothing remotely suspicious. He turned the page to the 9th and started down the list. He didn't have to check far. In OR 15, the same OR that Patty Owen had been treated in, there had been a corneal laceration repair at five in the morning. Jeffrey's pulse quickened. An ophthalmic emergency was promising indeed.

Jeffrey tore a piece of paper from a pad on the counter and quickly jotted down the patient's name. Then he closed the book and returned it to its spot on the shelf. Pushing his bucket along on its unsteady wheels, Jeffrey made his way down the hall to the anesthesia office. He opened the door and turned on the light. He ran to the anesthesia file drawer and pulled out the anesthesia record for the patient in question.

"Bingo!" Jeffrey whispered. The anesthesia record indicated that the patient had received retrobulbar anesthesia with .75% Marcaine! Jeffrey put the anesthesia record back in place and shut the file drawer. Kelly had been right. He could hardly believe it. Instantly he felt better about himself, and more confident about his judgment. He knew that what he'd found wouldn't have much import in court, but it meant the world to him. He hadn't misread the label on the Marcaine!

When the time for the lunch break arrived, David came looking for Jeffrey. Jeffrey had finished the main OR corridor and had cleaned the two operating rooms that had been used for the emergencies. He was busy in Central Supply when David found him.

"I'd just as soon keep working," Jeffrey said. "I'm not hungry. I'll head down to the labs and get started."

"You gotta slow down," David said with a bit less friendliness than he'd shown initially. "You'll make the rest of us look bad."

Jeffrey smiled sheepishly. "I guess I'm just eager because it's my first day. Don't worry, I'll calm down."

"I hope so," David muttered. Then he turned and left.

Jeffrey finished what he was doing in Central Supply, then pushed his cart the length of the OR corridor and out the swinging doors. Changing back to his housekeeping uniform, he pushed the cart down to the pathology department. He wanted to take advantage of the fact that David and the other cleaning personnel were lunching.

He tried the passkeys in the door that led to the administrative section of pathology. The third key opened the door.

Jeffrey was amazed where his uniform and passkeys could take him.

The place was deserted. The only people around in that whole section of the hospital were the technicians in the chemistry, hematology, and microbiology labs. Jeffrey lost no time. Propping his mop up against the massive file cabinets, he searched for the pathology file on Patty Owen. He found it easily.

He put the folder on a desk and opened it. Flipping through the pages, he found copies of the Medical Examiner's autopsy report. He turned to the toxicology section, which had graphs of the results of the gas chromatography-mass spectroscopy of blood, cerebrospinal fluid, and urine. The only compound that was listed as having been found was bupivacaine, the generic name for Marcaine. No other chemicals had been found in her body fluids, at least none that the tests had discovered.

Jeffrey went through the rest of the file, glancing at each page. He was surprised to find a number of eight-by-ten photos. Jeffrey pulled them free. They were electron micrographs made at Boston Memorial. Jeffrey's curiosity was piqued: electron micrographs were certainly not done for every autopsy. He was sorry he wasn't more skilled at interpreting electron microscope sections. As it was, he had a hard time deciding which end was up. After studying the micrographs carefully, he finally realized that he was looking at magnified images of nerve ganglia cells and nerve axons.

Reading the descriptions on the back of each photo, Jeffrey learned that the electron micrographs showed marked destruction of the intracellular architecture. He was intrigued. These photos had not been exhibited during pretrial discovery. With the hospital involved as a defendant in the same case as Jeffrey, the pathology department had not been acting with Jeffrey's best interest in mind. Jeffrey had not even been informed of the existence of these photos. If he and Randolph had, they might have been subpoenaed, not that Jeffrey had been particularly interested in possible axonal degeneration at the time of his trial.

Seeing the axonal degeneration evident in Patty Owen's electron micrographs made Jeffrey recall the axonal degeneration Chris Everson had described in his patient's autopsy.

What was so startling about the degeneration in both cases was that local anesthetics could not have been responsible. There had to be some other explanation.

Jeffrey took the file to the copy machine and copied the parts he thought he'd need. These included the electron microscopic reports, although not the photos themselves. It also included the toxicology section with the gas chromatography and mass spectroscopy graphs. To properly decipher the graphs, he knew he would have to spend more time in the library.

When he was finished with the copy machine, he found a large manila envelope and put the copies into it. Then he returned the original to its folder and refiled it. Jeffrey stowed the manila envelope on the lower shelf of his cleaning cart under some replacement rolls of toilet paper.

Then Jeffrey turned his attention back to cleaning. He was excited about what he had found. The idea of a contaminant was still viable indeed. In fact, given the results of the electron micrographs, it was almost a certainty.

As the night wore on, Jeffrey's energy waned. By the time the sky began to brighten, he was thoroughly exhausted. He'd been running on nervous energy for hours. At six-fifteen, he took the opportunity of a phone in an empty social service office to give Kelly a call. If she had to leave the house by six forty-five, she was sure to be up.

As soon as she came on the line, Jeffrey excitedly told her about the emergency eye case the morning of the Patty Owen disaster and that .75% Marcaine had been used. "Kelly, you were so right. I don't understand why no one thought to look into such a possibility. Randolph didn't, and I never did." Then he told her about the electron micrographs.

"Does that suggest a contaminant?" Kelly asked.

"It makes it almost certain. The next step is to try to figure out what it could be and why it didn't show up in the toxicology report."

"This whole thing scares me," Kelly said.

"Me too," Jeffrey agreed. He then asked her if she knew anybody in pathology at Valley Hospital.

"Not in pathology," Kelly answered. "But I still know several of the anesthesiologists. Hart Ruddock was Chris's best friend. I'm sure he'll know someone in pathology."

"Could you give him a call?" Jeffrey asked. "See if he'd be willing to get copies of whatever the pathology department has on Henry Noble. I'd be particularly interested in EM studies or histology of nervous tissue."

"What will I say if he asks why I want it?"

"I don't know. Tell him you're interested, that you were reading Chris's notes and read that there was axonal degeneration. That should pique his curiosity."

"All right," Kelly said. "And you better get back here and get some rest. You must be asleep on your feet."

"I'm exhausted," Jeffrey admitted. "Cleaning is a hell of a lot more tiring than giving anesthesia."

Early that morning, Trent made his way down the OR corridor of St. Joseph's Hospital with the doctored vial back in his briefs. He went through the same motions he had the previous morning, being especially sure no one was anywhere near Central Supply before he went in to switch the ampules. Since there were now only two ampules of .5% Marcaine in the open box, the chances that his ampule would be used that day were good, especially with two epidural cases listed on the big board. Of course, there was no guarantee Marcaine would be used, much less the .5%. But there was a good chance. The cases scheduled were a herniorrhaphy and a laparoscopy. If it was one or the other, Trent hoped his ampule would make it to the laparoscopy. It would be too perfect; that prick Doherty was listed as the anesthesiologist.

Casually strolling back to the locker room, Trent hid the good ampule in his locker. Closing and locking the door, he thought about Gail Shaffer. Dealing with her hadn't been as much fun as he'd anticipated, but in a way, Trent was grateful for the experience. Gail's spotting him had impressed upon him the need to be vigilant at all times. He couldn't afford to be careless. Too much was at stake. If he screwed up, there would be hell to pay. Trent couldn't help but feel the authorities would be the least of his worries.

The clock radio was set for six forty-five and tuned to WBZ. The volume was low, so Karen woke in stages. Finally her eyes blinked open.

Karen rolled over and sat on the edge of the bed. She still felt drugged from the medication that Dr. Silvan had given her to help her sleep. The Dalmane had worked better than she'd anticipated.

"Are you up?" Marcia called through the closed door.

"I'm up," Karen answered. She got to her feet unsteadily. Dizzy for a moment, she held on to her bed post to steady herself. Then she went into the bathroom.

Despite a cottony feeling in her mouth and a dryness in her throat, Karen was scrupulously careful not to drink anything. Dr. Silvan had warned her not to. She didn't even drink water when she brushed her teeth.

Karen wished the day were ending, not beginning. Then her procedure would be over and done with. She knew it was silly, but she still felt apprehensive. The Dalmane couldn't help that. She did her best to occupy her thoughts with the process of showering and dressing.

When it came time to head to the hospital, Marcia drove. For most of the drive, she did her best to keep up the conversation. But Karen was too distracted to respond. By the time they pulled into the hospital lot, they'd been driving in silence for some time.

"You're kinda scared, aren't you?" Marcia finally said.

"I can't help it," Karen admitted. "I know it's silly."

"It's not silly at all," Marcia said. "But I guarantee you won't feel anything. The discomfort will come later. But even then, it will be easier than you think. This is the worst part of it: the dread."

"I hope so," Karen said. She didn't like the fact that the weather had changed. It was raining again. The skies looked as gloomy as she was feeling.

There was a special day-surgery entrance. Karen and Marcia were left waiting for a quarter of an hour along with several dozen others. It was easy to pick out the patients in the crowd. Instead of reading their magazines, they merely flipped through the pages.

Karen had been through three magazines by the time she was called to a desk and greeted by a nurse. The nurse went over all the paperwork and made sure all was in order. Karen had been in for blood work and an EKG the day before. The consent form had already been signed and witnessed. An ID bracelet had already been printed up. The nurse helped Karen snap it on.

Karen was given a hospital johnny and a robe and shown to a changing room. She felt a mild wave of panic as she climbed onto the gurney and was moved to a holding area. At that point Marcia was allowed to join her for a few moments.

Marcia was holding the bag that contained Karen's clothes. She made some attempts at humor, but Karen was too tense to respond. An orderly came by and, after checking the chart at the end of the gurney as well as Karen's ID, he said, "Time to go."

"I'll be waiting," Marcia called as Karen was rolled away. Karen waved, then let her head fall back on the pillow. She thought about telling the orderly to stop pushing so she could get off. She could make it back to the dressing room, get her clothes from Marcia and put them back on, and calmly leave the hospital. The endometriosis wasn't that bad. She'd lived with it this long.

But she didn't do anything. It was as if she'd already been caught by an inevitable sequence of events that would play themselves out no matter what she did. Somewhere during the process of deciding on the laparoscopy she'd lost her freedom of choice. She was a prisoner of the system. The elevator doors closed. She felt herself being whisked upward, and the last chance for escape was cut off.

The orderly left Karen in another holding area with a dozen or so gurneys like her own. She glanced at the other patients. Most were resting comfortably with their eyes closed. A few were looking around just as she was, but they didn't look frightened, as she felt.

"Karen Hodges?" a voice called.

Karen turned her head. A doctor in surgical garb was by her side. He'd appeared so quickly she hadn't seen where he'd come from.

"I'm Dr. Bill Doherty," he said. He was about her father's age. He had a mustache and kind brown eyes. "I'm going to be your anesthesiologist."

Karen nodded. Dr. Doherty went over her medical history

again. It didn't take long; there wasn't much to go over. He asked the usual questions about allergies and past illnesses. He then explained that her doctor had requested epidural anesthesia.

"Are you familiar with epidural anesthesia?" Dr. Doherty asked.

Karen told him that her doctor had explained it to her. Dr. Doherty nodded but carefully explained it again, emphasizing its particular benefits in her case. "This kind of anesthesia will give lots of muscle relaxation, which will help Dr. Silvan with his examination," he explained. "Besides, epidural is safer than general anesthesia."

Karen nodded. Then she asked, "Are you sure it will work and that I really won't feel anything when they're probing around?"

Dr. Doherty gave her arm a reassuring squeeze. "I'm absolutely sure it will. And you know something? Everybody worries that anesthesia is not going to work for them the first time they have it. But it always does. So don't worry, okay?"

"Can I ask one other question?" Karen asked.

"As many as you like," Dr. Doherty answered.

"Have you ever read the book *Coma?*"

Dr. Doherty laughed. "I did, and saw the movie."

"Nothing like that ever goes on, does it?"

"No! Nothing like that ever goes on," he assured her. "Any more questions?"

Karen shook her head.

"All right then," Dr. Doherty said. "I'll have the nurses give you a little shot. It will calm you down. Then when we know your doctor is in the dressing room, I'll have you brought down to the operating room. And, Karen, you really won't feel a thing. Trust me. I've done this a million times."

"I trust you," Karen said. She even managed a smile.

Dr. Doherty left the holding area and went through the swinging doors into the OR suite. He wrote an order for Karen's tranquilizer, then went into the anesthesia office to take out his day's narcotics. Then he headed down to Central Supply.

In Central Supply, he picked up some IV fluids and, juggling the bottles, reached into the open box of .5% Marcaine and lifted out an ampule. Always careful about such things, he checked the label. It was .5% Marcaine all right. What Dr. Doherty didn't notice was the slight irregularity of the top, the part that he'd break off when he was about to draw up the drug.

Annie Winthrop was more tired than usual as she made her way up the walkway to the entrance of her apartment building. She had her umbrella up to shield her against the downpour. The temperature had dropped to the low fifties; it felt more like winter coming back than summer on its way.

What a night it had been: three cardiac arrests in the intensive care unit. It was a record for the last four months. Handling the three as well as taking care of the other patients had sapped everybody's strength—and patience. All she wanted to do was take a nice, hot shower, then climb into bed.

Arriving at her apartment door, she fumbled with her keys, dropping them in the process. Exhaustion made her clumsy. Picking them up, she put the right one into the lock. When she went to turn the key, she realized the door was already unlocked.

Annie paused. She and Gail always kept their door locked, even when they were inside the apartment. It was a rule that she and Gail had specifically discussed.

With mild apprehension, Annie turned the knob and pushed the door open. The lights were on in the living room. Annie wondered if Gail was home.

Annie's intuition made her hesitate on the threshold. Something was warning her of danger. But there were no sounds. The apartment was deathly quiet.

Annie pushed the door open wider. Everything seemed to be in order. She stepped over the threshold and immediately smelled a terrible odor. As a nurse she thought she knew what it was.

"Gail?" she called. Normally Gail was asleep when she got home. Annie walked toward Gail's bedroom and looked in through the open door. The light was on in there too. The smell got worse. She called Gail's name again, then stepped through the door. The door to the bathroom was open. Annie went to the bathroom and looked in. She screamed.

Trent's assignment for the day was to circulate in room four, where a series of breast biopsies were scheduled. He thought it would be an easy day unless some of the biopsies turned out to be positive, but that wasn't expected. He was pleased with the assignment because it gave him the freedom to keep an eye on his Marcaine vial, something he'd not been able to do the day before.

The first biopsy was just beginning to be performed when the nurse anesthetist asked Trent to run down and get her another liter of Ringer's Lactate. Trent was only too happy to oblige her.

There were a number of staff members in Central Supply when Trent walked in. He knew he'd have to be particularly circumspect when he checked for his vial. But they didn't pay attention to him. They were busy setting up surgical packs to replace the ones to be used that day. Trent walked back to the area where the IV fluids were kept. The non-narcotic drugs were to his left.

Trent took an IV bottle from the shelf. Through the door-less entranceway of this section of Central Supply, he could see the others as they counted instruments for each pack.

With one eye on his fellow nurses, Trent let his hand slip into the open Marcaine box. He felt a thrill. There was only one ampule left and its rounded top was smooth. His ampule was gone.

Barely able to contain his excitement, Trent left Central Supply and headed back to room four. He gave the nurse anesthetist the IV bottle. Then he asked the scrub nurse if she needed anything. She said that she didn't. The case was going smoothly. The biopsy had already been sent for frozen section and they were closing. Trent told the scrub nurse he'd be right back.

Emerging from room four, Trent hurried down to the big board. He was overjoyed at what he saw: the only epidural scheduled for seven-thirty was the laparoscopy, and Doherty was the anesthesiologist! The herniorrhaphy wasn't scheduled

until later in the day. His vial had to have been taken for the
laparoscopy.

Trent checked the laparoscopy's location. It had been assigned to room twelve. He hurried back up the corridor and
into the anesthesia alcove for room twelve. Doherty was there
and so was the patient. Sitting on the top of a stainless-steel
table was his ampule of Marcaine.

Trent couldn't believe his luck. Not only was the anesthesiologist Doherty, but the patient was a young, healthy girl.
Things couldn't have worked out better.

Not wanting to be seen loitering in the area, Trent didn't
linger. He returned to the OR he'd been assigned to, but he
was so agitated he could not stay still. He paced so furiously,
the biopsy surgeon had to ask him to sit or leave the room.

Normally such a command by a doctor would have enraged
Trent. But not today. He was too excited thinking about what
was about to happen and what he had to do. He knew he'd
have to return to room twelve as soon as all hell broke loose
and get the opened vial. That job was always a bit worrisome
for Trent, although on the previous occasions the general pan-
demonium the reaction caused had always adequately diverted
everyone's attention. Still it was the "weakest link" in the
whole operation. Trent did not want anyone to see him touch
the vial.

Trent looked up at the clock and watched the second hand
sweep around its face. It was all going to happen in a matter
of minutes. A shiver of pleasure swept down his spine. He
loved the suspense!

9

THURSDAY,
MAY 18, 1989
7:52 A.M.

With sirens blaring, the ambulance carrying Gail Shaffer turned into the emergency area of St. Joseph's Hospital and backed to the unloading dock. The EMTs had called ahead on the mobile phone to alert the emergency room as to what kind of case was coming in, requesting cardiac and neurological backup.

When the EMTs had initially reached Gail's apartment, after responding to the call placed by her roommate, Annie Winthrop, they had quickly deduced what had happened. Gail Shaffer had suffered a grand mal seizure while in the shower. They believed she'd had some warning the seizure was coming on since her roommate had insisted that the water had been turned off. Unfortunately, Gail hadn't been able to get out of the tub quickly enough, and she'd hit her head many times against the faucet and the tub. She had multiple scalp and facial wounds and a particularly deep gash high on her forehead at her hairline.

The first thing the EMTs had done was to get Gail out of the bathtub. As they did, they had noticed a total lack of muscle tone, as if she were completely paralyzed. They'd also detected a marked abnormality of her heart rate. Its rhythm was totally irregular. They'd tried to stabilize her by starting an IV and giving her 100% oxygen.

As soon as the ambulance doors were open, Gail was swiftly taken to one of the trauma units in the ER. Thanks to the EMTs' call, a neurology resident and a cardiology resident were on hand when she arrived.

The crew worked feverishly. Gail was clearly holding on to life by the thinnest of threads. The heart's electrical conduction system, responsible for coordinating its beating, was severely impaired.

The neurologist quickly corroborated the EMTs' initial impression: Gail was suffering from an almost total flaccid paralysis, which included the cranial nerves. What was particularly strange about the paralysis was that a few muscle groups still elicited some reflexive behavior, but there seemed to be no governing pattern as to which still did. It was random.

The consensus soon became that Gail had suffered a grand mal seizure secondary to an intracranial bleed and/or brain tumor. This was the provisional diagnosis despite the fact that the cerebrospinal fluid was clear. One of the internal medicine residents dissented. She thought the whole episode was due to some kind of acute drug intoxication. She insisted that a blood sample be drawn for an analysis of recreational drugs, particularly some of the newer synthetic types.

One of the neurology residents also had reservations about the provisional diagnosis. It was his feeling that a central lesion couldn't explain the paralytic problem. He sided with the internal medicine resident in suspecting an acute intoxication of some sort. But he wouldn't speculate further until he reviewed the results of additional tests.

Everyone agreed about the head trauma. The physical evidence was all too clear. A portal X-ray made everybody wince. The wound at the hairline had fractured into one of the frontal sinuses. But it was felt that not even such severe trauma was enough to explain Gail's condition.

Despite Gail's precarious cardiac status, an emergency NMR was scheduled. The neurology resident had been able to cut through the bureaucratic red tape and smooth the way. With several residents in tow, Gail was taken to radiology and slid into the huge, doughnut-shaped machine. Everyone was a bit worried that the magnetic field might affect her unstable cardiac conduction system, but the urgency of settling on an intracranial diagnosis superseded all other concerns. Everyone involved in the case remained glued to the screen as the first images began to appear.

Bill Doherty held the 5 cc glass syringe up to the light in the anesthesia alcove and gently tapped the edge. The few bubbles adhering to the sides floated to the surface. The syringe contained 2 cc's of spinal-grade Marcaine with epinephrine.

Dr. Doherty was far along in administering the continuous epidural on Karen Hodges. Everything was going smoothly and according to plan. The initial puncture had not given her the slightest pain. The Touhey needle had performed beautifully. He had demonstrated to his satisfaction that the Touhey needle was in the epidural space by the lack of resistance on the plunger of the small glass syringe when he pressed. A test dose he had administered had also confirmed it. And finally, the small catheter had slid into place with deceptive ease. All that remained was to confirm that the catheter was in the epidural space. Once he had, he could proceed with the therapeutic dose.

"How are you doing?" Dr. Doherty asked Karen. Karen was on her right side, turned away from him. He would turn her supine after administering the anesthesia.

"I guess I'm doing all right," Karen said. "Are you finished? I still don't feel anything."

"You're not supposed to feel anything yet," Dr. Doherty said.

He injected the test dose, then blew up the blood pressure cuff. The pressure didn't change, nor did the pulse. While he waited, he made a small bandage to fit around the catheter. After several minutes he tried the blood pressure again. It hadn't changed. He tested the sensation in her lower legs. There was no anesthesia, meaning that the catheter was surely not in the space where spinal anesthesia was given. He was pleased. The catheter had to be in the epidural space. All was ready for the main injection.

"My legs feel totally normal," Karen complained. She was still worried the anesthesia would not work on her.

"Your legs are not supposed to feel different at this point," Dr. Doherty assured her. "Remember what I told you when we started." He'd been careful to tell Karen what to expect. But he wasn't surprised that she'd forgotten. He was patient with her and knew she was apprehensive.

"How are we all doing?"

Dr. Doherty looked up. It was Dr. Silvan, dressed in scrubs.

"We'll be ready in ten minutes," Dr. Doherty said. He turned back to his stainless-steel table, picked up the 30 cc ampule of Marcaine, and checked the label again. "I'm just about to inject the epidural," he added.

"Good timing," Dr. Silvan said. "I'll scrub up and we'll get started. The sooner we do, the sooner we'll be finished." He patted Karen's arm, careful not to disturb the sterile drape Dr. Doherty had set up. "You relax, you hear?" he said to Karen.

Dr. Doherty broke the top off the ampule. He drew the Marcaine up with a syringe. From force of habit he tapped the edges of this larger syringe to remove any air bubbles, even though putting air into the epidural space would not cause a problem. The motion was more from force of habit.

Bending slightly, Dr. Doherty connected the syringe with the epidural catheter. He began a steady injection. The narrow gauge of the catheter provided some resistance, so he pushed firmly against the plunger. He had just emptied the syringe when Karen suddenly moved.

"Don't move yet!" Dr. Doherty scolded.

"I have a terrible cramp," Karen cried.

"Where?" Dr. Doherty asked. "In your legs?"

"No, my stomach," Karen said. She moaned and straightened out her legs.

Dr. Doherty reached for her hip to steady her. A nurse who'd been standing by for assistance reached over and grasped Karen's ankles.

Despite Dr. Doherty's attempts to restrain her with his free hand, Karen rolled over onto her back. She pushed herself up on one elbow and looked at Dr. Doherty. Her eyes were wide with terror.

"Help me," she cried desperately.

Dr. Doherty was confused. He had no idea what was going wrong. His first thought was that Karen had simply panicked.

He let go of the syringe. With both hands, he grabbed Karen by the shoulders and tried to force her back down onto the gurney. At her end, the nurse tightened her grip on Karen's ankles.

Dr. Doherty decided to give Karen a dose of IV diazepam, but before he could get it, Karen's face became distorted by undulating fasciculations of her facial muscles. At the same time, saliva bubbled out of her mouth and tears flowed from her eyes. Her skin was instantly wet with perspiration. Her breathing became stertorous and phlegmy.

Dr. Doherty went for the atropine. As he was administering it, Karen's back arched. Her body went rigid, then exploded in a series of convulsing fits. The nurse rushed to Karen's side to prevent the woman from throwing herself to the floor. Hearing the commotion, Dr. Silvan came in from the scrub sink to try to help.

Dr. Doherty got out some succinylcholine and injected it into the intravenous line. He then injected diazepam. He turned on the flow of oxygen and held the mask over Karen's face. The EKG began to register irregularities of conduction.

As word went out, help started to arrive. They wheeled Karen into the OR to have more room. The succinylcholine stopped her seizure. Dr. Doherty intubated her. He checked her blood pressure and found that it was falling. Her pulse was irregular.

Dr. Doherty injected more atropine. He'd never seen such salivation and lacrimation. He attached a pulse oximeter. Then Karen's heart stopped.

A code was called and more hospital staff descended on room twelve to offer assistance. After the number attending swelled to more than twenty, there were too many to notice out in the alcove when a hand reached for the half-full vial of Marcaine, dumped the contents down a nearby drain, and spirited away the empty vial.

Kelly put down the phone in the intensive care unit. The call left her feeling acutely distressed. She'd just been informed they were getting an admission from the emergency room. But that wasn't what had upset her. What bothered her was that the patient was Gail Shaffer, one of the OR nurses. A friend.

Kelly had known Gail for some time. Gail had dated one of the residents in anesthesia at Valley Hospital who'd been a student of Chris's. Gail had even been over to the Eversons' home for the annual dinner Kelly threw for the anesthesia residents. When Kelly had made the switch to St. Joe's, Gail had been nice enough to introduce her to a number of people there.

Kelly tried not to let her personal feelings get in the way. It was vital she remain professional. She called out to one of the other nurses who would help with the admission, telling her to get bed three ready for a new occupant.

A team of people brought Gail into the intensive care unit and helped get her set up with a monitor and a respirator. Her own breathing efforts were not satisfactory to keep her blood gases in a normal range. As they were working, Kelly was brought up to date.

There still was no diagnosis, which made Gail that much tougher to treat. The NMR had been negative except for the fracture into the frontal sinus. This ruled out a tumor and/or an intracranial bleed. Gail had not regained consciousness, and her paralytic state had deepened rather than resolved. The gravest, most immediate threat to Gail's condition was her unstable cardiac status. Even that had worsened. In radiology she'd scared everyone with runs of ventricular tachycardia that made people fear she was about to arrest. It was almost a miracle she had not.

By the time Gail was fully set up in the ICU the results of the cocaine test came back. It was negative. A broader screen for recreational drugs was pending, but Kelly was quite sure that Gail did not use drugs.

The team who'd brought Gail to the ICU was still there when Gail arrested. A countershock to her heart eliminated the fibrillation but resulted in asystole, meaning there was no electrical activity or beat whatsoever. A pacemaker threaded into her heart from a cutdown in her groin restored a heartbeat of sorts, but the prognosis was not good.

"I've faced a lot in this line of work," Devlin said angrily. "Guns, knives, a lead pipe. But I wasn't expecting to get shot in the ass with some Amazonian arrow poison. From a guy who was handcuffed, no less."

Michael Mosconi could only shake his head. Devlin was the most efficient bounty hunter he knew of. He'd brought in drug pushers, hit men, Mafioso dons, and petty thieves. How he could be having so much trouble with this piss-ant doctor was beyond Mosconi. Maybe Devlin was losing his touch.

"Let me get this straight," Mosconi said. "You had him in your car, handcuffed?" It sounded crazy.

"I'm telling you, he injected me with some stuff that paralyzed me. One minute I was fine, the next I couldn't move a muscle. There wasn't anything I could do about it. The guy's got modern medicine working for him."

"Makes me wonder about you," Mosconi muttered with irritation. He ran a nervous hand through his thinning hair. "Maybe you should think about changing your line of work. What about becoming a truant officer?"

"Very funny," Devlin said, but he clearly was not amused.

"How do you think you're going to be able to handle a real criminal if you can't bring in a skinny anesthesiologist?" Michael said. "I mean, this is a major screwup. Every time the phone rings I have palpitations that it's the court, saying they're forfeiting the bond. Do you understand the seriousness of all this? Now, I don't want any more excuses—I want you to get this guy."

"I'll get him," Devlin said. "I have someone tailing the wife. But more importantly, I put a bug on her telephone. He's got to call sometime."

"You have to do more than that," Michael said. "I'm scared the police might be losing interest in keeping him from getting out of the city. Devlin, I can't afford to lose this guy. We can't let him slip away."

"I don't think he'll be going anyplace."

"Oh?" Michael questioned. "Is this some new intuitive power you've developed, or is it wishful thinking?"

Devlin studied Michael from his seat on Michael's uncomfortable couch. Michael's sarcasm was beginning to get on his nerves. But he didn't say anything. Instead he leaned forward to get at his back pocket. He pulled out a bunch of papers.

Putting them on the desk, he unfolded them and smoothed them out.

"The doc left this stuff behind in his hotel room," he said, pushing them toward Michael. "I don't think he's going anyplace. In fact, I think he's up to something. Something that's keeping him here. What do you make of these papers?"

Michael picked up a page of Chris Everson's notes. "It's a bunch of scientific mumbo-jumbo. I don't make anything of it."

"Some of it's in the doc's handwriting," Devlin said. "But most of it isn't. I assume it was written by this Christopher Everson, whoever he is. His name is on some of the papers; does the name mean anything to you?"

"Nope," Michael said.

"Let me have the phone directory," Devlin said.

Michael handed it over. Devlin turned to the page where Eversons were listed. There was a handful, but no Chris. The closest was a K. C. Everson in Brookline.

"The man's not in the directory," Devlin said. "I suppose that would have been too easy."

"Maybe he's a doctor too," Michael suggested. "His number could be unlisted."

Devlin nodded. That was a good possibility. He opened the directory to the Yellow Pages and looked under Physicians. There were no Eversons. He closed the book.

"The point is," Devlin said, "the doctor is working on this scientific stuff while he's on the lam and holed up in a fleabag hotel. It doesn't make a whole lot of sense. He's up to something, but I don't know what. I think I'll find this Chris Everson and ask him."

"Yeah," Mosconi said, losing his patience. "Just don't take four years to go to medical school. I want results. If you can't deliver, just say the word. I'll get someone else."

Devlin got to his feet. He put the phone book down on Michael's desk and picked up Jeffrey's and Chris's notes. "Don't worry," he said. "I'll find him. It's getting to be sorta a personal thing at this point."

Leaving Michael's office, Devlin descended to the street. It was raining harder now than it had been when he'd arrived. Fortunately he'd parked close to an arcade, so he had only a short dash in the open to get to his car. He'd parked in a loading zone on Cambridge Street. One of the perks he enjoyed from having been on the police force was that he could park anywhere. Traffic cops turned a blind eye. It was a professional courtesy.

Getting into his car, Devlin worked his way around the State House to get on Beacon Street. The route was convoluted and complicated, as most Boston driving was. He turned left on Exeter and parked by the closest hydrant he could find to the Boston Public Library. Getting out of his car, he bolted for the entrance.

In the reference section he used city directories for Boston and all the outlying towns. There were plenty of Eversons but no Christopher Everson. He made a list of the Eversons he found.

Going to the nearest pay phone, he dialed the K. C. Everson in Brookline first. Although he figured the initials meant it was a female, he thought he'd give it a try anyway. At first he was encouraged: a sleepy male voice answered the phone.

"Is this Christopher Everson?" Devlin asked.

There was a pause. "No," said the voice. "Would you like to speak with Kelly? She's—"

Devlin hung up the phone. He'd been right. K. C. Everson was a woman.

Scanning his list of Eversons, he wondered which one was the next most promising. It was tough to say. There weren't even any others with a middle initial C. That meant he'd have to start making house calls. It would be a time-consuming process, but he couldn't think of what else to do. One of the Eversons was bound to know this Christopher Everson. Devlin still had a hunch that this was his best lead.

As tired as he was, Jeffrey could not get back to sleep after being awakened by the telephone. Had he been fully awake when it had rung, he probably wouldn't have answered it. He'd not discussed how to handle phone calls with Kelly, but he was probably safer not picking up. Lying in bed, Jeffrey remained vaguely troubled by the caller. Who could have been asking for Chris? His first thought was that it had been a cruel prank. But it could have been someone trying to sell something. They could have gotten Chris's name from some list. Maybe he wouldn't mention the call to Kelly. He hated to dredge up the past just when she was beginning to put it behind her.

Jeffrey's mind returned to considering the contaminant theory instead of dwelling on the mysterious caller. Rolling over on his back, he reviewed the details. Then he decided to get up and shower and shave.

While he was making coffee, he began to wonder if his anesthetic complication and Chris's were isolated episodes or if there had been other similar incidents in the Boston area. What if the killer had tampered with Marcaine other times besides the two Jeffrey knew of? If he had, Jeffrey would have thought reports of such bizarre reactions would have filtered through the grapevine. But then again, look what had happened to him and Chris. They'd each been served with malpractice suits instantly. At that point, defense of the case had become of paramount importance, dwarfing other issues.

Remembering that the role of the Board of Registration in Medicine in the state of Massachusetts had been statutorially expanded to keep track of "major incidents" in health care facilities, Jeffrey called the board.

After a brief runaround, Jeffrey was put through to a member of the Patient Care Assessment Committee. He explained the sort of incidents he was interested in. She put him on hold for a few minutes.

"You said you are interested in deaths during epidural anesthesia?" she asked, coming back on the line.

"Exactly," Jeffrey said.

"I can find four," the woman said. "All within the last four years."

Jeffrey was amazed. Four sounded like a lot. Fatalities during epidural anesthesia were extremely rare, especially after the .75% Marcaine was proscribed for obstetrical use. To have four occur in the last four years should have raised some red flags.

"Are you interested in knowing where they occurred?" the woman asked.

"Please."

"There was one last year at Boston Memorial."

Jeffrey wrote down "Memorial, 1988." That had to be his case.

"There was one at Valley Hospital in 1987," she said.

Jeffrey wrote that down. That case would have been Chris's.

"Then the Commonwealth Hospital in 1986 and at Suffolk General in 1985. That's it."

That's plenty, Jeffrey thought. He was equally amazed that all the episodes had been in Boston. "Has the Board done anything about these cases?" he asked.

"No, we haven't," the woman said. "If they had all occurred at one institution, it would have been put under review. But seeing that four different hospitals and four different doctors were involved, it didn't seem appropriate for us to get involved. Besides, it's indicated here that all four cases led to malpractice litigation."

"What are the names of the doctors involved at the Commonwealth and Suffolk?" Jeffrey asked. He wanted to discuss the cases with these doctors in great detail to see how similar their experiences were to his. In particular, he wanted to know if they had been using Marcaine from a 30 cc ampule for the local anesthetic.

"The doctors' names? I'm sorry, but that information is confidential," the woman said.

Jeffrey thought for a moment, then he asked: "What about the patients or the plaintiffs in those cases? What were their names?"

"I don't know if that is confidential or not," the woman said. "Just one moment."

She put Jeffrey on hold again. While he waited, Jeffrey again marveled about Boston having four deaths during epidural anesthesia and that he did not know it. He couldn't understand why such a series of complications hadn't become a topic of speculation and concern. Then he realized the explanation had to have been the unfortunate fact that all four had resulted in malpractice litigation. Jeffrey knew that one of the insidious effects of such litigation was the secrecy that the involved lawyers insisted on. He remembered his own lawyer, Randolph, had told him at the outset of his case that Jeffrey was not to discuss it with anyone.

"No one seems to know about this confidentiality issue," the woman said when she came back on the line. "But it would seem to me it's a matter of public record. The two patients were Clark DeVries and Lucy Havalin."

Jeffrey wrote the names down, thanked the woman, and hung up the phone. Back in the guest room Kelly had made up for him, Jeffrey pulled his duffel bag from under the bed and got out a couple of hundred-dollar bills. He would have to find the time to get some more clothes to replace the ones he'd had to leave at the Essex Hotel. Briefly he wondered what Pan Am had done with his small suitcase, not that it was a matter that was safe to pursue.

Next he called for a cab. He figured it was safe to take one as long as he did nothing to arouse the driver's suspicions. The weather hadn't improved since he'd come from the hospital that morning, so Jeffrey hunted for an umbrella in the front hall closet. By the time the cab arrived, he was waiting on the front steps, umbrella in hand.

Jeffrey's first objective was to buy another pair of plano dark-rimmed glasses. He had the cab wait while he went into an optician's along the way. His ultimate destination was the courthouse. It was eerie to be entering the building where only a few days earlier a jury had voted him guilty of the second-degree murder charge.

As he went through the metal detector, Jeffrey's anxiety increased. It reminded him too much of his episodes at the airport. He did his best to appear calm. He knew that if he seemed nervous, he'd only attract attention to himself. Despite his good intentions, however, he was visibly shaking as he entered the clerk's office on the first floor of the old building.

He waited for his turn at the counter. Most of the people waiting were lawyer types in dark suits whose pant legs were curiously too short. When one of the women behind the counter finally looked in his direction and said, "Next," Jeffrey stepped up and asked how to go about obtaining the record of a specific lawsuit.

"Settled or unsettled?" the woman asked him.

"Settled," Jeffrey said.

The woman pointed over Jeffrey's shoulder. "Gotta get the docket number from the Defendant/Plaintiff file," she said with a yawn. "That's those looseleaf books. Once you have the docket number, bring it back here. One of us can get the case from the vault."

Jeffrey nodded and thanked her. He went over to the shelves she had indicated. The cases were listed alphabetically year by year. Jeffrey started with the year 1986 and looked up Clark DeVries as the plaintiff. When he found the card for the case, he realized that the information he wanted was right there; he didn't need the whole record.

The information card listed the defendants, the plaintiffs, and the attorneys. The anesthesiologist in the case was a Dr. Lawrence Mann. Jeffrey used a handy copying machine to make a copy of the card in case he needed to refer to the docket number later.

He did the same with the card he found for Lucy Havalin's case. Her suit had been brought against an anesthesiologist by the name of Dr. Madaline Bowman. Jeffrey had had some professional dealings with Bowman, but hadn't seen her in years.

Removing the copy from the copy machine, he checked to make sure it was entirely legible. As he did so, he noticed the name of the attorney was Matthew Davidson.

Jeffrey winced. The copy almost slid from his hands. Matthew Davidson had been the attorney who'd sued Jeffrey for malpractice on behalf of Patty Owen's estate.

Jeffrey knew rationally that it was ridiculous to hate the man. After all, Davidson had only done his job, and the Patty Owen estate was entitled to legal representation. Jeffrey had heard all these arguments. But they didn't make any difference. Davidson had brought ruin to Jeffrey by bringing up the irrelevant minor drug problem that Jeffrey had had. The move had been unfair and had been done purely as a calculated maneuver to win the case. Justice and truth had not been the goal; there had been no malpractice. Jeffrey was certain of this now that he'd eliminated his own self-doubt and was more and more convinced a contaminant had been involved.

But Jeffrey had more to do at the moment than review past injustices. Changing his mind, he decided to look at the court records after all. Sometimes you didn't know what you were looking for until you found it, Jeffrey told himself. Going back to the counter where he'd started, he gave the woman who'd directed him before the docket numbers.

"You gotta fill out one of those request forms on the counter over there," she told him.

Typical bureaucracy, Jeffrey thought with some irritation, but he did as he was told. After he'd filled out the forms, he had to wait in line a third time. A different clerk handled his inquiry on this occasion. When he handed her the two forms, she looked at them and shook her head, saying, "It'll take about an hour, at the very least."

While he was waiting, Jeffrey sought out a bank of vending machines he'd seen on his way in. He got himself a quick snack of orange juice and a tuna sandwich. Then he parked himself on a bench in the rotunda and watched the comings and goings of the courthouse. There were so many uniformed policemen, Jeffrey actually started to grow used to seeing them. It was a kind of behavior therapy that went a long way in reducing his anxiety.

After a good hour had passed, Jeffrey returned to the clerk's room. The records he was interested in had been pulled for him. He took the large manila folders over to a side counter where he could have enough room to peruse the documents. There was a huge amount of material. Some of it was in too thick a form of legalese for Jeffrey to absorb, but he was interested in seeing what was available. There were pages and pages of testimony in the record as well as a variety of filings and briefs.

Jeffrey flipped through the testimony. He wanted to find out what local anesthetic was involved in each case. He scanned the papers pertaining to the Suffolk General case first. As he'd suspected, the local had been Marcaine. Now that he knew where in the record to look, he quickly found what he was looking for in the Commonwealth Hospital case. There, too, the local had been Marcaine. If Jeffrey's theory of a deliberate contamination was true, that meant that the killer, Boston's own Dr. or Mr. or Ms. X, had already struck four times. If only Jeffrey could come up with proof before the killer struck again.

Jeffrey was about to return the papers dealing with the

Commonwealth case to its manila envelope when he caught sight of the settlement decision. He shook his head in dismay. Like his, the settlement had been in the millions of dollars. What a waste, he thought. He checked the settlement in the other suit. It was even higher than Commonwealth's.

Jeffrey put the files in a basket reserved for returns. Then he left the courthouse. It had finally stopped raining, but it was still overcast and chilly and it looked like it might pour at any minute.

Jeffrey caught a cab on Cambridge Street and told the driver he wanted to go to the Countway Medical Library. He sat back and relaxed. He was looking forward to spending a rainy afternoon in the library. One of the things he wanted to do was to read up on toxicology. He wanted to brush up on the field's two main diagnostic tools: the gas chromatograph and the mass spectrograph.

Kelly unlocked her front door and pushed it open with her foot. Her hands were full between her umbrella, a small bag of groceries, and a large envelope.

"Jeffrey!" she called, setting the envelope and groceries on the foyer table, pushing her silver tea service to the side. She put her umbrella on the tile floor of the powder room, then stepped back out and shut the front door. "Jeffrey!" she called again, wondering if he was there or not. As she turned back into the room, she couldn't stifle a slight cry of surprise. Jeffrey was standing in the archway leading to the dining room. "You startled me," she said with a hand pressed up against her chest.

"Didn't you hear me?" he asked. "I answered back from the family room when you called my name."

"Phew," Kelly said, recovering her composure. "I'm just glad you're here. I have something for you." She picked up the envelope from the table and put it in Jeffrey's hands. "I've also got a lot to tell you," she added. She picked up the groceries and carried them into the kitchen.

"What's this?" he asked, following her with the envelope in hand.

"It's a copy of Henry Noble's pathology file from Valley Hospital," Kelly said over her shoulder.

"Already?" Jeffrey was impressed. "How on earth did you manage it so quickly?"

"It was easy. Hart Ruddock sent it over by messenger. He didn't even ask why I wanted it."

Jeffrey slipped the file out of the envelope as he was walking. There were no electron micrographs but then he didn't expect them. They were not part of a routine autopsy. Even so, the file seemed skimpy. Jeffrey spotted a notation that more material was on file at the Medical Examiner's office. So that explained it.

Kelly unpacked the groceries while Jeffrey retired to the couch in the family room with the files. He found a summary of the autopsy report that was at the Medical Examiner's office. Reading it quickly, he saw that a toxicology screen had been done but that the findings had not highlighted anything suspicious. He also saw that on microscopic section there had been evidence of histologic damage to the nerve cells of the dorsal root ganglia as well as to the cardiac muscle.

Kelly joined Jeffrey on the couch. He could tell she had something serious to tell him.

"There was a major anesthetic complication today at St. Joe's," she said. "No one wanted to say much, but I understand it involved an epidural case. The patient was a young woman named Karen Hodges."

Jeffrey shook his head sadly. "What happened?" he asked.

"The patient died," Kelly said.

"Marcaine?" Jeffrey asked.

"That I don't know for sure," Kelly said. "But I'll find out, probably tomorrow. The person that told me about it thought it was Marcaine."

"Victim number five," Jeffrey sighed.

"What are you talking about?"

Jeffrey told her of the fruits of his day's research, starting with his call to the Board of Registration in Medicine. "I think the fact that the deaths occurred at different hospitals increases the chances of a deliberate tampering. We're dealing with someone who's shrewd enough to know that more than one death during epidural anesthesia at any one institution would arouse suspicions and probably lead to an official inquiry."

"So you really think someone—some person—is behind all this?"

"More and more," Jeffrey said. "I'm almost certain a contaminant was involved. I went to the library today, and among other things I checked to be absolutely sure that local anesthetics in general and Marcaine in particular do not cause cellular damage; like the damage described in Henry Noble's autopsy or revealed in Patty Owen's electron micrographs. Marcaine just doesn't do it. Not Marcaine alone."

"Then what could have caused it?"

"I'm still not sure," Jeffrey said. "I did a lot of reading about toxicology and poisons at the library too. I'm convinced it couldn't be some traditional poison, since they would have shown up on the toxicology screen. What I'm tending to think is that it would have to be a toxin."

"Aren't they the same thing?"

"No," Jeffrey said. "A poison is more a general term. It applies to anything that causes damage to cells or interrupts cellular function. Usually when someone thinks of a poison they think of mercury or nicotine or strychnine."

"Or arsenic," Kelly added.

"Exactly," Jeffrey said. "They're all inorganic chemicals or elements. A toxin, on the other hand, although a type of poison, is the product of a living cell. Like the toxin that causes toxic shock syndrome. That comes from bacteria."

"Are all toxins from bacteria?" Kelly asked.

"Not all," Jeffrey said. "Some very potent ones come from vegetables, like ricin from the castor bean. But people are most familiar with toxins that come in the form of venoms, like from snakes, scorpions, or certain spiders. Whatever was put into the Marcaine, it had to be extremely potent. It had to be something that could be fatal in minute amounts and at the same time mimic local anesthetics to a great degree. Otherwise its presence would have been suspected. The difference, of course, would be that it destroys nerve cells, not just blocks their function like local anesthetics."

"So if it was injected along with the Marcaine, why wouldn't it show up with the toxicology testing?"

"For two reasons. First, it's probably introduced in such minute amounts there is very little in the tissue sample to be detected. Second, it's an organic compound that could hide among the thousands of organic compounds that normally exist in any tissue sample. What's used to separate all the compounds in a toxicology lab is an instrument called a gas chromatograph. But this instrument doesn't separate everything cleanly. There's always overlaps. What you wind up with is a graph featuring a series of peaks and valleys. Those peaks can reflect the presence of a number of substances. It's the mass spectrograph that actually reveals what compounds exist in a sample. But a toxin could be obscured in one of the gas chromatograph's peaks. Unless you suspected its presence and knew to search for it specifically, you wouldn't find it."

"Wow," Kelly said. "So if someone is behind this, he'd really have to know what he was doing. I mean, he'd have to be familiar with basic toxicology, don't you think?"

Jeffrey nodded. "I gave it some thought on my way home from the library. I think the murderer has to be a doctor, someone with a pretty extensive background in physiology and pharmacology. A doctor would also have access to a variety of toxins and to the Marcaine vials. To tell you the truth, my ideal suspect would likely be one of my closest colleagues: a fellow anesthesiologist."

"Any idea as to why a doctor would do such a thing?" Kelly asked.

"That might never be determined," Jeffrey said. "Why did Dr. X kill all those people? Why did the person put the poison in the Tylenol capsules? I don't think anyone knows for sure. Obviously they were unstable. But saying that poses more questions than it answers. Maybe the reasons would lie within the irrational psyche of a psychotic individual who is mad at the world or mad at the medical profession or mad at hospitals and in his distorted thinking believes that this is an appropriate way to exact revenge."

Kelly shivered. "It terrifies me to think of a doctor like that on the loose."

"Me too," Jeffrey said. "Whoever it is could be normal most of the time but suffer psychotic episodes. He or she might be the last person you'd suspect. And whoever it is, they would have to be in a position of trust to have access to so many hospital operating rooms."

"Do many doctors have privileges in such a range of hospitals?" Kelly asked.

Jeffrey shrugged. "I haven't the faintest idea, but checking is probably the next step. Could you get a printout from St. Joe's of the entire professional staff?"

"I don't see why not," Kelly said. "I'm very good friends with Polly Arnsdorf, the director of nursing. Would you want an employee list as well?"

"Why not," Jeffrey said. Her question made him think of the extraordinary access he had at Boston Memorial thanks to his position on the housekeeping staff. Jeffrey shuddered, realizing the magnitude of a hospital's vulnerability.

"Are you sure that we shouldn't go to the police?" Kelly asked.

Jeffrey shook his head. "No police, not yet," he said. "As convincing as all this sounds to us at the moment, we have to remember that we still don't have a lick of evidence to support our theory. So far it's pure speculation on our part. As soon as we get some evidence that's real, we can go to the authorities. Whether it would be the police or not, I'm not sure."

"But the longer we wait, the more chance there will be that the killer will strike again."

"I know," Jeffrey said. "But without more evidence or the slightest idea of who the killer is, we're not exactly in a position to stop him."

"Or her," Kelly said grimly.

Jeffrey nodded. "Or her."

"So what can we do to speed things up?"

"What are the chances you could get a professional staff and an employee list from Valley Hospital? It would be best if the list was contemporary to the period during which Chris lost his patient."

Kelly whistled. "That's a tall order," she said. "I could call Hart Ruddock back, or I could try a few of the nursing supervisors I know who are still there. One way or the other, I'll give it a shot tomorrow."

"And I'll try getting the same at the Memorial," Jeffrey said.

He wondered where in the hospital he'd have to go to get such a list. "The sooner we have this information the better."

"Why don't I call Polly right now?" Kelly suggested, checking the time. "She usually stays until five or so."

While Kelly went into the kitchen to use the phone, Jeffrey thought about the horror of another epidural disaster at St. Joe's that day. It confirmed his contaminant theory. He was surer than ever that a Dr. X was at large in the Boston area.

Although Jeffrey thought that a doctor was the most likely perpetrator, he acknowledged that anyone with pharmaceutical experience could have tampered with the Marcaine; it didn't have to be an M.D. The problem was access to the drug, and that made him wonder about someone in pharmacy.

Hanging up the phone, Kelly rejoined Jeffrey in the family room. She didn't sit down. "Polly said I can get the list. No problem. In fact, she said that if I wanted to come right over and get it, I could. So I said I would."

"Wonderful," Jeffrey said. "I only hope we get the same cooperation at the other hospitals." He got to his feet.

"Where are you going?" she asked.

"With you."

"No, you're not. You're staying here and relaxing. You look haggard. You were supposed to get some sleep today, and instead you went to the library. You stay here. I'll be back in a jiffy."

Jeffrey did as he was told. Kelly was right, he was exhausted. He lay down on the couch and closed his eyes. He heard Kelly start the car and pull out, then he heard the electric garage door close. The house became quiet save for the ticking of the living room's grandfather clock. Out in the yard a robin squawked.

Jeffrey opened his eyes. Sleep was out of the question; he was much too restless. Instead, he got up and went into the kitchen to use the phone. He called the Medical Examiner's office to ask about Karen Hodges. As an anesthetic complication, her fatality would have fallen into the Medical Examiner's province.

The secretary at the Examiner's office told him that Karen Hodges's autopsy was scheduled for the following morning.

Next, Jeffrey called information to get the numbers for

Commonwealth Hospital and Suffolk General. He called
Commonwealth first. When the operator there picked up, Jeffrey asked for the anesthesia department. Once connected, he
asked if Dr. Mann was still in the hospital.

"Dr. Lawrence Mann?"

"That's right," Jeffrey said.

"Hell, he hasn't worked here for well over two years."

"Could you tell me where he's working?" Jeffrey asked.

"I'm not sure exactly. Someplace in London. But he's not
practicing medicine anymore. I believe he's in the antiques
business."

Another casualty of the malpractice process, Jeffrey thought.
He'd heard of other doctors who'd given up medicine after
being sued, however frivolously. What a waste of education
and talent.

Next he placed a call to the anesthesia department of Suffolk
General Hospital. A cheerful female voice answered the department's phone.

"Is Dr. Madaline Bowman still practicing at the hospital?"
Jeffrey asked.

"Who is this?" the woman asked, her tone decidedly less
cheerful.

"Dr. Webber," Jeffrey said, making up a name.

"Sorry, Dr. Webber," the woman said. "This is Dr. Asher.
I didn't mean to sound rude. Your question took me by sur-
prise. Not many people have asked for Dr. Bowman recently.
I'm afraid she committed suicide several years ago."

Jeffrey slowly hung up the phone. The killer's casualties
weren't only the victims on the operating table, Jeffrey
thought grimly. What a trail of destruction! The more he
thought about it, the more he was sure someone was behind
this string of seemingly unrelated medical disasters: someone
with access to the ORs of the hospitals involved; and someone
familiar with at least basic toxicology. But who? Jeffrey was
more determined than ever to get to the bottom of it.

Walking back through the house, Jeffrey went into Chris's
study. He picked up the toxicology text that he'd glanced at
on his first visit to Kelly's and brought it back to the family
room. Stretching out on the couch, and kicking off his shoes,

he opened the book to the index. He wanted to check the listings under the entry for Toxins.

Devlin pulled up to the house and parked. Leaning over, he glanced at the façade. It was a nondescript brick house like so many others in the Boston area. He looked back at his list. The house was listed as the Brighton residence of one Jack Everson.

Devlin had already been to seven Everson addresses. So far he'd had no luck whatsoever, and he was beginning to wonder if the ploy would pay off. Even if he did find this Christopher Everson, who was to say for sure the man could lead him to Rhodes? It could all be a wild-goose chase.

Devlin was also finding the Eversons a decidedly uncooperative clan. You'd think he'd been asking these people about their sex lives and not merely if they knew a Christopher Everson. Devlin wondered what made the average person in the Boston area so damn paranoid.

At one house he had to literally grab the grubby, beer-bellied man and give him a good shake. That had brought the wife out, who was uglier than the man, which Devlin had thought was an accomplishment. Like some kind of cartoon character, she'd brought her rolling pin with her and threatened to hit Devlin with it unless he let go of her husband. Devlin had had to grab the rolling pin and throw it into the next yard, where there was a big, nasty German shepherd.

After that they had settled down and sullenly told Devlin they'd never heard of a Christopher Everson. Devlin had wondered why they couldn't have said that in the first place.

Devlin got out of his car and stretched. No sense putting off the inevitable, he thought, much as he might like to. He climbed the steps and rang the bell, scouting out the neighborhood while he waited. The houses were nothing splashy, but the yards were well-kept.

He again faced the door, which was covered by an aluminum storm door with two large glass panels. He hoped he wasn't experiencing his second empty house. It would mean he'd have to drive back here if he didn't get a tip on Christopher Everson someplace else. Devlin had already found one house empty. It had been in Watertown.

He rang the bell again. He was about to leave when he caught sight of the occupant looking at him through the side-light window to the right of the door. The man was another beauty with a beer-belly profile. He was wearing a tank-top undershirt that could not cover the full expanse of his abdomen. Tufts of Brillo-like hair stuck out from under each arm. A five-day stubble covered his face.

Devlin called out that he wanted to ask him a question. The man cracked the inner door open about an inch.

"Evening," Devlin said through the storm door. "Sorry to bother you—"

"Beat it, bud," the man said.

"Now, that's not very neighborly," Devlin said. "I just want to ask—"

"What's the matter with you—you can't hear?" the man asked. "I said beat it or there'll be trouble."

"Trouble?" Devlin questioned.

The man made a move to close the door. Devlin lost his patience. A quick, karate-style chop shattered the upper glass panel of the storm door. A swift kick with his boot took out the lower pane and kicked the inner door open.

In a blink of an eye, Devlin was through the aluminum door and had the man by the neck. The man's eyes started to bulge.

"I've got a question," Devlin repeated. "Here it is. I'm looking for Christopher Everson. You know him?" He released his hold on the man's throat. The man coughed and sputtered.

"Don't keep me waiting," Devlin warned.

"My name is Jack," the man said hoarsely. "Jack Everson."

"That I knew," Devlin said, regaining his composure. "What about Christopher Everson? Do you know him? Ever hear of him? He might be a doctor."

"Never heard of him," the man said.

Disgusted with his luck, Devlin went back out to his car. He crossed off Jack Everson and looked at the next name on his list. It was K. C. Everson in Brookline. He reached forward and started the car. From his phone call earlier he knew that the K stood for Kelly. He wondered what the C stood for.

He made a U-turn to get back to Washington Street. That ran into Chestnut Hill Avenue and then on into Brookline. He thought he could be at this K. C. Everson's in five minutes, ten tops, if there was traffic in Cleveland Circle.

"Ms. Arnsdorf will see you now," the secretary said. The secretary was male, about two or three years younger than Trent, or so Trent guessed. He wasn't bad-looking, either. He looked as if he pumped iron. Trent wondered how come the director of nursing had a male secretary. He thought it must have been a deliberate statement, some kind of a power trip on the part of the woman. Trent did not like Polly Arnsdorf.

Trent got up from the chair he'd been sitting in and stretched lazily. He wasn't going to rush into the woman's office after she'd kept him waiting for half an hour. He tossed the week-old *Time* magazine onto the side table. He glanced at the secretary and caught him staring.

"Something wrong?" Trent asked.

"If you want to talk to Ms. Arnsdorf I'd suggest you go right into her office," the secretary said. "She has a busy schedule."

Screw you, Trent thought. He wondered why everyone connected with administration thought their time was worth more than anybody else's. He would have liked to have said something cutting to the secretary, but he held his tongue. Instead he reached down, touched his toes, and stretched out his hamstrings. "Get kinda stiff sitting around," he said. He straightened up and cracked his fingers. Finally he walked into Ms. Arnsdorf's office.

Trent had to smile when he saw her. All nursing supervisors looked the same—like battleaxes. They never could decide what they wanted to be: nurses or administrators. He hated them all. Since he was only staying at each hospital for eight months or so, he'd gotten to see more of them than he cared to in the last few years. But today's meeting was of an order he always enjoyed. He loved to cause the directors trouble. With the severe nursing shortage, he knew how to do it.

"Mr. Harding," Ms. Arnsdorf said. "What can I do for you? Sorry to keep you waiting, but with the problem we had in the OR today, I'm sure you can understand."

Trent smiled to himself. He could understand about the

problem they had in OR. If only she knew how much he could understand.

"I'd like to give notice that I'm leaving St. Joseph's Hospital," Trent said. "Effective immediately."

Ms. Arnsdorf sat ramrod straight in her chair. Trent knew he'd gotten her attention. He loved it.

"I'm sorry to hear this," Ms. Arnsdorf said. "Is there some problem that we could discuss?"

"I don't feel I'm being used to my full potential," Trent said. "As you know, I was trained in the Navy and given significantly more autonomy there."

"Perhaps we could move you to a different department," Ms. Arnsdorf suggested.

"I'm afraid that's not the answer," Trent said. "You see, I like the OR. What I've begun to think is that I would be better off in a more academic environment, like Boston City Hospital. I've decided to apply there."

"Are you sure you won't reconsider?" Ms. Arnsdorf said.

"I'm afraid not. There's another problem, too. I've never gotten along well with the OR supervisor, Mrs. Raleigh. Just between you and me, she doesn't know how to run a tight ship, if you know what I mean."

"I'm not sure I do," Ms. Arnsdorf said.

Trent then gave her a prepared list of what he saw as problems in the organization and function of the OR. He'd always despised Mrs. Raleigh and hoped this chat with the director of nursing would give her some serious grief.

Trent came out of Ms. Arnsdorf's office feeling great. He thought about stopping and having a chat with her secretary to find out where the guy worked out, but there was someone else in the waiting room hoping to see the director. Trent recognized her. She was the day supervisor in the ICU.

Less than half an hour after his meeting with Ms. Arnsdorf, Trent walked out of the hospital with all his toiletries from his locker stuffed in a pillow case. He had rarely felt so good. Everything had worked out better than he could have hoped. As he walked toward the Orange Line of the MBTA, he wondered if he should go directly to Boston City to apply for a job. Glancing at his watch, he realized it was too late in the day. Tomorrow would be fine. Then he started to wonder where he would go after Boston City. He thought about San Francisco. He'd heard San Francisco was a place a guy could have fun.

When the doorbell rang the first time, Jeffrey's mind was able to neatly incorporate it into the dream he was having. He was back in college and facing a final exam in a course that he'd forgotten he'd taken and had never gone to the class. It was a terrifying dream for Jeffrey, and perspiration had formed along his hairline. He'd always been conscientious about his studying, ever fearful of failure. In his dream the doorbell had become the schoolbell.

Jeffrey had fallen fast asleep with the heavy toxicology book balanced on his chest. When the doorbell rang a second time, his eyes blinked open and the book fell to the floor with a crash. Momentarily confused as to where he was, he sat bolt upright and looked around. Only then did he get his bearings.

At first he expected Kelly to get the door. But then he remembered that she'd left to go to St. Joe's. He got to his feet, but too quickly. A little sleep on top of his general exhaustion made him suddenly dizzy, and he had to put a hand on the arm of the couch to steady himself. It took him a full minute to orient himself before he could pad his way on stocking feet through the kitchen and dining room to the front hall.

Grasping the doorknob, Jeffrey was about to open the door when he noticed the peephole. Leaning forward, he took a glance. Still groggy, he wasn't thinking quite straight yet. When he found himself staring straight at Devlin's bulbous nose and red, watery eyes, his heart leaped to his throat.

Jeffrey swallowed hard and warily took a second look. It was Devlin all right. Nobody else could be that ugly.

The door chimes rang again. Jeffrey ducked from the peephole and took a step back. Fear gripped him tightly around the throat. Where could he go? What could he do? How did Devlin ever manage to track him down? He was terrified of being caught or shot, especially now that he and Kelly had made progress. If they failed to discover the truth now, who was to say when the fiend responsible for so much death and anguish would be caught, much less stopped?

To Jeffrey's horror, the doorknob began to turn. He was

fairly confident the dead bolt was thrown, but from experience he knew that if Devlin aimed to get somewhere, you could bet he'd get there. Jeffrey watched as the knob began to turn the other way. He took another step back and brushed against the tea service on the foyer table.

Both the silver creamer and silver sugar bowl fell to the floor with a tremendous clatter. Jeffrey's heart leaped in his chest. The doorbell rang several times in a row. Jeffrey feared it was all over. He was through. Devlin had to have heard the crash.

Then he saw Devlin press his face against one of the narrow sidelights that lined the front door. It was covered on the inside by a lace curtain, so Jeffrey had no idea what Devlin could see. Quickly Jeffrey sidestepped through the archway into the dining room.

As if anticipating Jeffrey's movement, Devlin next appeared at the dining room window. Just as Devlin cupped his hands and leaned against the glass, Jeffrey dropped to his hands and knees and crawled behind the dining room table. Then, scurrying like a crab, he retreated into the kitchen.

Jeffrey's heart was racing. Once he'd made it to the kitchen, he got to his feet. He knew he needed to hide. The partially open door to the pantry beckoned. He rushed over and slipped into the aromatic darkness. As he did so, he clumsily bumped a mop that was leaning against the wall just inside the door. It fell out onto the kitchen floor.

Loud banging on the front door seemed to rattle the entire house. Jeffrey was half surprised Devlin didn't just shoot his way in. Jeffrey pulled the pantry door shut behind him. He worried about the mop, and debated if it was worth the risk to open the door to pull it back inside, but decided against it. What if Devlin was circling the house and caught a glimpse of him through one of the windows off the back?

Something brushed against Jeffrey's leg. He jumped and hit his head on a shelf of canned goods. Some of the cans fell to the floor. An awful feline screech resulted. It was Delilah, the pregnant tabby. What else could go wrong? Jeffrey wondered.

After the loud pounding on the front door had ceased, silence descended on the house. Jeffrey sweated and strained to hear anything that might give him a clue as to what Devlin was doing.

Suddenly there were heavy footfalls on the deck that extended off the back of the house. Then another door was rattled with a vehemence that promised to rend it off its hinges. Jeffrey guessed Devlin was at the door from the deck to the family room. He was sure that any minute he'd hear glass breaking to signal Devlin had come inside.

Instead, silence returned after the last clatter on the deck. Two minutes went by, then three. Jeffrey was not sure how much time passed after that. It could have been ten minutes by the time he relaxed his death grip on the inside panel of the pantry door. It seemed like an eternity.

Delilah seemed eager for attention. She kept brushing up against his leg. Jeffrey hoped to keep her quiet. He leaned over to give her a few strokes. Once he started to pet her, she gratefully arched her back and stretched. After a while, Jeffrey lost all sense of time. He could only hear his pulse in his ears. He could see nothing in the inky blackness. Sweat dripped down the back of his neck. The temperature in the small pantry was steadily rising.

Suddenly there was another noise. Jeffrey strained to listen. He was afraid it was the sound of the front door being opened! Then he heard a noise that he definitely recognized: the front door banged shut with a force that shook the house.

Jeffrey's exhausted fingers dug back into the wood-paneled door. Devlin had managed to get in! Maybe he had picked the lock. Jeffrey didn't need to hear the sound of the door slamming to know the man was angry.

Jeffrey began to worry again about the stupid mop lying on the kitchen floor like some sort of arrow pointing toward the pantry. He wished he'd pulled it in immediately after it had fallen. Jeffrey's only hope now was that Devlin would go upstairs, giving Jeffrey a chance to flee out the back door.

Light footfalls quickly toured the ground floor of the house, finally coming into the kitchen, where they abruptly stopped. Jeffrey held his breath. In his mind's eye he could see Devlin studying the mop as it pointed at the pantry and scratching his head. With the last bit of reserve strength in his fingers, Jeffrey pushed his nails into the wood of the pantry door. Maybe Devlin would try it and think it was locked.

Jeffrey's arms twitched as he felt the pantry door vibrate.

Devlin had his hand on the outer handle and was giving it a tug. Jeffrey strained, but the door still budged. The slight tug was followed by a definite yank that caused the door to open about an inch before slamming shut.

The next yank was overwhelming. It pulled the door open and yanked Jeffrey from the pantry. He stumbled into the kitchen, raising his hands to protect his head . . .

Reeling back from fright, Kelly clasped a hand to her chest and let out a short, high-pitched wail. She dropped the mop she'd picked up from the floor, along with the envelope she'd just brought home from St. Joe's. Delilah shot out of the pantry and disappeared into the dining room.

They stood looking at each other for a minute. Kelly was the first to recover.

"What is this, some sort of a game to scare me every time I come home?" she demanded. "I came through here tiptoeing around, thinking you might be asleep."

All Jeffrey could manage to say was that he was sorry; he hadn't meant to scare her. He grabbed her hand and pulled her against the wall separating the dining room and the kitchen.

"What are you doing now?" Kelly asked with alarm.

Jeffrey put a finger to his lips to shush her. "Remember the man I told you about, the one who shot at me? Devlin." He whispered.

Kelly nodded.

"He was here. At the front door. He even came around back and tried the door to the deck."

"Nobody was out there when I came in."

"Are you sure?"

"Pretty sure," Kelly said. "I'll check." She started to leave but Jeffrey grabbed her arm. Only then could she see how terrified he was.

"He may have a gun."

"You want me to call the police?"

"No," Jeffrey said. He didn't know what he wanted her to do.

"Why don't you get back in the pantry and I'll look around," Kelly suggested.

Jeffrey nodded. He didn't like the idea of Kelly facing Devlin alone, but since he was the one Devlin wanted, he thought he'd leave her alone. One way or another they had to find out if Devlin was lurking about the premises. Jeffrey went back to the pantry.

Kelly went to the front door and checked the front of the house. She looked up and down the street. Then, walking around the back of the house, she checked the rear. She found some muddy footprints across the back deck, but that was all. She went back inside and got Jeffrey to come out from the pantry. As soon as he did, Delilah scooted back inside.

Still unconvinced, Jeffrey warily made his own tour around the house, first inside, then out. Kelly tagged along. He was genuinely mystified. Why had Devlin retreated? Not that he wanted to question such an unexpected bit of luck.

Returning inside the house, Jeffrey said, "How the hell did he find me? I haven't told anyone I'm here—have you?"

"Not a soul."

Jeffrey headed directly to the guest room and pulled out his duffel bag from its hiding place under the bed. Kelly stood in the doorway. "What are you doing?" she asked.

"I've got to go before he comes back," he said.

"Wait a minute. Let's talk about this," Kelly said. "Maybe we could confer before you just decide to leave. I thought we were in this together."

"I can't be here when he comes back," Jeffrey said.

"Do you really think Devlin knows you're here?"

"Obviously," Jeffrey said almost irritably. "What do you think, he's going around ringing every doorbell in Boston?"

"No need to be sarcastic," Kelly said patiently.

"I'm sorry," Jeffrey said. "I'm not too tactful when I'm terrified."

"I think there is a reason why he came and rang the bell," Kelly said. "You left Chris's notes in your hotel room. They had his name all over them. He was probably just following up on it, wanting to ask me a few questions."

Jeffrey's eyes narrowed as he considered the possibility. "You really think so?" he asked, warming to the idea.

"The more I think about it, the more that seems the most reasonable explanation. Otherwise, why would he leave? If he knew you were here, he'd just park himself outside until you showed up. He would have been more persistent."

Jeffrey nodded. Kelly's argument was making sense.

"I think he may come back," Kelly continued. "But I don't think he knows you're here. All it means is that we have to be even more careful and we have to think up some explanation for your having Chris's notes with you, in case he asks me."

Jeffrey nodded again.

"Any suggestions?" she asked.

Jeffrey shrugged his shoulders. "We're both anesthesiologists. You could say Chris and I did research together."

"We might have to do better than that," Kelly said. "But it's a thought. Anyhow, you're staying, not going, so put your duffel bag back under the bed." She turned on her heels and left the guest room.

Jeffrey sighed with relief. He'd never actually wanted to leave. He tossed the bag back under the bed and followed Kelly.

The first thing Kelly did was draw the drapes in the dining room, kitchen, and family room. Then she went to the kitchen and put the mop back in the pantry. She handed Jeffrey the envelope from St. Joe's. It contained the printout of the professional staff and employee roster at St. Joe's.

Jeffrey took the envelope over to the couch and opened it. He slipped out the computer paper and unfolded it. There were a lot of names. What Jeffrey was interested in doing was reading over the professional staff to see if any of the people he knew at the Memorial had privileges at St. Joe's.

"Should we make some dinner?" Kelly asked.

"I guess," he said, looking up. After the episode in the pantry he wasn't sure he'd be able to eat. A half hour earlier he never would have guessed that about this time he'd be relaxing on the couch, thinking about dinner.

"Excuse me," Devlin began. A sixty-some-year-old woman with white hair had opened the door of her Newton home. She was impeccably dressed in a white linen skirt, a blue sweater, and a simple strand of pearls. As she tried to focus on Devlin, she reached for her glasses, which were dangling from a gold chain around her neck.

"My word, young man," she said after giving Devlin a good once-over. "You look like a member of the Hell's Angels."

"The resemblance has been noted before, ma'am, but to tell you the truth, I've never set foot on a motorcycle. They're just too darn dangerous."

"Then why dress in this outlandish style?" she asked, clearly puzzled.

Devlin looked in the woman's eyes. She seemed genuinely interested. Hers was a far cry from the reception he'd gotten at the other Everson residences. "Do you really want to know?" he asked.

"I'm always interested in what motivates you young people."

Being considered a young person warmed Devlin's heart. At

forty-eight, it had been a long time since he'd thought of himself as young. "I've found this manner of dress helps me in my work," he said.

"And, pray tell, what work do you do that requires you to look so . . ." The woman paused, searching for the right word. ". . . so intimidating."

Devlin laughed, then coughed. He knew he should stop smoking. "I'm a bounty hunter. I bring in criminals who are trying to evade the law."

"How exciting!" the woman said. "How noble."

"I'm not sure how noble it is, ma'am. I do it for money."

"Everyone has to be paid," said the woman. "What on earth brings you to my door?"

Devlin explained about Christopher Everson, emphasizing that he wasn't a fugitive but that he might have some information about a fugitive.

"No one in our family is named Christopher," she said, "but it seems to me someone mentioned a Christopher Everson a few years ago. I believe the man I'm thinking of was a physician."

"That sounds encouraging," Devlin said. "I had an idea Christopher Everson was a doctor."

"Perhaps I could ask my husband when he comes home. He's more acquainted with the Everson side of our family. After all, it's his. Is there some way I could get in touch with you?"

Devlin gave his name and Michael Mosconi's office phone number. He told her she could leave a message there. Then he thanked her for her help and went back to his car.

Devlin shook his head as he circled Ralph Everson's name on his list. He thought it might be worth a call back if no better leads turned up.

Devlin started his car and pulled out into the street. The next town on his list was Dedham. Two Eversons were listed there. His plan was to sweep around the south of the city to hit Dedham, Canton, and Milton before heading back into the city limits.

Devlin took Hammond Street to Tremont, and eventually to the old Route One. That would take him directly into the center of Dedham. As he drove, he laughed about the range of experiences he was having. It was going from one extreme to the other. He thought about the episode at Kelly C. Everson's. He'd been sure someone was at home, having heard a clatter of something hitting the floor just beyond the door. Unless it was a pet. He'd circled that address as well. He'd go back there if nothing better turned up elsewhere.

Finding this doctor was definitely not the easy job Devlin had thought it would be. For the first time he began to wonder what the circumstances were concerning Jeffrey's murder-two conviction. Normally he never bothered to find much out about the nature of the crime involved unless it suggested the type of firepower he'd need. And somebody's guilt or innocence was not a concern for Devlin.

But Jeffrey Rhodes was becoming a mystery as well as a challenge. Mosconi hadn't told him much about Rhodes except to explain his bail situation and to say that he didn't think Rhodes acted like the criminal type. And all of Devlin's requests for information that he'd put out through his network of underworld connections came back blank. No one knew anything about Jeffrey Rhodes. Apparently he'd never done anything wrong, a situation unique in Devlin's bounty-hunting experience. So why the huge bail? Just what had Dr. Jeffrey Rhodes done?

Devlin was also baffled by Rhodes's behavior since he'd tried to hightail it to Rio. Now Rhodes seemed to be altogether different. He wasn't acting like the usual fugitive on the run. In fact, since Devlin had taken away Jeffrey's ticket to South America, Jeffrey didn't seem to be running anyplace. He was working on something—Devlin knew it. He felt the papers he found at the Essex proved it. Devlin wondered if it would help to get one of the police surgeons to take a look at the material. With the Eversons not panning out, Devlin could use another angle.

Despite Kelly's insistence to the contrary, Jeffrey helped with the cleanup after their dinner of swordfish and artichokes. She was at the sink, scraping the dishes as he ferried them from the table in the family room.

"The OR wasn't the only place that had a tragedy today," Kelly said as she tried to wipe her forehead with the back of her forearm that showed above the rubber glove she was wearing. "We had our problems in the ICU as well."

Jeffrey took a sponge to wipe off the table. "What happened?" he asked absently. He was preoccupied with his own thoughts. He was worrying about Devlin's inevitable next visit.

"One of the hospital nurses died," Kelly said. "She was a good friend and a good nurse."

"Was she working when this happened?"

"No, she worked evenings in the OR," Kelly answered. "She came in this morning by ambulance sometime around eight."

"Auto accident?"

Kelly shook her head and went back to scraping the dishes. "Nope. Near as they could figure, she'd had a seizure at home."

Jeffrey held up from his sponging and stood upright. The word "seizure" evoked the memory of the whole sequence with Patty Owen. As if it were yesterday he could see her face as she looked at him for help just before her seizure had hit.

"It was terrible," Kelly continued. "She had this seizure or whatever it was in the bathtub. She hit her head something fierce. Enough to fracture her skull."

"How awful," Jeffrey said. "Is that what killed her?"

"It certainly didn't help," Kelly said. "But it wasn't what killed her. From the moment the EMTs got to her, she had an irregular heartbeat. The conduction system of her heart was shot. She died of an arrest in the unit. We had her going for a little while on a pacemaker. But the heart was just too weak."

"Wait a minute," Jeffrey said. He was stunned by the similarities between Kelly's description of this sequence of events and the sequence in Patty Owen's reaction to the Marcaine in her disastrous Caesarean. Jeffrey wanted to be sure he had it straight.

"One of the OR nurses was brought into the hospital after a seizure and some sort of cardiac problem?" he asked.

"That's right," Kelly said. She opened the dishwasher door and started loading the dirty dishes. "It was so sad. It was like having a member of your family die."

"Any diagnosis?"

Kelly shook her head. "Nope. They first thought of a brain

tumor but they found nothing with the NMR. She must have
had some developmental heart problem. That's what one of the
internal medicine residents told me."

"What was her name?" Jeffrey asked.

"Gail Shaffer."

"Do you know anything about her personal life?" Jeffrey
asked.

"A little," Kelly said. "Like I said, she was a friend."

"Tell me."

"She was single, but I believe she had a steady boyfriend."

"You know the boyfriend?"

"No. Just that he was a medical student," Kelly said. "Hey,
why the third degree?"

"I'm not sure," Jeffrey said, "but as soon as you started
telling me about Gail, I couldn't help thinking of Patty. It was
the same sequence. Seizure and cardiac conduction problems."

"You're not suggesting . . ." Kelly couldn't finish her sentence.

Jeffrey shook his head. "I know. I know. I'm starting to
sound like one of those crazies who sees a conspiracy behind
everything. But it's such an unusual sequence. I guess at this
point I'm just sensitive to anything that sounds even remotely
suspicious."

By eleven P.M. Devlin felt it was time to give up for the night.
It was too late to expect people to open their doors to a stranger. Besides, he'd done enough for one day and he was exhausted. He wondered if his intuition about Chris Everson's
even being in the Boston area was correct. He'd covered all the
Eversons in the southern suburbs of Boston without any appre-
ciable results. One other person said that he'd heard there was
a Dr. Christopher Everson, but he didn't know where the man
lived or worked.

Since he was in Boston proper, Devlin decided to pay a
quick visit to Michael Mosconi. He knew it was late, but he
didn't care. He drove into the North End and double parked,
along with everyone else, on Hanover Street. From there he
walked through the narrow streets to Unity Street, where
Michael owned a modest three-story house.

"I hope this means you have some good news for me,"

Michael said as he opened the door for Devlin. Michael was dressed in a maroon, satin-looking polyester robe. His feet were stuck into aged leather slippers. Even Mrs. Mosconi appeared at the top of the stairs to see who this late-night caller was. She had on a red chenille robe. Her hair was in pincurlers, which Devlin thought had gone out with the fifties. She also had some glop on her face, which Devlin guessed was to retard the inevitable aging process. God help any burglar who inadvertently broke into this house, thought Devlin. One look at Mrs. Mosconi in the dark and he'd die of sheer terror.

Mosconi took Devlin into the kitchen and offered him a beer, which Devlin accepted with enthusiasm. Mosconi went to the refrigerator and handed Devlin a bottle of Rolling Rock.

"No glass?" Devlin asked with a smile.

Mosconi frowned. "Don't push your luck."

Devlin took a long pull before wiping his mouth with the back of his hand.

"Well? Did you get him?"

Devlin shook his head. "Not yet."

"What is this, a social call?" Michael asked with his usual sarcasm.

"Business," Devlin said. "What is this Jeffrey Rhodes being sent up for?"

"Christ, give me patience," Michael said while looking heavenward and pretending to pray. Then, looking back at Devlin, he said, "I told you: murder-two. He was convicted of second-degree murder."

"Did he do it?"

"How the hell am I supposed to know?" Michael said with exasperation. "He was convicted. That's enough for me. What the hell difference does it make?"

"This case isn't run-of-the-mill," Devlin said. "I need more information."

Mosconi heaved an exasperated sigh. "The guy's a doctor. His conviction had something to do with malpractice and drugs. Beyond that, I don't know. Devlin, what the hell's the matter with you? What difference does all this make? I want Rhodes, understand?"

"I need more information," Devlin repeated. "I want you to find out the details of his crime. I think if I knew more about his conviction, I'd have a better idea as to what the guy's up to now."

"Maybe I should just call in reinforcements," Mosconi said. "Maybe a little friendly competition between, say, a half dozen of you bounty hunters would get quicker results."

Competition was not what Devlin wanted. There was too much money on the line. Thinking quickly, he said: "The one thing in our favor at the moment is the fact that the doc is staying in Boston. If you want him to run, like to South America, where he was headed when I stopped him, then bring in your reinforcements."

"All I want to know is when you'll have him in jail."

"Give me a week," Devlin said. "A week total. Five more days. But you have to get the information I need. This doctor is up to something. As soon as I figure out what it is, I'll find him."

Devlin left Mosconi's house and returned to his car. He could barely keep his eyes open as he drove back to his Charlestown apartment. But he still had to make contact with Bill Bartley, the fellow he'd hired to watch Carol Rhodes. He called on his car phone.

The connection wasn't a very good one. Devlin had to shout to make himself heard above the static.

"Any calls from the doctor?" Devlin yelled into the receiver.

"Not a one," Bill said. It sounded as if he were on the moon. "The only thing vaguely interesting was a call from an apparent lover. Some stockbroker from L.A. Did you know she was moving to L.A.?"

"You sure it wasn't Rhodes?" Devlin yelled.

"I don't think so," Bill said. "They even joked about the doctor in not too flattering terms."

Wonderful, thought Devlin after hanging up. No wonder Mosconi hadn't felt Carol and Jeffrey were lovey-dovey. It looked like they were splitting up. He had the feeling that he was throwing his money away keeping Bill on the payroll, but he wasn't willing to take the chance of not tailing Carol. Not yet.

As Devlin climbed the front steps of his apartment building that fronted Monument Square, his legs felt leaden, as if he had been through the battle of Bunker Hill. He couldn't remember the last time he'd been in his bed. He knew he'd be asleep before his head hit the pillow.

He turned on the light and paused at the door. His place was a mess. Magazines and empty beer bottles were strewn about. There was a musty, unlived-in smell. Unexpectedly, he felt lonely. Five years previously he had had a wife, two kids, a dog. Then there had been the temptation. "Come on, Dev. What's the matter with you? Don't tell me you couldn't use an extra five grand. All you have to do is keep your mouth shut. Come on, we're all doing it. Just about everybody on the force."

Devlin tossed his denim jacket onto the couch and kicked off his cowboy boots. Going into the kitchen, he got himself a can of Bud. Returning to the living room, he sat in one of the threadbare armchairs. Recalling the past always made him moody.

It had all been a trap, a sting operation. Devlin and a handful of other policemen were indicted and bounced off the force. Devlin had been caught red-handed with the money. He was putting a down payment on a small cottage in Maine so the kids could get out of the city for the summertime.

Devlin lit a cigarette and inhaled deeply. Then he coughed violently. Bending over, he ground the cigarette out on the floor and flicked it into the corner of the room. He took another pull on his beer. The cold brew helped soothe his raw throat.

Things had always been a little rough between him and Sheila, but in the past they'd always managed to work things out. At least until the bribery bust. She'd taken the kids and moved back to Indiana. There'd been a custody fight, but Devlin hadn't had a chance. Not with a felony conviction and a short stay in Walpole on his record.

Devlin wondered about Jeffrey Rhodes. Like Devlin's, his life had apparently come apart at the seams. Devlin wondered what kind of temptation Jeffrey had faced, what kind of mistake he'd made. Malpractice and drugs sounded like a weird combination, and Jeffrey certainly didn't look like any druggie to Devlin. Devlin smiled to himself. Maybe Mosconi was right. Maybe he was going soft.

*

Jeffrey cleaned with significantly less enthusiasm than he had the night before, which pleased David to no end. David even renewed the friendly overtures he had made at the outset. He showed Jeffrey a few clever cleaning shortcuts that were a cut above sweeping dust under a rug.

In light of Devlin's visit, Jeffrey viewed getting to work as an ordeal. He was sure Devlin was out there waiting to snap him up the minute he'd left Kelly's quiet neighborhood. Jeffrey had been so apprehensive, he entertained the idea of calling in sick.

Kelly had come up with the perfect solution. She kindly offered to drive him to work. Jeffrey liked that idea a whole lot better than trying to take mass transit or a cab. Still, he'd been reluctant to put Kelly's life in jeopardy. But he decided she'd be safe if he hid in her car before she pulled out of the garage. That way, if Devlin was watching, he'd think Jeffrey had remained in the house. So Jeffrey had lain low in the backseat of the automobile, and Kelly had thrown a blanket over him for good measure. Only after they'd driven a mile or so away from the house did he emerge and climb into the front seat.

Around three in the morning David announced it was time for "lunch." Jeffrey again begged off eating, a move which earned him a long look of disapproval. Once David and the others had left for the small housekeeping lunchroom, Jeffrey took his cleaning cart down to the first floor.

Pushing the cart along, Jeffrey went by the main entrance, then turned left up the center corridor. There were a few people wandering the halls, mostly hospital employees heading to the main cafeteria for their "lunch" breaks. As usual, no one paid the slightest attention to Jeffrey despite the noise his cleaning cart made as it rolled along.

Jeffrey stopped in front of the personnel offices. He wasn't sure if his passkeys would open the door. When he'd offered to clean in there, David had told him that all the administrative areas of the hospital were cleaned by the evening housekeeping shift.

Hoping no one familiar with the housekeeping routine would come along, Jeffrey tried the different keys on his ring

David had given him. It didn't take long to find one that fit.

All the lights were on. Jeffrey pushed his housekeeping cart in and closed the door behind him. Pushing the cart from room to room, he made sure that the place was deserted. Finally he pushed his way to Carl Bodanski's office.

The first place Jeffrey looked was Carl Bodanski's desk. He rifled through each drawer. Jeffrey wasn't sure the list he was looking for existed, much less where it would be kept. What he wanted was a list of the professional staff and employees that would be accurate for September 1988.

Next he tried Bodanski's computer terminal and played around with it for a quarter hour. But he had no luck. Jeffrey was well acquainted with the hospital's computer as far as patient records were concerned, but he wasn't familiar with the systems used by personnel and administration. He guessed code keys or passwords were involved, but not knowing what they were, he had little chance of accessing the right files. Eventually he gave up trying.

He turned his attention to a bank of file drawers built into one of the office's walls. Jeffrey clicked open a drawer he chose at random and pulled it out. It was then that he heard the main door to personnel open.

Jeffrey only had time to dash across the room and tuck himself behind the open door to Bodanski's office. He heard whoever had entered walk across the outer room and sit down at Bodanski's secretary's desk.

Peering through the crack between the door and the jamb, Jeffrey could just make out the outline of the figure poised over the desk.

The next thing Jeffrey heard was the phone being picked up, followed by the melodious beeps of tone dialing. Then he heard a voice: "Hello, Mom! How've you been doing? And how's that good old Hawaiian weather been?" There was a squeak of the secretary's chair and the person leaned back into Jeffrey's view. It was David Arnold.

Jeffrey had to wait for twenty minutes while David caught up on the news from home. At long last, he hung up and left personnel. Mildly unnerved by the interruption, Jeffrey went back to the file drawer he'd pulled out. It contained individual files for each employee, filed according to department, then alphabetically.

Opening the next drawer, Jeffrey scanned the plastic tabs that served as file organizers. He was about to close the drawer when he stopped at one that read United Fund.

Jeffrey pulled it out and opened it on a nearby desk. Inside were separate folders for each of the last six years. Jeffrey took the one for 1988. He knew the hospital ran its United Fund in October. It wasn't September, but it was close enough. In the file were lists of the hospital employees as well as the professional staff.

Taking the list out to the copy machine, Jeffrey made himself a copy. Then, after replacing the file exactly where he'd found it, he stowed the copy on the cart's supply shelf. He was in the main corridor a moment later.

Jeffrey didn't go directly back to the OR floor. Instead, he pushed his cart past the emergency room to pharmacy. On the spur of the moment he decided to see how far his housekeeping uniform would take him.

Pharmacy had a counter where the medications requested by the various departments were dispensed. It almost looked like a retail pharmacy. Beside the counter was a locked door. Parking his cart, Jeffrey tried his keys. One of them opened it.

Jeffrey knew he was taking a risk, but even so, he pushed his cart through the door and down the main corridor beyond. To the left and right of this main corridor were aisles and aisles of metal shelving extending from floor to ceiling. The ends of these shelves had attached cards describing the contained drugs.

Jeffrey pushed his cart along slowly, carefully reading each shelf's card. He was looking for local anesthetics.

One of the night shift pharmacists suddenly appeared from behind some shelving and came toward Jeffrey. She had an armload of bottles. Jeffrey stopped, expecting to have to account for himself, but the woman merely nodded a greeting and went on about her business, moving on to the counter that communicated with the hospital corridor.

Amazed again at the entrée his housekeeping position afforded him, Jeffrey continued his search for local anesthetics.

He finally found them toward the back of the room. They were on a low shelf. There were many boxes of Marcaine in several different-size doses, including the 30 cc variety. Jeffrey realized how accessible they were. Any one of the pharmacists could easily have had the opportunity to put a tampered vial in the supply. And a pharmacist would certainly have the kind of requisite knowledge as well.

Jeffrey sighed. It seemed that he was expanding the range of suspects, not narrowing them. How could he ever hope to find the criminal? In any case, he'd have to keep pharmacy in mind. What argued against a pharmacist being the culprit was that a pharmacist would not have the kind of mobility a physician would have. While he might enjoy complete access to supplies at one hospital, it was unlikely he would enjoy comparable access at another institution.

Turning his cleaning cart around, Jeffrey headed out of pharmacy. While he was walking, he acknowledged that not only would he have to keep pharmacy in mind, he'd have to consider housekeeping. Given the freedom he enjoyed on this, his second day in the hospital's employ, he realized how easy it would be for any member of the housekeeping staff to slip into the pharmacy just as he had. The only problem with housekeeping was that the people wouldn't have the requisite background in physiology or pharmacology. They might enjoy the access, but they probably lacked the know-how.

Suddenly Jeffrey stopped pushing the cart. Again he thought of himself. No one knew that he was an anesthesiologist with a wide range of knowledge. What was to prevent a comparably knowledgeable person from securing a position in housekeeping just as he had? The range of suspects widened again.

As seven finally approached, Jeffrey started to think about Devlin again, worrying that he might return and terrorize Kelly. If anything happened to her, he'd never forgive himself. At six-thirty he called her to see how she was, and to find out if there'd been any sign of Devlin.

"Haven't seen him or heard anything all night," Kelly assured him. "When I got up half an hour ago, I checked outside to make sure he wasn't around. There were no strange cars and nobody was in sight."

"Maybe I should go to a hotel just to be absolutely sure."

"I prefer you to stay here," Kelly said. "I'm convinced it's safe. To tell you the truth, I feel safer with you here. If you're worried about coming in the front door, I'll leave the back door unlocked. Have a cab drop you off on the street that runs behind my house and walk through the trees."

Jeffrey was touched that Kelly wanted him at her house as much as she did. He had to admit he infinitely preferred staying with her to staying at a hotel. In fact, he'd rather stay at her place than at his own home.

"I'll leave the drapes drawn. Just don't answer the door or the phone. No one will know you are here."

"Okay, okay," Jeffrey said. "I'll stay."

"But I have one request," Kelly said.

"Name it."

"Don't pop out of the pantry and scare me when I come home this afternoon."

Jeffrey laughed. "Promise," he said with a chuckle. He wondered who'd scared whom more in that episode.

At seven A.M., Jeffrey brought his cart back down to housekeeping. As the elevator descended, he closed his eyes. They felt like they were full of sand. He was so tired, he almost felt sick.

He parked his cart and went into the locker room to change from his uniform into his street clothes. He put the lists he'd copied from the United Fund file into his back pocket.

Closing his locker and giving the combination a twist, Jeffrey stood up. David came through the door and walked up to him.

"I got a page," he said, looking at Jeffrey suspiciously out of the corner of his eye. "You're supposed to see Mr. Bodanski in his office right now."

"I am?" Jeffrey felt a pang of fear. Had his cover been blown?

David studied Jeffrey, cocking his head to the side. "There's something fishy about you, Frank," he said. "Are you some kind of spy from administration trying to see if we're doing our jobs?"

Jeffrey gave a short, nervous laugh. "Hardly," he said. The fact that David might suspect such a thing had never occurred to him.

"Then how come the director of personnel wants to see you at seven o'clock in the morning? The man doesn't usually get here until after eight."

"I haven't the faintest idea," Jeffrey said. He stepped around David and went through the door. David followed. Together they went up the stairs.

"How come you don't eat lunch like normal people?" David asked.

"I'm just not hungry," Jeffrey said. But David's suspicions were the least of his concerns. He was worried about why Bodanski wanted to see him. At first Jeffrey felt sure that his true identity had been discovered. But if that were so, Bodanski's summoning him didn't make sense. Wouldn't they just have sent in the police?

Jeffrey got to the first floor and opened the door into the main hospital corridor. He might have turned and headed out the main entrance if David hadn't been trailing behind him, still carrying on about Jeffrey being some sort of spy for the administration. Jeffrey turned toward personnel.

Then he had another thought. Maybe someone had seen him in personnel that morning, perhaps while he was using the copy machine. Or maybe someone had mentioned seeing him in pharmacy. But if either of these were the case, wouldn't the problem have been referred to David, the shift supervisor? Or to Jose Martinez, head of housekeeping? Wouldn't he receive a reprimand or even dismissal from one of them?

Jeffrey was at a loss. He took a deep breath and pushed through personnel's door. The room appeared just as deserted as it had at three-thirty in the morning. All the desks were empty. The typewriters were silent. The computer screens were dark. The only sound came from the area near the copy machine where a coffeepot softly perked.

Walking over to the door to Bodanski's office, Jeffrey caught sight of the man sitting at his desk. Bodanski had a computer printout in front of him and a red pencil in his hand. Jeffrey knocked twice on the open door. Bodanski looked up.

"Ah, Mr. Amendola," Bodanski said, leaping to his feet as if Jeffrey were some important visitor. "Thank you for coming by. Please sit down."

Jeffrey sat down, as confused as ever as to why he'd been

summoned. Bodanski asked him if he'd like some coffee. When Jeffrey refused, he sat down as well.

"First, I'd like to say that all reports have indicated that you have already become a valuable employee of Boston Memorial Hospital."

"Glad to hear it," Jeffrey said.

"We'd like you to stay on as long as you'd like," Bodanski continued. "In fact, we hope you'll be staying on." He cleared his throat and played with his red pencil.

Jeffrey was getting the distinct impression that Bodanski was more nervous than he.

"I suppose you're wondering why I called you in here this morning. This is a bit early for me, but I wanted to catch you before you went home. I'm sure you're tired and would like to get some sleep."

Out with it, thought Jeffrey.

"Are you sure you don't want some coffee?" Bodanski asked again.

"To tell you the truth, I would like to go home to bed. Maybe you should just tell me why you wanted to see me."

"Yes, of course," Bodanski said. Then he got to his feet and paced in the small space behind his desk. "I'm not good at this sort of thing," he added. "Maybe I should have enlisted the help of the psychiatry department, or at least social service. I truly don't like to meddle in people's lives."

A red flag went up in Jeffrey's mind. Something bad was coming: he could sense it.

"Exactly what are you trying to say?" Jeffrey asked.

"Well, let me put it this way," Bodanski said. "I know you have been hiding."

Jeffrey's mouth went dry. He knows, he thought, he knows.

"I can appreciate the fact that you have had some big problems. I thought that in some small way I could help, so I made a call to your wife."

Jeffrey gripped the arms of his chair and pushed forward. "You called my wife?" he asked with incredulity.

"Now take it easy," Bodanski advised, holding out his hands, palms down. He'd known this would upset the man.

Take it easy, thought Jeffrey with alarm. Why Bodanski had called Carol was beyond him.

"In fact, your wife is here," Bodanski said. He pointed at the double doors. "She's eager to see you. I know she has some important things to discuss with you, but I felt it best to warn you she was here rather than let her surprise you."

Jeffrey felt a sudden rage build within him. He was angry at this meddlesome personnel director and at Carol. Just when he was making some progress, this had to happen.

"Have you called the police?" Jeffrey asked. He tried to prepare himself for the worst.

"No, of course not," Bodanski said, stepping over to the double doors.

Jeffrey followed. The question in his mind was whether he would be able to contain this catastrophe. Bodanski opened one of the doors, then stepped aside for Jeffrey to enter. His face had one of those patronizing smiles that galled Jeffrey all the more. Jeffrey stepped over the threshold into a conference room with a long table surrounded by academic-style chairs.

Out of the corner of his eye, Jeffrey saw a figure rushing toward him. In a flash, he decided it was a trap. Carol wasn't there, it was Devlin! But the figure rushing toward him was a woman. She fell on him, clutching him in her arms. She buried her head in his chest. She was sobbing.

Jeffrey looked toward Bodanski for help. It certainly wasn't Carol. This woman was nearly three times as heavy. Her tangled hair was like bleached straw.

The woman's sobs began to subside. She let go of Jeffrey with one hand and pressed a tissue to her nose. She blew loudly, then lifted her eyes.

Jeffrey stared into her wide face. Her eyes, which initially reflected a kind of joy, immediately flashed anger. The tears stopped as abruptly as they had begun.

"You are not my husband," the woman said indignantly. She pushed Jeffrey away.

"I'm not?" Jeffrey questioned, trying to make sense of the scene.

"No!" shouted the woman, again overcome with emotion. She came at Jeffrey with raised fists. Tears of frustration erupted and streamed down her cheeks.

Jeffrey retreated around the conference table as the shocked director tried to come to his aid.

The woman then turned her venom on Bodanski, screaming that he'd taken advantage of her. But after a minute she was overwhelmed by tears and she collapsed into his arms. That was almost more than the man could take, but with herculean effort, he managed to maneuver the mountain of a woman over to one of the academic chairs, where she collapsed in a sobbing mass.

A dumbfounded Bodanski took his white show handkerchief from his jacket pocket and wiped his mouth where the woman had struck him. A small amount of blood dotted the silk fabric.

"I never should have gotten my hopes up," the woman wailed. "I should have known Frank would never take a job cleaning in a hospital."

Jeffrey finally grasped the situation. This was Mrs. Amendola, the wife of the man in the tattered suit. Now that he'd thought of it, Jeffrey couldn't believe that it had taken him so long to understand. He also realized it wouldn't take Bodanski long to figure out what had happened. When he did, he might insist on calling the police. Jeffrey would have to do a lot of explaining to figure a way out of this one.

As the director tried to console Mrs. Amendola, Jeffrey backed out of the double doors. Bodanski called out for him to wait, but Jeffrey ignored him. Emerging from personnel, he ran for the main entrance, trusting that Bodanski would feel compelled to stay with Mrs. Amendola.

Once outside the hospital, Jeffrey slowed his gait. He didn't want to give the security people reason to pursue him.

Walking briskly, Jeffrey made his way to the cab stand and got in the first available taxi. He asked the driver to take him to Brookline. It was only after the cab began to turn right on Beacon Street that Jeffrey hazarded a look back. The front of the hospital appeared tranquil. The morning's rush of the sick to the clinics had not yet begun, and Carl Bodanski had not appeared.

After the cabbie crossed Kenmore Square, he eyed Jeffrey in his rearview mirror and said, "You're going to have to be more specific. Brookline is a big place."

Jeffrey gave the driver the name of the street behind Kelly's. He told the man he didn't know the number of the house, but that he'd recognize it.

With the concern about Devlin possibly being around

Kelly's house, Jeffrey was unable to recover from being rattled by the confrontation with Mrs. Amendola. His stomach was in a tight, painful knot, and he wondered how much longer his body would put up with the tension he'd been under for the last four or five days. Anesthesiology had its moments of terror, but they were short-lived. Jeffrey wasn't accustomed to such protracted anxiety. And on top of it all, he was exhausted.

Explaining that he was from out of town and had been in the area only once before, Jeffrey got the cabdriver to cruise the neighborhood around Kelly's house. He surreptitiously slouched down in his seat so that he couldn't be easily seen. At the same time he kept an eye out for Devlin. But there was no sign of the man. The only people Jeffrey saw were commuters leaving their homes for work. There were no cars parked near Kelly's house. Her home looked invitingly quiet.

Jeffrey eventually had the cabdriver drop him off at the house behind Kelly's. After the cab pulled away and turned around the next corner, Jeffrey skirted the house and slipped into the small thicket of trees that separated it from Kelly's property. From the shelter of these woods he surveyed the house for a few minutes before crossing the backyard and slipping into the door Kelly had left unlocked for him.

Jeffrey listened for a while before cautiously searching the entire house. Only then did he close and lock the back door.

In hopes of appeasing his contorted stomach, Jeffrey got out the milk and cereal. He carried them to the table in the family room. He also brought over the computer printout Kelly had gotten from St. Joe's. Taking the list he'd gotten from Boston Memorial that night out of his pocket, he put them side by side.

As he ate, Jeffrey compared the two staff lists. He was eager to see what physicians had privileges at both hospitals. He was immediately dismayed to see how many there were. On a separate sheet of paper Jeffrey began his own list of doctors whose names appeared twice. He was chagrined to see that the list swelled to more than thirty doctors. Thirty-four people were far too many to investigate in any depth, especially given his current circumstances. Somehow he had to narrow it down. That meant getting more hospital lists. Going to the telephone, Jeffrey called St. Joe's and asked to be put through to Kelly.

"I'm glad you called," Kelly said brightly. "Any problem getting into the house?"

"No problem," Jeffrey said. "The reason I called is to remind you to make that call to Valley Hospital today."

"I already did," Kelly told him. "I couldn't decide who to call, so I called several people, including Hart. He's such a dear."

Jeffrey told her about there being thirty-four doctors with privileges at both her hospital and the Memorial. She immediately understood the problem. "Hopefully I'll hear back from Valley this afternoon," she added. "That should help narrow things down some. There have to be fewer people with privileges at St. Joe's, the Memorial, *and* Valley."

Jeffrey was about to hang up when he remembered to ask Kelly to repeat the name of her friend who'd died the day before.

"Gail Shaffer," she said. "Why do you ask?"

"Sometime today I'm going to the Medical Examiner's office to check on Karen Hodges. While I'm there I'll see what I can find out about Gail Shaffer."

"You're frightening me again."

"I'm frightening myself."

After hanging up, Jeffrey went back to the remains of his cereal. Once he'd finished, he put the dishes in the sink. Then he returned to the table to look at his hospital list again. To be thorough, he thought he should compare the employee lists as well. This was harder than comparing the staff lists; those had been alphabetically arranged. The employee lists were organized differently. The one from St. Joe's listed the names by departments, the one from the Memorial had them by salary, probably since that list had been made for the purpose of soliciting contributions.

In order to compare them accurately, Jeffrey had to alphabetize both. By the time he got to the E's, his eyelids were sagging. His first find roused him. He noticed that a Maureen Gallop had worked at both hospitals.

Jeffrey searched the St. Joe's list for Maureen Gallop. He found that she was presently working in St. Joe's housekeeping department.

Jeffrey rubbed his eyes, again considering how easy it had
been for him to wander around the hospital pharmacy. He
added Maureen Gallop's name to the list of the physicians who
had privileges in both hospitals.

Galvanized by this unexpected find, Jeffrey went back to his
alphabetizing. On the very next letter he found another match:
Trent Harding. Taking the St. Joe's list again, Jeffrey searched
for Trent Harding. He found the name in the nursing department. Jeffrey added the name beneath Maureen Gallop's.

Jeffrey was surprised. He hadn't expected to find any hospi-
tal-employee names overlapping. He thought it was quite a
coincidence. More awake now, he finished the time-consuming cross-check, but there were no other matches. Maureen
Gallop and Trent Harding were the only names appearing on
both staff lists.

Jeffrey was so tired by the time he completed comparing the
lists that it was all he could do to get himself from the table to
the couch where he fell into a deep, dreamless sleep. He didn't
even stir when Delilah emerged from the pantry and leaped on
the couch to curl up with him.

There was something about Boston City Hospital that Trent
liked the moment he walked through the door. He guessed it
was the macho atmosphere of an inner-city hospital. There
would be no pussyfooting around here like there was in the
plush suburban hospitals. Trent was confident he wouldn't be
scrubbing on any nose jobs disguised as septal operations for
insurance coverage's sake. Instead he'd be seeing some chal-
lenging gunshot and stab wounds. He'd be in the trenches,
dealing with the fallout of urban terror in a kind of Don
Johnson–*Miami Vice* sort of way.

There was a line in the employment office, but that was just
for people seeking jobs in food service and housekeeping. As
a nurse, Trent was sent directly to the nursing office. He knew
why, too. Like all the hospitals, they were desperate for more
nurses. As a male nurse, he was in particular demand. There
was always an opening for a male nurse in those areas of the
hospital where some muscle was needed, like the emergency
room. But Trent didn't want the emergency room. He wanted
the OR.

After filling out the application form, Trent was given an interview. He wondered why they even bothered with this charade. The outcome was a foregone conclusion. At least he was enjoying himself. He liked the feeling that he was needed and wanted. When he was a child, his father had always told him he was a worthless sissy, especially after Trent had decided he didn't want to play in the junior football league his father had helped set up on the Army base in San Antonio.

Trent watched the woman's expression as she read over his application. The name tag on the front of her desk read: MRS. DIANE MECKLENBURG, R.N., SUPERVISOR.

Supervisor, bull crap, thought Trent. He guessed she didn't know her ass from a hole in the wall. That's what supervisor usually meant in Trent's experience. She probably got her nursing degree back when they were still using whiskey for anesthesia. Since then she'd probably taken a bunch of courses like Nursing in a Complex Society. Trent would have bet a hundred dollars she wouldn't know the difference between a pair of Mayo scissors and a Metzenbaum clamp. In the OR she'd be as much help as an orangutan.

Trent was already looking forward to the day he'd walk in and tender his resignation, thereby ruining this Mrs. Mecklenburg's day.

"Mr. Harding," Mrs. Mecklenburg said, turning her attention from the application to the applicant. Her oval face was partially obscured by large round glasses. "You've indicated on your application that you have worked at four other Boston hospitals. That's a bit unusual."

Trent was tempted to groan aloud. This Mrs. Mecklenburg seemed intent on playing this interview game to its bitter end. Although he felt he could say just about anything and still be hired, he decided to play it safe and be cooperative. He was always prepared for such questions.

"Each hospital offered me different opportunities in terms of education and responsibilities," Trent said. "My goal has been to maximize my experience. I gave each institution almost a year. Now I've finally come to the conclusion that what I need is the stimulation of an academic setting like the sort Boston City provides."

"I see," Mrs. Mecklenburg said.

Trent wasn't through. He added: "I'm confident that I can make a contribution here. I'm not afraid of work and challenge. But I do have one stipulation. I want to work in the OR."

"I don't think that will be a problem," Mrs. Mecklenburg said. "The question is, when can you start?"

Trent smiled. It was so goddamn easy.

Devlin's day wasn't going any better than the previous one. He was on the North Shore, and had visited two Everson households in Peabody, one in Salem, and was now on his way out the causeway to try one on Marblehead Neck. The harbor was to his left and the ocean to his right. At least the weather and the scenery were nice.

Fortunately people had been home at each of his stops. This round of Eversons had even been marginally cooperative, if wary. But no one had heard of a Christopher Everson. Devlin again began to question his intuition that had told him Christopher Everson was from the Boston area.

Reaching Harbor Avenue, Devlin turned left. He cast an admiring eye at the chain of impressive homes. He wondered what it would be like to have the kind of money it would take to live like this. He'd made some serious money over the last couple of years, but had blown it in Vegas or Atlantic City.

The first thing Devlin had done that morning was go to police headquarters on Berkeley Street and visit Sawbones Bromlley. Dr. Bromlley had been associated with the Boston Police Department since the nineteenth century, or so the legend had it. He gave officers physicals and treated simple colds and minor scrapes and scratches. He didn't inspire a lot of confidence.

Devlin had shown him the notes he'd picked up from Rhodes's hotel room and asked him what they were about. The result had been like turning on a water faucet. Sawbones had launched into a twenty-minute lecture on the nervous system, and the fact that it had two parts. One for doing things that you wanted to do, like drink or feel something; and another for doing the things that you didn't want to think about, like breathing or digesting a steak.

Up until that point Devlin had been doing fine. But then

Bromlley said that the part of the nervous system that did the things you didn't want to think about had two parts. One was called sympathetic and the other parasympathetic. These two parts fought against each other, like one made the pupil big, the other made it small; like one gave you diarrhea, the other stopped you up.

Devlin had done pretty well even to there, but Bromlley went on to talk about how nerves worked and how anesthetics screwed them up.

From then on, Devlin had had a hard time following, but he'd figured since his interest only went so far as the notes, it didn't much matter. Bromlley loved a captive audience, so Devlin had just let him roll on. When it had seemed Sawbones had arrived at a point of conclusion, Devlin reminded him of his initial question. "Great, Doc, great! But back to the notes for a minute. Is there anything about them that strikes you as surprising, or suspicious?"

Sawbones had looked befuddled for a moment. He'd studied the notes again, eyeing them through his thick bifocals. Finally he'd said a simple no; everything seemed quite clear, and who-ever had jotted down the information about the nervous system had gotten it right. Devlin thanked him and left. The trip had been useful only in that Devlin was more convinced than ever that like Rhodes, this Christopher Everson was also a doctor.

On Marblehead Neck, Devlin pulled up to a low, ranch-style house. He checked the number from his list. It was the one he wanted. He got out of his car and stretched. The house wasn't on the water, but he could make out its sparkles through the trees that lined the lane leading down to the harbor.

Devlin walked up to the door and rang the bell. An attractive blonde about Devlin's age answered the door. As soon as she caught sight of Devlin, she tried to shut it again, but Devlin gently eased the tip of his cowboy boot into the crack. The door stopped. The woman looked down.

"I think your boot is blocking my door," she said evenly. She looked him straight in the eye. "Let me guess: you're selling Girl Scout cookies."

Devlin laughed and shook his head in disbelief. He never

could anticipate people's reactions. But the one thing he appreciated more than anything else was a sense of humor. He liked this woman's.

"Excuse me for appearing so rude," he said. "I just want to ask you a simple question. One question. I was afraid you were about to shut the door."

"I have a black belt in karate," the woman said.

"No need to be nasty," Devlin said. "I'm looking for a Christopher Everson. Since this house is listed as belonging to an Everson, I thought that there was a remote possibility someone might have heard of this man."

"Why do you want to know?" the woman asked.

When Devlin explained, the woman eased up on the door.

"Seems to me I read about a Christopher Everson in the newspapers," she said, wrinkling her forehead. "At least I'm pretty sure it was Christopher."

"In a Boston paper?" Devlin asked.

The woman nodded. "The *Globe.* It was a while ago. A year or more. It caught my eye because of the name, obviously. There aren't that many Eversons around here. My husband and his family are from Minnesota."

Devlin didn't quite agree with her on the paucity of area Eversons, but didn't argue the point.

"Do you recall what the article was about?" Devlin asked.

"Yeah. It was on the obituary page. The man died."

Devlin got back in his car, feeling angry at himself. The idea that Christopher Everson was dead never occurred to him. Starting the car, he made a U-turn and headed back to Boston. He knew exactly where he wanted to go now. The drive took him half an hour. Parking at a hydrant on West Street, he walked to Tremont and went into the State Department of Public Health.

The Registry of Vital Records and Statistics was on the first floor. Devlin filled out a form for obtaining Christopher Everson's death certificate. For the year, he put 1988. He knew that could be altered if necessary. At the counter he paid his five dollars and sat down to wait. It didn't take long. The year wasn't 1988; it turned out it was 1987. Regardless, within twenty minutes Devlin was walking back to his car with Christopher Everson's death certificate.

Instead of starting the car, Devlin perused the document. The first bit of information that struck him was the fact that Everson had been married. His surviving spouse was a Kelly Everson.

Devlin remembered his trip to her house. That's where he'd heard that strange noise, like empty cans dropping on a tile floor, but no one had come to the door. He picked up his Everson list, where he'd circled K. C. Everson for a call back. He checked the address against the one on the death certificate. They were the same.

Devlin went back to the death certificate. Christopher Everson had been a physician. Glancing down at the cause of death, he saw it had been ruled a suicide. The technical cause of death was listed as respiratory arrest, but below that there was a note saying that this had been secondary to the self-administration of succinylcholine.

With sudden anger, Devlin crumpled the death certificate and tossed it onto the backseat. Succinylcholine had been the crap that Jeffrey Rhodes had injected into him. It was a wonder Rhodes hadn't killed him.

Starting the car, Devlin pulled forward and merged with the traffic on Tremont Street. Once again he was looking forward with particular relish to getting his hands on Jeffrey Rhodes.

The noontime traffic slowed Devlin's progress. It took him longer to drive from downtown Boston to Brookline than it had to drive all the way into town from Marblehead. It was almost one o'clock in the afternoon by the time he turned onto Kelly Everson's street and drove by her house. He saw no activity, but he did notice a definite change. All the curtains were drawn on the first floor. The day before they had been open. He remembered cupping his hands on the glass to peer in the dining room. Devlin smiled. As far as he was concerned, you didn't have to be a brain surgeon to know something was up.

After pulling a U-turn in the middle of the next block, Devlin passed a second time, trying to decide what to do. He made a second U-turn, then pulled to the side of the road and parked. He was two doors down from the Everson house, on the opposite side of the street. For the moment he couldn't decide on the best course of action. From experience he'd learned that if that was the case, it was best to do nothing.

FRIDAY,
MAY 19, 1989
11:25 A.M.

"Keep the change," Jeffrey said to the taxi driver as he got out in front of the city morgue. The driver said something to him he didn't hear. He bent closer.

"I'm sorry, what did you say?" Jeffrey asked.

"I said, what the hell kind of tip is fifty cents?" To punctuate his feelings the cabbie threw the change from his window, then took off with a screech of rubber.

Jeffrey watched the two quarters spiral on the sidewalk. He shook his head. Boston cabdrivers were a breed unto themselves. He bent down and picked up the coins. Then he looked up at the façade of the Boston city morgue.

It was an old building covered with a patina of filth that extended back to the time when coal was the major source of heat in the city. The edifice was embellished with stylized Egyptian motifs, but the effect was hardly regal. The structure looked more like something from the set of a Hollywood horror movie than a house of scientific medicine.

Jeffrey went through the front entrance and up the flight of stairs, following signs for the Medical Examiner's office.

"Can I help you?" a matronly woman asked as Jeffrey approached the counter. Behind her were five old-fashioned metal desks, haphazardly arranged. Each was piled high with an assortment of letters, forms, envelopes, and manuals. Jeffrey felt as if he'd stepped twenty years back into the past. The telephones, all grim black, were rotary.

"I'm a physician from St. Joseph's Hospital," Jeffrey said. "I'm interested in a case that I believe was scheduled for autopsy today. The name is Karen Hodges."

Instead of answering Jeffrey, the woman picked up a clipboard and ran her finger down the list. She got halfway down the page before she said, "That's one of Dr. Warren Seibert's cases. I'm not sure where he is. Probably up in the autopsy room."

"And where is that?" Jeffrey asked. Although he'd been practicing medicine in Boston for almost twenty years, Jeffrey had never been to the city morgue.

"You can take the elevator, but I don't advise it," said the woman. "Go around the corner and take the stairs. When you get upstairs, take your first right, then a left. You can't miss it."

Jeffrey did as he'd been told. He'd heard the phrase "you can't miss it" many times. This time it was true. Before he got anywhere near the autopsy room, he could smell it.

The door was ajar. Jeffrey timidly peered in from the threshold, half afraid to go farther. It was a room about forty feet long and twenty wide. A bank of frosted windows filled most of one wall. Fetid air swirled from an old-style rotating fan sitting atop a metal file cabinet.

There were three stainless-steel autopsy tables in the room, and all three were occupied by naked corpses. Two of the bodies were men. The third was a woman. The woman was young and blond, and her skin was like ivory but with a faintly bluish cast.

Each table had a two-person team working over it. The room was abuzz with cutting, slicing, sawing, and muted conversation. Jeffrey thought they were all men, but he wasn't sure. They were all dressed in scrub clothes covered by rubber aprons. They wore protective Plexiglas goggles over their eyes. Their faces were covered by surgical masks. On their

hands were heavy rubber gloves. In a corner stood a large
soapstone sink with continuously running water. A radio was
balanced on the edge of the sink and played incongruous soft
rock music. Jeffrey wondered what Billy Ocean would think
if he could see this scene.

Jeffrey stood by the door for almost a quarter of an hour
before one of the men in the room noticed him. He passed
Jeffrey on the way to the sink with what looked like a liver to
wash it under the running water. He stopped the moment he
saw Jeffrey. "Can I help you?" he asked suspiciously.

"I'm looking for Dr. Seibert," Jeffrey said, fighting a mild
sensation of nausea. He'd never appreciated pathology. Autopsies had always been an ordeal in medical school.

"Hey, Seibert, you got company," the man called over his
shoulder.

One of the men standing over the woman's corpse looked
up, then over at Jeffrey. He was holding a scalpel in one hand.
His other hand was deep inside the corpse's torso.

"What can I do for you?" he asked. His tone was a lot
friendlier than the first man's.

Jeffrey swallowed. He felt a little dizzy. "I'm a doctor from
St. Joseph's," he said. "From the department of anesthesia. I'm
interested to know what you found on a patient by the name
of Karen Hodges."

Dr. Seibert left the table after a nod to his assistant and came
over to Jeffrey. He was a good inch taller than Jeffrey, probably about six-one. "Were you the gas-passer on the case?" he
asked. He still had the scalpel in his hand. His other hand was
bloody. Jeffrey couldn't bear to look any lower than the man's
shoulders. His apron was unspeakably spattered. Jeffrey concentrated on Seibert's eyes. They were bright blue and rather
arresting.

"No, I wasn't," Jeffrey admitted. "But I'd heard the problem
occurred during epidural anesthesia. My interest in the case
stems from the fact that there have been at least four comparable cases in the last four years that I know of. Was the drug
involved with Karen Hodges Marcaine?"

"I don't know yet," Seibert said, "but the chart is in my
office—down the hall on the left just past the library. Be my
guest. I'll be through in here in fifteen or twenty minutes."

"The case you're working on now wouldn't be Gail Shaffer, would it?" Jeffrey questioned.

"Right on," Seibert said. "First time in my career I've had two good-looking young females in a row. It's been my lucky day."

Jeffrey let that comment go. He'd never been comfortable with pathology humor. "Any clues on gross pathology as to the cause of death?"

"Come on over," Seibert said with a wave of his bloodied hand. He started back toward the table.

Jeffrey followed hesitantly. He didn't want to get too close.

"See this?" Seibert questioned after he'd introduced Jeffrey to his assistant, Harold. He pointed with the handle of the scalpel to the gash high on Gail's forehead. "That was one hell of a blow. Fractured the skull into the frontal sinus."

Jeffrey nodded. He began to breathe through his mouth. He couldn't bear the smell. Harold was busy removing the entrails. "Could the blow have killed her?" Jeffrey asked.

"Possibly," Seibert said, "but a NMR was negative. We'll see when we get the brain out. Apparently she also had some cardiac trouble, even though there was no previous history. So we'll be looking at the heart pretty carefully."

"Will you be testing for drugs?"

"Absolutely," Seibert said. "We'll be doing a full toxicology screen on blood, CSF, bile, urine, and even what we aspirated out of her stomach."

"Here, let me help," Seibert said to his assistant when he saw that Harold had succeeded in freeing the abdominal organs. Seibert grabbed a long flat pan and held it while Harold lifted the mass of slippery organs and transferred them into the container.

Jeffrey turned away for a moment. When he looked back, the body had been gutted. Harold was on his way to the sink with the organs. Seibert was casually poking around inside the abdominal cavity. "You always have to be on the lookout for the unexpected. You never know what you're going to find in here."

"What if I suggested to you that both these women were poisoned?" Jeffrey said suddenly. "Would you do anything differently? Would you run any other tests?"

Seibert stopped abruptly. At that moment he was deep into Gail's pelvis with his gloved right hand. He slowly raised his head to take another look at Jeffrey, almost as if to reevaluate his opinion of the man. "Do you know something that I should know?" he asked, his tone more serious.

"Let's say I'm posing it as a hypothetical question," Jeffrey said evasively. "Both women had seizures and cardiac problems without a history of either—or so I understand."

Withdrawing his hand, Seibert stood up and faced Jeffrey across the gutted hull of Gail Shaffer's body. He thought for a moment, then looked down at the dead woman.

"No, I wouldn't do anything differently," he said. "There isn't really a difference between self-poisoning, euphemistically known as recreational-drug use, and being poisoned—at least not from a pathology point of view. Either the poison is in the deceased's system or it isn't. I suppose if I were told a specific poison was involved, it would influence how I processed some of the individual tissues. There are certain stains for certain poisons."

"What about a toxin?" Jeffrey asked.

Seibert whistled. "Now you're talking serious stuff. You mean like phytotoxins or tetrodotoxin. You've heard of tetrodotoxin, haven't you? It's from puffer fish. Can you believe they're licensing sushi bars to serve that stuff? Hell, I wouldn't touch it."

Jeffrey could tell he'd touched on one of Seibert's areas of interest. Seibert's enthusiasm for toxins was clear.

"Toxins are phenomenal," Seibert went on. "Man, if I wanted to do away with somebody, there's no doubt in my mind I'd use a toxin. Lots of times no one thinks to look for signs of them. The cause of death seems natural. Hey, you remember that Turkish diplomat that was knocked off in Paris? That had to be a toxin. It was hidden in the end of an umbrella and somebody just walked by the guy and gave him a little jab in the ass. Bingo, the guy was writhing around on the platform. Dead in minutes. And did they figure out what it was? Hell, no. Toxins are murder to identify." Seibert grinned at his joke.

"But *can* you detect them?" Jeffrey asked.

Seibert shook his head with uncertainty. "That's why I'd use 'em if I were to knock somebody off: they're a bitch to trace. As to whether you can detect them, I'd have to say yes and no. The big problem is that a very little bit of some of these toxins goes a very long way. They only need a few molecules to do their dirty work. I'm talking about nano-nano moles. That means our usual old standby, the gas chromatograph, combined with a mass spec, often can't pick the toxin out of all the other organic compounds floating around in the sample soup. But if you know what you're looking for, like tetrodotoxin, say, because the deceased dropped dead at a sushi party, then there are some monoclonal antibodies tagged with either fluorescein or a radioactive marker that can pick the stuff up. But I'm telling you, it ain't easy."

"So sometimes you can't find the toxin unless you know specifically what it is," Jeffrey said, suddenly disheartened. "That sounds like a real Catch-22."

"That's why it can be the perfect crime."

Harold came back from the sink with the tray of organs. Jeffrey took the opportunity to study the lab's ceiling.

"Harold, you want to get the brain out?" Seibert asked his assistant. The man nodded, put down the tray on the end of the table, then walked around to the head.

"I'm sorry to be interrupting like this," Jeffrey said.

"Hey, no problem," Seibert said. "This kind of interruption I can stand. This autopsy crap gets a little boring after a while. The fun of this job is in the analysis. I never liked to clean fish when I went fishing, and there's not a lot of difference between that and doing an autopsy. Besides, you've sparked my curiosity. How come the questions about a toxin? A busy man like you didn't come down here to play twenty questions."

"I told you there have been at least four other deaths during epidural anesthesia. That's very unusual. And for at least two of them, the initial symptoms were subtly different than one would expect from a reaction to a local anesthetic."

"How so?" Seibert asked.

One of the other pathologists raised his head and called over, "Hey, Seibert, you goin' to make that case your life's work just because she's got a good body?"

"Up yours, Nelson," Seibert called over his shoulder. Then, to Jeffrey, he said, "He's just jealous I got two in a row. But it evens out. My next one will probably be a sixty-year-old alcoholic who'd been floating in Boston Harbor for three weeks. You should see what that's like. Ugh! The gas that comes out you could run your car on for a week."

Jeffrey tried to smile, but it was difficult. The mental images these men talked in were almost as bad as the actualities.

Responding to the goading of the other pathologist, Seibert picked up a thick suture material swagged onto a strong cutting needle and began to suture Gail Shaffer's Y-shaped autopsy wound. "Now where were we?" he said. "Oh yeah. How were the symptoms different?"

"Right after the Marcaine was given, the patients got a sudden and striking parasympathetic reaction with abdominal pain, salivation, perspiration, and even miotic pupils. It was only for a few seconds, then they had grand mal seizures."

Harold had cut around Gail's head with a scalpel. Then, with an awful ripping sound, he pulled the scalp down over the woman's face. The skull was now exposed. Jeffrey tried to turn sideways to keep from seeing.

"Don't you see those kinds of symptoms with a toxic reaction to local anesthetics?" Seibert asked. He was lifting the needle up over his head like a cobbler after each running stitch to take up the slack.

"Yes and no," Jeffrey said. "The seizures for sure. Also the miotic pupils have been described in the literature, although for the life of me, I can't explain it physiologically, and I've never seen it. But the transient salivation, the sweating and lacrimation, I've never even read about."

"I think I'm getting the picture," Seibert said. There was a sudden whirring noise and Gail's body began to vibrate. Harold was using a power saw to cut off the crown of the head. Soon he'd be lifting out the brain. Seibert had to speak louder to be heard. "As I recall, local anesthetics block transmission at synapses. Any initial stimulation you might get is because inhibitory fibers can be blocked first. Am I remembering this right?"

"You're impressing me," Jeffrey said. "Go on."

"And the blockage comes from keeping sodium ions from crossing membranes, am I right?"

"You must have gotten an A plus in neurophysiology in med school."

"Hey, this is the kind of stuff I'm interested in," Seibert said. "I was reviewing this for a case of myasthenia gravis. It also came up in a paper I read about tetrodotoxin. Did you know that stuff mimics the local anesthetics? In fact, some people were hypothesizing it might be a natural local anesthetic."

Jeffrey vaguely remembered reading something to that effect, now that Seibert mentioned it.

The whirring of the power saw abruptly stopped. Jeffrey didn't want to watch the next step, so he turned completely around.

"Anyhow," Seibert said, "what I remember is that with epidural anesthesia, any alteration you'd expect to see would be with the sympathetic system, not the parasympathetic system, because of the risk of inadvertently injecting the stuff where spinal anesthesia goes. Is that right?"

"Right on the nose," Jeffrey said.

"But isn't the real worry that you can mistakenly inject the anesthetic agent directly into the bloodstream?"

"Exactly," Jeffrey said. "And that's where the problems with seizures and cardiac toxicity come into play. But there is no way to explain sudden marked parasympathetic stimulation. It makes you think there is some other drug involved. Something that not only causes seizures and heart toxicity, but also, for a brief instance, parasympathetic stimulation."

"Wow!" Seibert exclaimed. "This is my kind of case. It's like something a pathologist would think up."

"I suppose," Jeffrey said. "To tell the truth, I was thinking of an anesthesiologist."

"Wouldn't be a contest," Seibert said, waving a pair of toothed tongs. "The pathologist is much more qualified to think up the best way to kill people."

Jeffrey started to argue, then stopped, aware of the ridiculousness of deciding which specialty cultivated a more sophisticated killer. "There is something else about the two cases I'm talking about. At autopsy both showed damage to nerve cells and nerve axons. One of the cases even had some electron micrographs taken, showing marked ultrastructure damage to nerve and muscle."

"No kidding?" Seibert said. He held up on his sewing. Jeffrey could tell he was fascinated. "So all we got to do is come up with a toxin that causes seizures and cardiac toxicity by screwing up nerve and muscle cells plus causes marked parasympathetic stimulation! At least initially. Hey, you know something—you're right. This is like a test question on a first-year neurophysiology exam. I'm going to have to think about it for a while."

"Do you know if Karen Hodges had the same type of initial symptoms?" Jeffrey asked.

Seibert shrugged. "Not yet. My usual modus operandi is to study the chart in detail after I've done the autopsy. I like to keep an open mind. That way I'm less apt to miss anything."

"You don't mind if I go look at the chart?" Jeffrey asked.

"Hell, no! As I said, be my guest. I won't be long here."

Glad to escape the oppressive smell of the autopsy room, Jeffrey made his way down to Seibert's tiny office. The room was the homiest Jeffrey had seen in the morgue, with lots of personal touches. The desk was laden with a matching leather blotter, an in-and-out basket, a pen and pencil set, and picture frame. The picture in the frame was of Seibert with an attractive woman with a pixie haircut, and two smiling children. Clad in skiwear, the family had been posed with a wintry white mountain in the background.

In the center of the desk blotter were the two charts. The top one was for Gail Shaffer. Jeffrey put it aside. The bottom one was Karen Hodges'. He picked it up and sat down in a vinyl chair. The anesthesia record was what he was most interested in.

The anesthesiologist's name was William Doherty. Jeffrey vaguely knew him from medical meetings. Glancing down the page, Jeffrey saw that the anesthetic had indeed been Marcaine .5%. Judging by the dose, Jeffrey deduced that Doherty had been using a 30 cc ampule. Next Jeffrey perused a terse summary of the events. The summary instantly brought thoughts of the Patty Owen disaster to mind. Jeffrey shuddered as he read. Karen Hodges had initially suffered the same baffling parasympathetic symptoms before the onset of her seizure.

Jeffrey was overwhelmed with empathy for Doherty. He knew only too well what the man was going through. On an impulse, he used Seibert's phone to place a call to St. Joseph's Hospital. He asked for anesthesia, then waited for Dr. Doherty.

When Doherty picked up, Jeffrey told him how sorry he was for his experience the day before, saying that he could appreciate his anguish; he'd been through a similar episode.

"Who is this?" Dr. Doherty asked before Jeffrey could say another word.

"Jeffrey Rhodes," Jeffrey said, using his real name for the first time in days.

"Dr. Jeffrey Rhodes from Memorial?" Doherty asked.

"Yes," Jeffrey said. "I did want to ask you one question about the case. When you gave the test dose . . ."

"I'm sorry," Dr. Doherty interrupted, "but I have very explicit orders from my attorney not to discuss the case with anyone."

"I see," Jeffrey said. "Has there already been a malpractice action filed?"

"No, not yet," Dr. Doherty said. "But unfortunately we're all expecting it. I really cannot discuss it further. But I appreciate your call. Thank you."

Jeffrey hung up the phone, frustrated that he couldn't have the benefit of Dr. Doherty's fresh experience. But he could understand the man's motives for remaining so guarded. Jeffrey had received the same prohibition from his attorney with respect to Patty Owen's case.

"I already have some ideas," Seibert said as he breezed into his office dressed in a fresh scrub suit. Without the surgical gown, mask, and hat, Jeffrey got a good look at him for the first time. Seibert had an athletic build. His hair was sandy blond to go with his blue eyes. He had an angular, handsome face. Jeffrey guessed he was in his early thirties.

Seibert went behind his desk and sat down. Leaning back, he lifted his feet and rested them on the corner of his desk. "What we are talking about is some kind of histotoxic depolarizing blocker. That would give an initial jolt as if you injected a bolus of acetylcholine into all the ganglionic synapses and motor end plates. Presto: parasympathetic symptoms before all hell breaks loose secondary to the nerve and muscle cell destruction. The only trouble is, it would also cause muscle twitches."

"But there were muscle fasciculations!" Jeffrey said with growing interest. It sounded as if Seibert was really onto something.

"Doesn't surprise me," he said. Then he took his legs off the desk and tipped forward, looking at Jeffrey. "What about this latest patient? Did Karen Hodges have the kind of symptoms we're talking about?"

"Exactly the same," Jeffrey said.

"And you're sure they couldn't be caused by local anesthetics?"

Jeffrey nodded.

"Well, it's going to be interesting to see the toxicology results."

"I've had a look at the autopsies for two of the other four epidural fatalities. Toxicology was negative on both."

"What were the names of the four cases?" Seibert asked, taking out a pen and legal pad.

"Patty Owen, Henry Noble, Clark DeVries, and Lucy Havalin," Jeffrey said. "I've reviewed the autopsies for Owen and Noble."

"I'm not familiar with any of these cases. I'll have to check to see what we have in the files."

"Any chance that some body fluid might still be available on any of them?" Jeffrey asked.

"We save frozen samples on selected cases for about a year. Which case was the most recent?"

"Patty Owen," Jeffrey said. "If you got serum, could you run some tests for toxin?"

"You make it sound easy," Seibert said. "Like I told you before, it's pretty tough to find a toxin unless you're lucky enough to have the specific antitoxin in some labeled form. You can't just try a bunch of antitoxins shotgun style and hope for the best."

"Is there any way of narrowing the range of possibilities?"

"Possibly," Seibert said. "Maybe it would be worthwhile to come at the problem from another angle. "If there was to be a toxin, how would these patients have gotten it?"

"That's another issue entirely," Jeffrey admitted. He was reluctant to outline his Doctor X theory just yet. "Let's hold off on that for a moment. When you first came in here a moment ago, I thought you had something specific in mind."

"I did," Seibert said. "I was thinking of a whole class of toxins that have some toxicologists abuzz. They come from the skin glands of dendrobatid frogs from Colombia, South America."

"Would they fill the specifications of the mystery toxin we've been discussing?"

"I'll have to do some reading to be sure," Seibert admitted. "But as near as I can remember, they would. They were discovered much the same as curare was. The Indians used to grind these frogs up and use an extract on their poison darts. Hey, maybe that's what we got here: one of those Colombian Indians on the warpath." Seibert laughed.

"Can you give me any references?" Jeffrey asked. "I'd like to do some reading myself."

"Absolutely," Seibert said. He started toward his file cabinet, then stopped in his tracks and turned around. "This discussion has got me thinking about the perfect crime cocktail. If I were to choose what to put in a local anesthetic, I'd use that sushi poison, tetrodotoxin. Since it has the same apparent effect as local anesthetics, no one would ever suspect anything. It's the transient parasympathetic symptoms that have you worried. With tetrodotoxin you wouldn't have any."

"You're forgetting something," Jeffrey said. "I believe tetrodotoxin is reversible. It paralyzes the ability to breathe, but during anesthesia that doesn't matter. You can breathe for the patient."

Seibert snapped his fingers in disappointment. "You're right, I forgot about that. It's got to destroy the cells as well as block their function."

Seibert continued to his file cabinet and pulled out the top drawer. "Now where the hell did I file that stuff?" he muttered.

He shuffled through the files for a few minutes, obviously frustrated. "Ah, here it is," he said, triumphantly pulling a folder from the drawer. "I'd filed it under 'frogs.' What an idiot."

The folder contained a series of reprinted articles from a number of journals, some of which were common publications like *Science*. Others were more esoteric, like *Advances in Cytopharmacology*. For a few minutes the men were silent as they leafed through the many articles.

"How is it you happen to have all these?" Jeffrey asked.

"In my business, anything that causes death is interesting, especially something that does it as efficiently as these toxins. And how can you resist the names? Here's one: histrionicotoxin." Seibert put an article in front of Jeffrey. Jeffrey picked it up and began reading the extract.

"Here's a lulu," Seibert said, picking up an article and slapping it with his free hand. "This is one of the most toxic substances known to man: batrachotoxin."

"Let me see that one," Jeffrey said. He remembered the name from the many he'd come across in the chapter on toxins in Chris's toxicology book. Jeffrey took the article and read the abstract. It sounded promising. As Seibert suggested, it functioned as a depolarizing agent on nerve junctions. It was also said to cause extensive ultrastructure damage to nerve and muscle cells.

Looking up from reading, Jeffrey held the article toward Seibert. "What about looking for this one in the serum of some of these cases?"

"That would be a tough one for sure," he said. "It's so goddamn potent. It's a steroidal alkaloid, which means it can easily hide in the lipids and steroids of the cell. Maybe a muscle-tissue extract would be better than a serum sample, since the toxin is active on motor end plates. Probably the only way to find something like batrachotoxin is to figure out a way to concentrate it in a sample."

"How would you go about doing that?"

"As a steroid, it would be metabolized by being gluconated in the liver and excreted by the bile," Seibert explained. "So a bile sample might be good except for one minor problem."

"And what's that?" Jeffrey asked.

"The stuff kills so quickly, the liver never has a chance to process it."

"One of the cases didn't die as quickly as the others," Jeffrey said, thinking of Henry Noble. "He apparently got a smaller dose and lived for a week. You think that would help?"

"If I had to guess, I'd say yes," Seibert said. "His bile most likely would have had the highest concentration of anyplace in his body."

"He died almost two years ago. I suppose there wouldn't be any chance that his body fluid would still be around."

Warren shook his head. "Not a chance. We only have so much room in our freezer."

"Would it do any good to get to it by exhuming the body?" Jeffrey asked.

"Possibly," Seibert said. "It would depend on the extent of decomposition. If the body was in reasonable shape, say if it had been buried in a shady spot and reasonably embalmed, it might work. But exhuming a body isn't the easiest thing to do. You have to get a permit and that ain't always so easy. You have to get a court order or permission from the next of kin. As you might imagine, neither the courts nor the relatives are that willing."

Jeffrey glanced at his watch. It was already after two. He held up the article he was holding. "Any chance that I could borrow this?" he asked.

"As long as I get it back," Seibert said. "I can also give you a call about the toxicology results on Karen Hodges and on the serum sample from Patty Owen. Only trouble is, I don't know your name."

"I'm sorry," Jeffrey said. "The name is Peter Webber. But it's always hard to get me at the hospital. It would be easier if I called you back. When do you suggest I try?"

"How about tomorrow? When we're this backed up we work weekends. I'll see if I can speed things up since you're so interested."

Leaving the morgue, Jeffrey had to walk over to Boston City Hospital to get a cab. Climbing in, he told the driver to take him to St. Joseph's. His idea was to try to time his day so that he could ride home with Kelly. As a supervisor, she had a parking place at the hospital.

During the ride, Jeffrey managed to skim the article on batrachotoxin. It was difficult reading because the article was highly technical. But he did learn that the toxin definitely caused irreversible damage to nerve and muscle cells, and while it didn't specifically say that it produced salivation, lacrimation, and miotic pupils, it was highly suggestive. It did say that the toxin stimulated the parasympathetic system and produced muscle twitches.

At St. Joe's, Jeffrey found Kelly at her usual location, the nurses' station in the ICU. She was very busy. The ICU had recently gotten a new admission and the shift was changing.

"I've only got a second," she said. "But I forgot to give this to you." She handed Jeffrey a St. Joseph's Hospital envelope.

"What is it?" he asked as Kelly turned back to her work.

"The lists from Valley Hospital. Hart came through again. He faxed it over this afternoon. He was a little curious this time, though."

"What did you tell him?" Jeffrey asked.

"I told him the truth," Kelly said. "That there was something about Chris's case that still bothered me. But, Jeffrey, I can't talk right now. Go in the back room. I'll be off duty in a few minutes."

Jeffrey went into the narrow room and sat down. In marked contrast to the busy ICU, the only noise was from the compressor of a small refrigerator and the omnipresent coffeepot. Jeffrey opened the envelope and took out the fax.

There were two separate sheets. One was a list of doctors issued parking stickers for the year 1987 and was organized by department. The other was a payroll manifest for the same year for all employees of the hospital.

Eagerly, Jeffrey took out his own list of the thirty-four doctors who had privileges at both Memorial and St. Joseph's. Checking down the list of names, Jeffrey was able to narrow the list of thirty-four down to a list of six. One of the six was a Dr. Nancy Bennett. She was from Valley Hospital's department of anesthesia. For the moment she became Jeffrey's prime suspect. Now he would have to get equivalent lists from Commonwealth Hospital and Suffolk General. Once he had those he was confident his list would be even smaller. In fact, he hoped he would be down to a single individual.

The door from the ICU opened and Kelly came in. She looked as tired as Jeffrey felt. She came over and took a chair next to Jeffrey. "What a day!" she sighed. "Five admissions on our shift alone."

"I've got some encouraging news," Jeffrey said eagerly. "Using the Valley professional staff list, we're down to only six doctors. Now if we could just think of a way to get lists from the other two hospitals."

"I don't think I can help there," Kelly said. "I don't know a soul at either Commonwealth or Suffolk."

"What would you think of just going out there and visiting the nursing office?"

"Wait a second!" Kelly said suddenly. "Amy worked at Suffolk in their ICU."

"Who's Amy?" Jeffrey asked.

"She's one of my nurses," Kelly said. "Let me see if she's left yet." Kelly sprang from the chair and disappeared into the ICU again.

Jeffrey's eyes went back to his list of six doctors, then to the list of thirty-four. It was encouraging progress, indeed. Six was a lot more reasonable number of people to consider. Then he spotted the two names to the right of the list of M.D.s. He'd forgotten about the employees. Moving over to the Valley Hospital employee roster, he looked for Maureen Gallop's name. As he expected, it was not there. Next he checked Trent Harding. To his utter amazement, the man's name was on the Valley Hospital roster. He'd actually worked in their nursing department in 1987!

Jeffrey's heartbeat quickened. The name shouted at him from the page. Trent Harding had worked at Valley Hospital, Memorial, *and* St. Joseph's.

Stay cool, Jeffrey advised himself as his excitement soared. It was probably just a coincidence. But it was one hell of a coincidence and a lot less easy to explain than a doctor's having multiple privileges.

The door to the ICU opened and Kelly reappeared. She

dropped back into her seat, pushing her hair off her forehead. "I missed her," she said with disappointment. "But I'll be seeing her tomorrow. I'll ask her then."

"I'm not sure it will be necessary," Jeffrey said. "Look what I found!" He placed the Valley employee list in front of her and pointed to Trent Harding's name. "This guy's worked in all three hospitals at the critical times," he said. "I know it's circumstantial, but it's hard to believe his having been at each of the three at the right time is mere coincidence."

"And he's working here at St. Joseph's now?"

"According to the list you brought me."

"Do you know where in the hospital?"

"I don't know where but I know the department," Jeffrey said. "He's in the same department as you: nursing."

Kelly drew in a sharp breath. "No!" she said.

"That's what was indicated on the list. Do you know him?"

Kelly shook her head. "I've never even heard his name before, but then I certainly don't know everybody."

"We have to find out where he works," Jeffrey said.

"Let's go see Polly Arnsdorf," Kelly said, quickly getting to her feet.

Jeffrey grabbed her arm. "Hold on. We have to be careful. I don't want Polly Arnsdorf scaring this guy. Remember, we have no proof. It's all circumstantial. If this Harding character suspects we're onto him, he could run, and that's the last thing we want. And besides, we can't use my real name. She might recognize it."

"But if Harding is the killer, we can't have him stalking the halls of this hospital."

"The interval between the anesthetic complications has been eight or more months," Jeffrey said. "A couple of days won't matter."

"What about Gail?" Kelly demanded.

"We still don't know what was behind her death."

"But you implied—" Kelly began.

"I said I was suspicious," Jeffrey interrupted. "Calm down. You're getting more worked up than I am. Remember, all we know for sure is that this Harding fellow has worked at all three hospitals at the time of the anesthetic problems. We're going to need a lot more than that to put the finger on him. And it might turn out we're wrong. I'm not saying we shouldn't talk to Polly. We just have to get our story straight. That's all."

"All right," Kelly said. "How should I introduce you?"

"I've been using the name Webber but I'm afraid I haven't been consistent with the first name. Let's call me Dr. Justin Webber. And as far as this Harding fellow is concerned, let's say that we are concerned about his competence."

Together they went downstairs and into the administration office. When they arrived outside Polly Arnsdorf's office they were told she was on a long distance telephone call. They sat in the waiting area until she could see them. From the flurry of activity around her office, it was clear how busy she was.

When they were finally let in to see her, Kelly introduced Jeffrey as Dr. Justin Webber, according to plan.

"And what can I do for you?" Polly asked. Her tone was friendly but businesslike.

Kelly looked briefly at Jeffrey, then started. "We wanted to inquire about one of the nurses here," she said. "His name is Trent Harding."

Polly nodded and waited. When Kelly didn't speak, she said, "And what is it you'd like to know?"

"First, we're curious as to where in the hospital he works," Jeffrey asked.

"Worked," Polly corrected. "Mr. Harding quit yesterday."

Jeffrey felt a pang of disappointment. Oh no, he thought; would he lose this man after coming this close? On the positive side, Harding's quitting right after the latest anesthetic complication was another circumstantially incriminating piece of information.

"Where in the hospital did he work?" Jeffrey asked.

"The OR," Polly answered. She looked back and forth between Jeffrey and Kelly. Her instincts told her that something was up, something fairly serious.

"What shift did he work?" Kelly asked.

"For the first month he worked evenings," Polly said. "But then he'd been shifted to days. He'd been on days until yesterday."

"Was it a surprise that he quit?" Jeffrey asked.

"Not really," Polly said. "If there wasn't such a shortage of good nurses, I would have asked him to leave some time ago. He's had a history of normative problems with respect to getting along with superiors, not only here but in other institutions where he'd worked. Mrs. Raleigh had her hands full with him. He was always telling her how to run the OR. But as a nurse he was superb. Extremely intelligent, I might add."

"Where else has the man worked?" Jeffrey asked.

"He's worked at most of the Boston hospitals. I believe the only major hospital he has yet to work in is Boston City."

"He worked at Commonwealth and Suffolk General?" Jeffrey asked.

Polly nodded. "To my best recollection."

Jeffrey could barely contain himself. "Would it be possible to look at his file?"

"That I can't let you do," Polly told him. "Our files are confidential."

Jeffrey nodded. He'd expected as much. "What about a photo? Surely that would be all right."

Polly used her intercom to call out to her secretary, asking him to locate a photo of Trent Harding. Then she asked, "May I ask what this interest in Mr. Harding is all about?"

Both Jeffrey and Kelly started to speak at the same time. Then Jeffrey nodded for her to go on. "There is some question about his credentials and competence," she said.

"That's not the part I'd question," Polly said as her secretary came in with a photo. She took it and handed it across to Jeffrey. Kelly leaned over to look at it as well.

Jeffrey had seen the man in the Memorial OR on many occasions. He recognized his startling blond crewcut and stocky build. Jeffrey had never spoken with him directly as far as he could remember, but he remembered him as having always been deferential and conscientious. He certainly didn't look like a killer. He looked rather all-American, like a football player from a college in Texas.

Looking up from the photo, Jeffrey asked, "Do you have any idea of the man's plans?"

"Oh, yes," Polly said. "Mr. Harding was quite specific. He

said he was going to apply to Boston City because he wanted a more academic program."

"One other thing," Jeffrey asked. "Could you give us Trent Harding's address and phone number?"

"I suppose that would be all right," Polly said. "I'm sure it's in the phone book." She took out a piece of paper and pencil. She reached across and took the photo of Trent Harding from Kelly, turned it over, and copied the information from the back, then handed the paper to Jeffrey.

Jeffrey thanked Polly for her time. Kelly did the same. Then they left administration. Walking out the front door to the hospital, they went to Kelly's car.

"This could really be it!" Jeffrey said excitedly once they were out of earshot. "Trent Harding could be the murderer!"

"I agree," Kelly said. They got to the car and faced each other over the top. Kelly had yet to open the door. "I also think we have an obligation to go to the police right away. We've got to put a stop to him before he strikes again. If he's the man, he must be insane."

"We can't go to the police," Jeffrey said with some exasperation. "And for the same reasons I told you last time. As incriminating as we think this information is, it's still circumstantial. Remember, we have no proof. None! There isn't even any proof the patients were poisoned. I've got the Medical Examiner looking for a toxin, but the chances of his isolating one are not good. There are limits to toxicological capability."

"But the idea someone like this is walking around terrifies me," Kelly said.

"Hey, I agree with you—but the fact of the matter is at this point the authorities wouldn't be able to do anything even if they believed us. And at least for the moment he's not in the hospital."

Kelly reluctantly opened the door to her car. Both of them climbed in.

"What we need is proof," Jeffrey said. "And the first thing we have to do is make sure that this character is still in town."

"And how are we going to do that?" Kelly asked.

Jeffrey unfolded the piece of notepaper Polly had given him. "We're going to drive over to his apartment and make sure it's still occupied."

"You're not going to try to talk with him, are you?"

"Not yet," Jeffrey said. "But I'll probably have to at some point. Let's go. The address is Garden Street on Beacon Hill."

Kelly did as she was told, even though she didn't like the idea of going anywhere near this fiend's home. Proof or no proof, she was already convinced of Harding's guilt. What other reason could there be for his being at each of those hospitals at precisely the right time?

Kelly drove onto Storrow Drive, then turned right on Revere Street, which took them straight up to Beacon Hill. At Garden Street they turned down toward Cambridge Street. They didn't speak again until they came to the address. Kelly double-parked. She pulled on the emergency brake. It was a steep hill.

Jeffrey leaned across Kelly's lap to look up at the building. In contrast to those neighboring it, Harding's building was built of yellow, not red, brick. But, like the others, it was a five-story tenement. Because of the steepness of the street, the rooflines stepped down from building to building like a giant stair. Trent's building was capped with a decorative parapet sheathed in copper that was weathered to the familiar greenish patina. It would have been attractive except that the right corner had split and a large section hung down. The front door, the fire escape, and all the trim were badly in need of repair, and, like its neighbors, the building had a dilapidated appearance.

"It doesn't look like a good area," Kelly said. There was trash littering the street. The cars parked on either side were junky and battered except for one: a red Corvette.

"I'll be right back," Jeffrey said as he made a move to open his door.

Kelly grabbed his arm. "Are you sure you should do this?"

"Do you have a better idea?" Jeffrey said. "Besides, I'm just going to check in the foyer and see if his name's listed. I'll be right back."

Kelly's concern gave Jeffrey pause. He stood in the street for a moment, wondering if he was doing the right thing. But he had to make sure Harding was still in Boston. Setting his jaw, he crossed between parked cars and tried the yellow building's outer door. It opened into a small foyer.

Jeffrey stepped inside. The building was even shabbier on

the inside. A cheap fixture dangling from an exposed wire hung from the foyer ceiling. At one time the inner door must have been forced open with a crowbar and never repaired. A ripped plastic trash bag had been tossed in the foyer's corner. Trash had spilled from the tear, adding the disagreeable smell of garbage to the air.

There were six apartments listed by the intercom. Jeffrey guessed that meant there was one apartment per floor, including the basement. Trent Harding's name was at the top of the list. His name was also on the front of one of the mailboxes. Jeffrey saw that all the locks on the mailboxes were broken. He reached up and opened Harding's box to see if there was any mail. The instant his hand touched the box, the inner door to the building was pulled open.

Jeffrey found himself face to face with Trent Harding. He had not remembered how strong the man appeared. There was also a meanness about him that Jeffrey had never appreciated when he'd seen him in the Memorial OR. His eyes were blue and cold and deeply set beneath thick brows. Harding also had a scar that Jeffrey had forgotten about and that hadn't been apparent in the photograph.

Jeffrey was able to pull his hand off the mailbox in the split second before Harding could see. At first Jeffrey was afraid Harding would recognize him. But with an expression akin to a sneer, the man gruffly pushed past Jeffrey without a pause.

Jeffrey took a deep breath. He leaned against the wall of mailboxes for a moment to catch his breath. The brief, unexpected encounter had momentarily unnerved him. But at least he'd accomplished what he'd set out to do. He knew Trent Harding had not left town. He might have quit St. Joe's, but he was still in Boston.

Emerging from the building, Jeffrey stepped between the parked cars and climbed back into Kelly's car. Kelly was livid.

"The guy just came out of the building!" she snapped. "I knew you shouldn't have gone in. I knew it!"

"Nothing happened," Jeffrey assured her. "At least we know he hasn't skipped town. But I admit he startled me. I can't say for sure if he's the murderer, but he's pretty scary-looking up close. He's got a scar under his eye that didn't show up in the photo and there's something wild about his eyes."

"He's got to be crazy if he's been putting something in the anesthetic," Kelly said as she reached forward and started the car.

Jeffrey leaned over and put his hand on her arm. "Wait," he said.

"What now?" Kelly questioned.

"Just a second," Jeffrey said. He jumped out of the car again and jogged up to the corner of Revere Street. Looking down Revere, he could just make out Harding's form receding in the distance.

Jeffrey trotted back to Kelly, but instead of getting in the car, he appeared at her driver's-side window. "This is too good an opportunity to pass up," he said.

"What do you mean?" Whatever it was, Kelly was sure she wasn't going to like it.

"The inner foyer door to Trent's building is open. I think I'll take a quick look around his apartment. Maybe I'll find some sort of evidence to confirm our suspicions."

"I don't think it's a good idea," Kelly said. "Besides, how will you get into his apartment?"

Jeffrey pointed up at the roof. Kelly craned her neck.

"See that window by the fire escape on the top floor?" Jeffrey said. "It's open. Trent Harding lives on the top floor. I can go to the roof, climb down the fire escape, and get inside."

"I think we should just get out of here," Kelly said.

"A few minutes ago you were the one who was so concerned about this guy on the loose," Jeffrey said. "If I can get the proof we need to stop him, isn't it worth the risk? I don't think we can pass up the opportunity."

"What if Mr. Muscle Beach comes back while you're in there? He could tear you apart with his hands."

"I'll be quick," Jeffrey said. "Besides, in the unlikely event that he does come back while I'm still there, just let him go inside. Wait for five seconds, then come in and ring his buzzer. His name is right by the button. If I hear the buzzer, I'll go back out the window and up to the roof."

"Something could go wrong," Kelly said, shaking her head.

"Nothing will go wrong," Jeffrey said. "Trust me."

Before Kelly could agree or disagree, Jeffrey patted her arm and went back to the apartment building. He entered the foyer and pushed open the inner door. A narrow stair led up to the right. A single bare bulb illuminated each landing. Jeffrey could look up the stairwell and see a frosted skylight above.

He climbed the stairs rapidly. By the time he reached the headhouse door to the roof, he was out of breath. It took a little coaxing to get the door open, but Jeffrey was finally able to do it.

The roof was tar and gravel. There was about a four-foot wall separating it from the roof of the next building up the hill. The same with the building beyond that. Each building had its own headhouse. A few were painted and appeared in good repair. Many were dilapidated, with some of the doors off their hinges. Some of the roofs had makeshift decks with rusty lawn furniture.

Going over to the edge of the roof and looking down to the street, Jeffrey could see Kelly's car. He'd never been fond of heights, and it took all his courage to step out on the metal grate that comprised the fire escape. Between his feet he could look straight down five stories to the brick sidewalk.

Moving carefully, Jeffrey descended the one flight of steps to the landing outside Trent's window. He felt exposed, and suddenly worried if any of the neighbors were watching. The last thing he needed was for anyone to call the police.

Jeffrey had to wrestle with the ancient screen before he could clear his way to climb in. Once he made it through, he leaned back out the window. He gave Kelly a thumbs-up. Then he turned into the room.

Trent eyed the *Playgirl* magazine in the rack. He thought about reaching up and flipping through just to see what girls liked in a male body. But he didn't. He was standing in Gary's Drug Store on Charles Street and he knew the proprietor was at the counter to his left. Trent didn't want to give the man any wrong ideas about why he'd be interested in *Playgirl*. Instead, he picked up a travel magazine that had a cover story about vacations in San Francisco.

Going over to the counter, Trent tossed the magazine down

and put a *Globe* on top of it. Then he asked for two packs of filterless Camel cigarettes, his usual brand. As far as Trent was concerned, if he was going to smoke, he wanted something powerful.

After he'd paid for his purchases, Trent stepped out on the street. He debated going down to Beacon Hill Travel to talk about going to San Fran on a little vacation. Being between jobs, he had the time, and he had money to burn. But he felt lazy. Maybe he'd go to the travel agent tomorrow. Instead, he turned and crossed the street and went into a liquor store. He wanted to pick up some beer.

What he decided to do was go back home and take a nap. That way he'd be able to stay out late that night. Maybe he'd take in a movie and then go see if he could find some fags to push around.

Jeffrey stood and gazed around the living room, getting his bearings. He surveyed the mismatched furniture, the empty beer bottles, and the Harley-Davidson poster. He wasn't at all sure of what he was looking for or expecting to see; it was a pure fishing expedition. And even though for Kelly's benefit he'd pretended that coming into the apartment would be a snap, he was a lot more nervous than he'd let on. He couldn't help but wonder if any of the neighbors had called the police. He was afraid he'd hear police sirens in the distance at any moment.

The first thing that Jeffrey did was take a rapid tour around the whole apartment. It occurred to him he'd better make sure no one else was there. When he was convinced he was alone, he went back to the living room and started examining everything more closely.

On the coffee table he saw a number of mercenary and survivalist journals as well as some X-rated S&M magazines. There was also a pair of handcuffs, with the key in the lock. Against the common wall with the bedroom stood a wooden bookcase. The books were mostly chemistry, physiology, and nursing textbooks, but there were a few volumes on the Holocaust as well. Next to the couch was a fish tank with a large boa constrictor inside. Jeffrey thought that was a nice touch.

There was a desk against one wall. In contrast with the rest
of the apartment, its surface was quite orderly. Additional
reference books were neatly positioned on it between brass
bookends shaped like owls. There was also an answering machine.

Jeffrey went to the desk and pulled out the center drawer.
Pencils and paper were neatly arranged. There was a stack of
three-by-five cards, an address book, and a checkbook. Jeffrey
flipped through the address book. On the spur of the moment
he decided to take it. He slipped it in his pocket. Picking up
the checkbook, he glanced through. He was surprised at the
balance. Harding had over ten thousand dollars in his account.
Jeffrey put the checkbook back.

Leaning over, he opened the first of the deeper drawers. Just
as he did so the phone rang. Jeffrey froze. After a few rings,
the machine kicked on. Jeffrey regained his composure and
continued his search. The drawer contained manila files. Each
was labeled for a different subject, such as Surgical Nursing,
Anesthesia for Nurses, and so on. Jeffrey began to wonder if
he hadn't jumped to mistaken conclusions about the man.

After the outgoing message was completed, the answering
machine clicked again and Jeffrey heard Trent's caller leaving
a message.

"Hello, Trent! This is Matt. I'm just calling to tell you how
pleased I am. You're fantastic. I'll call back. Take care."

Jeffrey vaguely wondered who Matt was and why he was so
pleased. He moved into the bedroom. The bed was unmade.
The room was sparsely furnished with a night table, a bureau,
and a chair. The closet door was open. Jeffrey could see a rack
of Navy uniforms, all pressed and ready to go. Jeffrey fingered
the material. He wondered why Harding had them.

There was a TV on top of the bureau. Scattered by it were
a dozen or so X-rated videos, mostly of a sadomasochistic
variety. Photos of men and women in chains adorned the
boxes. On the night table next to the bed was a paperback
called *Gestapo*. On the cover was a picture of a large bearded
man in a Nazi uniform standing over a naked blond woman
in chains.

Jeffrey opened the top drawer of the bureau and found a

sock filled with marijuana. He also found a collection of women's lingerie. Real stable guy, Jeffrey thought sarcastically. By the lingerie, Jeffrey saw a stack of Polaroids. They were shots of Trent Harding. He'd apparently taken them himself. He was posed on his bed in various stages of undress. In a few, he appeared to be sporting some of the lingerie in the drawer. Jeffrey was just putting them back in place when he had a thought. Selecting three from the stack, he put them in one of his pockets. Then he put the rest of the photos back and closed the drawer.

Jeffrey wandered into the bathroom and turned on the light. He walked over to the medicine cabinet and opened the mirrored door. There was the usual complement of aspirin, Pepto-Bismol, Band-Aids, and the like. Nothing unusual, like ampules of Marcaine.

Closing the medicine cabinet, Jeffrey wandered out of the bedroom area and into the kitchen. One by one, he started looking through the cabinets.

Kelly drummed her fingers on the steering wheel. She didn't like this waiting one bit. She hadn't wanted Jeffrey to go into that apartment. Nervously she glanced up at the open fifth-floor window. Some blue curtains were sticking out and flapping in the breeze. The aged screen was leaning up against the brickwork where Jeffrey had left it.

Kelly looked down Garden Street. She could see the traffic going by on Cambridge Street down below. She shifted her position and looked at the clock on the dash. Jeffrey had been in the apartment for almost twenty minutes. What on earth was he doing?

Unable to sit still for another minute, Kelly started to get out of the car. She had the door half open and her foot on the pavement when she caught sight of Trent Harding. He was back! He was two doors up from his building, and heading right for the door. There was no doubt about it: he was on his way home.

Kelly froze. The man came toward her. She could see the look that Jeffrey had described in his eyes. They were like cats' eyes in their unblinking intensity. He seemed to be staring right at her, but he didn't break his stride. He reached his door and yanked it open with a thoughtless tug. Then he disappeared from view.

It took Kelly several beats before she could break the paralyzing spell the man's appearance had caused. In full panic she pushed the car door completely open and leaped out into the street. She dashed for the building, grasping the door, fully intending to pull it open. But she didn't. She wondered if Trent had had time to pass through the foyer. After another second's hesitation, she cracked the door an inch and peered within. Seeing the foyer was empty, she quickly entered and madly searched for Trent's name on the intercom board. Finding it on the top, she reached with a trembling index finger and pushed the button.

"No!" Kelly cried. Tears of fear and frustration welled in her eyes. The button wouldn't budge. Looking closely, she could see that the buzzer had long been disconnected. The severed wire was clearly exposed. The button was permanently smashed in. If the wire hadn't been cut, Harding's apartment would have been perpetually abuzz. Kelly pounded the intercom panel with her fist. She had to think of something. She considered her options. There weren't many.

She dashed back outside and ran to the middle of the street. Cupping her hands around her mouth, she shouted up to the open window: "Jeffrey!" There was no response. Then she yelled even louder, repeating his name twice.

If Jeffrey heard, he gave no sign. Kelly was at a loss. What could she do? She pictured Harding climbing the stairs. He was probably at his door that instant. Running over to her car, Kelly hopped in and leaned on her horn.

Jeffrey straightened up and stretched. He'd searched most of the undercounter cabinets in the kitchen and had found nothing unexpected besides a rather sizable colony of cockroaches. In the distance he heard a car horn sound steadily. He wondered what the trouble was. Whatever it was, the driver was pretty insistent.

Jeffrey had hoped by now to have come across something incriminating in Trent's apartment, but he'd come up with

nothing. All he'd succeeded in establishing was some evidence
of a weird and possibly violent personality, combined with
some serious questions about his sexual identity. But that certainly didn't make him a serial killer who'd tampered with vials
of local anesthetics.

Jeffrey began to open the kitchen drawers. There was nothing unusual, just the usual flatware, knives and openers, and
other kitchen gadgets. Then he went to the sink and opened
the cabinet under it. There he found a garbage can, a box of
S.O.S. pads, a bunch of discarded newspapers, and a propane
torch.

Jeffrey lifted the torch from the cabinet and looked at it more
closely. It was the type used by do-it-yourself plumbers. A
portable tripod was folded against its side. Jeffrey's first
thought was whether the torch could have been used in tampering with the Marcaine vials. He recalled his own makeshift
experiment using Kelly's stove. A torch like this would have
been better in directing the heat. But while the torch might
have been useful for such a purpose, in itself it hardly con-
stituted proof that was the reason Trent had it under his sink.
There were a lot of uses for a propane torch besides tampering
with glass medicinal ampules.

Jeffrey's heart skipped a beat. The sound of heavy footfalls
coming up the stairs reached his ears. Quickly he put the
propane torch back in place and closed the doors to the cabinet.
Then he started for the living room in case he had to beat a
hasty retreat. He'd not heard the buzzer, but he thought it best
to be prepared in the unlikely event Harding had gotten in
without Kelly seeing him.

The sound of a key slipping into a lock made him freeze.
The open window was twenty feet away, directly past the door
to the hall. Jeffrey knew he wouldn't make it out in time. All
he could do was flatten himself against the kitchen wall and
hope to stay out of sight.

His heart racing, Jeffrey heard the door slam and the sound
of magazines being dropped onto the coffee table, followed by
the same heavy footfalls across the room. Soon the deep, per-
cussive pulse of rock music filled the apartment.

Jeffrey wondered what he could do. The window in the
kitchen looked out on a courtyard, but there was no fire escape

there. It was a straight five-story drop to the ground. His only route of escape was the window in the front, unless he could get to the hall door in time. Jeffrey doubted he could do it, and even if he did make it to the door, he'd noticed the full complement of locks securing it. He'd never be able to unlock them fast enough. But he had to do something. It was only a matter of time before Trent noticed the missing screen.

Before Jeffrey could think of what to do, Trent surprised him again by walking directly past, heading to the refrigerator. He had a six-pack of beer in his hand.

Knowing he'd be discovered in the next few seconds, Jeffrey took advantage of the moment by dashing through the door, heading for the open window.

The sudden movement startled Trent, but only momentarily. With a burst of profanity, he let go of the beer, which crashed to the linoleum, and leaped after Jeffrey.

Jeffrey had one goal in mind: to get out the window. Reaching it, he practically dove through, hitting his hip on the sill. Grabbing the wrought-iron balustrade of the fire escape, he attempted to pull his legs from the room, but he wasn't quite fast enough. Trent got hold of his right leg at the knee and began to pull.

A tug-of-war resulted, with both men grunting and heaving. Jeffrey was no match for the younger man's strength. Realizing he was about to be yanked back into the apartment, Jeffrey cocked his free leg and kicked Trent as hard as he could in the chest.

The blow loosened Trent's grip on Jeffrey's leg. With a second kick, Jeffrey was freed. He cleared the sill and scrambled up the fire escape on all fours.

Trent leaned out the window, to see Jeffrey going up. Deciding to head him off, he ducked back into the apartment to use the main stairs. En route he grabbed a claw hammer he kept on his bookcase.

Jeffrey had never moved so quickly in his life. Once he made it to the roof, he lost no time. He ran directly at the wall of the neighboring house and vaulted to its roof. He rushed to the headhouse and frantically tugged on the door. It was locked! Running for the next wall, he heard the door to the headhouse of Trent's building burst open and smash against the wall.

Jeffrey glanced over in time to see Trent charging in his direction with a determined grimace of anger contorting his face. Jeffrey saw that he was clutching a claw hammer.

Jeffrey reached the second headhouse, two buildings up from Trent's. He gave the door a tug. To his utter relief, it opened. In a second he was inside, pulling the door shut behind him and fumbling with the lock, which was broken. But there was a hook and eye. Jeffrey's hands were trembling so badly that he had trouble putting the hook through. He slipped it home just as Trent smashed into the door's other side.

Trent rattled the door viciously, trying to open it. Jeffrey backed away, hoping the slender hook would hold. When Trent gave vent to his frustration by pounding the door with his hammer, several of the blows penetrated the thin door with a splintering sound. Jeffrey turned and fled down the stairs. He was two flights down when he heard the door crash open.

Rounding the third landing, Jeffrey tripped in his haste. Had it not been for his grip on the banister, he would have fallen. Fortunately he was able to regain his balance and continue his descent.

Reaching the ground floor, he pushed through the doors to the street. Kelly was standing next to the car.

"Let's go!" Jeffrey shouted as he dashed for the car. By the time he got in, Kelly had the car started. At that moment, Harding appeared, his hammer clenched in his hand. Kelly spun the tires. There was a dull thud on the roof of the car. Trent had thrown the hammer.

Jeffrey braced himself against the dash as Kelly accelerated down Garden Street. The tires screeched in complaint as she braked at the foot of the hill. Without stopping, she turned right onto Cambridge Street's busy thoroughfare and headed for downtown Boston.

Neither of them spoke until they were forced to stop for a light at New Chardon Street. Then Kelly turned to Jeffrey. She was enraged. " 'Nothing will go wrong. Trust me,' " she said, parodying Jeffrey's earlier reassurance. "I told you not to go in there!" she yelled.

"You were supposed to buzz!" Jeffrey yelled in return, still catching his breath.

"I tried," Kelly snapped. "Did you check to make sure the

buzzer worked? Of course not. That would have been asking too much. Well, the buzzer was busted and you could have gotten yourself killed. That idiot had a hammer. Why did I let you go in there?" she wailed, hitting her forehead with an open palm.

The light changed. They moved forward. Jeffrey remained silent. What could he say? Kelly was right. He probably shouldn't have gone into Trent's apartment. But it had seemed like such an ideal opportunity.

They drove in silence for a few miles more. Then Kelly asked, "Did you at least find something to justify the gamble?"

Jeffrey shook his head. "Not really," he said. "I found a propane torch, but that's hardly evidence."

"No poison vials on the kitchen table?" she asked sarcastically.

"Afraid not," Jeffrey said, beginning to feel a little angry himself. He knew Kelly was shaken up, and had reason to be irritated at his amateur sleuthing, but he thought she was carrying it a bit far. Besides, he'd been the one who risked his neck, not her.

"I think it's time we call the police, proof or no proof. A hammer-toting madman is proof enough for me. The police should be in that creep's apartment, not you."

"*No!*" Jeffrey shouted, this time with real anger. He didn't want to go through this discussion again. But as soon as he'd raised his voice, he felt sorry. After everything she'd gone through for his sake, Kelly deserved better. Jeffrey sighed. He'd go through it one more time. "The police wouldn't even be able to get a search warrant with only pure speculation."

They drove toward Kelly's Brookline home in silence. When they got close, Jeffrey said, "I'm sorry I yelled at you. That fellow really scared me. I hate to think what he would have done to me if he'd caught me."

"My nerves are a bit raw, too," Kelly admitted. "I was terrified when I saw him go in the building, especially after I realized I couldn't warn you. I felt so helpless. Then when I saw you struggling on the fire escape, I was beside myself. How did you manage to get away?"

"Luck," Jeffrey said, realizing how much danger he'd been in. He shuddered as he tried to ban from his mind the image of Trent coming at him with the claw hammer in his hand.

As they turned onto Kelly's street, Jeffrey remembered his other problem: Devlin. He thought about climbing into the backseat, but there wasn't time. Instead, he slid down so that his knees were against the dash.

Kelly saw him out of the corner of her eye. "Now what?"

"I almost forgot about Devlin," Jeffrey explained as Kelly pulled into her driveway. She pressed her automatic garage door opener, and as soon as she'd pulled in, she pressed it again. The door closed behind them.

"All I need at this point is for Devlin to lunge out of nowhere," Jeffrey said as he got out of the car. He didn't know whom he feared more, Trent or Devlin. They went into the house together.

"How about some herbal tea?" Kelly suggested. "Maybe it will settle us both down."

"I think I need about 10 mgs of intravenous Valium," Jeffrey said. "But I'll settle for tea. It would be nice, actually. Maybe we could put a little shot of cognac in it. That might help."

Kicking off his shoes, Jeffrey slumped onto the family room couch. Kelly put the water on to boil.

"We've got to come up with some other way of finding out if Trent Harding is the culprit or not," Jeffrey said. "The problem is that I don't have a lot of time. Devlin's going to find me one of these days. Probably sooner than later."

"There's always the police," Kelly said. As soon as Jeffrey started to protest, she added: "I know, I know. We can't go to the police, et cetera, et cetera. But remember, you're a fugitive, I'm not. Maybe they would listen to me."

Jeffrey ignored her. If she didn't understand by this time, he wasn't going to try to explain it to her again. Until there was some concrete evidence, it was ridiculous to go to the authorities. He was that much of a realist.

Lifting his feet to the top of the coffee table, Jeffrey settled back into the depths of the couch. He was still shaking from his experience with Trent Harding. The vision of the man coming at him with the hammer would haunt him for the rest of his life.

Jeffrey tried to review where he was in his investigation.

Although he had no proof of a contaminant in the Marcaine, his instincts told him it had been there. There was no other explanation for the array of symptoms all those patients evidenced. He didn't have high hopes of Dr. Seibert's finding anything, but his conversation with the man had made Jeffrey feel relatively certain that some kind of toxin, maybe batrachotoxin, was involved. And at least Dr. Seibert was interested enough to be looking for one.

Jeffrey was also pretty certain that Harding was the murderer. His working at all five of the involved hospitals was too much of a coincidence. But Jeffrey had to be sure. If it was just coincidence, then he'd have to get busy on getting the staff lists for the remaining two hospitals.

"Maybe you should just call him up," Kelly said from the kitchen.

"Call who?" Jeffrey asked.

"Harding."

"Oh, sure!" Jeffrey said, rolling his eyes. "And say what? Hey, Trent! Are you the guy who's been putting poison in the Marcaine?"

"It's no more stupid than you going up to his apartment," Kelly said, taking the kettle from the stove.

Jeffrey turned to look at Kelly to make sure she was serious. She raised her eyebrows at him as if to challenge him to disagree with her last statement. Jeffrey faced around again and stared out at the garden. In his mind he played a hypothetical telephone conversation with Trent Harding. Maybe Kelly's suggestion wasn't so stupid after all.

"Obviously you couldn't ask him directly," Kelly said, coming around the couch with the tea. "But maybe you could just be suggestive and see if he implicates himself."

Jeffrey nodded. As much as he hated to admit it, Kelly might have hit on something. "I did find something in the drawer of his nightstand that might be significant in this regard," Jeffrey said.

"And what was that?"

"A bunch of kinky Polaroids. Nudie pictures."

"Of whom?"

"Himself," Jeffrey said. "There were other things in his apartment—handcuffs, lingerie, violent porn videos—that

make me think that in addition to being a serial killer, Nurse
Harding has a gender-identity problem and some serious sex-
ual hangups. I took some of the Polaroids with me on a hunch.
Maybe we can use them as leverage."

"How so?"

"I'm not sure," Jeffrey said. "But I can't imagine he'd want
too many people seeing them. He's probably pretty vain."

"You think he is gay?" Kelly asked.

"I think there is a chance," Jeffrey said. "But I have the
feeling he's not at all sure, like he's confused and fighting it.
It could be the problem that's driving him to do crazy things.
That is, if he's doing them."

"He sounds charming," Kelly said.

"The kind of son only a mother could love," Jeffrey said. He
reached into his pockets, searching for the three Polaroids.
Finding them, he extended them toward Kelly. "Take a gan-
der," he said.

Kelly took the photos. She took one look and gave them
back to Jeffrey. "Ugh!" she said.

"Now the only question is whether a tape recording would
be admissible in court if we happen to get lucky. Maybe it's
time I give old Randolph a call."

"Who's Randolph?" Kelly asked. She checked to see if the
tea had adequately steeped, then poured two cups.

"My lawyer."

Jeffrey went into the kitchen and called Randolph's office.
After identifying himself, he was put on hold. Kelly brought
a cup of tea over to him and put it on the counter. He took a
sip. It was very hot.

When Randolph came on the line he was not particularly
friendly. "Where are you, Jeffrey?" he asked abruptly.

"Still in Boston."

"The court is aware of your attempted flight to South America," Randolph said. "You're about to forfeit your bail. I cannot
urge you more strenuously to give yourself up."

"Randolph, I have other things on my mind right now."

"I'm not sure you understand the gravity of your situation,"
Randolph said. "There is a formal warrant out for your apprehension and arrest."

"Shut up for a minute, will you, Randolph!" Jeffrey yelled. "And let me tell you something. I've had a full appreciation of the seriousness of this affair from day one. If anyone has erred in that regard it is you, not I. You lawyers think of this as all a game, all in a day's work. Well, let me tell you something: it's my life that's in the balance. And let me tell you something else. I'm not running around on Ipanema Beach having a good time these days. I think I'm onto something that can potentially negate my conviction. At the moment all I want to do is ask you a legal question and maybe get something for all the money I've thrown at you."

There was a momentary silence. Jeffrey was afraid the man had hung up on him.

"Are you still there, Randolph?"

"What is your question?"

"Is a tape recording admissible as evidence in court?" Jeffrey asked.

"Does the person know he is being tape-recorded?" Randolph asked.

"No," Jeffrey said. "He doesn't."

"Then it would not be admissible," Randolph said.

"Why the hell not?"

"It has to do with the right to privacy," Randolph said, starting to explain the law to Jeffrey.

Disgusted, Jeffrey hung up on the man. "Still batting zero," he told Kelly. Jeffrey carried his tea over to the couch and sat down next to her.

"I can't believe that man," Jeffrey said. "You'd think he'd be able to come through on one thing."

"He didn't make the law."

"I'm not so sure," Jeffrey said. "Seems to me most of the lawmakers are lawyers. It's like a private club. They make their own rules and thumb their noses at the rest of us."

"So what if you can't tape-record?" Kelly said. "I can listen on the extension. I'm no tape recorder, but I certainly could be introduced as evidence. I could be a witness."

Jeffrey studied her face with admiration. "That's right—I never thought of that. Now all we have to think about is what I'll say to Trent Harding."

FRIDAY,

MAY 19, 1989

7:46 P.M.

Devlin was jolted out of his indecision by his car phone. He was still sitting in his car two doors down from Kelly Everson's house. Twenty-five minutes earlier he'd seen the car pull into the drive and disappear into the garage. He'd caught a glimpse of the driver: a cute brunette with long hair. He'd guessed she was Kelly.

Earlier he'd gone up to the house and rung the bell, but no one had come to the door. The place seemed empty. He hadn't heard so much as a pin drop, not like he had on his first visit. Devlin had retired to the car to wait. But now that Kelly had come home, he didn't know whether to go right up there and talk to her or sit tight for a while to see if she had any visitors or went anyplace. Unable to decide, he sat some more, which he knew was a decision in itself. One thing for sure was that she'd not opened any of the drawn drapes. That didn't seem normal at all.

It was Mosconi on the phone. Devlin had to hold the phone at arm's length while Michael carried on. The bond was about to be forfeited.

"Why haven't you found the doctor yet?" Mosconi demanded after his hysterical monologue had run out of steam.

Devlin told him that his week still wasn't up, but the reminder fell on deaf ears.

"I've put in calls to some other bounty hunters."

"Now why did you do that?" Devlin asked. "I told you I'd get him, and I will. I've made some progress, so when those calls come back, tell the men they're not needed."

"Can you promise me something in the next twenty-four hours?"

"I have a good lead. I have a feeling I'll be seeing the doctor tonight."

"You didn't answer my question," Michael said. "I want some results in twenty-four hours. Otherwise I'm out of business."

"All right," Devlin said. "Twenty-four hours."

"You're not giving me a load of crap just to humor me, are you, Devlin?"

"Would I ever do that?"

"All the time," Michael said. "But this time I'm going to hold you to it. Understand?"

"Have you found out anything else about the doctor's trial?" Devlin asked. Mosconi had already told Devlin the essentials of the case earlier that afternoon. When Devlin had heard more of the story, he felt something close to sympathy for Rhodes. To have made a mistake once with something like morphine and then to get over it only to have it kicked in your face at the first wrong turn seemed unfair. Knowing what kind of "murderer" Rhodes was, Devlin even felt guilty about having shot at him back at the Essex. Part of the reason Devlin had played such hardball had been because he thought he'd been dealing with a real criminal—a bona fide bad guy of the white-collar variety Devlin always had it in for. But knowing more about the nature of the crime made Devlin feel like he was just another hit of the bad luck already plaguing the guy.

But Devlin wasn't about to let his empathy get out of control. He would be professional about this, he reminded himself. He had to be. He'd bring in Dr. Jeffrey Rhodes all right, but he'd be sure to bring him in alive, not dead.

"Quit worrying about the man's conviction," Mosconi snapped. "Just bring the bastard in or I'm getting somebody else. You hear me?"

Devlin hung up his car phone. Sometimes Mosconi could get on his nerves and this was one of them. Devlin certainly didn't want to lose the reward on this case, and he disliked being threatened with the possibility. He also hated to have been forced into a promise that he might not be able to deliver on. He'd try his best. But now he didn't have the luxury of waiting for things to happen. He had to make them happen. He started his car and drove into Kelly's driveway. Getting out, he went to the front door and rang the bell.

Jeffrey had been deep in thought when the doorbell rang and it startled him. Kelly got up and started for the door. Jeffrey leaned over the back of the couch and said, "Make sure who it is."

Kelly stopped at the door to the dining room. "I always make sure who it is," she said with an edge to her voice.

Jeffrey nodded. He was sorry both their nerves were getting so frayed. Maybe he should do Kelly the favor of moving to a hotel after all. The situation was fraught with more tension than he could expect her to endure. For the moment, he turned his thoughts back to Trent Harding and what he might say to him on the telephone. There had to be a way to bait the guy. If he could only get him talking . . .

Just then Kelly tiptoed back into the room. "At the door," she whispered. "It's not anyone I know. I think it might be that Devlin character. Ponytail, denim clothes, Maltese cross earring. I think you should come see."

"Oh, no!" Jeffrey said as he lifted himself from the couch and followed Kelly through the dining room and into the foyer. He wasn't up to another confrontation. Just as they arrived at the door, its chimes were rung again several times in rapid succession. Jeffrey warily advanced and gingerly put his eye to the peephole.

Jeffrey's blood ran cold. It was Devlin, all right! Jeffrey ducked away from the door and motioned Kelly to follow him into the dining room.

"It's Devlin, all right," he whispered. "Maybe if we stay quiet he'll think no one is at home and go away like he did last time."

"But we just drove in," Kelly said. "If he'd seen the car, he'd know someone is home. Then if we pretend otherwise, he'll guess you are here."

Jeffrey looked at her with renewed admiration. "Why do I have the feeling you're better at this stuff than I am?" he asked.

"We can't let him get suspicious," Kelly said. She started back toward the door. "You hide. I'll talk to him, but I won't let him in."

Jeffrey nodded. What else could he do? Kelly was right. Devlin had probably been watching the house. Jeffrey only hoped he'd crouched low enough in the car so Devlin hadn't seen him.

Frantically, he searched for a place to hide. He didn't want to go back to the pantry. Instead, he slipped into the hall closet built under the stairs and pushed in behind the coats.

Kelly went to the door and called out: "Who is it?"

"Sorry to bother you, ma'am," Devlin called through the door. "I'm working for law enforcement and I'm looking for a dangerous man, a convicted felon. I would like to talk to you for a moment."

"I'm afraid this is a bad time," Kelly said. "I've just come from the shower and I'm all alone. I don't like to open the door to strangers. I hope you understand."

"I can understand," Devlin said. "Especially the way I look. The man I'm looking for is named Jeffrey Rhodes, although he has used aliases. The reason I want to talk to you is because someone specifically told me that you were recently seen with this man."

"Oh!" Kelly said, nonplussed that someone had told that to Devlin. "Who told you such a thing?" she stammered. Kelly quickly tried to guess who Devlin possibly could have been talking with. A neighbor? Polly Arnsdorf?

"I'm not at liberty to say," Devlin said. "But the fact is that you know him, isn't that true?"

Kelly quickly regained her composure, realizing that Devlin had been fishing, trying to get her to commit herself just as she and Jeffrey had thought of trying to do to Trent Harding.

"I've heard the name," Kelly said. "Some years ago, before my husband died, I believe he did some research with a Jeffrey Rhodes. But I haven't seen the man since my husband's funeral."

"In that case, I'm sorry to bother you," Devlin said. "Perhaps my contact isn't reliable. I tell you what. I'll slip a telephone number under the door. If you see or hear from Jeffrey Rhodes, give me a call."

Kelly looked down as a card came under the door.

"Did you get it?" Devlin asked.

"I did, and I'll be sure to call if I see him." Kelly pulled aside the lace curtain over the sidelight of the door and watched Devlin descend the few steps in front of her house. He disappeared from view. Then she heard a car start. A black Buick Regal backed into the street and accelerated away. Kelly waited a moment, then went out the door and peeked around the corner of the house. She watched the car disappear toward Boston. Running back into the house, she closed and locked the front door. Then she opened the door to the front closet. Jeffrey was way in under the stair. He blinked when he emerged into the light.

Devlin had to smile. Sometimes even smart people could be so dumb. He could tell Kelly had been thrown the minute he'd told her she'd been seen with Jeffrey Rhodes. She'd recovered, but too late. Devlin knew she'd been lying, which meant she was trying to hide something. Besides, he'd seen her peeking around the side of her house as he'd driven away.

As soon as he was well out of sight of Kelly's house, he pulled a quick U-turn. Then he maneuvered through the small side streets until he approached her house from the opposite direction. Devlin pulled into the crushed-gravel drive of a nearby home that looked deserted and killed his engine. He had a good view of Kelly's house through a stand of birch trees.

From the way Kelly had acted, he knew she knew something. The question was how much. Devlin thought there was a good possibility she'd be getting in touch with Jeffrey to warn him that Devlin had been there. Devlin wished he'd had an opportunity to put a bug on her phone. He thought about going around the back of her house and finding her telephone junction box, but he couldn't do that in the daylight. He'd have to wait for dark for that kind of stunt.

If he was really lucky, and Devlin thought he was due for a little luck, Kelly would go visit Jeffrey, wherever the hell the

guy was hiding. There was a slim chance that the doc would
even show up there on Kelly's doorstep. Devlin would wait and
see. Whatever else might happen, one thing was for sure: the
next time he ran into him, the good doctor wasn't getting away.

"Didn't you hear what he said?" Kelly asked.

"No," Jeffrey said. "I could hear you, but not him."

"He said that someone told him they'd seen us together. I
said that I hadn't been in touch with you since Chris's funeral.
He left his name and number in case I heard from you. I'm sure
he doesn't know you're here. If he did, he wouldn't have given
up so easily, and he certainly wouldn't have bothered leaving
his telephone number."

"But it's the second time he's come here," Jeffrey said. "He
must know something, otherwise he wouldn't keep coming
back. We've been lucky so far. He carries a gun, which he
thinks nothing of shooting at will."

"He's fishing," Kelly said confidently. "I'm telling you, he
doesn't know you're here. Trust me!"

"It's Devlin I don't trust. He's real trouble. I feel guilty
about jeopardizing your safety."

"You're not jeopardizing my safety. *I'm* jeopardizing my
safety. I'm an active participant in this. You're not about to
scare me out of it any more than Devlin or Harding are.
Besides," she said, softening a bit, "you need me."

Jeffrey studied Kelly's face. He looked deep into her dark-
brown eyes, noticing flecks of gold. For the first time he almost
felt everything he'd gone through in the last few days had been
worth it just to reach this moment with her. He'd always
thought of her as attractive; suddenly she was beautiful. Beautiful, warm, caring, and oh, so feminine.

They were sitting on the gingham couch, having come there
after Kelly had pulled Jeffrey from the depths of the front
closet. With the curtains of the family room still drawn, the
only source of the late-afternoon light was the mullioned casement windows over the sink. It made the illumination in the
room gentle and even. The sound of songbirds drifted in from
the backyard.

"Despite the danger, you really want me to stay?" Jeffrey
queried. He had one arm over the back of the couch.

"You can be so thickheaded," Kelly said with a smile. "Just like a man." She laughed her crystalline laugh. Her eyes and teeth sparkled in the soft light. "So it's settled," she said. Playfully she leaned her head against Jeffrey's arm and reached out with her hand. She ever so gently touched the end of his nose, then the tip of his upper lip. "I have some idea of how alone you must have been feeling these days, these months. I know because I've felt the same. I could see it in your eyes the night you came here from the airport."

"It was that obvious?" Jeffrey asked. But he didn't expect an answer. It was a rhetorical question, as he felt a change coming over him. The universe was shrinking. Suddenly the room was all there was. Time slowed, then stopped. Gently leaning forward, Jeffrey kissed Kelly's upturned mouth. As if in slow motion they came together in a tender, emotional, love-starved way. At first their coupling was slow, then eager, then ravenous. It was a joyous union, as mutual need was sated by mutual gratification.

Eventually the sound of the songbirds re-entered their consciousness. As overwhelming and as unexpected as their lovemaking had been, reality drifted back in stages. For a brief instant they'd been the only people on the earth, and space and time had stood still. With some embarrassment akin to a loss of innocence they pulled apart enough to look into each other's eyes. They giggled. They felt like teenagers.

"So," Kelly said, at last breaking the silence. "You'll stay?" Both laughed.

"I'll stay," Jeffrey agreed.

"How about some dinner?"

"Wow, what a transition," Jeffrey said. "I haven't been thinking much about food. Are you hungry?"

"I'm always hungry," Kelly admitted, detaching herself.

They made dinner together, Kelly doing the lion's share of the work but giving Jeffrey odd jobs like cleaning and spin-drying the lettuce.

Jeffrey was amazed at how calm he felt. The fear of Devlin was still there, but it was now under control. With Kelly by his side he didn't feel as if he was alone. Plus he decided she was right. Devlin couldn't have known he was there. If he had, he would have come through the door whether Kelly had opened it or not.

Noticing the hour, Jeffrey took time out from his chores to call the Medical Examiner's office. He hoped Dr. Warren Seibert would be still there. Jeffrey wanted to ask if he'd been able to identify any toxins.

"No luck so far," Seibert told him once he got on the line. "I ran samples from Karen Hodges, Gail Shaffer, and even Patty Owen through the gas chromatograph."

"I appreciate your trying," Jeffrey said. "But from what you said this morning, I suppose it's not surprising. And just because you haven't found a toxin, doesn't mean that one's not there. Right?"

"Right," Seibert said. "Even though I didn't find it, it could be hiding in one of the peaks. But I put in a call to a pathologist from California who's been doing some research on batrachotoxin and its family of toxins. Hopefully, he'll be getting back to me to let me know where the stuff would come out of the column. Who knows, maybe he might know where we could get a tagged antitoxin. I did some more reading, and with all the stipulations you've given me, I think batrachotoxin is the prime candidate."

"Thanks for all your help in this," Jeffrey said.

"Hey, no problem," Seibert said. "This is the kind of case that made me go into the field. It's got me all excited. I mean, if your suspicions are right, this is big-time stuff. We'll get a couple of great papers out of it."

After Jeffrey hung up the phone, Kelly asked, "Any luck?"

Jeffrey shook his head. "He's excited, but he hasn't found anything. It's so frustrating to be this close but still have no proof of either the crime or the guilt of the main suspect."

Kelly stepped over and gave Jeffrey a hug. "Don't worry, we'll get to the bottom of it one way or another."

"I sincerely hope so," Jeffrey said. "And I hope we do it before Devlin or the police catch up with me. I think we better go ahead and make this call to Trent Harding."

"After dinner," Kelly said. "First things first. Meanwhile, how about opening some wine? I think we could use a little."

Jeffrey got out a bottle of chardonnay from the refrigerator and took off the foil seal. "If this Trent turns out to be the person responsible, I'd love to find out about his childhood. There has to be some kind of explanation, even if it's irrational."

"The problem is he looks so normal," Kelly said. "I mean, his eyes are pretty intense, but maybe we're reading that into them. Otherwise he looks like the fellow who was the captain of the football team in my high school class."

"What bothers me most is the indiscriminate nature of the killings," Jeffrey said as he got out the corkscrew. "Killing another person is bad enough, but tampering with drugs and killing randomly is so sick it's hard for me to conceive of it."

"If he's the culprit, I'm going to wonder how he can function so well in the rest of his life," Kelly said.

With a grunt, Jeffrey popped the cork on the wine bottle. "Especially becoming a nurse," he said. "He has to have had some altruistic motivations. Nurses more than doctors have to be motivated by a desire to help people in a true, hands-on manner. And he's got to be intelligent. If the contaminant turns out to be something like this batrachotoxin, its choice is diabolically ingenious. I wouldn't have ever thought of a contaminant if it hadn't been for Chris's suspicions."

"That's kind of you to say," Kelly said.

"Well, it happens to be the truth," Jeffrey said. "But if Trent is the guilty one, I'm certainly not going to admit that I'll ever understand his motivations. Psychiatry was never one of my strong points."

"If you're finished opening the wine, how about setting the table?" Kelly asked. She bent over and turned on the oven.

The meal was delicious, and though Jeffrey hadn't realized he was hungry, he ate more than his share of the breaded Dover sole and steamed broccoli.

Taking a second helping of salad, he said, "If Seibert is not able to isolate a toxin from any of the current bodies, we talked about exhuming Henry Noble."

"He's been dead and buried for almost two years," Kelly said.

Jeffrey shrugged his shoulders. "I know it sounds a bit ghoulish, but the fact that he lived for a week after his adverse reaction might be helpful. A toxin like this batrachotoxin gets concentrated in the liver and is excreted in the bile. If it's what Harding used, the best place to find the stuff may be in Henry Noble's bile."

"But two years after the fact?"

"Seibert said that if the body had been reasonably embalmed and perhaps buried in a shady spot, it would still be traceable."

"Yuck," Kelly said. "Can't we talk about something else, at least until we're finished dinner? Let's get back to what we're going to say to Trent Harding."

"I think we have to be direct. Let him know what we suspect. And I can't help but think we can use those Polaroids to our advantage. He can't want pictures like that to get into circulation."

"What if it just makes him mad?" Kelly said, recalling Harding's angry hammer throw. The roof of her car had a dent in it the size of a baseball.

"I hope it does. If he gets angry, maybe he'll say something to give himself away."

"Like threaten you?" Kelly said doubtfully. " 'I've killed before, I'll kill again.' That sort of thing?"

"I know it's a long shot," Jeffrey said, "but do you have any better suggestions?"

Kelly shook her head. Jeffrey's idea was worth a try. There certainly wasn't anything to lose at this point.

"I'll bring an extension in here," she said. "There's a phone jack over by the TV set." She went to get it.

Jeffrey tried to prepare himself for the call. He tried to put himself in Trent's position. If he was innocent, he'd probably hang up immediately. If he was guilty, then he'd be nervous and want to try to find out what the caller knew. But it was all pure guesswork. If Trent stayed on the phone, it certainly wouldn't qualify as proof of guilt.

Carrying a dusty red telephone, Kelly returned to the kitchen. "Somehow I thought it would be fitting if we used the phone from Chris's office," she said. She pulled out the TV stand, bent over, and plugged in the jack. Picking up the phone, she made sure there was a dial tone.

"You want to use this one or the one in the kitchen?" she asked Jeffrey.

"The one in the kitchen," Jeffrey said, not that it made much difference. This was going to be one tough call, no matter where he made it.

Jeffrey pulled out the slip of paper Polly Arnsdorf had given him, with Trent's phone number and address. He dialed Harding's number, then motioned to Kelly to pick up as soon as it started to ring.

The phone rang three times before Trent answered. His voice was a lot softer than Jeffrey had anticipated. He said, "Hello . . . Matt?" before Jeffrey had a chance to say anything.

"This isn't Matt," Jeffrey said.

"Who is it?" Harding demanded. His voice turned cold, even angry.

"An admirer of your work."

"Who?"

"Jeffrey Rhodes."

"Do I know you?"

"I'm sure you do," Jeffrey said. "I was an anesthesiologist at Boston Memorial, but I was put on leave after a problem occurred. A problem in the OR. Does that ring any bells?"

There was a pause. Then Harding raged. "What the hell you calling me for? I don't work at Boston Memorial anymore. I quit there almost a year ago."

"I know," Jeffrey said. "Then you went to St. Joseph's and you've just recently quit there. I know a bit about you, Trent. And what you've been up to."

"What the hell are you talking about?"

"Patty Owen, Henry Noble, Karen Hodges," Jeffrey said. "Those names ring any bells?"

"I don't know what you're talking about, man."

"Oh, sure you do, Trent," Jeffrey said. "You're being modest, that's all. Plus I can imagine you don't want many people to know. After all, you went to all that trouble to choose just the right toxin. You know what I mean?"

"Hey, man, I don't know what you mean. And I haven't the faintest idea why you're calling me."

"You do know who I am, don't you, Trent?" Jeffrey asked.

"Yeah, I know you," Trent said. "I remember you from Boston Memorial and I read about you in the papers."

"I thought so," Jeffrey said. "You read all about me. Only

maybe it won't be too long before people are reading about you, one way or another."

"What do you mean?"

Jeffrey knew he was upsetting him, and the fact that Trent was still on the phone was encouraging. "These things have a way of getting found out," Jeffrey continued. "But I'm sure I'm not telling you anything you don't already know."

"I don't know what you're talking about," Trent said. "You've got the wrong guy."

"Oh, no," Jeffrey said. "I've got the right guy. Like I said, one way or the other you're going to make the news. I've got some pictures that would look great in print. Let's say copies of them spread all over Boston City. Your colleagues there could be treated to a whole new side of you."

"What pictures are you talking about?" Trent demanded.

"They were a treat for me," Jeffrey said, ignoring him, "and quite a surprise."

"I still don't know what you're talking about," Trent said.

"Polaroids," Jeffrey said. "Color glossies of you and not much else. Check your bureau drawer, right by your sack of pot. I think you'll find you're missing a few photos."

Trent muttered a few curses. Jeffrey thought he heard him put down the phone. In a minute Trent was back, shouting into the receiver. "So it was you in here, huh, Rhodes. Well, I'm warning you—I want those pictures back."

"I'm sure you do," Jeffrey said. "They are fairly . . . revealing. Great lingerie. I liked the pink teddy the best."

Kelly gave Jeffrey a disgusted look.

"What is it you want?" Trent asked.

"I'd like to get together," Jeffrey said. "Meet you in person." It was clear to Jeffrey he wouldn't be able to draw anything out of Trent over the phone.

"And what if I don't want to meet you?"

"That's your prerogative," Jeffrey said. "But if we aren't able to get together, I'm afraid I just can't vouch for where all the copies of these photos might end up."

"That's blackmail."

"Very good," Jeffrey said. "I'm glad we understand one another. Now, do we have an appointment or not?"

"Sure," Trent said, suddenly changing his tone. "Why don't

you come over. I know I don't need to tell you where I live."

Kelly waved her arms and mouthed the word No.

"Much as I like the idea of something up close and personal," Jeffrey said, "I don't think I'd feel all that welcome in your apartment. I'd feel more comfortable with people around."

"Name the place," Trent said.

Jeffrey could tell he really had Harding now. He thought for a moment. Where was a safe, public place they could meet? He remembered his wandering down by the Charles River. There were always plenty of people and lots of open space. "How about the Esplanade, down by the Charles River?" Jeffrey suggested.

"How will I recognize you?" Trent asked.

"Don't worry," Jeffrey said. "I'll recognize you. Even with your clothes on. But I tell you what. Look for me on the stage of the Hatch Shell. How does that sound?"

"Name a time," Trent said. He could barely contain his rage.

"How about nine-thirty?"

"I assume you'll be alone."

"I don't have too many friends these days," Jeffrey said. "And my mother's busy."

Harding didn't laugh. "I just hope you haven't been spreading your cockamamy stories to anyone else. I won't tolerate any slander."

I'm sure you won't, thought Jeffrey. "See you on the Esplanade." He hung up before Trent could say another word.

"Are you crazy?" Kelly fumed once they'd hung up. "You can't go meet that lunatic. That wasn't part of the plan."

"I had to improvise," Jeffrey said. "The guy's smart. I wasn't making any headway. If I talk to him in person I'll be able to see his face, judge his reactions. There'll be a much better chance he'll implicate himself."

"The guy is a maniac. He was just chasing you with a hammer."

"That was a different circumstance," Jeffrey said. "He caught me in his apartment. He had a right to be angry."

Kelly looked to the ceiling in astonishment. "And now he's defending this serial killer?"

"He wants his pictures," Jeffrey said. "He won't do anything to me until he has them. And I won't even take them. I'll leave them here."

"I think we should go back to the idea of digging up Henry Noble. That sounds like a Sunday picnic compared with a face-to-face meeting with this madman."

"Finding a toxin in Henry Noble would solve Chris's case and clear his name, but it wouldn't implicate Trent. Trent is the key to this whole grisly affair."

"But it will be dangerous—and don't tell me again that nothing will go wrong. I know better."

"I'll admit there is some danger. I think it would be foolish to think otherwise. At least we'll be meeting in public. I don't think Trent will try anything in a crowd."

"You're forgetting one big difference. You're thinking rationally. Harding isn't."

"He's been a very shrewd killer so far," Jeffrey reminded her.

"And now he's a very desperate one. Who knows what he'll try?"

Jeffrey pulled her to him. "Look," he said. "Seibert's coming up with nothing. I've got to try. It's our only hope. And I don't have much time."

"And just how am I supposed to eavesdrop? Even if you get lucky and Harding confesses, you'll still be without your precious proof."

Jeffrey sighed. "I hadn't thought of that."

"You didn't think of a lot of things," Kelly said through tears of frustration. "Like the fact that I don't want to lose you."

"You'll be losing me if we can't prove Harding's our man," Jeffrey said. "We have to figure a way for you to hear our conversation. Maybe if I took Harding for a walk . . ." His voice trailed off. He really didn't have any idea.

The two of them sat in glum silence.

"I know," Kelly said at last. "At least, it's an idea."

"What?"

"Well, don't laugh, but there's a gizmo I saw, browsing through the Sharper Image catalogue. It's a thing called the

Listenaider. It looks like a Walkman, but what it does is pick up sound and amplify it. Hunters and bird-watchers use it. Theatergoers too. It might work perfectly if you are standing on the Hatch Shell stage."

"Sounds fantastic," Jeffrey said, suddenly enthused. "Where's the closest store?"

"There's one at Copley Place."

"Great," Jeffrey said. "We can pick it up on our way."

"There's still one problem."

"What?"

"Keeping you safe!"

"No guts, no glory," Jeffrey said with a wry smile.

"I'm serious," Kelly said.

"Okay, I'll take something under my coat in case he gets unruly."

"Like what? An elephant gun?"

"Hardly," Jeffrey said. "Do you have a tire iron in your car?"

"I haven't the slightest idea."

"I'm sure you do," Jeffrey said. "I'll take that. It will give me something 'up my sleeve' so that if he gets abusive, I can get the hell out of there. But I honestly don't think Harding will try anything in public."

"And if he does?"

"Let's not worry about it. We can't eliminate all risk. If he does try anything, it might give us a leg up on establishing that proof. But come on. We don't have much time. We've got to be at the Hatch Shell by nine-thirty and we have to stop off at Copley Place in the meantime."

"Goddammit!" Trent roared. He cocked his arm and made a fist, then drove it like a piledriver against the wall above the telephone. With a crunch that surprised him, his fist went clean through the plaster wall and lath. Pulling his hand free, he inspected his knuckles for damage. There wasn't even a scrape.

Turning into the room, Trent kicked his coffee table, snapping off one of its legs and sending the rest of it hurtling across the floor to crash into the wall. Magazines, handcuffs, and several books went flying.

Looking around for something else to give vent to his rage, he spotted an empty beer bottle. He snatched it and threw it against the wall of the kitchen with all his might. It shattered, spraying shards of glass across the floor. Only then did Trent begin to regain control of himself.

How had this happened? he wondered. He'd been so careful. He'd thought of every angle. First it had been that goddamn nurse and now it was this crazy-ass doctor. How the hell did he know so much? And now he had those Polaroids. Trent knew he shouldn't have taken them. He'd just been fooling around. He'd only wanted to see how he'd look . . . Not that anyone would understand. He just had to get those pictures back from that damn doctor. He couldn't believe the guy had actually had the nerve to search his place.

Trent froze in his tracks. Another horrid thought suddenly dawned on him. With a new surge of panic, he rushed to his kitchen. He threw open the door to the cabinet next to the refrigerator and pulled the glasses out in one quick swipe. Several smashed as they fell to the countertop.

With trembling fingers he removed the false back and peered into his hiding place. He sighed a breath of relief. Nothing appeared to have been disturbed. All was in order.

Reaching in, Trent lifted out his beloved .45 pistol. He wiped the barrel on the front of his shirt. The gun was clean, oiled, and ready for work. Reaching back into the hiding place, he pulled out the clip. After checking that it was fully loaded, he shoved it into the handle until there was a resounding click.

Trent's biggest worry was whether Jeffrey had told anyone else what he'd learned. The guy was a fugitive, so Trent figured that he probably hadn't. Trent would try to find out for certain. But either way, Rhodes had to go. Trent laughed. Rhodes clearly had no idea who he was dealing with.

Returning to his makeshift safe, Trent removed a small 5 cc syringe and, just as he'd done for Gail Shaffer, drew up a tiny bit of the yellow fluid and diluted it with sterile water. Then he replaced the vial. In his mind's eye he could see Jeffrey Rhodes having a grand mal seizure on the Hatch Shell stage. The image brought a smile to his lips. It would be quite a performance.

Picking up the piece of plywood, Trent carefully fitted it

into the back of the cabinet and replaced the glasses that hadn't broken. The rest he left as they lay; he'd clean the place up after he got back from the Esplanade.

With his preparations complete, Trent checked the time. He still had an hour and a half until the rendezvous. Moving into the living room, he eyed the telephone and wondered what he should do. Rhodes's meddling was the kind of potential interference Trent had been warned about. He debated whether or not to call. In the end, he picked up the receiver. He was calling as instructed, he told himself as he dialed, to notify, not for help.

FRIDAY,

MAY 19, 1989

8:42 P.M.

"Ah, here we go," Devlin whispered to himself as he saw
Kelly's garage door beginning to rise. Kelly's Honda shook as
the engine started. Then the car backed out into the street at
twice the expected speed. Laying a patch of rubber, it barreled
off toward Boston.

Devlin fumbled with the ignition of his car. He'd not expected to see her leave so fast. By the time he got going, Kelly's
car was almost out of sight. Devlin had to gun his Buick to
catch up.

"Well, well!" Devlin said once they'd gotten several miles
from Kelly's home. A second head had mysteriously popped
up in the backseat. Then the figure had climbed over the seat
to join Kelly in the front.

Devlin warned himself not to get too excited about this
unexpected but interesting development, but he needn't have
bothered. When Kelly pulled up to the front entrance of the
Copley Place shopping mall, Jeffrey Rhodes jumped out and
ran inside.

"Goodie, goodie," Devlin said ecstatically as he pulled past
Kelly and over to the curb. He thought his luck had finally

changed. Jeffrey was already well inside, halfway up the escalator, as Devlin cut his engine and slid across the front seat. Devlin was about to get out of his car when he noticed the window had suddenly filled with a patch of navy blue. There was also a black leather belt and holstered .38 Smith and Wesson.

"Sorry, but there's no parking here," the policeman said.

Devlin looked the patrolman in the eye. He appeared about eighteen. A rookie, thought Devlin, but then who else would get such a beat on a Friday evening? Devlin groped for the card that allowed him to park anywhere in the city, but the rookie refused to look at it.

"Move on," he said with less cordiality.

"But, I'm . . ." Devlin started to explain who he was. Yet it was no longer important. Jeffrey had disappeared from view.

"I wouldn't care if you were Governor Dukakis," the young policeman said. "You can't park. Now move on!" He pointed forward with his nightstick.

Resigned to a change in plans, Devlin slid back across the seat and restarted the car. Quickly he drove around the block. Seeing Kelly's car, he stopped worrying. The little run-in with the policeman might have been for the better. Devlin might not have lost Rhodes in the shopping-mall crowd, after all. Instead, he pulled up to the curb half a block behind Kelly's car and again cut his engine. Then the two of them—Devlin in his car and Kelly, unaware, in hers—waited for Jeffrey to reappear.

Putting on the earphones, the salesperson directed Jeffrey to turn the unit on. Jeffrey turned the small knob. Then the salesperson told Jeffrey to point the unit toward a couple at the opposite end of the store. Jeffrey did as he was told.

"Wouldn't that look impressive on our coffee table?" the man asked the woman. They were standing in front of a glass sphere that looked like it belonged on the set of an old Frankenstein movie. It contained a plasma that was emitting light like miniature bolts of blue lightning.

"Yeah," the woman said, "but look at the price. I could get a pair of Ferragamo shoes for that."

Jeffrey was impressed. He'd also heard the dull murmur of other peripheral voices as well, but he'd been able to understand every word of the couple's conversation.

"Do you know the Hatch Shell on the Esplanade?" Jeffrey asked the salesperson.

"Sure do."

"What do you think you could hear with this thing back by the concession stand?"

"A pin drop."

Jeffrey bought the device, then jogged back to Kelly's car. She was in the same spot he'd left her in.

"Did you get it?" she asked as he closed his door.

Jeffrey held up the parcel. "We're all set," he said. "It really works. I had a demonstration."

Kelly pulled away and headed for the Esplanade.

Neither of them looked back. They remained unaware of the black Buick Regal following them three cars behind.

Kelly took Storrow Drive to get to Beacon Hill. Just after they emerged from an underpass, Jeffrey caught a brief glimpse of the grassy area in front of the Hatch Shell on the Esplanade. The sun had set, but it was still light out, and Jeffrey was able to see plenty of people enjoying the spring weather. That made him feel a bit more at ease.

They turned right on Revere Street, then again on Charles. They passed most of the shops on Charles Street and turned right again on Chestnut. They parked near the foot of Chestnut Street and got out of the car.

For the last few minutes of driving neither had spoken. The excitement of the preparations and of getting there had abated and was being replaced by anxiety about whether things would go as planned. Jeffrey broke the silence by asking to use the car keys. Kelly flipped them to him over the top of the car. She'd just locked the doors.

"Forget something?" she asked.

"The tire iron," Jeffrey said. He went around to the trunk and opened it. It wasn't a tire iron. It was a combination wrench for the lug bolts and an arm to operate the jack. It was a steel rod about eighteen inches in length. Jeffrey slapped it into the palm of his hand. It would do fine if he needed it. A good whack across the shins would slow anybody down. He hoped it wouldn't come to that.

They crossed to the Esplanade by way of the Arthur Fiedler pedestrian bridge. It was a pleasant midspring evening. Jeffrey noticed the colorful sails of a few sailboats heading for their respective yacht clubs. In the distance, an MBTA train rumbled across the Longfellow Bridge.

Devlin cursed. It was even hard to find a free parking spot by a hydrant on Beacon Hill. By the time he found an empty no-parking zone on the entrance onto Storrow Drive, Jeffrey and Kelly were heading across the footbridge over to the Esplanade. Devlin grabbed his handcuffs from the car and ran down to the base of the bridge.

Devlin was mystified as to what the hell was going on. He thought an evening along the Esplanade was strange behavior for a convicted felon and a fugitive who knew he was being pursued by a professional bounty hunter. With the girl in tow, Jeffrey acted like he was on a date. Devlin had a strong suspicion that something was about to happen, and his curiosity was piqued. He could remember telling Mosconi that he thought Jeffrey was up to something. Maybe this was it.

Crossing the bridge, Devlin descended the off ramp and stepped out onto the lip of green spring grass. He didn't feel like he had to rush to apprehend Jeffrey, since the location was so perfect. He effectively had Jeffrey cornered between the Charles River on one side and Storrow Drive on the other. Besides, the Charles Street Jail was conveniently located only a stone's throw away, just beyond Charles Circle. So Devlin didn't mind indulging his curiosity for a few minutes to try to figure out exactly what Jeffrey was up to.

Out of the corner of his eye, Devlin saw something coming at him from behind and to his right. By reflex he moved to his left, whirling around to a crouch position. His hand shot into his denim jacket and onto the butt of the pistol tucked in his shoulder holster.

Devlin felt his face redden as a Frisbee sailed past him, followed closely by a black Lab, who caught it before it hit the ground.

Devlin straightened and took a breath. He hadn't realized how keyed up he was.

The Esplanade was occupied by two or three dozen people, all doing their thing at the twilight of the day. Besides the

Frisbee players, there were people playing touch football and a group kicking around a Hacky Sack. Directly across the expanse of grass, on the pavement in the front of the Hatch Shell, was a group of roller skaters moving to the beat of a ghetto box cassette player; on the macadam walkway were the joggers and cyclists.

Devlin took in the whole scene, wondering what had brought Jeffrey and Kelly. They weren't participating in any of these activities. Instead they were just standing and talking with each other in the shadows of the trees surrounding the closed concession stand. Devlin could just make out Jeffrey helping Kelly put on a Walkman-like cassette player.

Devlin put his hands on his hips. What the hell was going on? While he watched, he saw Jeffrey do something else unexpected. He saw Jeffrey bend down and kiss Kelly. "Naughty, naughty," Devlin whispered. For a moment Jeffrey and Kelly held hands with their arms outstretched. Finally Jeffrey let go. Then he bent down and picked up a thin rod from the ground.

With the rod in his hand, Jeffrey started to run eagerly out across the grass toward the stage. Devlin started to make a move to follow, afraid Rhodes might disappear around the Hatch Shell, but he stopped when Rhodes ran up to the stage and mounted it from the right side.

While Devlin looked on, his curiosity deepening, Jeffrey went directly to the center of the stage. Facing toward the concession stand, he started to speak. Devlin couldn't hear him, but his lips were moving.

From the concession stand, Kelly shot Rhodes an emphatic thumbs up. What was going on? Devlin wondered. Was the guy reciting Shakespeare? And if he was, what was Kelly doing? The girl still had the Walkman on. Devlin scratched his head. This case was getting weirder by the minute.

Trent Harding tucked his .45 automatic in his belt exactly as he had when he'd gone off to Gail Shaffer's. He put the syringe, its cap tightly in place, in his right front pocket. He checked the time. It was a little after nine. Time to get going.

Trent walked down to Charles Circle via Revere Street. To

get over to the Charles River embankment, he took the footbridge just west of the Longfellow Bridge.

It was late evening as he walked down the darkened walkway lined with granite balustrades. Above was a dense canopy
of newly leafed trees. The Charles River shimmered, aglow
with the reflected dusty-rose light of the evening sky. The sun
had set about a half hour before.

Earlier, Trent had been nervous and upset about this Jeffrey
Rhodes debacle, not knowing what the man wanted. His
blackmail threat was as unexpected as it was shocking. But now
that he was prepared, Trent's anxiety had abated considerably.
He wanted his photos, and he wanted to be sure that Rhodes
was acting on his own. Beyond that, Trent wasn't interested
in the man, and he'd give him the injection. Having seen what
it did to Gail Shaffer, he knew it would work quickly and
effectively. Someone would call an ambulance and that would
be that.

A pair of joggers whisked past Trent in the half-light and
made him jump. He felt like pulling out his pistol and dropping
the bastards in their tracks. He'd do it just the way they did
on *Miami Vice:* legs spread apart, arms stiff, both hands holding
the gun.

Ahead loomed the huge hemisphere of the Hatch Shell.
Trent was approaching the stage from the convex rear. He felt
a sudden thrill as adrenaline coursed through his system. He
was looking forward to meeting Dr. Jeffrey Rhodes. Reaching
back under his jacket, his hand closed around the handle of his
.45. His finger slipped around the trigger. It felt terrific.
Rhodes was in for one hell of a surprise.

Trent stopped. He had to make a decision. Should he go
around the right or left side of the Hatch Shell? He tried to
remember the layout of the stage, wondering if it made any
difference. He decided he'd prefer to have Storrow Drive to his
back. After he'd taken care of Jeffrey, if he had to run, he'd
make a run for the highway.

Jeffrey nervously paced the stage, staying to the right of center.
The skaters who'd congregated in the small expanse of macadam between the stage and the grass also stayed to the right,
and Jeffrey wanted to be as close to them as possible without

making Trent feel they could overhear. At first the skaters had eyed Jeffrey suspiciously. But after a few minutes they'd ignored him.

What had surprised Jeffrey about the listening device was that it was able to ignore the skaters' music. Jeffrey assumed it had something to do with the fact that the cassette player was off to the side and not within the acoustical shadow of the Hatch Shell's large concave surface. He guessed it was the same with the noise of the traffic passing so close on Storrow Drive.

The light was now fading rapidly. The sky was still a light, silvery blue, but stars had begun to appear and the shadows under the trees had turned a deep purple. Jeffrey could no longer see Kelly. Most of the Frisbee and ball players had concluded their games and left. But there were still a few people out on the grass. There was also a smattering of joggers using the walkway to the far right, as well as an occasional cyclist.

Jeffrey looked at his watch. It was nine-thirty, time for Harding to arrive. When it got to be a bit past, Jeffrey began to wonder what he'd do if Trent didn't show up. For some reason, up until that moment Jeffrey had not even considered the possibility.

Jeffrey told himself he had to calm down. Trent would come. As sick as the guy had to be, he'd be dying to get the photos back. Jeffrey stopped pacing and gazed out over the grassy expanse in front of the stage. If Trent decided to get rough, Jeffrey had a lot of room to run. He also had Kelly's lug wrench literally tucked up his right sleeve. It might come in handy even if he only used it as a threat.

Jeffrey squinted into the distance. Try as he might, he couldn't see Kelly in the darkness under the trees near the concession stand. That meant Harding wouldn't be able to either. There was no way Trent could think there was a witness to their conversation.

A siren in the distance made Jeffrey start. He held his breath and listened. It was coming closer. Could it be the police? Had Harding alerted them? The sirens grew louder with their approach, but then Jeffrey saw the source: an ambulance sped past on Storrow Drive.

Jeffrey sighed. The tension was wearing him down. He started to pace again, then abruptly stopped. Trent Harding was looking at him from the stage steps to the left. He had one hand at his side, the other behind his back beneath a leather jacket.

Jeffrey's bravado drained from him as he stared at Trent, who for the moment was motionless. Trent was dressed in a collarless, lightweight black leather jacket and acid-washed jeans. In the half-light of the fading day, his hair appeared blonder than before, almost white. His unblinking eyes sparkled.

Jeffrey stood facing the man he suspected of at least six murders. Again he wondered about the man's motivations. They seemed unfathomable. Even with the lug wrench up his sleeve and all the potential witnesses, Jeffrey felt suddenly afraid. Trent Harding was a wild card. There was no predicting what his reaction to this blackmail ruse might be.

Trent mounted the stage steps slowly. Before he took the final step that would put him on a plane with Jeffrey, he took a look around. Seemingly satisfied, he set his gaze on Jeffrey. He approached with a cocky, confident step, an expression of disdain on his face.

"Are you Jeffrey Rhodes?" he asked, finally breaking the silence.

"You don't remember me from Memorial?" Jeffrey said, his voice cracking. He cleared his throat.

"I remember you," Trent said. "Now I want to know why you're bothering me."

Jeffrey's heart was pounding. "Call me curious," he said. "I'm the one taking the fall for your handiwork. It's a done deal. I'm twice convicted. I'd just like to know a little bit about the motivation." Jeffrey felt like a piano wire stretched to its limit. His muscles were tense, and he was ready to flee at any moment.

"I don't know what you're talking about."

"And I suppose you don't know anything about the Polaroids, either."

"I want those back. I want you to give them to me. Now."

"In good time. All in good time. Why don't you tell me

about Patty Owen or Henry Noble first." Come on, Jeffrey urged, please talk to me. Talk.

"I want to know who you've shared your nutty theories with."

"No one," Jeffrey said. "I'm an outcast. A fugitive from justice. A man with no friends. Who would I have to tell?"

"And you brought the photos with you?"

"Isn't that what we're here for?" Jeffrey said evasively.

"That's all I wanted to know," Harding said.

Smoothly but suddenly he pulled his hand from behind his back and brandished his pistol. Grasping the gun with both hands, just the way Crockett did on *Miami Vice,* he aimed the barrel at Jeffrey's forehead.

Jeffrey froze. His heart skipped a beat. He'd not expected a gun. He stared with utter terror at the dark black hole at the end of the barrel. The lug wrench was a joke compared with such a weapon.

"Turn around," Harding commanded.

Jeffrey couldn't move.

Trent fished for the syringe, still pointing the gun at Rhodes.

Trent let go of the gun with his right hand and fished a syringe from his pocket. Jeffrey eyed it with horror. Then, out in the blackness he heard a scream. It was Kelly! Oh God, thought Jeffrey, imagining her running across the grass toward the stage.

"I thought you came alone," Trent snarled. He took a step forward and locked the arm with the gun. Jeffrey could see his trigger finger begin to move.

Before Jeffrey could react, there was a gun blast, followed by screams from the skaters as they stumbled in all directions.

Jeffrey's legs went limp. The lug wrench fell from his sleeve with a clatter. But he felt no pain. He thought he'd been shot, but instead a hole appeared in Trent's forehead. The man staggered. Then there was a second, more sustained blast of multiple, rapid shots. Jeffrey felt the sound had come from over his shoulder, downstage right.

Trent was thrown back by the additional shots that had struck him square in the chest. Jeffrey looked down, mute with

shock, as Trent's pistol came skidding across the stage to bump
to a stop at his foot. The syringe bounced on the wood floor
and lay still. It was almost too much to take in. Jeffrey glanced
at Trent. He knew he was dead. Part of the back of his head
was gone.

The moment the rifle shot sounded and the blond guy staggered as if he'd been hit, Devlin hit the grass. At that point he'd
been halfway across the grassy area. The instant he'd seen the
blond guy draw the pistol, Devlin started for the stage. He'd
been careful to stay low to the ground, half bent over in an
effort to come to the pair by surprise. He'd heard Kelly scream,
but he'd ignored it. Then there had been the additional burst
of shots. From his experience from his days on the Force, but
mainly in Vietnam, he knew a rifle shot when he heard one,
especially a high-caliber automatic assault type.

Devlin hadn't recognized the blond fellow. He'd assumed he
was the out-of-town talent that Mosconi had been threatening
to bring in. Devlin was determined not to be cheated out of the
reward money. He'd have more than a word with Mosconi
when he saw him next. But first he'd have to deal with the
matter at hand, which was turning into a carnival in its com-
plexity. The rifle business meant a third bounty hunter was in
the picture. Devlin had been in with some pretty stiff competition before, but he'd never known even the toughest of
bounty-hunting SOBs to take out a competitor without so
much as a word.

From his spot flat out on the lawn, Devlin raised his head
and peered at the stage. He couldn't see the blond from that
angle. The doctor was just standing there like a fool, with his
mouth hanging open. Devlin had to suppress an urge to shout
to him to hit the deck. But he didn't want to draw attention
to himself without knowing more about the origin of the rifle
shots.

With another scream and clearly no thought for her safety,
Kelly recovered from the burst of gunfire and ran past Devlin
on her way toward the stage. Devlin rolled his eyes. Quite a
pair, these two, he thought. He wondered which one would
manage to get killed first.

But at least Kelly's screams seemed to snap Rhodes out of

his trance. He turned toward her and, raising his hand, yelled at her to stop. She did. Devlin lifted himself, hunkering down on the grass. From that position he could see the blond guy lying in a crumpled heap center stage.

The next thing Devlin knew, two men casually stepped out of the shadows and mounted the stairs to the stage. One of them was carrying an assault rifle. Both were in dark business suits with white shirts and conservative ties. As if they had all the time in the world, they calmly approached the doctor, who'd turned to face them. Devlin thought that for bounty hunters, their style was unusual, but it was as effective as it was ruthless. It was obvious they were after Jeffrey Rhodes.

Pulling his own gun from its holster and gripping it with both hands, Devlin ran for the stage. "Freeze!" he yelled with authority, pointing his gun at the chest of the man with the assault rifle. "Rhodes belongs to me! I'm taking him in, understand?"

The two men froze in their tracks, obviously taken by surprise by Devlin's appearance. "I'm just as surprised to see you guys," Devlin whispered, half to himself, half to the men in suits.

The men were only about twenty feet away. It was point-blank range. Jeffrey was to Devlin's right, just at the periphery of his vision. Suddenly Devlin recognized one of the men. He wasn't a bounty hunter.

Jeffrey's heart was in his mouth, and his mouth was so dry he couldn't swallow. His pulse hammered at his temples. Devlin's sudden appearance had surprised him as much as the arrival of the two men in suits.

If only Kelly had the sense to stay clear of whatever was developing. He never should have involved her in this mess in the first place. But this was no time to berate himself. The men in suits had stopped their relentless approach. Now their full attention was on Devlin, who was at the lip of the stage, holding his pistol with both hands. Devlin was watching the men with total intensity. No one spoke and no one moved.

"Frank?" Devlin said finally. "Frank Feranno—what the hell is going on?"

"I don't think you should be interfering, Devlin," the man with the rifle said. "This doesn't concern you. We just want the doctor."

"The doctor belongs to me."

"Sorry," Frank said.

The two men slowly started to move apart.

"Nobody move!" Devlin yelled.

But the men ignored him. They steadily inched apart.

Jeffrey began to back up. At first he edged away only a step at a time. But once he saw that at least temporarily the three men were caught in something of a Mexican standoff, he decided to take advantage of it. For the moment he wasn't the target. The instant he reached the stairs, he turned on his heels and ran.

Over his shoulder Jeffrey heard Devlin order the men to stay still or he'd shoot. Jeffrey ran out into the grass and caught Kelly where she'd stopped at the point where the lawn met the macadam. He grabbed her hand and together they ran for the Arthur Fiedler bridge.

Reaching the ramp, they ran up, rounding several turns. Sudden gunfire from the direction of the stage made them flinch, but they never looked back. At first there was just a single shot, but that was immediately followed by the rapid, sustained sound of an automatic weapon. Jeffrey and Kelly tore across Storrow Drive, then down the other side. Panting, they reached Kelly's car. She frantically searched for her keys while Jeffrey thumped the roof of the car with his palm.

"You have them!" Kelly shouted, suddenly remembering.

Jeffrey pulled the keys from his own pocket. He tossed them over the car. Kelly unlocked the doors and both jumped in. Kelly got the car going, and they shot forward, turning onto Storrow Drive. She quickly gunned the car to sixty. When they came to the end of Storrow in a matter of minutes, Kelly pulled into a maze of narrow city streets.

"What on earth is going on?" Kelly demanded once they'd both regained their breath.

"I wish I knew!" Jeffrey managed. "I have no idea. I think they were fighting over me!"

"And I let you talk me into this plan," Kelly said with

irritation. "Once again I should have listened to my intuition."

"There's no way we could have anticipated what happened," Jeffrey said. "It wasn't a bad plan. Something very screwy is going on. Nothing makes sense except that the one person who was capable of restoring my life is now dead." Jeffrey shivered, recalling the gruesome image of Trent Harding being shot through the forehead.

"Now we *have* to go to the police," Kelly said.

"We can't."

"But we saw a man killed!"

"I can't go, but if you have to go for yourself, do it," Jeffrey said. "For all I know they'll probably indict me for Trent Harding's murder. That would be the final irony."

"What will you do?" Kelly asked.

"Probably what I set out to do a number of days ago," Jeffrey said. "Leave the country. Go to South America. With Trent dead, I don't think I have much choice."

"Let's go back to my place and think," Kelly said. "At this point neither one of us is in any shape to make such a major decision."

"I'm not sure we can go back there," Jeffrey said. "Devlin must have followed us from your house. He must know I've been staying there. I think you'd better drop me off at a hotel."

"If you go to a hotel, then I'm going too," Kelly said.

"You really want to stay with me after what just happened?"

"I made a commitment to see this through."

Jeffrey was touched, but he knew he couldn't let her run any more risks than she already had. At the same time he wanted her near him. They'd only been together a couple of days, but already he didn't know what he'd do without her.

She was right about one thing: he was in no shape to make a decision. He closed his eyes. He felt shell-shocked. Too much had happened. He was emotionally drained.

"How about driving out of town and staying at a small inn?" Kelly suggested when Jeffrey didn't make any suggestions.

"Fine." He was already distracted, his mind involuntarily taking him back to the horrid and tense moments on the stage. He remembered Devlin recognizing one of the other men. He'd called him Frank Feranno. Jeffrey guessed they were all bounty hunters greedily fighting over the sizable reward money on his head. But why kill Harding? That didn't make sense, unless of course they'd thought he was a bounty hunter. But even then, did bounty hunters kill each other?

Jeffrey opened his eyes. Kelly was making her way through the Friday night traffic.

"Are you okay to drive?" Jeffrey asked her.

"I'm fine," she said.

"If there's a problem, I can drive."

"After what you just went through, I think you should just try to relax," Kelly said.

Jeffrey nodded. He couldn't argue with that. He then told her his idea that the men in suits were bounty hunters like Devlin, and that they had been fighting over him for the reward money.

"I don't think so," Kelly said. "When I first saw those men, I thought they were with Trent. They came right after he did. But then as I watched, I could tell they were *after* Trent Harding, not with him. They shot him very deliberately. They didn't have to shoot him. They wanted to. You weren't the target."

"But why kill Trent?" Jeffrey asked. "It doesn't make sense." He sighed. "Well, in one way it does make sense. There is some benefit. I'm convinced Trent Harding was the killer, even if we don't have the proof. The world will be far better off without him."

Jeffrey laughed suddenly.

"What can you possibly find funny?" Kelly asked.

"I'm just marveling at my own naiveté. That I actually thought I could get Harding to implicate himself by meeting with him. Thinking back, I bet he saw it as an opportunity to kill me from the start. I didn't tell you, but he had a syringe with him. I suppose he didn't plan on shooting me with a bullet. He was going to shoot me with his toxin."

Kelly suddenly slammed on the brakes and pulled to the side of the road.

"What's the matter?" Jeffrey asked, alarmed. He half expected Devlin to loom out of the night. The man's appearances were always so startling.

"I just thought of something," Kelly said excitedly.

Jeffrey stared at her in the dim light. Cars passed, filling their car briefly with their headlights.

Kelly turned to him. "Maybe Trent's killing has a hidden benefit."

"What are you talking about?"

"Maybe his death provides us with a clue that we wouldn't have had unless he'd been killed."

"I don't follow you," Jeffrey said.

"Those men in suits were primarily out to shoot Harding, not you. I'm sure of it. And it wasn't a humanitarian gesture. That tells us something." Kelly was becoming more animated by the second. "It means that somebody thought that Harding was a threat. Maybe they didn't want him talking to you. I think those men with their fancy suits and guns were professional killers." She took a breath. "I think this whole thing might be more complicated than we've imagined."

"You mean you think that Harding wasn't just a crazy person acting alone?"

"That's exactly what I mean," Kelly said. "What's happened tonight makes me think of some sort of conspiracy. Maybe it has something to do with hospitals. The more I think about it, the more I believe there has to be another dimension that we've completely missed by concentrating on the idea of a lone psychopath. I just don't think he was acting alone."

Jeffrey's thoughts went back to the exchange between Frank Feranno and Devlin. Frank had said, "This doesn't concern you, and we just want the doctor." They had wanted Jeffrey, but they had wanted him alive. They'd certainly had the opportunity to shoot him, along with Harding.

"What about insurance companies?" Kelly asked. She'd always disliked insurance companies, especially after Chris's suicide.

"Now what are you talking about?" Jeffrey asked. With everything that he'd experienced, his mind was numb. He couldn't keep up with her line of thinking.

"Somebody benefits from these murders," Kelly said. "Remember, the hospitals have all been sued as well as the doctors. In Chris's settlement, the hospital's insurance paid as much if not more than Chris's insurance did. But it was the same insurance company."

Jeffrey thought for a moment. "That seems like a pretty far-out idea. Insurance companies do benefit, but it's too far down the line. In the short run they lose and lose big. It's only in the long run that they can recoup the cost of such extravagant settlements by raising premiums to doctors."

"But they would ultimately benefit," Kelly said. "And if insurance companies benefit, I think we should keep them in mind as being involved in all this."

"It's a thought," Jeffrey said, unconvinced. "I hate to put a damper on your brainstorming, but with Trent out of the picture, it's all academic. I mean, we still have no proof of any kind about anything. Not only do we not have proof that Trent was involved, but we don't even have proof of a toxin. And despite Seibert's interest, we might not get any."

Jeffrey remembered the syringe Trent had menaced him with on the stage. If only he'd had the presence of mind at the time to pick it up. Then Seibert would have had an adequate amount for his tests. But Jeffrey knew he couldn't be too hard on himself. After all, at the time, he was terrified he was about to be killed.

Just then Jeffrey thought of Trent's apartment. "Why didn't I think of this before?" he said excitedly. He tapped his forehead with his fist. "We still have one more chance to prove Trent's involvement in the deaths and the existence of the toxin. Trent's apartment! Someplace in that apartment there has to be incriminating evidence."

"Oh, no," Kelly said, slowly shaking her head. "Please tell me you're not suggesting we go back to his apartment."

"It's our only chance. Come on—let's do it. We certainly don't have to worry about running into Trent. Tomorrow the authorities might be there. We have to go tonight. The sooner the better."

Kelly shook her head in disbelief, but she put her car in gear and pulled away from the curb.

Frank Feranno felt terrible. As far as he was concerned, this had been the worst night in his life. And it had started out so promisingly. He and Tony were going to clear ten grand for wiping out a blond kid named Trent Harding and drugging a doctor named Jeffrey Rhodes. Then all they had to do was drive to Logan Airport and put the doctor on a waiting Learjet. It was going to be so simple, since the kid and the doctor were meeting at the Hatch Shell on the Esplanade at nine-thirty. Two birds with one stone. It couldn't have been an easier setup.

But it hadn't come off as planned. They certainly hadn't planned on Devlin showing up.

Frank came out of Phillips's drugstore on Charles Circle and walked over to his black Lincoln Town Car and climbed in. He used the vanity mirror on the flip side of the sun visor to see as he cleaned the graze along his left temple with the alcohol he'd just purchased. It stung something fierce, and he bit his tongue. Devlin had almost nailed him. The thought of how close he'd come made him sick to his stomach.

He broke the seal on his other purchase, a bottle of Maalox, and popped two tablets into his mouth. Then, picking up the car phone, he called his contact in St. Louis.

There was a bit of static when a man answered.

"Matt," Frank said. "It's me, Feranno."

"Just a minute," Matt said.

Frank could hear Matt tell his wife that he was going to take this call in the other room and to hang up when he'd gotten it. A minute later, Frank heard an extension picked up. Then he heard Matt yell to his wife that he had it. There was a click as she hung up.

"What the hell is going on?" Matt said. "You weren't supposed to use this number unless there was trouble. Don't tell me you boys screwed this up."

"There was trouble," Frank said. "Big trouble. Tony got hit. He's dead. You forgot to tell us something, Matt. There must be a price on this doctor's head. One of the meanest bounty hunters in the business showed up, and he wouldn't have been there unless money was involved."

"What about the nurse?" Matt asked.

"He's history. That was easy. It was getting the doctor that was the hard part. What kind of money is involved with him?"

"Bail was set at half a million."

Frank whistled. "You know, Matt, that's not an insignificant detail. You should have warned us. We might have handled the situation a little differently had we known. I don't know how important the doctor is to you, but I got to tell you, my price just went up. I figure you got to match the reward at a minimum. Plus, I lost one of my best hatchetmen. I have to say I'm very disappointed, Matt. I thought we understood each other. You should have told me about the bail in the beginning."

"We'll make it up to you, Frank," Matt said. "The doctor is important to us. Not as important as getting rid of Trent Harding, but important nonetheless. I tell you what—if you can get the doctor to us, we'll up the fee to seventy-five thousand. How does that sound?"

"Seventy-five thousand has a nice ring. Sounds like your doctor's pretty important. Any idea where I can find him?"

"No, but that's part of the reason we're willing to pay so much. You've told me how good you are—here's a chance to prove it. What about Harding's body?"

"I did like you asked," Frank said. "Luckily I hit Devlin after he shot Tony, but I don't know how bad I hit him. I didn't have a lot of time. But the body is clean. No identification. And you were right: there was a syringe. I got it. I'll put it on the plane."

"Excellent, Frank," Matt said. "What about Harding's apartment?"

"That's next on the list."

"Remember—I want it scrubbed," Matt said. "And don't forget the hiding place in the cabinet next to the refrigerator. Get everything out of it and put it on the plane too. And look for the kid's address book. He was such a hardheaded stupid ass that he might have put something in it. If you can find it, put it on the plane with the rest of the stuff. Then trash the place. Make it look like a robbery. Did you get his keys?"

"Yeah, I got his keys," Frank said. "No problem getting into the apartment."

"Perfect," Matt said. "Sorry about Tony."

"Well, life's a risk," Frank said. He was feeling better, thinking about seventy-five grand. Frank hung up the phone, then made another call.

"Nicky, this is Frank. I need some help. Nothing big, just got to trash a place. How does a few C notes sound? I'll pick you up on Hanover Street in front of the Via Veneto Café. Bring your piece just in case."

Making a left turn onto Garden Street, Kelly had an unpleasant sense of déjà vu. She could still picture Trent Harding coming at them with the hammer in his hand. She pulled over to the right side of the street and double-parked. Leaning out the window, she looked up at Trent's apartment.

"Uh-oh," she said. "The lights are on."

"Trent probably left them on, thinking he'd be gone for only half an hour or so."

"You sure?" Kelly asked.

"Of course I'm not sure," Jeffrey said, "but it seems like a reasonable assumption. Don't make me more nervous about going up there than I already am."

"Maybe the police are already there."

"I can't imagine they'd have made it to the Hatch Shell yet, let alone here. I'll be careful. I'll listen before I go inside. If the police come while I'm up there, lean on your horn, then drive around the block to Revere Street. If it comes to it, I'll cross the roofs and come out one of the buildings over there."

"I tried blowing the horn last time," Kelly said.

"This time I'll be listening."

"What are you going to do if you find anything incriminating?"

"I'll leave it there and call Randolph," Jeffrey said. "Then maybe he can get the police to come in with a search warrant. At that point I'd turn over the investigation to the experts. Let the legal system crank through its slow gears. In the meantime I think I'd be better off out of the country. At least until I'm exonerated."

"You make it sound so easy," Kelly said.

"It will be if I find the toxin or something equivalent," Jeffrey said. "And, Kelly, if I do leave the country, I'd like you to think about joining me."

Kelly began to speak but Jeffrey stopped her. "Just think about it," he said.

"I'd love to go," Kelly said. "Honestly."

Jeffrey smiled. "We'll talk about it more. For now just wish me luck."

"Good luck," Kelly said. "And hurry!"

Jeffrey got out of the car and peered up at Trent's open window. He could see that the screen had not been replaced. That was good. It would save time.

He crossed the street and made his way through the front door. He was able to push through the inner door without difficulty. There was the smell of fried onions and the sound of several simultaneous stereo systems. As he climbed the littered stairway, his apprehension rose. But he knew he didn't have time to indulge his fears. With newfound resolution he went to the roof and down the fire escape.

Jeffrey stuck his head into the living room and listened. All he could hear was the muted stereo music he'd heard in the hallway. Satisfied that the place was empty, Jeffrey climbed in.

Jeffrey immediately noticed that the place was more of a mess than it had been the previous evening. The coffee table, minus a leg, was overturned. Everything that had been piled atop it was scattered about the floor. By the telephone there was a round hole through the plaster wall. Shards of glass were strewn all over the floor near the kitchen door. Jeffrey spotted a broken beer bottle among the wreckage.

Moving quickly, Jeffrey made sure no one was there. Then, going to the door to the hall, he secured the chain lock. He was not about to take any chances of being surprised. With these chores accomplished, he started his search. What he planned to do first was look for correspondence. He wouldn't read it there, but rather take it with him and go over it at his leisure.

The most promising place for correspondence was the desk. But before going to the desk, he stepped into the kitchen to see if he could find an empty bag of some sort to put correspondence into. In the kitchen he found more broken glass.

Jeffrey stared at the glass in the kitchen. It was on the countertop next to the refrigerator. It appeared to be a bunch of clean glasses that had been deliberately broken. Stepping over to the counter, he opened the cabinet immediately above. Inside on the first shelf were more of the same kind of glasses. On the shelf above were dishes.

Jeffrey wondered what had gone on inside the apartment

before Trent had left. Then his eye caught a discrepancy in the depth of the cabinet. The glass portion was half the depth of the dish portion.

Reaching into the cabinet, Jeffrey pushed the glasses out of the way and rapped on the back with his knuckle. As he did so, he felt the wood move. He tried to pry the rear wall of the cabinet forward, but it wouldn't budge. Changing tactics, he tried pushing against the wood. When he pushed against the far right-hand corner, the wooden panel rotated. Jeffrey grabbed its free end and pulled it out.

"Hallelujah!" Jeffrey cried as he peered in at an unopened box of 30 cc ampules of Marcaine, a cigar box, a supply of syringes, and a rubber-stoppered vial of a viscous yellow fluid. Jeffrey glanced around the kitchen for a towel. Finding one hanging from the refrigerator handle, he used it to pick up the vial. It seemed to be of foreign manufacture. Jeffrey recognized the vial as the type used to contain some sort of sterile injection medication.

Using the same towel, Jeffrey lifted the cigar box from the space and, placing it on the countertop, lifted its lid. Inside was an impressive stack of crisp hundred-dollar bills. Recalling his own stack of hundred-dollar bills, Jeffrey estimated that the cigar box contained between twenty and thirty thousand dollars.

Jeffrey put everything back where he'd found it. He even wiped off the wooden back and the glasses he'd handled so that he'd leave no fingerprints behind. He felt excited and encouraged. He had no doubt that the yellow fluid in the vial was the phantom toxin, and that an analysis of it would reveal what Seibert should look for in Patty Owen's serum. Even the money heartened him. He viewed it as strong evidence that Kelly's guess of some sort of conspiracy was correct.

Flushed with success, Jeffrey was eager for more. Somewhere in the apartment had to be evidence hinting at the nature of the conspiracy. Quickly searching the rest of the kitchen cabinets, Jeffrey ferreted out what he'd originally come for: a brown paper shopping bag.

Going back into the living room, he rifled through the desk rapidly, finding a number of letters and bills. He put them all in the paper bag. Then, going into the bedroom, he started through the bureau. In the second drawer he found a cache of *Playgirl* magazines. He left them alone. In the third drawer he found a number of letters, more than he'd bargained for. Pulling a chair over, he started a rough sorting.

Kelly was nervously drumming her fingers on the steering wheel and fidgeting in her seat. A car had moved out of a parking place two doors down from Trent's building, and she'd passed a few minutes backing into it. Glancing up at Trent's open window, she wondered what was keeping Jeffrey. The longer he took, the more nervous she became. What could he be doing up there? How long could it take to search a one-bedroom apartment?

Garden Street was not a busy street, but while Kelly waited, a half dozen cars turned at Revere Street and drove by. The drivers seemed to be searching for parking places. So Kelly wasn't surprised when an additional pair of headlights suddenly appeared from Revere Street and crept toward her. What caught her attention was that the car stopped directly in front of Trent's building and double-parked. The car's headlights snapped off and the parking lights came on.

Kelly twisted around to see a man in a dark sweater get out of the passenger side of the car and walk around to the sidewalk. He stretched as the driver got out. The driver was wearing a white shirt with the sleeves rolled up. He was carrying a satchel. The two men laughed about something. They seemed in no hurry. The younger one finished a cigarette and threw the butt into the gutter. Then the two men went into Trent's building.

Kelly looked at the car. It was a big, shiny, black Lincoln Town Car whose back bristled with a variety of antennae. The car appeared distinctly out of place and gave her a bad feeling. She wondered if she should lean on her horn, yet she hated to alarm Jeffrey needlessly. She made a move to get out of her car, then decided to stay put. She looked back up at Trent's window, as if her staring alone could bring Jeffrey safely out.

"If you can prove to me I can count on you, I got big plans for you, Nicky," Frank said as they climbed the stairs. "With

Tony gone there's a gap in my organization. You know what I mean?"

"All you gotta do is tell me something once and it's done," Nicky said.

Frank was wondering how the hell he was going to find this doctor. He was going to need somebody to do a lot of running around. Nicky was perfect even if he was a little stupid.

They arrived at the fifth floor. Frank was out of breath. "I gotta cut down on the pasta," he said as he pulled Harding's keys out of his pocket. He looked at the lock and tried to guess which key was the right one. Unable to decide, he stuck the first one into the lock and tried to turn it. No luck. He tried the second one and it turned. He pushed the door in but it was stopped abruptly by its chain. "What the hell?" Frank questioned.

Jeffrey had heard the first key rattling in the lock. He'd sat bolt upright in terror. His first thought was totally irrational: Trent had not been killed. By the time Frank tried the second key, Jeffrey was rushing past the door in a panic. By the time Nicky, having crashed through the door, came stumbling into the room, Jeffrey was already at the window.

"It's the doctor!" Jeffrey heard someone yell. He sprang over the windowsill as if he were running the high hurdles. This time he cleared it in a single bound. In seconds, Jeffrey was scrambling up the fire escape.

Reaching the roof, he followed his previous path, vaulting to successive rooftops. But this time he passed the headhouse he'd used yesterday, fearing its hook lock would still be as he'd left it. Behind him, he could hear the clatter of pursuing footsteps. Jeffrey guessed these strangers were the same men who had been at the Hatch Shell, men Kelly thought were professional killers. In coming to Trent's apartment, he hadn't thought of them.

Jeffrey frantically tried several headhouses, but each one's door was secured. It wasn't until he got to the corner building that he found one ajar. Rushing inside, Jeffrey yanked the door closed and felt for a lock to secure behind him. But there wasn't one there. He turned and started down the stairs. The men behind had gained ground. As he neared street level, he could tell they were not far behind him.

When he reached the street, Jeffrey made a snap decision. He knew he would not have time to reach Kelly and get into her car before the men were on him, so instead he turned and ran down Revere Street. He was not about to jeopardize Kelly's safety any more than he already had. He'd try to lose his pursuers before returning to get her.

Behind him he heard the men reach the street and start after him. He didn't have much of a lead. Jeffrey turned left on Cedar and ran past a laundry and a convenience store. There was a handful of people on the sidewalk. Jeffrey began to distinguish the footfalls of the faster of his pursuers. It seemed one was in much better shape than the other and was closing distance.

Turning again on Pinckney Street, Jeffrey ran down the hill. His familiarity with Beacon Hill was not extensive. He only prayed he wouldn't end up in a blind alley. But Pinckney Street opened up into Louisburg Square.

Jeffrey realized he'd have to find a way to hide if he wanted to evade his pursuers. He'd never outrun them. Seeing the wrought-iron fence that surrounded the central green of Louisburg Square, he ran directly to it and scrambled up, braving its chest-high, pointed spikes. Leaping into the grass beyond, his shoes sank deep into the turf. Rushing forward, he ran headlong into dense shrubbery and dove to the moist earth. Then he held his breath, waiting.

Jeffrey heard the men coming down Pinckney Street. The sounds of their feet slapping against the pavement echoed off the façades of the elegant brick buildings. One of them soon appeared, running into the square. Having lost sight of his quarry, the man immediately slowed, then stopped. The other joined him moments later. They spoke briefly between gasping breaths.

In the light of the gas lamps that surrounded the square, Jeffrey caught a glimpse of the two men as they split up. One went to the left, the other to the right. Jeffrey recognized the man on the upper roadway from the Hatch Shell stage. The other man was a stranger, and he was holding a pistol.

The men methodically searched entranceways and stairwells as well as under cars as they moved down the square. Jeffrey didn't stir even after the two had disappeared from view. He was afraid any movement might catch their attention.

When he guessed the men were near to the opposite end of the square, he thought briefly of scaling the fence and running back to Kelly. But he decided against it. He was afraid he'd be too easily seen going over the fence.

The nearby meow of a cat made Jeffrey jump. Two feet from his face was a gray tabby. Its tail stood ramrod straight in the air. The cat meowed again and moved closer to rub itself against Jeffrey's head. It began to purr loudly. Jeffrey remembered the fright Delilah had given him in Kelly's pantry. Cats had never paid much attention to him before; now they seemed to appear every time he tried to hide!

Turning his head and peering through the shrubbery, Jeffrey could see the two men conferring at the Mount Vernon end of the square. A lone pedestrian was walking along the sidewalk. Jeffrey thought about screaming for help, but the pedestrian entered one of the houses and rapidly disappeared. Jeffrey then thought about screaming for help anyway but decided against it, thinking it would probably do little but bring on a few lights. Even if someone had the presence of mind to call 911, it would take ten, fifteen minutes for the police to arrive under the best of circumstances. Besides, Jeffrey wasn't sure he wanted the police.

The two men split up again, coming back toward Pinckney Street. As they walked, they were now peering into the grassy area. Jeffrey felt his panic returning. Especially with the cat still persisting in its demands for attention, Jeffrey realized he couldn't stay put. He had to move.

Getting his feet under him, Jeffrey sprinted to the fence. He climbed over as quickly as before, but when he landed on the cobblestones on the other side, his right ankle twisted. A stab of pain went up Jeffrey's spine.

Mindless of his ankle, Jeffrey hurled himself down Pinckney Street. Behind him he heard one of the men yell to the other. Soon their footsteps filled Pinckney Street. Jeffrey passed West Cedar and raced down to Charles. Desperate for aid, he ran directly into the street and tried to hail a passing motorist, but the drivers coming by wouldn't stop.

With his pursuers coming rapidly down Pinckney Street, Jeffrey crossed Charles and continued down to Brimmer, where he turned left. He ran to the end of the block. Unfortunately, the faster of the two men was gaining considerably.

Desperately Jeffrey turned into the Church of the Advent, hoping he could hide somewhere inside. Reaching the thick door in its gothic archway, he grasped the heavy handle and yanked. The door wouldn't budge. It was locked. Jeffrey turned back to the street just as one of the men appeared—the man with the gun. A few moments later, the other man arrived, more winded than the first. He was the one Jeffrey had seen before. Together they slowly advanced toward him.

Jeffrey turned back to the door of the church and pounded on it in frustration. Then he felt the barrel of a gun pressed to his head. He heard the more winded man say, "Good-bye, Doctor!"

Kelly slapped her hand against the dash. "I don't believe this!" she said aloud. What could be taking him so long? She looked up at Trent's window for what felt like the hundredth time. There was still no sign of Jeffrey.

Getting out of the car, she leaned on the roof and thought about what she could do. She could use the car-horn signal, but she was reluctant to interrupt him just because she was anxious and apprehensive. For him to be taking this long, he had to be onto something. She had half a mind to go up to the apartment herself, but was afraid that her knock at the door might scare Jeffrey into fleeing.

Kelly was at her wits' end when the shiny black Lincoln returned. Not ten minutes earlier, Kelly had seen one of the men come back to get the car. But he'd come from down the street, not from Trent's apartment building. Kelly watched the car double-park in the same spot it had before. Then the same two individuals got out of the car and went back inside Trent's building.

With her curiosity piqued, Kelly straightened up from leaning on her car and strolled over to the Lincoln to take a better look. She put her hands in her pockets as she approached the car, hoping to appear like a casual passer-by in case either of the men should suddenly reappear. When she got alongside the Lincoln, she looked up and down the street as though she were doing something wrong by indulging her curiosity. She bent over and looked in at the dash. The car had a mobile phone, but otherwise looked normal. Taking two more steps, she looked in the back, wondering why the car had so many antennas.

Kelly quickly straightened up. Someone was curled up, sleeping in the backseat. Leaning forward slowly, she looked again. One of the man's hands was twisted unnaturally behind his back. My God, thought Kelly, it was Jeffrey!

In a frenzy, she tried the door. It was locked. She ran around to the other doors. They all were secured. Desperate, she looked for something heavy, like a rock. She pried one of the bricks from the sidewalk. Running back to the Lincoln, she dashed the brick against the window on the back door. She had to smash it several times before it finally shattered in a million pieces of gravel-sized pieces of glass. Reaching in, she unlocked the door.

As she bent in and tried to rouse Jeffrey, she heard someone yell from above. She assumed it was one of the men who'd gotten out of the car. They must have heard the window break.

"Jeffrey, Jeffrey!" she cried. She had to get him out of the car. Hearing his name, he began to stir. He tried to speak but his voice was slurred. His eyelids rose slightly as he wrinkled his forehead in effort.

Kelly knew she had little time. Grasping him by his wrists, she pulled him toward her. His limp legs drooped to the ground. His body was a dead weight. He seemed to be passed out. Letting go of his wrists, she grabbed him around the chest in a bear hug and dragged him from the car.

"Try to stand, Jeffrey!" she pleaded. He was like a rag doll. She knew that if she let him go he'd slump to the pavement. It was as if they'd drugged him.

"Jeffrey!" she cried. "Walk! Try to walk!"

Summoning all her strength, Kelly dragged Jeffrey down the pavement. He tried to help, but it was as if he was a quadriplegic. He couldn't seem to put any weight on his legs, much less stand.

By the time she was abreast of her car, Jeffrey was able to support himself to some degree, but he was still too groggy to grasp their situation. Kelly leaned him against the car, bracing him with her body. She got the back door open, then she managed to push him in. Kelly made sure he was all the way in before she slammed the door.

Opening the driver's door, she jumped in. She heard the door to Trent's building burst open and smash against its doorstop. Kelly started her engine, turned the wheel sharply to the left, and accelerated. She hit the car in front of her with enough force to throw Jeffrey to the floor in the backseat.

Putting the car in reverse, Kelly backed up, smashing the car behind her. One of the men had reached her car. He had her car door open before she could think to lock it. He seized her left arm roughly. "Not so fast, lady," he snarled in her ear.

With her free hand Kelly put the car in drive and floored the accelerator. She clutched the steering wheel as she felt herself being dragged sideways by the brute at her door. Her car shot forward, missing the car directly in front by inches. Kelly threw the steering wheel to the left, grazing her open door on the parked cars on the opposite side of the street. The man who'd had her by the arm only moments before shouted in pain as he was crushed between a parked automobile and Kelly's flailing door.

Kelly kept the accelerator floored. She plummeted down Garden Street with her door still open. She stomped on the brake just in time to avoid a half dozen pedestrians crossing at the busy intersection of Garden and Cambridge streets. The people scattered as Kelly's car careened sideways with a screech of rubber, missing a few by inches.

Kelly closed her eyes, expecting the worst. When she opened them, she'd stopped, but the car had swung in a one-hundred-eighty-degree turn. She was pointed the wrong way up Cambridge Street, facing a line of angry motorists. Some had already gotten out of their cars and were approaching. Kelly put her car in reverse and, arcing around, was able to turn back in the right direction. It was then she saw the black Lincoln flying down Garden Street, to fall in directly behind her. The car was on her tail, inches from her rear bumper.

Kelly decided her only hope was to lose the big Lincoln in

the tiny streets of Beacon Hill, where her little Honda would be more maneuverable. She took the next left off Cambridge Street. In making the turn, she inadvertently cut across the curb, hitting a refuse container. Her door swung open widely, then slammed shut. Kelly accelerated up the hill. At the top she braked enough to make a left-hand turn onto narrow Myrtle Street. Looking in her rearview mirror, she could tell that her ploy was already working. The Lincoln had dropped behind. It was too big to negotiate so sharp a turn at so high a speed.

Having lived in Beacon Hill for a number of years before she was married, Kelly was well acquainted with the labyrinth of narrow one-way streets. Turning right against the traffic on one-way Joy Street, Kelly took a gamble that she could reach Mount Vernon. At Mount Vernon, she took another right and headed down the hill toward Charles. Kelly's plan was to shoot through Louisburg Square, then disappear against traffic up Pinckney. But after braking for the square, she saw that both roadways were temporarily blocked, one with a taxi, the other with a car discharging a passenger.

Changing her mind, Kelly continued down Mount Vernon. But the pause had cost her. In her rearview mirror, she saw that the Lincoln was back on her tail. Looking ahead, Kelly saw she would not make the green at Charles Street. She turned left at West Cedar instead.

Turning right on Chestnut Street, Kelly accelerated. The light ahead at Charles turned yellow, but she didn't slow. Shooting out into the intersection, she saw a taxi coming at her from her right. The driver was running the lights. Kelly braked and threw the wheel to her left, sending her car into another skid. Instead of a direct collision, Kelly was jolted by a mere glancing blow. Her engine didn't even stall.

Kelly didn't stop even as the cabbie leaped from his vehicle, waving an angry fist and screaming at her. Continuing down Chestnut, she got to Brimmer and turned left. As she was turning she caught a glimpse of the Lincoln detouring around the stalled taxi.

Kelly felt a stab of panic. Her ploy wasn't working as she'd hoped. The Lincoln was staying with her. The driver seemed to know Beacon Hill.

Kelly realized she had to think of something out of the

ordinary. She turned left onto Byron Street, then left again into the Brimmer Street parking garage. She drove past the attendant's glass booth, veered sharply to the right, and drove directly onto an auto elevator.

The two attendants who'd stood and watched dumbfounded as she drove by came running onto the elevator. Before they could speak, she yelled: "I'm being chased by a man in a black Lincoln. You've got to help me! He wants to kill me!"

The two attendants looked blankly at each other. One raised his eyebrows, the other shrugged and got off the elevator. The one who stayed on reached up and pulled the cord. The elevator doors scraped together like the upper and lower jaws of a huge mouth. The elevator rose with a groan.

The attendant walked back and bent down at Kelly's window. "How come somebody wants to kill you?" he asked calmly.

"You wouldn't believe it if I told you," Kelly said. "What about your friend? Will he put the man off if he comes into the garage?"

"I guess so," the attendant said. "It's not every night we get to rescue a lady in distress."

Kelly closed her eyes in relief, leaning her forehead on the steering wheel.

"What's wrong with the guy on the floor of the backseat?" the attendant asked.

Kelly didn't open her eyes. "Drunk," she said simply. "Too many margaritas."

When Frank called the second time, he had to wait while Matt went through the same rigmarole of changing phones. Frank was sitting in his own home at the time and the line was considerably better than when he'd called from the car phone.

"More trouble?" Matt asked. "You're not impressing me, Frank."

"There's no way we could have anticipated what happened," Frank said. "When Nicky and I got to Trent's apartment, the doctor was in there."

"What about the stuff in the cabinet?" Matt demanded.

"No problem," Frank said. "It was there, not disturbed."

"Did you get the doctor?"

"That was the problem," Frank said. "We chased him all over Beacon Hill. But we got him."

"Terrific!" Matt said.

"Not completely. We lost him again. We drugged him with the stuff you sent in the plane, and it worked like a charm. Then we loaded him into my car while we went up to take care of the apartment and get the stuff you wanted. We thought, why make two trips to Logan? Anyhow, the guy's girlfriend came along and broke into my car. Smashed the goddamn window with a brick. Naturally, we ran down the stairs to stop her, but the kid's apartment was on the fifth floor. Nicky, one of my associates, ran out into the street to stop her but she pulled away before he could. Broke Nicky's arm. I chased her by car, but I lost her."

"What about the apartment?"

"No problem there," Frank said. "I went back and trashed it, and I put the stuff you wanted on the plane. So everything is done except I don't have the doctor. But I think I can get him if you use some of your influence. I got the girlfriend's license number. Think you could get me her name and address?"

"That shouldn't be any trouble," Matt said. "I'll call you with it tomorrow, first thing."

Jeffrey regained consciousness in stages, remembering weird and wild dreams. His throat was so parched it hurt as he breathed, and he found it difficult to swallow. His body felt heavy and stiff. He opened his eyes and began to take a look around to get his bearings. He was in a strange room with blue walls. Then he noticed the IV. With a start, he checked his left hand. Whatever had happened the night before, he'd wound up on intravenous!

As his mind began to clear, Jeffrey rolled over. Morning sunlight was streaming in through the blinds of his window. Beside him was a bedside table with a pitcher and a glass. Greedily, Jeffrey took a drink.

Sitting up, he surveyed the room. It was a hospital room, complete with the usual metal bureau, the track for the curtain on the ceiling above the bed, and in the corner, an uncomfort-able-looking vinyl-covered armchair. In the chair was Kelly. She was curled up and fast asleep. One arm hung off the chair at an angle. Below her hand was a newspaper on the floor that appeared to have fallen from her grasp.

Jeffrey swung his legs over the side of the bed, planning on getting up and going to Kelly, but the IV restrained him.

Looking behind him, he noticed it was sterile water and barely running.

With a jolt, Jeffrey suddenly remembered his flight from the men in Beacon Hill. His terror came back with astonishing clarity. He remembered being pressed against the door to the Church of the Advent, a gun pointed to his head. Then he'd been injected in the back of his thigh. That was all he could recall. From that moment on, his mind was a total blank.

"Kelly," Jeffrey called softly. Kelly murmured but didn't wake. "Kelly!" Jeffrey called more loudly.

Kelly's eyes fluttered open. She blinked a few times, then leaped from her chair and rushed to Jeffrey. She grasped him by both shoulders and stared into his face. "Oh, Jeffrey, thank God you're all right. How do you feel?"

"Fine," Jeffrey said. "I'm fine."

"Last night I was terrified. I had no idea what they had given you."

"Where am I?" Jeffrey asked.

"St. Joe's. I didn't know what to do. I brought you here to the emergency room. I was afraid something would happen to you, like you'd have trouble breathing."

"And they admitted me without asking questions?"

"I improvised. I said you were my brother from out of town. No one questioned it. I know everybody in the ER, both doctors and nurses. I emptied your pockets, including your wallet. There was no problem, except when the lab said you'd taken ketamine. I had to improvise some more. I had to tell them you're an anesthesiologist."

"What the hell happened last night?" Jeffrey asked. "How did I end up with you?"

"It was just a bit of luck," Kelly said. Sitting on the edge of Jeffrey's bed, Kelly told him everything that had happened from the moment he'd disappeared into Trent's building until she pulled into St. Joe's emergency.

Jeffrey shuddered. "Oh, Kelly, I never should have gotten you involved. I don't know what possessed me. . . ." His voice trailed off.

"I got myself involved," Kelly said. "But that's not important. The important thing is, we're both all right. How did you make out in Harding's apartment?"

"Fine, before they surprised me," Jeffrey said. "I found what we've been looking for. I stumbled onto a secret stash of Marcaine, syringes, a lot of cash, and the toxin. They were tucked in a false back to a kitchen cabinet. There's no doubt about our suspicions about Trent Harding now. It's the evidence we've been hoping for."

"Cash?" Kelly said.

"I know exactly what you're thinking," Jeffrey said. "As soon as I saw the money, I thought of your conspiracy theory. Harding had to be working for someone. God! I wish he weren't dead. At this point he could probably solve everything. Give me back my old life." Jeffrey shook his head. "We'll just have to work with what we've got. It could be better, but it's already been worse."

"What's our next move?"

"We'll go to Randolph Bingham and tell him the whole story. He's got to get the police up to Trent's apartment. We'll let them worry about the conspiracy aspect."

Swinging over to the other side of the bed, where the IV was hung, Jeffrey put his feet on the floor and stood up. He was dizzy for a moment as he fumbled to hold his johnny to his body. It wasn't tied in the back. Seeing him wobble, Kelly came around the bed and gave him a steadying hand.

Regaining his balance, Jeffrey looked at Kelly and said, "I'm beginning to think that I need you around all the time."

"I think we need each other," Kelly said.

Jeffrey could only smile and shake his head. It was his opinion that Kelly needed him about as much as she needed to be run over by a truck. Hadn't he brought her nothing but trouble? He only hoped he'd be able to make it up to her.

"Where are my clothes?" Jeffrey asked.

Kelly stepped over to the closet. She opened the door. Jeffrey untaped the IV and removed it with a wince. Then he joined Kelly. She handed him his clothes.

"My duffel bag!" Jeffrey said with surprise. It was hanging on one of the hooks in the closet.

"I went home early this morning," Kelly said. "I got clothes for myself, fed the cats, and got your duffel bag."

"Going home was taking a chance," Jeffrey said. "What about Devlin? Was there anyone there watching the house?"

"I thought about that," Kelly said. "But when I got the paper early this morning, I felt it would be okay." She walked over to get the *Globe* on the floor by the chair. Carrying it back, she pointed at a small cover story of the Metro section.

Taking the newspaper from her, Jeffrey read a description of the incident at the Hatch Shell. It reported that a nurse recently employed at St. Joseph's Hospital had been gunned down by a reputed underworld crime figure, Tony Marcello. A former Boston police officer, Devlin O'Shea, had shot and killed the assailant but had been critically wounded in an ensuing gun battle. Devlin had been admitted to Boston Memorial Hospital and was reputed to be in stable condition. It went on to say that the Boston police were investigating the incident, which they believed to have been drug-related.

Putting the paper on the bed, Jeffrey took Kelly in his arms and hugged her. "I'm truly sorry for putting you through all this," he said. "But I think we're close to the end."

Relaxing his grip, Jeffrey leaned back and said, "Let's get to Randolph's. Then we'll see if we can't get away. Drive to Canada, then fly to someplace quiet while a real investigation goes on."

"I don't know if I can leave," Kelly said. "When I was home I realized Delilah's close to term."

Jeffrey stared at Kelly in disbelief. "You'd stay behind because of a cat?"

"Well, I can't just leave her in my pantry," Kelly said. "She's due any day."

Jeffrey recognized how attached she was to her cats. "Okay, okay," he said, quickly giving in. "We'll think of something. Right now we have to get to Randolph's. What do we have to do to get me out of here? And maybe you'd better let me know my name."

"You're Richard Widdicomb," Kelly told him. "Wait here. I'll go out to the nurse's desk and get things squared away."

When Kelly left, Jeffrey finished dressing. Except for a dull headache, he felt fine. He wondered how much ketamine they'd injected him with. With as deep a sleep as he'd had, he wondered if there could have been something like Innovar mixed in.

Opening the duffel bag, Jeffrey found his toilet articles, some clean underclothes, the money, a number of pages of handwritten notes he'd made at the library, the information pages he'd copied from the defendant/plaintiff file at the courthouse, his wallet, and a small black book.

He put the wallet in his pocket and picked up the black book. He opened it and, for a few moments, couldn't figure out why it was in his duffel bag. It was clearly an address book, but it didn't belong to him.

Kelly came back with a resident physician in tow. "This is Dr. Sean Apple," she said. "He has to check you before you can sign out."

Jeffrey allowed the young doctor to listen to his chest, take his blood pressure, and do a cursory neurological exam which included Jeffrey walking a straight line across the room, putting one foot directly in front of the other.

While the doctor was examining him, Jeffrey asked Kelly about the black book.

"It was in your pocket," Kelly said.

Jeffrey stayed quiet until after Dr. Apple had declared Jeffrey fit to leave and walked out of the room.

"This book isn't mine," Jeffrey said, holding the address book aloft. Then he remembered. It was Trent Harding's address book. With all that had happened, it had slipped his mind. He told Kelly, and together they glanced through a few pages.

"This might be important," Jeffrey said. "We can give it to Randolph." Jeffrey slipped it into his pocket. "Are we ready?"

"You'll have to sign out at the nurse's desk," Kelly said. "Remember, you're Richard Widdicomb."

Leaving the hospital was as uneventful as Jeffrey could have hoped. He carried his duffel bag over his shoulder. Kelly also carried a small bag with her things in it. They got in her car. Jeffrey began to give her directions once she'd pulled out of the lot. He'd gotten her halfway to Randolph's office when he suddenly turned to her. The look on his face immediately frightened her.

"What's the matter?" she asked.

"You said those men went back into Trent's apartment after they dumped me in their car?" Jeffrey asked.

"I don't know if they went into his apartment, but they went back into his building."

"Oh, God!" Jeffrey said. He turned to face forward. "The reason they got in so easily when I was there was because they had keys. Obviously they were going in there for something specific."

Jeffrey turned back to Kelly. "We have to go to Garden Street first," he said.

"We're not going back to Trent's apartment?" Kelly couldn't believe it.

"We have to. We have to be sure the toxin and the Marcaine are still there. If they're not, we're back to square one."

"Jeffrey, no!" Kelly cried. She couldn't believe he wanted to go back a third time. Every time they'd gone, they'd encountered a new danger. But Kelly had come to know Jeffrey only too well. She knew there'd be no talking him out of yet another illicit visit. Without another word of protest, she simply headed for Garden Street.

"It's the only way," Jeffrey said, as much to convince himself as to convince Kelly.

Kelly parked a few doors down from the yellow brick building. The two of them just sat there for a few moments, collecting their thoughts.

"Is the window still open?" Jeffrey asked. He scanned the area to see if there were any people watching the building or who looked in any way out of place. Now he was worried about the police.

"The window's still open," Kelly said.

Jeffrey started to say he'd be back in two minutes, but Kelly cut him off. "I'm not waiting down here," she said in a tone that said there'd be no discussion.

Without a word, Jeffrey nodded.

They went through the front door, then through the inner door. The building was eerily quiet until they reached the third floor. Through a closed door they could just barely hear the crashing mayhem of Saturday morning cartoons.

Arriving on the fifth floor, Jeffrey motioned Kelly to be as quiet as possible. Harding's door was ajar. Jeffrey moved over beside the door and listened. All he could hear were sounds of the city coming through the open window.

Jeffrey pushed the door farther open. The scene that greeted his eyes was not encouraging. The apartment was worse than

ever, much worse. It had been torn apart. Everything had been
rudely dumped into the center of the room. All the drawers
from the desk had been removed.

"Damn!" Jeffrey whispered. Stepping inside, he rushed to
the kitchen. Kelly stayed at the doorway, surveying the debris.

Jeffrey was back in a second. Kelly didn't have to ask; his
face reflected what he'd found. "It's all gone," he said, close to
tears. "Even the false back to the cabinet is gone."

"What are we going to do?" Kelly asked, putting a consol-
ing hand on his arm.

Jeffrey ran his fingers through his hair. He choked back
tears. "I don't know," he said. "With Harding dead and his
apartment cleaned . . ." He couldn't continue.

"We can't give up now," Kelly said. "What about Henry
Noble, Chris's patient? You said that the toxin might be in his
gallbladder."

"But that was two years ago."

"Wait a minute," Kelly said. "Last time we talked about this,
you were convincing me. You sounded hopeful. What happened to your statement that we have to work with what we
have?"

"You're right," Jeffrey agreed, attempting to get control of
himself. "There's a chance. We'll go to the Medical Examiner's
office. I think it's time we told Warren Seibert the whole
story."

Kelly drove them to the city morgue.

"Think Dr. Seibert will be here on a Saturday morning?"
Kelly asked as they alighted from the car.

"He said when they were busy they worked pretty much
every day," Jeffrey answered, holding the morgue's front door
for her.

Kelly eyed the Egyptian motifs in the entrance hall. "Re-
minds me of *Tales from the Crypt*," she said.

The main office door was closed and locked. The place
looked deserted. Jeffrey led Kelly around to the stairway to the
second floor.

"There's a strange smell in here," Kelly complained.

"This is nothing," Jeffrey said. "Wait until we get upstairs."

By the time they reached the second floor, they still hadn't seen a soul. The door to the autopsy room was open, but it was devoid of people, alive or deceased. The smell wasn't nearly as bad as it had been on Jeffrey's initial visit. Turning down the hall, they passed the dusty library. Peering into Dr. Seibert's office, they discovered him hunched over his desk, a large coffee mug at his side, a stack of autopsy reports in front of him.

Jeffrey knocked on the open door. Seibert jumped, but when he saw who it was, a smile spread across his face. "Dr. Webber—you scared me."

Jeffrey apologized. "We should have called," he said.

"No matter," Seibert said. "But I haven't heard from California yet. I doubt if it will be until Monday."

"That wasn't exactly why we've come," Jeffrey said. He took a moment to introduce Kelly. Seibert stood to shake her hand.

"Why don't we go into the library?" Seibert said. "This office isn't big enough for three chairs."

Once they were settled, Seibert encouraged them, saying, "Now what can I do for you folks?"

Jeffrey took a deep breath. "First," he said, "my name is Jeffrey Rhodes."

Jeffrey then told Seibert the whole incredible story. Kelly helped at certain points. It took Jeffrey almost a half hour to finish. "So now you see our predicament. We've got no proof, and I'm a fugitive. We haven't much time. Our last hope seems to be Henry Noble. We have to find the toxin before we can document its existence in any of these cases."

"Holy Moses!" Seibert exclaimed. It was the first words he'd said since Jeffrey had begun. "I thought this case was interesting from the start. Now it's the most interesting I've ever heard. Well, we'll pull up old Henry and see what we can do."

"What kind of time frame are you talking about?" Jeffrey asked.

"We'll have to get an exhumation permit as well as a reinterment permit from the Department of Health," Seibert said. "As a medical examiner, I'll have no problem obtaining either. As a courtesy, we should notify the next of kin. I imagine we can do that in a week or two."

"That's too long," Jeffrey said. "We've got to do it right away."

"I suppose we could get a court order," Seibert said, "but even that would take three or four days."

"Even that's too long," Jeffrey sighed.

"But that's the shortest I can imagine," Seibert said.

"Let's find out where he was buried," Jeffrey said, moving on to other issues. "You said you have that information here."

"We have his autopsy report and we should have a copy of his death certificate," Seibert said. "The information should be there." He pushed back his chair. "Let me get it."

Seibert left the room. Kelly looked at Jeffrey. "I can tell you have something on your mind," she said.

"It's pretty simple," Jeffrey said. "I think we should just go and dig the guy up. Under the circumstances, I don't have much patience for all this bureaucratic rigmarole."

Seibert came back with a copy of Henry Noble's death certificate. He put it on the table in front of Jeffrey and stood over his right shoulder.

"Here's the place of disposition," he said, pointing to the center of the form. "At least he wasn't cremated."

"I'd never thought of that," Jeffrey admitted.

"Edgartown, Massachusetts," Seibert read. "I haven't been here long enough to know the state. Where's Edgartown?"

"On Martha's Vineyard," Jeffrey said. "Out on the tip of the island."

"Here's the funeral home," Seibert said. "Boscowaney Funeral Home, Vineyard Haven. The licensee's name is Chester Boscowaney. That's important to know because he'll have to be involved."

"How come?" Jeffrey asked. He wanted to keep everything as simple as possible. If he had to, Jeffrey thought he'd go out there in the middle of the night with a shovel and crowbar.

"He has to be the one to ascertain it is the right coffin and the right body," Seibert said. "As you can imagine, like everything else, there've been screw-ups, especially with closed-coffin funerals."

"The things you don't know about," Kelly said.

"What do these exhumation permits look like?" Jeffrey asked.

"They're not complicated," Seibert said. "I happen to have one on my desk right now for a case where the family was concerned their kid's organs were taken. Want to see it?"

Jeffrey nodded. While Seibert was getting it, Jeffrey leaned over to Kelly and whispered: "I wouldn't mind a little sea air, would you?"

Seibert came back in and put the paper in front of Jeffrey. It was typed up, like a legal document. "Doesn't seem to be anything special," Jeffrey said.

"What are you talking about?" Seibert asked.

"What if I came in here with one of these forms and asked you to exhume a body for me and check it out for something I was interested in?" Jeffrey asked. "What would you say?"

"We all do some private work on occasion," Seibert said. "I suppose I'd say it would cost you some money."

"How much?" Jeffrey asked.

Seibert shrugged. "There's no set fee. If it were simple, maybe a couple of thousand."

Jeffrey grabbed his duffel bag and pulled out one of the packets of money. He counted out twenty hundred-dollar bills. He put them on the table in front of Seibert. Then he said, "If I can borrow a typewriter, I'll have one of these exhumation permits in about an hour."

"You can't do that," Seibert said. "It's illegal."

"Yeah, but I take the risk, not you. I bet you never verify that these permits are bona fide. As far as you're concerned, it will be. I'll be the one breaking the law, not you."

Seibert gnawed his lip for a moment. "This is a unique situation," he said. Then he picked up the cash. "I'll do it, but not for money," he said. "I'll do it because I believe the story you've told me. If what you say is true, then it's certainly in the public interest to get to the bottom of it." He tossed the money into Jeffrey's lap. "Come on," he said. "I'll open the office downstairs and you can make us an exhumation permit. While you're at it, you might as well make a reinterment permit as well. I'd better call Mr. Boscowaney and have him start lining up the people and make sure the sexton of the cemetery isn't out bluefishing."

"How long will all this take?" Kelly asked.

"It's going to take some time," Seibert said. He looked at

his watch. "We'll be lucky to get out there by the middle of the afternoon. If we can get a backhoe operator, we could be done sometime tonight. But it might be late."

"Then we should plan to stay overnight," Kelly said. "There's an inn out in Edgartown, the Charlotte Inn. Why don't I make some reservations?"

Jeffrey said he thought that was a good idea.

Seibert showed Kelly into a colleague's office so she could use the telephone. Then he took Jeffrey down to the office, where he left him at a typewriter.

Kelly called the Charlotte Inn and was able to get reservations for two rooms. She thought that was an auspicious beginning to their quest. She hated to admit it, but the only thing that troubled her about the proposed venture was Delilah. What if she delivered? Last time Delilah had had kittens, she'd gone into calcium shock. She'd had to be rushed to the vet.

Picking up the phone again, she called Kay Buchanan, who lived in the house next door. Kay had three cats. The two had exchanged cat-sitting favors on many occasions.

"Kay, are you planning on being around for the weekend?" Kelly asked.

"Yup," Kay said. "Harold has work to do. We'll be here. Want me to feed your monsters?"

"I'm afraid it's more than that," Kelly said. "I have to go away and Delilah's close to term. I'm afraid she's about to have kittens any day."

"She almost died the last time," Kay said with concern.

"I know," Kelly said. "I was going to have her spayed, but she beat me to it. I wouldn't leave now but I haven't any choice."

"Will I be able to get in touch with you if something goes wrong?"

"Sure," Kelly said. "I'll be at the Charlotte Inn on Martha's Vineyard." Kelly gave her the number.

"You're going to owe me for this one," Kay said. "Plenty of cat food over there?"

"Absolutely," Kelly said. "You'll have to let Samson in. He's out."

"That I know," Kay said. "He just had an argument with my Burmese. You have a good time. I'll take care of the fort."

"I really appreciate this," Kelly said. She hung up the phone, thankful she had such a friend.

"Hello?" Frank said into the telephone, but he couldn't hear a thing. His kids had the Saturday morning cartoons on, with the volume turned way up, and it was driving him crazy. "Hold on," he said, setting the receiver down. He walked over to the family room's threshold. "Hey, Donna, quiet those kids or that set's going out the window."

Frank pulled the sliding door closed. The volume was cut in half. Frank shuffled back to the phone. He was dressed in his blue velveteen robe and velour slippers.

"Who's this?" he said into the phone when he'd picked it up from the counter.

"It's Matt. I got the information you needed. It took me a little longer than I expected. I forgot today was Saturday."

Frank got a pencil from the drawer. "All right," he said, "give it to me."

"The license number you gave me is registered to a Kelly C. Everson," Matt said. "The address is 418 Willard Street in Brookline. Is that far from you?"

"Just around the corner," Frank said. "That's a big help."

"The plane is still there," Matt said. "I want that doctor."

"You got him," Frank said.

"It takes me awhile to get mad," Devlin told Mosconi. "But let me warn you, I'm mad now. There's something about this Dr. Jeffrey Rhodes case that you haven't told me. Something that I should know."

"I've told you everything," Michael said. "I've told you more about this case than I've told you about any other that you've been involved with. Why would I hold back? Tell me that. I'm the one that's being put out of business."

"Then how come Frank Feranno and one of his goons showed up at the Hatch Shell?" Devlin asked. He winced as he changed positions in the hospital bed. He had a trapeze hanging down from a frame over the bed, which he used to lift himself up. "He's never been in the bounty-hunting business as far as I know."

"How the hell should I know?" Mosconi said. "Listen, I

didn't come down here to take abuse from you. I came down here to see if you were as bad as they suggested in the papers."

"Bull crap," Devlin said. "You came down here to see if I was too far out of commission to bring in the doc like I promised."

"How bad is it?" Mosconi asked, glancing at the graze wound above Devlin's right ear. They had shaved off most of the hair on that side of his head in order to suture the laceration. It was an ugly wound.

"Not as bad as you'll be if you're lying to me," Devlin said.

"Did you really take three bullets?" Mosconi said. He looked at the elaborate bandage covering Devlin's left shoulder.

"The one that grazed my head missed," Devlin said. "Thank God. Otherwise, it would have been curtains. But it must have knocked me out. I got hit in the chest but my Kevlar vest stopped the bullet. All I got out of that one is a sore spot on my rib cage. The one that hit my shoulder went clean through. Frank had a goddamn assault rifle. Least he wasn't using soft-nosed bullets."

"It's a little ironic that I can send you after serial killers and you come back without a scratch, but when I send you after a doctor who's being sent up for having some kind of problem administering anesthesia, you almost get yourself killed."

"Which is why I think there's something else to this affair. Something that involved that kid who was wasted by Tony Marcello. When I first saw Frank, I thought maybe you'd talked to him."

"Never," Mosconi said. "That guy's a criminal."

Devlin gave Mosconi a "who's kidding who" look. "I'll let that pass," he said. "But if Frank's involved, something big time is going down. Frank Feranno's never around unless it's serious money or big players. Usually both."

With a crash that surprised Mosconi, the side rail on the bed collapsed. Devlin had released it. Wincing, Devlin used his good arm to raise himself to a sitting position. Then he swung his legs over the side of the bed. He had an IV attached to the back of his left hand, but he just grabbed the tube and pulled it out. The needle came away with its adhesive tape and began squirting onto the floor.

Mosconi was horrified. "What the hell are you doing?" he asked, backing up.

"What the hell does it look like I'm doing?" Devlin said as he stood up. "Get my clothes out of the closet."

"You can't leave."

"Just watch me," Devlin said. "Why stay around here? I got my tetanus shot. And like I said, I'm mad. Plus, I promised you the doctor in twenty-four hours. I still got a little time."

Half an hour later, Devlin had signed himself out of the hospital, against medical advice. "You're taking full responsibility," a prim nurse had warned him.

"Just give me the antibiotics and the pain pills and save the lecture."

Michael gave him a ride over to Beacon Hill so Devlin could get his car. It was still parked in the no-parking zone at the very foot of the hill.

"Keep that check-writing hand warmed up," Devlin advised Mosconi as he got out of his car. "You'll be hearing from me."

"You still don't think I should call in somebody else?"

"Be a waste of time," Devlin said. "Plus, it might just get me mad at you as well as Frank Feranno."

Devlin got in his car. His first destination was police headquarters on Berkeley Street. He wanted his gun and he knew it would be there. With that accomplished, he called the detective type he'd hired to watch Carol Rhodes back when he thought she'd lead him to Jeffrey. This time he asked the man to go out to Brookline to watch Kelly Everson's house. "I want to know everything that happens there, understand?" Devlin told the man.

"I won't be able to get out there until later this afternoon," the man said.

"Make it as soon as you can," Devlin said.

That taken care of, Devlin drove to the North End. After double parking on Hanover Street, he went into the Via Veneto Café.

As soon as Devlin entered, there was a shuffle of feet toward the back of the café, just beyond the mural depicting a section of the Roman Forum. A wire-backed chair fell to the floor. Devlin heard the strands of a beaded curtain tinkle against each other.

Wasting no time, Devlin sprinted from the café to the street. He wove his way around pedestrians to Bennet Street and took a left. Turning into a narrow alleyway, he plowed into a short, balding man with round features.

The man tried to elude Devlin, but Devlin grabbed his jacket before he had taken two steps. Still squirming, the man tried to slip out of the jacket, but Devlin pinned him against the wall.

"Not so happy to see me, are you, Dominic?" Devlin said. Dominic was a small part of Devlin's network of informers. Devlin was now particularly interested in talking with him because of his longtime association with Frank Feranno.

"I had nothing to do with Frank's shooting you," Dominic said, visibly quaking. He and Devlin went back a long way as well.

"If I thought you had, I wouldn't be talking with you," Devlin said with a smile that Dominic immediately understood. "But I'm interested to know what Frank is up to these days. I figured you'd be the one to tell me."

"I can't tell you anything about Frank," Dominic said. "Give me a break. You know what would happen to me."

"That's only if I say anything to anybody," Devlin said. "Have I ever said anything about you to anybody, even the police?"

Dominic didn't respond.

"Besides," Devlin said, "for the moment, Frank is a hypothetical concern. Right this minute, I'm your worry. And I have to tell you, Dominic, I'm not a happy camper." Devlin reached into his jacket and pulled out his gun. He knew it would make its intended impression.

"I don't know much," Dominic said nervously.

Devlin slipped the gun back into its holster. "What might not be much to you might mean a lot to me. Who is Frank working for? Who got him to waste that kid last night on the Esplanade?"

"I don't know."

Devlin reached in to grasp his gun for the second time.

"Matt," Dominic said. "That's all I know. Tony told me before they went to the Esplanade. He's working for some guy named Matt. From St. Louis."

"What was the deal? Drugs, something like that?"

"I don't know. I don't think it was drugs. They were supposed to kill the kid and send the doctor to St. Louis."

"You're not yanking my chain, are you, Dominic?" Devlin asked menacingly. This was a far cry from the scenario he'd imagined.

"I'm telling it to you straight," Dominic said. "Why should I lie?"

"Did Frank send the doctor to St. Louis?" Devlin asked.

"No, they missed him. Frank took Nicky after Tony was shot. This time the doctor's girlfriend clipped him with her car. Broke his arm."

Devlin was impressed. At least he wasn't the only pro having trouble with the doctor. "So Frank's still involved?" Devlin asked.

"Yeah, as far as I know," Dominic said. "I understand he's talked to Vinnie D'Agostino. There's supposed to be big money involved."

"I want to know about this guy from St. Louis," Devlin said. "And I want to know what Frank and Vinnie are up to. Use the usual phone numbers. And, Dominic, if you don't call, my feelings will be hurt. I think you know how I get when I have hurt feelings. I don't suppose I have to draw you any pictures."

Devlin let Dominic go. He turned and left the alley without looking back. The guy had better deliver. Devlin was in no mood to dick around, and he was determined to find out what Frank Feranno was up to.

Frank's euphoria evaporated when he caught sight of Kelly's house. The place looked deserted, with all the curtains drawn. Frank sighed. That seventy-five grand was further away than he'd thought.

For about half an hour he just sat and watched the place. No one came in or out. There was no sign of life except for a Siamese cat lolling in the middle of the front lawn like he owned the place.

Finally Frank got out of the car. First he walked around the side of the house to see if there were any windows in the garage. There were. Cupping his hands, he peered in. No red Honda Accord like he'd hounded last night on Beacon Hill. Returning to the front of the house, Frank decided to ring the bell and see what happened. For reassurance, he felt his gun. Then he rang the bell.

When nothing happened, he put his ear to the door and pushed the button again. He could hear the chimes within, so at least the doorbell worked. Cupping his hands again, he looked through the sidelight of the door. He couldn't see much because of a lacy curtain on the other side.

Damn, he thought as he turned to face the street. The Siamese was still crouched in the middle of the lawn.

Walking out onto the grass, Frank bent down and stroked the large cat. Samson eyed him suspiciously, but didn't dart away.

"You like that, huh, pussy?" Frank said. Just then a woman came out of the house next door and walked toward him.

"Have you made a friend, Samson?" she asked.

"Your kitty, ma'am?" Frank asked in his most gracious voice.

"Hardly," the woman said with a chuckle. "He's the mortal enemy of my Burmese. But as neighbors, we have to learn to get along."

"Nice big cat," Frank said, standing up. He was about to ask the woman about Kelly Everson, when she started for Kelly's front door.

"Come on, Samson," she called to the Siamese. "Let's go check Delilah."

"Are you going into Kelly's house?" Frank asked.

"Yes, I am," she said.

"Wonderful," Frank said. He walked over to her. "I'm Frank Carter, a cousin of Kelly's. I took a chance on finding her home."

"I'm Kay Buchanan," she said, extending her hand. "I'm Kelly's neighbor and sometime cat-sitter. I'm afraid you're going to have some wait. Kelly's gone away for the weekend."

"Darn," Frank said, snapping his fingers. "My mother gave me her address so I could say hello. I'm from out of town. Here just for a couple of days on business. When will Kelly be coming back?"

"She didn't say exactly," Kay said. "What a pity."

"Especially with my not having much to do today," Frank said. "Any idea where she went?"

"Just out to Martha's Vineyard. Edgartown, I think," Kay said. "She said she had to go. I have a sneaking suspicion it was more of a romantic thing. But I didn't complain. To tell the truth, I was glad for her. She needs to get out more. She's been in mourning long enough, don't you think?"

"Oh, absolutely," Frank said, hoping not to get further into it than that.

"Well, nice meeting you," Kay said. "I've got to see to these cats. It's the other one who's the big worry. You think Samson's big, you should see Delilah. She gives new meaning to the term 'fat cat.' Due any day. Say, maybe you should stop back on Monday if you're still in town. I imagine Kelly will be back by then. She better be. I'm not playing nursemaid to a whole litter!"

"Maybe I could give her a call," Frank said. He liked the idea of her trip being romantic. That probably meant the doctor had probably gone along as well. "Any idea where she's staying?"

"She told me the Charlotte Inn," Kay said. "Come on, Samson, let's go."

Frank flashed Kay one of his most sincere smiles as she went to the front porch and fished the key from the carriage lamp. Frank went back to his car.

Once he had the car started, he made a quick U-turn. One thing he'd decided about the seventy-five grand was that he wasn't going to tell Donna about it. He'd stash it someplace. Maybe take a trip down to the Caymans.

The idea of a little side trip to Martha's Vineyard also appealed. And he had a bright idea. Since he had to put the doctor on Matt's plane, why not take the plane to the island? That was calling using your noodle, he told himself.

As he drove back into town, Frank started to think about whom he should take with him if he couldn't find Vinnie D'Agostino. There was no doubt he would miss Tony. It was a shame what had happened. Frank also wondered about Devlin and whether he should go visit him in the hospital to tell him there were no hard feelings. But he decided against it. There just wasn't time.

Driving down Hanover Street, Frank pulled up and triple-parked in front of the Via Veneto Café. He leaned on his horn. Before long, someone ran out of the café and moved his car, allowing Frank to pull in. The traffic that had backed up on Hanover Street funneled past. Several of the cars honked at him for delaying them. "Hey, screw you!" Frank called out his window. It was amazing how inconsiderate some people were, he thought.

Frank walked into the café and shook hands with the owner, who'd rushed out from behind his register to greet him. Frank took a table near the front which had a little reserved sign on it. He ordered a double espresso and lit a cigarette.

When his eyes had adjusted to the dim light in the café, Frank twisted around and scanned the room. He didn't see Vinnie, but he did see Dominic. Frank motioned for the owner. He told him to ask Dominic to come and talk to him.

A nervous Dominic approached Frank's table.

"What's the matter with you?" Frank asked, looking at Dominic.

"Nothing," Dominic said. "Maybe I've had too much coffee."

"Know where Vinnie is?" Frank asked.

"He's at home," Dominic said. "He was in here half an hour ago."

"Go ask him to come over. Tell him it's important," Frank said.

Dominic nodded and went out the front door.

"How about a sandwich?" Frank said to the owner. While Frank ate, he tried to remember where the Charlotte Inn was in Edgartown. He'd only been there a couple of times. It wasn't that big a town, the way he remembered it. In fact, the biggest thing was the cemetery.

Vinnie came in with Dominic. Vinnie was a young, muscle-bound guy who thought that all women were after him. Frank had always been a little afraid to use him because he seemed a little reckless, like he was always trying to prove himself. But with Tony gone and Nicky out of commission, Frank was getting down to the bottom of the barrel. He knew he couldn't use Dominic. Dominic was an ass. He'd always been too nervous. He was a liability, especially if anything went wrong. Frank had found that out the hard way.

"Sit down, Vinnie," Frank said. "How'd you like a free trip to the Charlotte Inn in Edgartown?"

Vinnie took a chair and sat on it backwards, hunching forward over the back so that his muscles bulged. Frank thought he had a lot to learn.

"Dominic," Frank said, "how about you take a powder?"

Dominic slipped out of the back of the café and ran over to the candy store on Salem Street. There was a pay phone in the back of the magazines. He took out Devlin's numbers and dialed the first of the two. When Devlin came on the line, he cupped the receiver with his hand before he started speaking. He didn't want anyone to hear.

16

SATURDAY,

MAY 20, 1989

7:52 P.M.

"It's a good thing we didn't try to fly," Kelly said to Jeffrey as a jet rumbled in the distance. "We wouldn't have gotten here yet. It looks like the fog is just lifting now."

"At least it stopped raining," Jeffrey said. He watched the scoop of the backhoe dig into the soft earth.

They had come across to the island on the Steamship Authority ferry from Woods Hole. It was a good thing they'd taken Seibert's official Medical Examiner's van, complete with the official seal on the door. They never would have managed to get on the ship with a vehicle had it not been for Seibert's insisting they were traveling on official business. Having his truck rather than Kelly's Honda helped him make his case. Even then, there had been some grumbling. Theirs was the very last vehicle to board.

The trip had been uneventful. Between the fog and slight drizzle they had stayed belowdecks, finding a nonsmoking corner to sit in. Jeffrey and Kelly had spent most of the time going over Trent's address book, but they hadn't turned up any clues.

The only listing that had caught Jeffrey's attention was a Matt, listed under the Ds. Jeffrey wondered if it was the same

Matt who'd left a message on Trent's machine when Jeffrey had been there the first time. The area code was 314.

"Where's 314?" Jeffrey asked Kelly.

Kelly didn't know. Jeffrey asked Seibert, who was skimming one of the dozen professional journals he'd brought along for the ride.

"Missouri," Seibert said. "I have an aunt in St. Louis."

Once they had arrived at Vineyard Haven, the largest town on Martha's Vineyard, they'd gone directly to the Boscowaney Funeral Home. Thanks to Seibert's call that morning, Chester Boscowaney had been expecting them.

Chester was in his late fifties, overweight, with cheeks so ruddy they looked rouged. He was dressed in a dark suit and vest complete with pocket watch and fob. His manner was unctuous, even servile. He'd snapped up the several hundred dollars that Jeffrey had offered on Seibert's advice with the eagerness of a hungry dog.

"Everything's been arranged," he'd said in a whisper as if a funeral was in progress. "I'll meet you out there at the site."

Kelly, Jeffrey, and Warren had driven to Edgartown and had checked into the Charlotte Inn. Kelly and Jeffrey registered as Mr. and Mrs. Everson.

The only remaining stumbling block had been the backhoe operator, Harvey Tabor. He'd been out on Chappaquiddick digging a septic system for a beach house and couldn't get back to Edgartown until after four. And even then, he'd not been able to get to the cemetery. He'd explained that his wife had made a special dinner for his daughter's birthday, and that he couldn't join them at the cemetery until after that.

The whole affair had gotten under way a little after seven. The first thing Jeffrey had pointed out to Seibert was that no one had asked to see the permits. Boscowaney hadn't even asked if they had them. Seibert had said that it was still good to have them in hand. "It ain't over till it's over," he'd added.

The sexton of the cemetery was a man named Martin Cabot. His face was craggy, his build slim. He looked more like a weathered mariner than a cemetery caretaker. He'd eyed Seibert for a full minute before saying: "You're kind of a young fella to be a coroner."

Warren told him that he'd managed to skip the third grade,

so that he'd been able to cut the duration of his schooling. He also told him that he was a physician and a medical examiner and not a coroner. Jeffrey guessed that Warren was sensitive about the issue.

The sexton and the backhoe operator obviously didn't get along too well. Martin kept telling Harvey where he should be and what he should be doing. Harvey told Martin that he'd been operating his backhoe long enough and didn't need any advice.

Groundbreaking had occurred just past seven-thirty, behind Henry Noble's granite headstone. It was a pleasant site under a large maple tree. "This is encouraging," Seibert had said. "With this shade, there should be less deterioration and putrefaction."

Kelly had felt her stomach turn.

There was a sharp screech from the ground.

"Ease up!" Martin shouted. "You'll bust through the top of the vault." A line of stained concrete appeared in the fresh earth.

"Shut up, Martin," Harvey said as he lowered the backhoe into the pit. It struck the concrete gently. Harvey drew the hoe toward him and up. A large portion of the top of the vault became visible.

"Don't break the handles," Martin cried.

Kelly, Jeffrey, and Seibert were standing on one side of the grave, Chester and Martin on the other. The sun was still up, although low in the sky, and it was obscured by dark rain clouds. Wisps of fog swirled about the cemetery grounds by the force of the sea breeze. Martin had looped an extension cord around one of the maple tree's branches. The sight of it made Jeffrey think of a hangman's knot, even though the only thing dangling was the solitary bare bulb of a drop light. Its light shone directly down into the trench that the backhoe was digging.

Kelly shivered, more from the endeavor than from cold, although it had grown progressively cooler. The cozy room with its Victorian wallpaper at the Charlotte Inn seemed a long way away. She reached out and clutched Jeffrey's hand.

It took another fifteen minutes to clear away the rest of the dirt covering the cement slab. When it was clear enough, Harvey and Martin got down on its surface to shovel the remaining dirt from the grave.

Then Harvey climbed back onto his backhoe and positioned the scoop directly above the slab. He and Martin scrambled back into the hole to run steel cables from the slab's handles to the teeth of the scoop.

"All right, Martin, out of the hole," Harvey said, taking pleasure in giving Martin an order for a change. He climbed back on his machine. Then, looking at Jeffrey, Kelly, and Seibert, he said: "You folks will have to move. I'm going to swing the top your way." The three of them did as they were told. Once they were out of the way, Harvey again set to work.

The backhoe engine grunted and strained. Then, with a popping noise, the top of the vault came away. Jeffrey could see that it had been sealed with a tarlike substance. The backhoe swung the slab to the side and lowered it to the earth.

Everyone crowded to the edge of the hole. Within the vault rested a silver coffin.

"Isn't it a beauty?" Chester Boscowaney said. "It's one of our top of the line. Nothing better than a Millbronne casket."

"No water in the vault," Seibert said. "That's another good sign."

Jeffrey's eyes swept the graveyard. It was an eerie sight. Night was falling fast. The headstones cast narrow, purple shadows across the cemetery.

"Well, what do you want us to do, Doc?" Martin asked Seibert. "You want us to lift the coffin out or you want to jump down there and open it in place?"

Jeffrey could tell Seibert was debating.

"I never have liked to get down in those vaults," he said, "but lifting the coffin will only take more time. I say the sooner we get this over with, the better. I'm looking forward to a nice dinner."

Kelly's stomach turned again.

"Can I help?" Jeffrey asked.

Seibert looked at Jeffrey. "Have you ever done anything like this before? It might be a little gruesome, and I can't guarantee what it will smell like, especially if there's any water inside."

"I'll be okay," Jeffrey said, despite his misgivings.

"That's a Millbronne casket," Chester Boscowaney said with pride. "It's got a rubber gasket all the way around. There won't be any water."

"I've heard that before," Seibert whispered. "All right, let's do it."

Jeffrey and Seibert stepped down to the concrete edge of the vault and lowered themselves in at either end of the casket. Seibert was at the casket's foot, Jeffrey at its head.

"Let me have the crank," Seibert said.

Chester handed it down to him.

Seibert felt along the back of the casket with his hand until he felt the spot. Then, inserting the crank into the hole, he tried to turn it. He had to put his weight into it before it would budge. Finally it turned with an agonizing screech. Kelly winced.

The coffin's seal broke with a hissing sound.

"Hear that air?" Chester Boscowaney said. "There's not going to be any water in there, mark my word."

"Get your fingers under the edge," Seibert said to Jeffrey, "and lift."

With a creaking sound the lid of the coffin opened. Everyone looked in. Henry Noble's face and hands were covered by a fine web of white fuzz. Beneath, his skin was a dark gray. He was dressed in a blue suit, white shirt, and paisley tie. His shoes appeared shiny and new. On the white satin of the interior was a rash of green mildew.

Jeffrey tried to breathe through his mouth to avoid the odor, but to his surprise, it wasn't all that bad. The smell was musty rather than rank, like a cellar that hadn't been opened for a long time.

"Looks very good," Seibert said. "My compliments to the funeral director. No water whatsoever."

"Thank you," Chester Boscowaney said. "And I can assure you that you are looking at the body of Henry Noble."

"What's the white fuzz?" Jeffrey asked.

"Some kind of fungus," Seibert said. He asked Kelly to hand him down his kit. Kelly passed him his black bag.

Seibert worked his way along the side of the coffin. There

was barely enough room for his feet, but he managed. Setting his bag down on Henry Noble's thighs, he opened it and took out a pair of heavy rubber gloves. After putting on the gloves, he began to unbutton the man's shirt.

"What can I do?" Jeffrey asked.

"Nothing right now," Seibert said. He exposed the sutured incision made at the time of the man's autopsy. Taking a pair of scissors from his bag, he cut the sutures, then spread the sides of the wound. The tissue was dry.

Jeffrey straightened up. The smell was more obnoxious now, but Seibert seemed indifferent to it.

Seibert got the wound open, then reached inside the body cavity and pulled out a heavy clear plastic bag. The contents were darkened. The bag contained a good deal of fluid. Holding the bag up to the light, Seibert twirled it slowly, examining its contents.

"Eureka!" Seibert said. "Here's the liver." He pointed, for Jeffrey's benefit. Jeffrey wasn't sure he wanted to look, but he humored Seibert. "My guess is that the gallbladder will still be attached."

Seibert rested the bag on Henry Noble's torso and undid the cinch. A very disagreeable odor filled the damp night air. Seibert reached in and pulled out the liver. Turning it over, he showed Jeffrey the gallbladder. "Perfect," he said. "It's even still moist. I thought it would be dried out." He palpated the small organ. "It's got some fluid in it, too." Putting the liver and the gallbladder down on top of the plastic bag, Seibert went back into his black bag and pulled out a syringe and several specimen bottles. He punctured the gallbladder and suctioned as much bile as he was able. He squirted some in each of the sample jars.

Everyone had been watching Seibert's efforts so intently, they were oblivious to other goings-on. They hadn't noticed a blue rental Chevrolet Celebrity pull into the cemetery with its lights out. They hadn't heard the doors open, or the sound of the two men approaching.

For Frank it had not been a smooth afternoon. Once again what he thought would be an easy operation had turned into

a major headache. He'd looked forward to riding in a private
jet, something he'd never done before. But after getting into
the plane and strapping himself into the seat, he'd had a bout
of claustrophobia. He'd never realized just how small these
private planes were. And then to make matters worse, they
weren't able to take off right away because of the volume of
incoming traffic at Logan. Then the weather changed.

At first, a fog bank had engulfed the Cape and the islands,
then a severe thunderstorm had swept in from the west, pelting
the city with marble-sized hailstones. Frank had gotten off the
plane to wait out the storm in the general aviation terminal. By
the time they had clearance to leave and adequate visibility to
land on the Vineyard, it was almost six o'clock.

Then, to make matters worse, the flight had been a nightmare. With all the turbulence, the plane had bounced around
like a cork in a bubbling brook. Frank had gotten airsick and
had to puke in a paper bag. The whole time, Vinnie had been
carrying on about how great the plane was. He'd munched on
peanuts and potato chips nonstop.

By the time they'd arrived on Martha's Vineyard, Frank
was weak. He'd sent Vinnie to get the rental car while he
stayed in the men's room. Only after eating some soda
crackers and drinking a Coke had he started to feel like his
old self again.

They'd gone directly to the Charlotte Inn. At the front desk
they'd inquired about Kelly Everson. Frank had used the same
ploy about being a relative, but now he'd embellished his story
by saying he was trying to surprise his cousin. He and Vinnie
had exchanged winks at that little ruse. They certainly did have
a surprise in mind. Both were armed with guns discreetly
hidden in shoulder holsters, and Frank had another dose of the
tranquilizer in his pocket.

But the surprise had turned out to be for Frank. The woman
at the desk at the Charlotte Inn had told them that she believed
the Eversons were in the Edgartown cemetery. She said that
Mr. Everson had spent some time on the phone next to the
check-in desk, trying to arrange a rendezvous with Harvey
Tabor, the backhoe operator.

Back in the car, Frank had said to Vinnie: "The cemetery?
I don't like the sound of this."

They'd circled the cemetery first. It was a big place, but it was easy to see the group in the center. There was a light in a tree that illuminated the four people standing in front of a backhoe.

"What should I do?" Vinnie had asked. He was driving.

"What the hell do you think they are doing?" Frank had asked.

"Looks like they're digging somebody up," Vinnie had answered with a macabre laugh. "Like in a horror movie."

"I don't like this," Frank had said. "First Devlin shows up at the Esplanade, now this doctor is in a cemetery at night, digging up dead people. This doesn't feel right. Besides, it gives me the creeps."

Frank had had Vinnie drive around the cemetery a second time while he thought about what to do. It had been a good decision. From the opposite side they'd been able to see that there were two more people, down in the open grave. Finally Frank had said: "Let's get it over with. Kill the lights and drive in halfway. Then we'll walk."

Devlin hadn't had much better luck than Frank. He'd flown commercial and had spent most of the time sitting on the runway in Boston. Even once they'd gotten going, the plane had made a stop in Hyannis that lasted forty minutes. Devlin hadn't reached the Vineyard until after seven. Once there he'd had to wait for his gun, which airport security had prevented him from carrying on the plane. By the time he got to the Charlotte Inn, it was almost nine.

"Excuse me," he said to the woman at the front desk. She'd been reading by the light of an antique brass lamp.

Devlin knew he looked worse than usual with the large, sutured incision. With all the hair they'd cut off, he'd been unable to form his usual ponytail. Instead he'd tried to comb the hair from the other side of his head over the suture site. He had to admit the result was startling at best.

The woman looked up and did a double-take when she saw Devlin. On top of everything else, Devlin guessed that not too many guests at the Charlotte Inn sported a Maltese cross earring.

"I'd like to inquire about several of your guests," Devlin

began. "Unfortunately, they may be using aliases. But one's a young woman named Kelly Everson." Devlin described her. "The other is a man about forty years of age. His name is Jeffrey Rhodes. He's a doctor."

"I'm sorry, but we don't give out information about our guests," the woman curtly replied. She'd gotten up from her chair and had taken a step back as if she'd expected Devlin to grab her and shake the information from her.

"That's unfortunate," Devlin said. "But maybe you could tell me if a large, rather overweight man with dark hair and puffy, deeply set eyes was here inquiring about the same couple. His name is Frank Feranno, but he's not choosy about what name he goes by when he's working."

"Maybe you should talk to the manager," the woman said.

"That's okay," Devlin said. "You'll do fine. Was this gentleman in here? He's about this high." Devlin held his hand out to show about five-ten.

The woman was clearly flustered, and she relented, hoping that if she did, Devlin would go away. "A Frank Everson, a cousin of Mrs. Everson's, was here," she said. "But no Frank Feranno. At least not while I've been at the desk."

"And what did you tell this purported cousin?" Devlin said. "That wouldn't be telling me anything about a guest, now would it?"

"I told him that the Eversons were most likely over at the cemetery."

Devlin blinked. He studied the woman's face for a moment to see if she'd waver with her story, but she held his gaze. The cemetery? Devlin didn't think the woman was lying. Was this yet another bizarre twist to this already strange case?

"What's the quickest way to the cemetery?" Devlin demanded. Whatever was happening, he had the feeling he didn't have a lot of time.

"Just go down the street and take the first right," the woman said. "You can't miss it."

Devlin thanked the woman and ran out to his car as fast as his bandaged arm would allow.

Jeffrey watched Seibert balance Henry Noble's liver in his left hand. Holding it at an arm's length so that the embalming fluid

wouldn't drip on his clothes, he opened the plastic bag containing the rest of Henry Noble's decomposing internal organs.
Jeffrey winced as Seibert unceremoniously dropped the liver
back into the sack and cinched the top of the bag so no fluid
would escape.

Seibert was about to return the bag to its place in Henry
Noble's body when a voice said, "What the hell is going on
here?"

Along with everybody else, Jeffrey looked up in the direction the voice had come from. A man stepped into the circle
of light. He was dressed in dark slacks, white shirt, sweater,
and dark windbreaker. In his hand was a gun.

"My God!" Frank said with revulsion. He was transfixed by
the gruesome sight of the open grave. The nausea he'd suffered
earlier returned with a vengeance.

Jeffrey recognized the man instantly from the Esplanade and
the doors of the Church of the Advent. How had he tracked
them? And what did he want?

Jeffrey wished he had a weapon, any means of defending
himself. Last time they'd gone to extraordinary lengths to drug
him.

Frank retched from the horrid sight and offensive smell. He
clasped his free hand to his mouth and turned to face Kelly,
Chester, and Martin. With a wave of his gun he ordered Jeffrey
and Seibert out of the grave.

Seibert scrambled out of the vault, wondering if this intruder
was related to Henry Noble. "I'm the Medical Examiner," he
said, hoping to sound official and take charge of the situation.
Seibert had dealt with irate family members before. Nobody
was keen on autopsies, especially relatives. He stepped between Frank and the others.

Jeffrey had noticed Frank's reaction to having seen Henry
Noble and he saw him turn his head. Reaching forward, he
grasped the plastic bag containing Noble's organs. It had to
weigh thirty-five to forty pounds. Climbing out of the vault
and up onto the grass, he held the bag to his side and slightly
behind.

"I'm not interested in you," Frank said to Warren, giving
him a rough shove to the side. "Get over here, Dr. Rhodes."

Frank put his gun into his other hand, then dug in his pocket

until he came up with the syringe. "Turn around!" he ordered
Jeffrey. "Vinnie, you cover . . ."

Jeffrey swung the plastic bag with both hands, bringing it
over his head and down on top of Frank's with as much force
as he could muster. The bag burst on impact, knocking Frank
to his hands and knees. The syringe flipped into the pile of dirt;
the gun skidded into the grave, falling with a clank into the
vault and landing in the coffin.

At first Frank was dazed and unsure of what had hit him.
Then he looked with horror at what was smeared over him and
all around him on the ground. Recognizing the brain and the
blackened loops of intestines, he threw up wildly. In between
retching fits, he tried to brush the gore off his shoulders and
head.

Jeffrey was still holding the empty plastic bag when Vinnie
dashed forward into the sphere of light from the darkened
periphery. Tense and nervous, he was holding his gun with
both hands. "Nobody move!" he shouted. "Anybody moves,
they're dead!" He rotated his gun in jerky arcs from one person to the other.

Jeffrey hadn't seen Frank's accomplice. If he had, he probably wouldn't have risked hitting Frank.

Keeping his gun trained on the group, Vinnie stepped over
to Frank, who had gotten shakily to his feet. He was standing
with his arms outstretched, shaking fluid from his hands.

"You all right, Frank?" Vinnie asked.

"Where the hell's my gun?" was all Frank said by way of an
answer.

"It went into the grave," Vinnie said.

"Get it!" Frank ordered. He unzipped his jacket and carefully pulled it off, then threw it on the ground.

Vinnie stepped over to the grave and nervously peered
down, trying to spot the gun. It was in plain view, between the
corpse's knees. Henry Noble seemed to be looking up at him.

"I've never been in a grave before," Vinnie said.

"Get the gun!" Frank shouted. He glared at Jeffrey and said:
"You bastard. You think I'm going to let you get away with
that little trick?"

"Nobody move," Vinnie said. He stepped down to the edge

of the grave. Looking away for just a moment, he jumped down. Instantly he looked back. His head was still above the level of the ground. Vinnie's gun was pointed directly at Chester, who stood weak-kneed between Kelly and Martin. Harvey was to Martin's left. Jeffrey was closer to Frank, and Seibert was between Frank and the others.

When Vinnie bent down to grab the gun, Jeffrey gambled on two things: one, that he could get away into the darkness fast enough to evade Vinnie, and two, since he was the one they were really after, both would come after him and leave the others alone. He was right only on the first count.

As Jeffrey ran along the cemetery road into the darkness, he heard Frank yell, "Toss me the gun, you ass!"

Leaving the circle of light, Jeffrey was immediately enveloped in darkness. It took a few moments for his eyes to adjust. When they did, he realized it wasn't quite as dark as he'd believed. Reflections from the lights of the surrounding town shimmered off the moist grass. The silhouettes of tombstones served as an eerie reminder that this was the home of the dead.

A parked, dark car suddenly loomed in front of Jeffrey. He paused long enough to check for keys in the ignition, but none were there. Looking back toward the point of light over Henry Noble's grave, Jeffrey could make out Frank's lumbering bulk heading in his direction. Vinnie remained behind, keeping watch on the others.

Jeffrey sprinted past the car, heading into the night. He remembered that Frank's girth was deceptive and that he was surprisingly agile and fast. Jeffrey was not confident that he could merely outrun Frank. He had to think of something. A plan. Could he make it to the center of town? On a Saturday night Edgartown should have some activity, even though it was not yet tourist season.

Behind him, Jeffrey heard the deadly crack of a gunshot. Frank had fired at him. Jeffrey heard a bullet hiss by his head. He veered in the other direction, to the left and off the cemetery road.

Crouching low to the ground, Jeffrey began to weave among the headstones. He did not want to be an easy target. He had the sickening feeling that Frank was no longer so concerned about taking him alive. Now that he was off the road, the footing wasn't as sure. Rocks and flat grave markers slowed Jeffrey's progress. He tripped at one point and staggered. He stayed on his feet only by grabbing a granite obelisk in a bear hug. The obelisk teetered on its plinth, threatening to topple. That was when Frank fired the second time.

The bullet struck the side of the obelisk just below Jeffrey's arm. Jeffrey backed up a step. Looking in the direction of the muzzle flash, he could just make out Frank coming in his direction. He was gaining on him!

Jeffrey raced on, his panic increasing. He was breathing heavily and felt a stitch in his side. He was lost among the graves. He didn't know in which direction he should head. He wasn't sure that he was still heading for town.

Out of the corner of his eye, Jeffrey saw the silhouettes of a cluster of single-story buildings which he guessed were mausoleums. He decided to head there. Veering in their direction, he stumbled onto another of the cemetery's several gravel roads. Once he reached the row of mausoleums, Jeffrey ducked between the first two. Edging behind them, he moved down the row, then turned back toward the road. Peering around a corner, he looked for Frank.

The man wasn't fifty feet away. He'd pulled up short in front of the first mausoleum. He hesitated a moment, then started walking in Jeffrey's direction. Jeffrey was about to turn when Frank suddenly stepped between two of the tombs and disappeared from Jeffrey's line of sight.

Jeffrey tried to think what to do. One wrong move and he would be at Frank's mercy. Remembering Frank's expression after he'd hit him with the bag of decomposing organs, Jeffrey didn't think Frank would have much mercy.

Directly across from where Jeffrey was standing was a marble mausoleum that appeared older than the others. Even in the darkness, Jeffrey could tell that its iron door was slightly ajar.

After checking the road again for any sign of Frank, Jeffrey dashed to the open door. He pushed it open enough to slip into the mausoleum's cool interior. He tried to close it behind him, but when he pushed, the door grated on the floor. Jeffrey stopped immediately. He wouldn't risk making any more noise. The door was still open about three inches, slightly less than it had been when Jeffrey first spotted it.

Surveying the interior of his narrow cell, Jeffrey saw that the only light came from a small, elliptical window set high in the mausoleum's rear wall.

Jeffrey groped toward the window's dim light, inching ahead with his right foot and bringing his left up with each step. He could feel square depressions in the wall and realized they were for coffins.

When he reached the back wall, he squatted in the corner. As his eyes adjusted to the deeper darkness, he was able to make out the thin strip of vertical light that came in through the open door.

He waited. There wasn't a sound. After what he guessed was five minutes, he began to think about how long he would wait until venturing back out.

Then, with an agonizing screech of metal scraping rock, the ancient door to the mausoleum was shoved open. It clanged against the stone wall. Jeffrey leaped to his feet.

A cigarette lighter flared and illuminated Frank's fleshy face. He held the light out at arm's length. Jeffrey could see Frank squint, then smile. "Well, well," Frank said. "Isn't this convenient? You're already in a crypt." His shirt was stained and his hair was matted from the embalming fluid. Frank's sardonic smile changed to a sneer. He sauntered into the mausoleum, gun in one hand, cigarette lighter in the other.

When he was about six feet away, Frank stopped. He aimed his gun at Jeffrey's face. In the light of the small flame, Frank's features were grotesque. His deep eye sockets looked empty. His teeth appeared yellow.

"I was supposed to send you to St. Louis alive," Frank snarled, "but your hitting me with that stinking slop changed that. You're going to St. Louis, all right, but in a pine box, my friend."

For the second time in his life and in so many days, Jeffrey was forced to helplessly watch the end of a gun move forward and jiggle slightly as pressure was applied to the trigger.

"Frank!" a harsh voice called. The name echoed in the small chamber.

Frank spun away from Jeffrey, whipping his gun around. A

blast rocked the tiny chamber. Then a second blast reverberated within the mausoleum. Jeffrey hit the ground. Frank's
lighter went out. A ringing silence and utter blackness descended.

Jeffrey stayed perfectly still with his hands over his head and
face pressed to the cold stone floor. Then he heard the sound
of a flint being struck.

Jeffrey slowly raised his head, terrified at what he might see.
Frank was just in front of him, sprawled out on the floor,
facedown. His gun was on the floor in front of him, just
beyond his reach. Beyond Frank was a pair of legs. Raising his
head further, Jeffrey looked up into the face of Devlin O'Shea.

"What a surprise," Devlin said. "If it isn't my favorite doctor." He was holding a lit cigarette lighter in one hand and a
gun in the other, just as Frank had.

Jeffrey struggled to his feet. Devlin went to Frank and rolled
him over. Squatting, he felt for a carotid pulse. "Damn," he
said. "I got too good an aim. I really didn't want to kill him.
At least I think I didn't want to kill him." Devlin straightened
up and stepped over to Jeffrey. "No poison darts, now," he
warned.

Jeffrey backed up against the wall. Devlin looked worse than
Frank.

"Like my new hairstyle?" Devlin asked, aware of Jeffrey's
reaction. "It's thanks to that goon on the floor." Devlin ges-
tured toward Frank. "Listen, Doc," he said, "I got good news
for you and I got bad news. Which do you want to hear first?"

Jeffrey shrugged. He knew it was all over now. He was only
sorry that Devlin had to step in now when they were so close
to getting their much-needed proof.

"Come on," Devlin warned. "We don't have all night.
There's still a young hoodlum out there holding your friends
at gunpoint. Now do you want to hear the good news or bad?"

"The bad news," Jeffrey said. He wondered if Devlin would
respond by shooting him point-blank. The good news, which
he'd never live to hear, would be that at least he'd be killed
quickly.

"And I would have bet good money you would have wanted
the good news first. Considering what you've been going

through, I think you need some. However, the bad news is that I'm going to take you to jail. I want to collect that reward money from Mosconi. But let me tell you the good news. I've uncovered some information that will probably get your conviction overturned."

"What are you talking about?" Jeffrey asked, dazed by this revelation.

"I don't think this is the time or place for a friendly chat," Devlin said. "There's still wiseass Vinnie D'Agostino out there with a firearm. Now I'm going to make a deal with you. I want you to cooperate with me. That means no running away, no sticking me with needles, or hitting me with briefcases. I'll take care of Vinnie so no one gets hurt if you would be so good as to create a little diversion. After I get Vinnie's gun, I'll handcuff him to that vault lid that's sitting on the ground. Then we'll call the Edgartown police. This will be more excitement than they've seen since all those rubbers washed up on the beach at Chappaquiddick Island. Then we'll all go and have some dinner. What do you say?"

Jeffrey could hardly answer, he was so dumbfounded and confused.

"Come on, Doc!" Devlin said. "We don't have all night. Do we have a deal or don't we?"

"Yes," Jeffrey said. "It's a deal."

The Charlotte Inn had a charming restaurant overlooking a tiny inner courtyard with a fountain. The tables were covered with white tablecloths and the chairs were comfortable. A team of attentive waiters and waitresses responded to the diners' every need.

If someone had described the scene that Jeffrey was now enjoying to him at some earlier time, he would have laughed it off as an impossibility. There were four people at the table. To Jeffrey's right was Kelly. She was obviously still anxious, but she looked radiant. To Jeffrey's left was Seibert. He wasn't particularly calm either, worried about the forged exhumation documents and the fact that the episode at the graveyard would be investigated. Across from Jeffrey was Devlin, who was the only one at the table who appeared completely relaxed. Instead of wine he was drinking beer, and he was already on his fourth.

"Doc!" Devlin said to Jeffrey. "You're one patient man. You still haven't asked me about the liberating information I mentioned back at the mausoleum."

"I've been afraid to," Jeffrey answered honestly. "I've been afraid to break the spell that I've been under since we walked out of there."

Everything had happened as Devlin had said it would. Jeffrey had made a commotion as if he and Frank were having a knock-down drag-out fight near the rental car. When Vinnie moved closer to see if he could help his boss, Devlin had walked up behind and disarmed him in the blink of an eye. Then on went the cuffs.

The only departure from the original plan had been that Devlin had not handcuffed Vinnie to the vault lid. Instead, he cuffed him directly to one of the handles of the casket. "You and Henry can keep each other company," he'd said to the terrified kid.

Then the rest of them had gone back to the Charlotte Inn, where, true to his word, Devlin called the Edgartown police. Although they'd been invited to stay for dinner, Chester, Martin, and Harvey politely declined, each preferring to unwind in their respective homes after the cemetery ordeal.

"Then I'm going to tell you whether you ask me or not," Devlin said. "But let me preface what I'm about to say with a few comments. First, I'd like to apologize for shooting at you in that fleabag hotel. At the time, I was pissed and I thought you were a real criminal. A kind I'd learned to hate. But as time went on, I learned more about your case, bit by bit. Mosconi wasn't all that helpful, so it wasn't easy. Anyway, I knew something was up when you stopped acting like the usual bail-jumper. Then, when Frank entered the picture, I really knew that something strange was happening, especially when I got the word that he was supposed to get seventy-five grand for shipping you to St. Louis. That didn't make any sense at all until I found out that the people who had hired Frank were interested in interrogating you for something you'd learned.

"At that point I decided to find out who these big out-of-town spenders were. I figured with the kind of money in-

volved it had something to do with drugs. But then I found out
it didn't. Here's the part I discovered that you'll find interesting. What would you think if I told you that the guy who hired
Frank Feranno is a guy by the name of Matt Davidson? A Matt
Davidson of St. Louis?"

Jeffrey let his spoon drop to the table. He looked at Kelly.
"The Matt in Harding's address book," she said.

"More than that," Jeffrey said. He reached under the table
for his duffel bag. He fished inside for some papers and came
up with two copies from the defendant/plaintiff book he'd
made at the courthouse. He set them on the table so everyone
could see.

Jeffrey pointed to Matthew Davidson's name where it appeared as the plaintiff attorney for the malpractice case at Suffolk General Hospital. "Matthew Davidson was also the
plaintiff attorney on my case," Jeffrey told them.

Kelly snapped up the other paper, containing the information on the Commonwealth suit. "The plaintiff attorney on
this case, Sheldon Faber, was the same as on my husband's,"
she said. "Now that I think of it, he was from St. Louis."

"Let me check something," Jeffrey said, pushing back from
the table. To Devlin he added, "Stay put, I'll be right back."
Devlin had started to follow. Jeffrey left the group to go to the
public phone. Calling information in St. Louis, he asked for the
business phone numbers for each of the two attorneys. The
numbers were the same!

Jeffrey came back to the table. "Davidson and Faber are
partners. Trent Harding had been working for them. Kelly,
you were right. It was a conspiracy. This whole mess was
being run by the plaintiff attorneys, creating their own demand
and their own cases!"

"That's about the way I have it figured," Devlin said. He
laughed. "I've heard of ambulance chasers, but these guys are
making their own accidents. Needless to say, I think all this
will have a positive effect on your appeal."

"That puts the burden on me," Seibert said. "Me and my gas
chromatograph. These malpractice attorneys must have re-
cruited Trent Harding to contaminate Marcaine ampules and
place them in OR supplies. All I can say is that I hope Henry

Noble comes through this one last time. I've got to isolate the toxin."

"I wonder if these lawyers are involved in any other cities?" Kelly asked. "How extensive is their operation?"

"I'm only guessing," Jeffrey said, "but I would think it all depends on how many psychopaths like Trent Harding they're able to find." He shook his head.

"I never did like lawyers," Devlin said.

"Kelly," Jeffrey said, suddenly overcome with emotion. "You know what this means?"

Kelly smiled. "No South America."

Jeffrey drew her into his arms. He couldn't believe it. He was getting his life back after all. And just in time to share it with the woman he loved.

"Hey!" Devlin called to one of the waiters. "Bring me another Bud and how about a bottle of champagne for the lovers?"

EPILOGUE

Randolph adjusted his glasses so he could read. He cleared his throat. Jeffrey was seated at a simple oak table directly across from him, drumming his fingers on its scarred surface. Randolph's leather briefcase was on the table to Jeffrey's right. It was open. Jeffrey could just see that it contained a pair of squash sneakers as well as a wealth of legal papers and forms.

Jeffrey was dressed in a light-blue denim shirt and dark-blue cotton pants. As Devlin had promised, he'd brought Jeffrey back to Boston, where he'd turned him over to the authorities.

Jeffrey had not enjoyed his time in jail, but had tried to make the best of it. He lifted his spirits by repeatedly reminding himself that his stay would be temporary. He'd even had time to start playing pickup basketball, something he'd not done since his days in medical school.

Jeffrey had gotten in touch with Randolph from the Charlotte Inn after the celebration dinner with Devlin. Randolph had gotten right on things, or so he'd said. That had been over a week ago. Now Jeffrey found himself losing patience.

"I know you think that this should all be done overnight," Randolph said, "but the reality is that the wheels of justice take time to turn."

"Tell me the bottom line," Jeffrey said.

"The bottom line is that I have now formally filed three motions," Randolph said. "The first and most important is the one I have filed for a new criminal trial. I've filed that with Judge Janice Maloney, asking her to set aside the verdict on the ground of errors in the trial . . ."

"Who cares about the errors in the trial?" Jeffrey cried, exasperated. "Isn't it more important that the whole affair was caused by a couple of plaintiff attorneys filling their coffers?"

Randolph removed his glasses. "Jeffrey, will you allow me to finish? I know you are impatient, and with good reason."

"Finish," Jeffrey said, mustering as much patience as he could.

Randolph replaced his glasses, then looked back at his notes. He cleared his throat again.

"As I was saying," he continued, "I filed a motion for a new trial on the basis of errors in the trial and on the basis of newly discovered evidence that warrants review."

"My God!" Jeffrey said. "Why can't you say that in plain English? Why this beating around the bush?"

"Jeffrey, please," Randolph said. "There are procedures to be followed in this kind of situation. You can't demand a new trial just for any kind of new evidence. I have to make it clear that this new evidence we have is not something I could have learned with reasonable diligence. They don't give new trials for lawyers' malpractice. May I go on?" he questioned.

Jeffrey nodded.

"The second motion that I have filed is to amend the record on appeal of the malpractice judgment," Randolph said. "This is a Petition of Extraordinary Equitable Relief because of newly discovered evidence."

Jeffrey rolled his eyes.

"The third motion I have filed is for a new bond hearing. I've spoken with Judge Maloney to explain that there had been no harmful intent on your part, and that you had not jumped bail but had simply been conducting a commendable and eventually successful investigation leading to the uncovering of the new evidence."

"I think I could have worded that a bit simpler," Jeffrey said. "So what did she say?"

"She said she'd consider the motion," Randolph said.

"Wonderful," Jeffrey said sarcastically. "While I rot here in prison, she'll consider the motion. That's wonderful. If all the lawyers became doctors, all the patients would die before they got through the paperwork!"

"You have to be patient," Randolph advised, accustomed to Jeffrey's sarcasm. "I imagine I'll hear tomorrow about the bond hearing. We should have you out in another day or so. The other issues will take a little longer. Lawyers, like doctors, are not supposed to give guarantees, but it is my belief that you will be totally exonerated."

"Thank you," Jeffrey said. "What about Davidson et al.?"

"I'm afraid that's a different story," Randolph said with a sigh. "We will of course cooperate with the district attorney in St. Louis, who has assured me that there will be an investigation. But I'm afraid he feels the chances of an actual indictment are slim. Other than hearsay, there is just no evidence of any business association between Davidson and Trent Harding. The only evidence of an association is the entry in Mr. Harding's address book, which does nothing to demonstrate or prove the nature of that association. By the same token, there is no evidence directly linking Trent Harding to the batrachotoxin that Dr. Warren Seibert has found in all the cases after having isolated it from the gallbladder of Mr. Henry Noble. With Mr. Frank Feranno dead, and any alleged association between him and Davidson also based on hearsay, so far the case against Davidson and Faber is quite weak."

"I don't believe this," Jeffrey said. "So for Davidson and his colleagues, it will soon be back to business as usual, although probably not in Boston."

"Well, I don't know about that," Randolph said. "As I mentioned, there will be an investigation. But if it doesn't turn up any new and convincing evidence, I suppose Davidson might try it again. His firm is certainly highly regarded in the malpractice field. And the field remains highly lucrative. But maybe next time they will make a mistake. Who knows?"

"What about my divorce?" Jeffrey asked. "You must have some good news."

"I'm afraid that also could be trouble," Randolph said, putting his papers in his briefcase.

"Why?" Jeffrey asked. "Carol and I have no disagreements. It's a mutual and amicable divorce."

"It may have been," Randolph said. "But that was before your wife retained Hyram Clark as her divorce attorney."

"What difference does it make who she uses?"

"Hyram Clark goes for the jugular as a matter of course," Randolph said. "He'll consider the silver in your dental fillings as part of your assets. We'll have to be prepared and retain someone equally aggressive."

Jeffrey groaned aloud. "Maybe you and I should get married, Randolph. That's how much it sounds like we'll be together."

Randolph laughed in his contained, Boston Brahmin fashion. "Let's talk about the lighter side," he said. "What are your general plans?" Randolph stood up.

Jeffrey brightened. "As soon as I get out of here, Kelly and I are going on a vacation. Someplace in the sun. Probably the Caribbean." Jeffrey stood up also.

"What about medicine?" Randolph asked.

"I've already spoken with the chief of anesthesia at the Memorial," Jeffrey said. "They'll be working quicker than the wheels of justice. I'll be reinstated shortly."

"So you'll go back there?"

"I doubt it," Jeffrey said. "Kelly and I have pretty much decided to move on to a new state."

"Oh?" Randolph questioned. "Sounds like a serious relationship."

"It most certainly is," Jeffrey said. "As serious as it gets."

"Well then," Randolph said. "Perhaps I should draw up a preliminary premarital agreement."

Jeffrey stared at Randolph in disbelief, but then he saw the corners of Randolph's mouth curl up into a smile.

"It's a joke," Randolph said. "What's happened to your sense of humor?"